One of us is lying

Also by Patricia Wendorf

ONE OF US IS LYING

Patricia Wendorf

Hodder & Stoughton

Wendorf, Patricia, 1928–
One of us is lying
1. English fiction – 20th century
I. Title
823.9'14 [F]

ISBN 0 340 67171 8

Typeset by Palimpsest Book Production Limited,
Polmont, Stirlingshire
Printed and bound in Great Britain by
Mackays of Chatham PLC, Chatham, Kent

Hodder and Stoughton
A division of Hodder Headline PLC
338 Euston Road
London NW1 3BH

To Sheila Gorst

Maya
_____

A Saturday afternoon in late August, the sun hot in a blue sky, Bruce Springsteen singing 'The River' on an old tape.

They had left Milwaukee soon after midday, had eaten lunch in a truckers' pull-in. 'For the experience,' Louann had said. 'Every visitor from England should eat at least one meal in such a dive.' The truckers were large and silent men, their heads bent to steak plates piled high with pancakes drenched with maple syrup, and flanked by sausages and eggs. Maya ordered something called a Turkey Melt which tasted of nothing much save tomato ketchup. Louann, the sophisticated American woman, had not eaten but had drunk decaffienated coffee.

By early afternoon they were driving on the northside of Chicago, down a long straight road on either side of which stood white clapboard houses set in green lawns. Morning-glories climbed trellised arches and old shady trees grew from clipped grass verges.

They passed through a built-up area of shops and churches. In front of a red-brick building, men and boys stood about in chattering, gesticulating groups.

'Hasidic Jews,' Louann said, explaining the tall hats and strange black garments, the spray-fixed kiss curls which made the men look like animated dolls.

Maya relaxed into her seat, happy to play the tourist for this weekend. Normal business would be resumed on Monday morning when Louann, commission agent, would introduce her to important store buyers in Chicago, who, she hoped, might wish to view her samples and purchase her designs.

It happened at an intersection, just as the car was rolling slowly out into a right turn. The tape had moved on; a muted Frank Sinatra was singing 'My Way' when Maya jerked abruptly forward, her face saved only by the seat belt from impact with the windscreen. She hung there

Patricia Wendorf

for a moment, motionless, eyes closed. Then she fell back, her head and neck supported by the headrest.

Louann, now deep in heavy traffic, cried out, 'What *was* that? What happened? Are you OK? Was it something that I did?'

Maya said, 'It's nothing that you did. It happens sometimes. I feel a little faint and then it passes. I'm fine now.'

Louann glanced sideways. 'My God! You don't look fine. Hang on in there, Maya. Ten minutes, I promise you, and we'll be at the motel.'

Maya looked at her wristwatch, made a calculation. Two in the afternoon Chicago time would be eight in the evening back in England.

The motel was expensive, exclusive. They parked among Jaguars and Mercedes. The parking attendant wore plum-coloured uniform heavy with gold braid. Inside the motel the plum and gold motif was repeated in the decor. Maya handed in her sample cases at reception and was assured by a superior young man that her valuables would be locked away at once in his impregnable safe. Through a screen of sculpted glass she could almost feel the damp heat from an indoor swimming pool which was fringed by potted palms and edged with waiter-serviced tables.

'The Chicago Bears stop over here,' Louann whispered reverently, 'when they're playing a home game.'

The only available room was a double. Maya felt drained, disorientated; she would have forgone dinner but Louann was persuasive. She was pushing lemon sole around a plum-coloured, gold-rimmed plate when Louann said, 'So what is it with you? That was no faint back there in the car. If we're going to continue doing business together, then I think you'd better level with me.'

Maya had heard about American directness. This was her first experience of it. She laid her knife and fork carefully across the plate. She spoke sharply, irritation rising in her voice. 'It wasn't an epileptic fit, if that's what you're thinking. Neither am I an alcoholic. There is nothing wrong with me. I'm perfectly healthy and normal.'

Louann made placatory gestures across the table. 'OK. Calm down. It was just – well, I thought, we'll be meeting some pretty important people in the next few days. I don't want you to fold up on me.'

'I won't. Look. I'm sorry if I frightened you. It happens only rarely. It's nothing serious.'

'Could be fatal if it happened when you're driving.'

'It never does. Never will.'

'How can you be that sure?'

'I know it will never happen in potentially dangerous situations because I can control it.'

2

Louann leaned across the table, causing the candle flame to flicker. 'That's freaky,' she said softly. 'That's really freaky.'

Maya wanted to rise and leave the table, but there was nowhere she could go. She and Louann were sharing a room; the pool was probably full of baseball players. She ate a piece of fish to gain time, drank some wine, crumbled a dry roll. Weariness seeped through her, weakening reserve. For the first time in her life she was tempted to confide, to trust. Four days ago Louann had been a stranger; she was still no more than an acquaintance. After next week they would almost certainly never meet again.

Maya said, 'When it happens, it's like a shutter that flips up in my mind; but if I don't want it to open, then I can control it.'

'So what happens when the shutter opens?'

'I see things.'

'Like visions?'

'Not exactly. This afternoon, in the car, I was off guard, relaxed. Listening to Sinatra. Leaving myself wide open to anything that came.'

'Your face, afterwards. It was like you'd just seen something terrible happening.'

'That's exactly how it is. I see the major disasters of the world. Where they happen, how they happen, as they happen. Earthquakes. Rail and air crashes. Floods. Motorway pile-ups. I get a re-run that same evening or the next day on TV or in the newspapers.'

'That's terrible.'

'Like I told you, I learned early on how to block it out.'

'So how long —'

'Since I was seven. I began to sleepwalk, then came the sightings. I wasn't really frightened to begin with. I thought it probably happened to everybody.'

'What about your parents? Did they take you to doctors?'

'My parents? They were never around much. I was brought up by au pairs, obliging neighbours, my father's mother. I learned when I was very young to keep my own counsel. In fact, you are the first person I have ever told about it.'

Louann had that stricken sympathetic look which meant that at any moment now she would begin to cry. Maya felt guilty and embarrassed. She had always suspected that confidentiality was dangerous.

She pushed her plate away and folded her napkin. 'Look,' she said, 'it's been a long day. We're both very tired. Let's take a bottle of wine back up to the room. Make quite sure we can sleep without having bad dreams.'

'You haven't told me yet what it was you saw this afternoon.'

'Tomorrow,' said Maya. 'I'll tell you tomorrow.'

The telephone rang at twenty past five in the morning. She waited for Louann to wake, pick up the receiver, deal with the matter. It was, after all, her city, her country. When she failed to stir, Maya sat up and switched on the lamp. The plum-coloured telephone vibrated, she snatched up the handset. A voice said, 'Is that you, Maya?'

'Polly! Do you know what time it is here?'

'Yes, I do. I've just roused Louann Kominski's boss who was not at all pleased. She said I might find you at the Paradise Motel.'

'Well, if this is a business call, you needn't have bothered. 'Everything is going well. I have three appointments for tomorrow in Chicago —'

'It isn't business. Maya.'

'What then?'

'It's your parents. I'm so sorry. There's no easy way to do this. I wanted your Aunt Alice to make this phone call, but she says she hardly knows you.'

'They're dead, aren't they?'

'It was very quick. They would hardly have known what was happening.'

'My mother crashed the car.'

'How did you know that?'

'I guessed.'

'How soon can you get back to London?'

'How urgent is it?'

'Well, you *are* the next of kin, Maya. There'll be an inquest, things to be sorted out.'

'I'll come as soon as I can get a flight.'

'Let me know when and I'll meet you at Heathrow.'

Maya laid down the handset. Louann, now awake and listening, said, 'Bad news?'

'My partner, phoning from London. My mother crashed the car. She and my father are both dead.'

Without make-up and her hair mussed. Louann looked younger, less sophisticated. 'Oh,' she whispered. 'Why, that's awful!' Her pale lips parted and now there was horror in her face. 'You saw it all. didn't you? Back there at the intersection. You saw their car crash?'

'I saw *a* car crash. I saw the bonnet of a red car hit the trunk of a large tree. I saw the explosion, the fire.' She paused. 'Something's changed. It's the first time I've witnessed a personal disaster. There was a large white van involved. Two men. One of them wore a blue shirt.'

'You didn't recognise the motor?'

'How could I? I haven't seen my parents in the past five years.'

Within minutes Louann had brewed coffee in the elegant percolator that came with the pricey room. She found biscuits in a tin on the bedside table and miniature brandies in the mini-fridge. At seven o'clock she phoned the airport. 'No flight available until this evening,' she reported.

'Book it,' said Maya.

Later on she said, 'We'll be able to keep our appointments in the city. I'll be much better working until my flight leaves.'

'You could be right. Anyway, you're still in deep shock.'

Deep shock, if that is what it was, saw her through her first and last day in Chicago. She glanced at the Sears Building (tallest in the world), at the blue of Lake Michigan, down the canyons of streets where sunlight never penetrated.

She sat in mahogany-panelled offices and showed her samples to keen-eyed buyers. Different, they said, as she laid before them coral and jet set in silver, amber set in rose-gold, pendants and earrings. brooches and bangles, chokers and rings. Victorian designs adapted for the nineteen nineties.

Louann now changed from empathising friend to rampant business-woman. Maya watched her as she bargained like a cheapjack in a street market, clinched deals and noted orders, and she knew that without Louann she might as well have stayed at home.

They ate hamburgers at a McDonald's on West Adams Street. Maybe, said Louann, she would come to London in the spring. They must surely keep in close touch; after all, they had been through so much together.

They arrived at O'Hare Airport with only minutes to spare. After phoning Polly and saying her farewells to Louann, Maya was the final passenger to board the aircraft. She stored her sample cases underneath her seat and attempted to relax.

Her neighbour in the window seat clutched a rosary in one hand, a dark green passport in the other. His eyes were closed. He recited Hail Marys until well after they were airborne.

Maya also closed her eyes and locked the shutter in her mind. If the Irishman had a premonition of disaster, she did not wish to know about it.

Heathrow Airport on a Tuesday morning; they landed at noon in heavy rain. She had not slept, had not even dozed. Polly waited for her at the barrier. They did not speak but walked together to the Coffee Shop. They hunched over steaming cappuccino. Polly's voice was hesitant, her manner awkward. She glanced once at Maya's face, and then swiftly away. She said, 'I *had* to ring you. You being next of kin. Your Aunt Alice was insistent. You see, I had this phone call at two in the morning. The Dorsetshire constabulary; Alice had given them my name and number.' Polly lifted an eyebrow. 'I didn't even know you had an aunt.'

Maya shrugged. 'We've never met. We exchange cards and phone calls at birthdays and Christmas. I must have mentioned at some time that you are my business partner.'

Polly said, 'The police told me what happened.' She paused. 'On a clear night, on a good road, your mother drove at speed into an oak tree.'

'Yes,' said Maya, 'I guessed that's how it was.' She sipped her coffee, set the cup very carefully into the saucer. 'What were they doing in Dorset?'

'Nobody knows. It seems that they were just out driving. They have a house on the Somerset-Dorset border, a lovely place according to your aunt, miles from the nearest village. I'll drive you down there when you're ready.'

'I'll need to go back to the flat, pick up my mail and some fresh clothes.'

'You should also get some sleep.'

'I'll sleep in the car.'

Obsessive tidiness can have its compensations; routine and neatness observed in the very smallest details of daily living can have unexpected benefits when life itself becomes disorganised and messy. Sometimes she thought her flat to be the only tranquil place in a mad world. She opened the doors and surveyed with pleasure the rooms which she had left in perfect order. It took only minutes to empty her suitcase and repack it. She placed clothes to be washed in the dirty-linen basket; her suits and dresses were put on hangers and hung in a wardrobe, her shoes on trees. She refilled her case with sweaters and trousers, clean underwear, a silk robe and pyjamas. At the very last moment she added a plain black suit and shoes, a grey silk shirt. There would be a funeral. Beyond that point her thoughts would not reach.

On her way out she picked up the scatter of mail which lay on the hall carpet. Downstairs, in the workroom she and Polly shared, Maya placed the sample cases in a safe, left the paperwork of the orders gained in Chicago on the desk that Polly used.

Before the car had reached the outskirts of the city, she was deep in sleep.

She awoke as they drove into the village. She opened her eyes to the blueness of the early September twilight, through the open window of the car she breathed in the soft air, the scents of roses.

Polly said, 'I think this is the right place. I've been lost for hours driving around these damned lanes. I'm not sure now if we're in Somerset or Dorset.'

'You should have woken me.'

'You wouldn't have been much help in your present state, would you? You're jet-lagged, Maya. And shocked.' Polly drove very slowly. 'According to the directions your Aunt Alice gave me, her house is called Jasmine Cottage, and it stands opposite the pub. I rang her on the car phone about two hours ago, told her that we're on our way. She sounded relieved – and very nice.' Polly glanced sideways. 'I'm glad you won't be on your own here. I would have stayed with you, but those American orders mean lots of extra work. In any case, Alice is family. She'll be more useful to you than I could ever be.'

She awoke soon after daybreak to the sounds of footfalls on the stairs, doors opening and closing. The cottage was tiny and Alice was an early riser. Last night Maya had taken little notice of her surroundings; she had been greeted warmly by her aunt, shown her bedroom and the bathroom, and then left to sleep.

Now she watched the sun rise through the branches of a large tree. The room was furnished with stripped pine, a sheepskin rug lay on the floor of polished boards. The quilt was a patchwork of every shade of blue; the walls and the curtains were white. The framed sampler which hung above a chest of drawers bore the uncompromising message, 'The Lord giveth, and the Lord taketh away.'

She watched the sunlight climb slowly up the leafy oak. Oak was the only tree she recognised; she was not, and never had been, a country person. Her thoughts moved to Polly who had last night accepted coffee and a sandwich from Alice but declined the offer of a bed, turned the car round and drove straight back to London. How long would it take to organise a funeral, dispose of the contents of a house, and then sell that house? Do the necessary business with the lawyers? There would be a lot of extra work for both of them as a result of the American orders.

Maya had rarely been absent from the workshop in the five years of her partnership with Polly. They had been friends since schooldays, had studied jewellery design at the same London college of art. At previous busy times they had brought in Jonah who was always willing to help out. At a price. The price of Jonah had, however, recently risen to levels unacceptable to Maya. She thought it more than likely that he was evil. She believed in evil. Goodness in others was a kind of aberration not too often encountered. She could count on the fingers of one hand those people of her acquaintance who fitted that category. There was Polly, of course; and Alice who had always been a benign although unseen constant in her life. She remembered Louann, and thought with surprise that she too was almost certainly a good person. Sometimes she wondered how much she herself was possessed by circumstances long out of her control. How often were the bad things that happened in her life spontaneous occurrences, and how many times had she made them happen?

The white linen suit in which she had travelled from Chicago was creased and grubby. She put on laundered jeans, a soft blue shirt, pulled her long straight hair hard back from her face and tied it with a dark blue ribbon. It was time to face Alice, and the day.

The kitchen was spacious. The floor was of red tile, the table and chairs, the old-fashioned dresser were of black oak. There was a shiny dark-red Rayburn, above which hung a clothes airer that worked on a pulley system. The dresser was crammed with attractive, unmatched Victorian china. She admired a set of seven, rosebud-encrusted jugs in diminishing sizes, and a circular white and gold cheese dish. In a corner by the door leaned a besom, a horseshoe was nailed above the lintel. In a padded basket beside the Rayburn slept the largest black cat she had ever seen.

The last food she had eaten had been the Turkey Melt in the truckers' pull-in, and an inch of lemon sole in the Paradise Motel. She sat down at the table. Alice turned to greet her.

'Good morning, Maya. Did you sleep well?'

'Very well, thank you.'

'What about breakfast? Boiled eggs?'

'Just tea and toast. I don't usually eat breakfast.'

The toast came in a white china rack, the pale farm-churned butter in a brown crock; homemade marmalade was in a yellow dish. Maya started to eat, slowly at first and then with unexpected hunger. Across the table Alice filled two cups with strong tea. She said abruptly, 'You look nothing like your father. Nothing like your mother, either.' Even as she spoke, pink colour stained her fine-lined face. 'I'm sorry. That was not very considerate, was it?'

Maya said, 'It's all right. You can talk to me about them. There will have to be a lot of talking, won't there? So much that I don't know about it all. Them. Their lives.'

Alice said, 'You've been out of touch for such a long time.'

Maya buttered a slice of toast and spread marmalade on it. 'You could say the same of them,' she said sharply. '*They* always knew where *I* was. I didn't even know they were back in England.'

Alice nodded. 'Yes. I do know how it's been for you. I tried to talk to Geoffrey about it, but my brother was not an easy man, and as for your mother —'

'I'd like to know what happened. The accident.'

'There isn't much that I can tell you. They were driving near Hunger Hill. Well, your mother was driving. Geoffrey's sight was becoming very poor. It was about eight in the evening, not dark. A camper was approaching, but not close enough to be involved. They were found by a farmer. He'd been out shepherding earlier in nearby fields and was on his way home from the pub. He heard the crash. They were both dead when he got to them.' Alice sighed. 'A bright red Triumph Stag sports car seemed a very odd choice of vehicle for people of their age. Perhaps your mother lost control, or there was some mechanical fault. The police are investigating of course.'

'Did you have to identify them?'

'Yes. Well, there was no one else.'

'I'm sorry. I came as soon as I could get a flight.'

'I know you did. It wasn't too bad. Their ... faces were almost unmarked.'

Maya studied Alice. Tall and very thin, her silver hair curled short about her head, the familial likeness to her brother Geoffrey was marked. They had the same deep-set blue eyes, the mild and deprecating manner. Maya felt a rare pang of regret. She might have loved her father had she ever been given the chance to know him. She said, 'I suppose you're retired now.'

'Last year.'

Alice had taught music at a nearby minor public school. When young she had toured abroad with a famous orchestra.

'Do you miss it?'

Alice smiled. 'Not one little bit. I was glad to finish. I have a large garden. I keep bees and hens and two goats. I belong to several local societies and clubs.'

'Sounds idyllic.' And so it did, except that there was something about Alice which led Maya to suspect that her aunt had once led a more interesting and secret life.

They returned to the subject that neither of them wanted to discuss.

Alice said, 'There has already been a postmortem. The inquest has been adjourned for five weeks.'

'Is there anything I should be doing?'

'Well, you'll need to see your parents' solicitors in Yeovil, and then there's the house. Nobody has been there since the accident. I have a spare set of keys. I kept an eye on the place when they went away.'

'What about funeral arrangements?'
'The police say we can hold the funeral as soon as we wish.'

Alice drove an old, well-cared-for Rover. The road to Yeovil lay downhill through narrow shaded lanes. The little town, attractively pedestrianised, its lampposts hung with baskets of petunias and trailing ivy, seemed vaguely familiar to Maya. She questioned Alice on the subject.

'My parents – your grandparents – lived in Crewkerne. It's quite possible that when you were little they brought you shopping into Yeovil.'

The solicitor's office was in a quiet corner beside the parish church. He was middle-aged, sympathetic, helpful. He volunteered the information for which Maya could not bring herself to ask. Except for a small bequest to Alice, Maya was the sole beneficiary. There was not a lot of money, but there was the house, upon which considerable sums had been spent in the past five years. Should she wish to sell, he felt sure there would be no difficulty in disposing of it.

They walked out of the gloom of the solicitor's office into bright autumn sunshine. On the short turf of St John's churchyard, young people ate picnic lunches, small children played. The beautiful church of mellow stone stood out sharply against the blue sky.

Maya said, 'I'll make the funeral arrangements.'
'I'll come with you.'
'No. This is something I must do myself. You've been through enough already. Just point me in the right direction. We'll meet for lunch in about an hour.'

Alice nodded. 'Well, if you're quite sure. I need to shop for a black dress. Meet me in the Manor Hotel, anyone will tell you how to find it.'

Maya's sense of unreality increased as she chose caskets, opted for burial rather than cremation, decided upon a date and time. This was a service one did not expect to have to perform for strangers. She had questioned Alice about her parents' preferences in such matters but the subject, said Alice, had never been discussed.

The funeral director's office was furnished in bleached wood, the curtains and carpet were pale grey. Bowls of brilliantly coloured dahlias stood on windowsill and desk. She sat on a hard, upright chair, and a part of her mind was with Polly in the familiar clutter of the workroom. Another three days and all this nightmare would be over, settled. She thought about Jonah who had pointed ears and a faun face, and who was not to be trusted.

'No,' she told the undertaker, 'no particular hymns or prayers. As far as I know, they were not religious people.'

The Manor Hotel was old and comfortable, and gracious. No indoor swimming pool, no uniformed car park attendant. Alice sat in the foyer on a chintz-covered sofa, her head leaning back against the cushions. She looked weary and vaguely apprehensive, as if present troubles were still minor and the worst was yet to come. Maya seated herself in a facing armchair. She studied Alice carefully across the coffee table. She wondered how deeply her aunt mourned the death of Geoffrey, her brother; or if she mourned at all. Alice had said, as they left the solicitor's office, 'If you like, I could drive you over to the house this afternoon and pick you up again later.' Then she had hesitated. 'I have some rather urgent things to attend to later on. And anyway, I think it will be better if you go into the house by yourself.'

They ate chicken sandwiches and drank coffee from thin, flowered china. Maya said, 'It's all arranged. Burial on Monday morning at the village church. I wondered about flowers. What do you think?'

'Two wreaths,' said Alice. 'One for each coffin. You and I will be the only mourners.'

Every road out of Yeovil seemed to slope uphill. They were cresting Babylon Hill when Alice said, 'I ought to warn you. They say your parents' house – your house now – is haunted.'

Maya said, 'Do you believe that?'

'Yes, my dear. I think I do believe it. The place stood empty for many years, it was said to be unlucky. Some story about a Gypsy curse – but you know what country people are. Nevertheless, there is something strange about it, I feel uneasy underneath that roof.'

'Tell me about it.'

'Well, it's pretty isolated. It stands directly on the Somerset-Dorset border, and close to Hunger Hill.'

'But that's where the accident happened.'

'Oh yes. Your parents were almost home when the car crashed.' She paused. 'The estate agents called it a minor manor house. The sort of place inhabited in the last century by gentlemen farmers who had pretensions to a higher station in life. In fact, I would say it was no more than a rather superior farmhouse. In the war years it was used as a convalescent home for wounded airmen. In the nineteen twenties it had been a small private school. By the time it finally came up for auction the whole place was in a bad state. I could never understand why Geoffrey bought it. It's called the Monks House, I believe a Priory once stood upon the site.'

Maya said, 'I thought they were still living in Brazil.'

'They came back to England five years ago. To begin with they lived in a hotel in London. They came down to see me on a visit that was to have lasted for three weeks. At the end of that time your mother announced that they had decided to settle in the area. I could hardly believe it. Oh, I knew that Geoffrey would be happy. After all, he was born and brought up here. But your mother! Whatever would she do with herself?' Alice smiled. 'I gave them six months in that house. I was wrong. Very wrong, as it turned out.'

'I can't imagine Bruenette living in the country.'

Alice said, 'I went with them to the auction. It was your mother who led the bidding. I watched her face. She was determined to have that house; I had the feeling that she would have sold her soul to the Devil to get possession of it.'

Alice dropped her off at the entrance to a long sloping driveway. 'I won't come down. Give me a ring when you're ready to leave and I'll come over and collect you.'

From the road, only the rims of chimneys were to be seen between tall trees. Maya walked very slowly down the hedged and rutted drive. On either side stubbled fields stretched away to touch deep woods. The silence of the hot afternoon disturbed her; she stood for a moment and looked at the surrounding countryside for signs of human habitation, but there was none. She moved on, her breathing shallow, her hands damp.

As the house came into view she was unprepared for the size of it, its sense of importance. Once again she halted, needing to look at the house, to think about the unexpectedness of such a gift when she had expected nothing. The word 'home' came into her mind, which was surprising since she had never had occasion to use that particular description of any dwelling. She came down to a rough lawn and a neglected terrace of cracked flagstones which fronted the long, low house. Built of the local Ham stone, its walls had mellowed with the centuries from pale gold to a shade of dark honey. The windows were small and mullioned, with diamond-leaded panes. The door of thick oak stood well back beneath a porch, inside which wooden benches were set on either side. She tried to imagine her parents sitting in the porch on long summer evenings, her father smoking the pipe he would have taken up since living in the country, her mother reading, or working on an improbable tapestry or piece of knitting.

The large iron key turned easily in the lock. The door swung open noiselessly on oiled hinges. Now that the moment had come, Maya found it difficult to enter. Her role in their lives had always been that of an intruder. Now here she was, the sole beneficiary of all they had to give.

A square hall, dark-panelled, with six doors opening off, and to one side a broad curved staircase. On an oaken table a copper bowl of wilted marigolds was reflected in a gilt-framed mirror. An Indian rug lay on polished floorboards. A trug and gardening gloves stood on an antique chest, a frayed Panama hat hung on a wall hook.

She closed the outer door as soundlessly as it had opened. She moved to stand in the centre of the hall, her vision adjusting to the sudden gloom. She imagined her mother on that last evening, casually throwing down the gardening gloves and trug, her father tossing the battered straw hat up on to the hook. And neither of them dreaming that they would never again return to the house.

She found it difficult to move on in any direction. She thought she knew now why Alice would not come here.

The rear door she guessed would lead into the kitchen; she opened it on to sunlight slanting across a flagstoned floor. No attempt had been made at modernisation, the old soapstone sink and wooden draining board were still in position. A hand-operated pump placed above the sink provided water. There were ashes in an open fireplace, beside which stood two wicker armchairs which held bright coloured cushions. She could just make out the indentation of a head in the cushions of one chair, a scatter of cigarette ash on the arms of the other.

Here, the Rayburn was dark blue. Blue checked gingham curtains hung at the windows. The long scrubbed table top must once have seated a farming family and its servants; a square blue gingham tablecloth made an island at one end of the table. On it stood two willow-patterned plates, two used cups and saucers, a teapot and milk jug, the remains of a Madeira cake. Maya picked up the china and carried it to the sink, rinsed it under ice-cold pump water and set it to dry on the wooden drainer. She shook the crumbs from the tablecloth and folded it into a drawer, acting without thought, keeping her hands busy in an attempt to quieten the chaos in her mind. The plate which held the wedge of Madeira cake she carried to an old-fashioned wooden cupboard, but the shelves were already filled with a complete tea and dinner service. Other cupboards held iron saucepans and the kind of copper utensils that were used before the invention of plastic and Teflon. The only modern gadgets appeared to be an electric kettle and toaster, and a washing machine tucked away in an alcove. A door at the end of the kitchen led to a large walk-in pantry; the white painted shelves were stacked with jams and pickles and preserved fruit. A thick marble slab formed a shelf beneath which a refrigerator hummed. She opened the fridge door. There was half an apple pie in a white dish, custard in a blue pitcher; a bowl of cooked green peas on a lower shelf, the remains of a leg of lamb, and a sauce boat half full of congealed gravy.

13

Their last meal, she thought. The dinner they ate before setting out on that fatal, final drive. The sight of the leftover food distressed her. She fetched the slice of Madeira cake and put it on a shelf beside the apple pie. She closed the fridge door and walked out of the pantry. It would all have to be disposed of. But not today.

The telephone was fixed to the kitchen wall. She dialled the number Alice had given her. 'I'd like to come back as soon as possible,' she said. 'Can you come and collect me?'

From the kitchen window she could see outbuildings, a stable block, a paddock, a small, walled garden; she felt the pull of the view, the urge to explore. But what would be the point?

When Polly phoned later that evening, Maya said, 'I've looked at the house. No, I shan't be keeping it. I shall put it on the market before I leave for London. The funeral is on Monday. I'll be back at work on Tuesday morning.'

The weather had been warm and sunny all through August and into the first week of September. On the day of the funeral they awoke to blustery winds and heavy rain. Alice found a Burberry for Maya to wear over the black suit and grey silk shirt.

Bruenette and Geoffrey were to be buried in the churchyard of the village nearest to their home. The solicitor from Yeovil had offered to drive his clients there and to bring them back. They walked with him through the churchyard, following the trestles which bore the two plain caskets, each with its wreath of white and yellow roses. He stood with them at the graveside while the coffins were lowered into the wet earth. Maya held the big black umbrella over Alice, while her aunt dabbed at her eyes and blew her nose. It was a lonely funeral. Three mourners, one a stranger, one a virtual stranger, and only Alice regretful enough to shed tears. The final prayer was said, a handful of soil scattered on the coffins, and it was over. The solicitor and Alice walked slowly back towards the car. The young clergyman accompanied Maya. 'A tragedy,' he said, 'to lose both one's parents at the same time. It must have been a great shock.'

'Yes. Yes, it was a shock. But quite fitting that they should die together. I am sure they would not have had it any other way.'

'Devoted, were they?'

'Oh yes. Devoted.' She turned upon him all the force of her suppressed anger. 'Somebody said – I can't remember who – that the children of lovers are orphans. My parents were lovers all their lives.' She swung away from him, her narrow heels stabbing at the soft turf, and now there were tears mixed in with the rain which beat against her face.

The mistake had been to come here in the first place. She should have stayed in Chicago, conducted the whole business by telephone, remained uninvolved.

She walked quickly now towards the waiting car; as she came to the lych gate, she looked back into the churchyard. Two men were standing by the open grave. The flowers they carried were a brilliant red against the greyness of the morning. Even as she watched, each man threw his bouquet of scarlet carnations down on to the coffins. There was something almost ritualistic about their actions. She paused just long enough to note that they were youngish, sharp dressers, strangers. The only other vehicle parked before the church gates was an expensive Winnebago camper, the vanity number plate of which spelled out LIAS 7. She looked towards the car where Alice and the solicitor sat waiting. Perhaps they knew the men, had expected that they would be present at the funeral. She looked back again at the open grave, but the unknown mourners had disappeared.

The London train was late by twenty minutes. Maya stood with Alice on the windy platform at Yeovil Junction. Alice looked tired. In the past few days the fine lines around her mouth and eyes had deepened; the stoop of her shoulders was more pronounced. Maya put a hand out awkwardly towards her aunt. 'It'll all be over soon,' she said. 'There's just the inquest to be gone through, and then your life can get back to normal.'

'It will never be quite the same. I didn't see much of Geoffrey, but I always knew that he was there.' Alice paused and looked away down the line at the approaching train. 'I suppose you are decided about selling the house.'

'My life is in London. I could hardly regard the place as a weekend cottage, could I? A house of that size needs to be lived in, and in any case, I'm not a country sort of person.'

'What kind of person are you, Maya? I'd rather hoped that we might get to know each other better. You are my only living relative now, as I believe I am yours.'

'Well, yes, I suppose you are. I'd never really thought much about it, family and all that.' As the train drew into the station, she turned towards her aunt. 'I'll be back for the inquest, and then there will be the house to sort out, furniture to dispose of. We'll spend some time together then. I promise.'

The business which Maya owned equally with Polly was housed in what had once been a rope factory, a small rundown structure that stood close

15

to the River Thames. In the first three years of their occupation they had rented the building. Four years ago they had bought the freehold. Changes had been made. The ground floor now accommodated a garage, offices and workrooms. The upper floor had been converted to house two self-contained flats. All that remained of the original structure was the roof and the rose-coloured brickwork of the outer walls.

Polly had been born in Wapping. The river, the docks, the network of small Victorian streets were her familiar territory. Maya, after seven years of almost constant residence, still felt herself to be the incomer, the one who had lived in many places but had settled nowhere.

She went in through the private entrance that led up to the flats. She paused beside the window which lit the turn in the staircase and gazed out upon the oily river, the towpath, the river craft and houseboats. It was a view that until now had given her a sense of deep satisfaction, framing as it did the success that she and Polly had achieved. But today her thoughts turned back to the house in Somerset which was now hers. She recalled her first sighting of it, the feeling she now acknowledged as being one of *déjà vu*, of painful recognition. But in which life? she wondered. In which of her reincarnations? For Maya had privately believed for as long as she could remember that in a different time and place she had been another person.

She entered her flat without her usual sense of satisfaction with its simplicity and order. On this damp and cloudy morning the blues and blacks and silvers looked dull and unimpressive. Jonah had said that the flat reflected accurately the coldness of her personality and nature. He had lived in it with her for a fortnight and then departed back to his own scruffy bedsit in a dilapidated Victorian villa near the Tube station. Since that time she had allowed a distance to develop between herself and Jonah. Sometimes she knew things without ever knowing how she knew them. If she permitted her feelings of dislike and fear to develop towards Jonah, she thought that something terrible might happen to him; as it had to her husband, and perhaps, in the end, to her parents.

She unpacked her suitcase, loaded the machine with her soiled clothing, hung the black suit in the wardrobe, returned jars and bottles to the bathroom shelves. She made instant coffee in a mug and sat in a black leather armchair to drink it. In the long mirror on the facing wall she could see her reflection: the straight, shining, white-blonde hair that reached to her shoulders, the yellow eyes set slanting and cat-like in her pale face; and just for a moment it seemed to her that the woman in the mirror was a stranger.

Jango

*H*e came awake abruptly, startled too soon into the new day. He lay very still, tried to identify what it was that had roused him, and could not. He liked to come slowly out of sleep, to lie for a long time, eyes closed, breathing in the scents of grass and the smell of wood smoke from last night's fire. It had become a ritual with him, this slow lifting of his lids to a wide sky, the gradual assimilation of peripheral objects; the bulk of the Winnebago camper looming up behind him, Lias sleeping on the far side of the dead fire, wrapped in a plaid blanket. The day was already flawed for Jango because of the abrupt awakening.

He stood up, barefoot in the damp grass, and pulled his blanket close about him. The October days were sliding gradually towards winter; another week or two and Lias and he would be sleeping nights in the Winnebago. They were not as hardy as the old ones in their family, as the father and grandfather who, if family tales were to be believed, had slept underneath the stars in frost and snow, had bathed – when they bathed – in the nearest river, and shaved with a cutthroat razor and in cold water. Jango liked the notion of his forebears' toughness and was secretly shamed by his own inclination towards the softness of Gorgio living. He shaved with an electric razor, ate meat he had not snared and skinned with his own two hands, and was fastidious about his personal cleanliness and appearance.

As he moved towards the Winnebago, the dogs crept silently out from beneath the camper to walk beside him one on either hand. Absent-mindedly he fondled their silky ears and smooth heads. He climbed the three steps, opened the door of the camper, reached inside to pick up the kettle and then carried it to the churn which stood in the deep shade of the hedge. He ladled water into the kettle; on the edge of his vision he was aware of Lias moving coming instantly awake as was his habit. But for the abrupt awakening, it would have been Lias who filled the kettle.

17

Jango went back into the camper; he lit the gas jet, put the water on to boil for tea. His jeans and plaid shirt hung on hooks above the bunk seats; he dressed, noting with satisfaction that jeans and shirt were uncreased. He shook dried dog food into two bowls, took a third bowl to the churn and filled it with water. He stood in the faint warmth of the October sunshine and curled his bare toes into the grass. He watched the greyhounds as they ate and drank, observing their glossy coats and bright eyes, assessing their chances for the coming winter's racing season.

Lias, who did not hang his shirt and jeans on hooks, stood at the cooker, dressed in his creased clothes. He chopped mushrooms and tomatoes into a pan. The camper was filled with the smell of frying bacon. Jango had brought in more water in a plastic jug; from the cupboard beneath the sink unit he removed a red bowl and filled it. He washed his hands and dried them, pulled out the folding table, and set two places with cutlery and plates. He picked up the bowl, walked with it to the open door, and threw the soapy water out on to the surrounding grass.

Lias brought the large brown teapot to the table; he shovelled bacon, mushrooms and tomatoes on to each plate. Jango cut thick slices from a brown loaf and spread them with butter. They ate in silence, without once glancing at each other. They were half-brothers. They had always lived together. The essential communication which ran between them was like an underground stream; they required no words. They had been born on the straw in an old-fashioned bender tent, beside a heavy, brightly painted, horse-drawn wagon. They still remembered and spoke about the colours of it, the reds and greens and yellows, the horses' heads carved upon the sides and doors, the little tin chimney that carried the smoke from the black iron stove.

It was not until breakfast had been eaten, cigarettes lit and the teapot emptied that Lias spoke. 'How much longer can we pitch here?'

'Farmer said one week. I offered to pay extra but he said the locals wouldn't like it.'

'So that gives us three more nights.'

Jango looked out and up through the beechwoods where the sun struck copper in the turning leaves. 'I could stand a winter here.'

'No, you couldn't. You'd get restless for Derbyshire. You always do.' Lias tamped out his cigarette. He took a blue bowl from the sink unit cupboard, half filled it with hot water from the kettle, added a dash of liquid soap. He washed the breakfast china and dried it on a soft cloth. The crockery was old and thin and valuable, a gift to his grandparents on their wedding day; irreplaceable. He packed it carefully away into cupboards especially designed for the safe transport of breakable objects.

He dried the blue bowl in which he had washed the dishes and replaced it in the sink unit cupboard. The kettle and frying pan he stowed in a recess underneath the cooker. He said, irritation in his voice, 'It's a waste of time, you know, going to this inquest. We could have been gone from here weeks ago, doing good business down the coast.'

'We've done well in the local markets.' Jango spoke above the whir of his electric shaver.

'Oh, I'll give you that much. But our lines are a bit of a novelty in these parts, we were bound to do good for a few weeks. Now it's time to move on.' Lias lit another cigarette, drew smoke deeply into his lungs and then trickled it slowly out through his nostrils. 'It's the girl, isn't it? The tall blonde at the funeral.'

'What if it is?'

'There's nothing for you there.'

'You don't know that.'

'I'm telling you! That's a classy dame, little brother.'

Jango switched off the shaver, rubbed a hand across his jaw and chin. 'We should have leaned harder on that detective.'

'He couldn't tell us what he didn't know.' Lias stood. He whistled the dogs up into the camper. He laid out the blanket on which they travelled. 'We'll have to decide what to do about things. Might be better to do nothing.'

Jango said, 'We'll talk about it after the inquest.' He moved to the strip of mirror which was bolted to the camper wall. From a shelf he took a bottle of expensive aftershave. smiled approvingly at his own reflection, and began to slap the liquid onto his shaven skin.

The trailer was ready loaded with the merchandise by which they made their living. They pulled out of the woodland clearing soon after eight; the morning road was almost clear of traffic. Lias drove while Jango read the signposts; within half an hour they were in Yeovil, camper and trailer parked.

The inquest was to be held in the Magistrate's Court in Petters' Way. They walked through the sloping streets of the little town, found a cluster of market stalls behind the public library, and cast a professional eye across the goods on offer.

The court stood close beside the market, an imposing building, its entrance doors bearing an attractive fanlight, and flanked by pillars topped with white-painted iron lamps.

The inquest was held in the Family Court. The waiting rooms were small, the seating insufficient. People who expected to be called crouched in corners and leaned against the walls.

Evidence was given by the police, the emergency services, the farmer who had helped to pull the burning bodies from the car. Also called was the doctor who performed the postmortem, and an elderly white-haired woman who was the sister of the dead man, who said that as far as she was aware, both victims of the accident had been of sound mind and in good health.

Lias and Jango were not, after all, required to give evidence. They were thanked for their attendance and paid a nominal sum towards their expenses. As they left the court, Jango spoke to the blonde-haired, bereaved daughter. 'Meet me tomorrow night,' he said, 'at the pub on the village green in Halstock. I have something important to tell you about your mother.'

'You knew my mother?'

'Not exactly knew. She wrote us a letter, my brother and me. I think you ought to know about it.'

The pub was called the Quiet Woman. The painted inn sign which swung above the door showed a girl in a blue dress, her decapitated head tucked tidily underneath her arm.

Jango parked the camper carelessly, leaving it slewed crossways in the middle of the almost empty car park. He awarded the headless female on the inn sign a two-fingered salute, and dipped his head and shoulders to accommodate the low lintel of the doorway.

The bar was typical of this corner of Dorset, dark and private, never mind the landlord's smile of welcome, his cheerful greeting. This place belonged to the cider drinkers in the corner, the old men who occupied by right the chairs which stood closest to the log fire. Jango ordered Bacardi and Coke. He carried the tall glass to a seat beside the window, from which he could view the steep and winding road down which the girl would have to come.

From time to time the old men set their tankards down and turned their heads in the direction of the stranger. He could hear the low, incomprehensible rumble of their voices and found the sound oddly reassuring. There was something secretive about the inn, the village. He looked out on to the darkening fields and trees, and the stillness of the view increased his unease. He twirled his glass, interlinking the wet rings it had made on the polished table. He extended his legs to their full and considerable length, and studied the tan leather boots into which were tucked the blue designer jeans. His shoulders twitched inside the Armani jacket; he lit a cigarette and blew the smoke out in a long plume. He had felt relief and a shamed satisfaction when Lias had refused to come with him.

He walked to the bar, ordered straight Bacardi, a double this time. The second drink saw him calmer; as tranquil as it was ever possible for him to be. He settled back into his chair and recalled the black humour of the inn sign.

When she finally came, it was half an hour after the agreed time of meeting. He watched the small black foreign car drive sedately into the car park, saw the deliberate precision of her parking which seemed to him like a rebuke for his own slapdash method. Her walk across to the inn door was unhurried. She looked up at the inn sign but did not smile.

Her outstretched hand was cool and slim and suntanned. There was no apology for her late arrival. She said, 'I'm Maya.'

'Jango,' he said, taking her hand. 'Jango Heron.' He picked up his empty glass. 'What will you have?'

'Grapefruit juice,' she said, glancing at his glass. 'I never drink alcohol when I'm driving.'

Standing in the courtroom between her solicitor and aunt, she had seemed slighter, less compelling. As they stood together at the bar, she turned slowly towards him, and her gaze was direct and almost level with his own. Her looks were of a type he did not usually find attractive, but seen close to, he found himself mesmerised by the fall of the straight, white-gold hair, the yellow eyes tilted cat-like at their corners, the full red lips and white skin. Her voice was low, amused and cultured.

'I hope,' she said, 'that you have something interesting to tell me. I've delayed my return to London in order to meet you.'

He followed her back to the window table. She wore black tailored trousers and a shirt of coral-coloured wool. Her jewellery was gold set with coral: a pendant, drop-earrings, a ring of intricate design. She sat directly beneath the pink glow of a wall lamp. She said, 'You mentioned a letter. A letter sent to you by my mother.' In the lamp glow, her eyes looked less yellow and more tawny amber. He became aware that he was staring at her. 'Sorry,' he said. 'Yes, the letter. It's a weird kind of story.' He drank some Bacardi then set his glass down. 'I'd better begin by explaining about Jango and me. We're travellers, brothers, Romanichals. We live and work together. We're market traders.'

'Romanichals?'

'Gypsies – Romany – the old sort. Not didicoys, not Irish tinkers.'

She said, looking at his jacket, 'I would never have mistaken you for an Irish tinker.'

'Your mother put a detective on us. A private detective.'

'Why ever would she do that?'

'You don't know?'

'No. I don't know.'

'Then you won't like what I have to tell you.'

'For goodness sake, man, get on with it!'

'Your mother was a relative of ours.'

Her laughter was spontaneous, and yet he sensed that she was a person who did not often laugh.

She said, 'My mother had no relatives. She was not a family sort of person.' She leaned forward, her gaze intent and her voice accusing. A small thrill of fear whispered down his backbone. She said, 'You were at the inquest and the funeral. You threw red flowers on her coffin.'

'That was Lias and me.' His need to implicate Lias was urgent; he could not, he thought, ever stand alone against this woman. 'We only did what was right and proper, according to our custom.'

'Your custom?' The ridicule was in her voice, in the curl of her lip.

He said, 'Scarlet is the colour of mourning among our people. She claimed to be our kin, and why should she do that if it wasn't true?'

'Why indeed.' The ridicule was still there, but now she watched him closely. 'Tell me,' she said, 'exactly what was your involvement with my mother?'

He sat back in his chair and sipped at the neat rum. He studied her long legs and small waist, the swell of her breasts beneath the woollen shirt, the long stem-like neck and triangular face. He looked into her eyes and memories that were not his own began to stir within him. Strange images flashed briefly across the blank screen of his mind. He saw a dark night, a swollen river, masonry falling, people running across a narrow bridge. He tried to break the link with her but could not. She held him with her eyes, and as he looked into the yellow irises, he had the frightened thought that they were lasers, cutting a sharp path into his brain, giving her access to that part of him that was his core, the centre of his being.

'My mother,' she said. 'You were going to tell me about your connection with her.'

When he spoke, the words came out carefully and slowly. 'We've got this base, Lias and me, in Derbyshire. A farmhouse. We don't really live there, only go there in the wintertime, and then for just a few months. Last February it was, when this mush came ferreting around the place. Lias thought at first he was a copper or Inland Revenue or VAT but the fellow said he was a private investigator, showed us identification; said a relative of ours had employed him to find us. Well, we didn't believe him. Any kin of ours would know that we could be found regularly at the big horse fairs – Brough, Appleby, Stow. We couldn't imagine anything so urgent that it would merit the hiring of a private detective. Lias told him to push off, but he pulled out this letter and threw it at me. It had our names on the envelope. The woman had certainly done her homework. She listed our great-grandparents' names and some of our grandparents and parents. She even knew where their graves were – and one of them is buried at a crossroads outside Gloucester! Now how could she have known that if she was not born into our family?'

'Do you still have this letter?'

He reached into his jacket pocket. The envelope was creased, the two pages of writing worn from frequent study. She took it from him and read it.

'It's my mother's handwriting, she said. 'But I don't recognise any of these names. She told me once that she had been abandoned when a baby. That she grew up in a children's home. It explained her lack of family, and a lot of other things.' She laid the note down on the table. She tapped it with her index finger. 'It says here that she is anxious to meet you.'

'We talked it over, thought about it. Lias is the careful one. He reckoned that a woman who could afford to employ a private detective wasn't short of the readies. So what did she want with the likes of us?'

'A very good question. So what did you do?' She leaned towards him as she spoke; the straight white-gold hair lay like swathes of silk across the collar and sleeves of her shirt; she smelled of sunshine and honeysuckle. Once again the trickle of fear ran along his spine and he thought he knew then who and what she was.

Lias

*L*ias lay on the soft grey quilted leather of the bunk top, his face turned towards the television set which hung suspended from a bracket in a corner of the camper. He smoked a thin black cigarillo and drank a herbal tea called Chrysanthemum. From time to time he lifted the white net curtain which covered the etched glass of the window at his side. From his place on the bunk he could see clearly the marble-topped table at which Jango sat with the blonde woman. Even at a distance he could sense his brother's unease, read the unaccustomed signs of nervous compliance in the bow of his shoulders, the dip of his head.

He saw the woman stand, pushing her chair back with an irritable gesture. She began to walk away from the table. Jango followed. They came out from beneath the low lintel of the doorway and walked towards her car. As far as Lias could see, no conversation passed between them. Jango watched until the woman and the lights of her car were out of sight. Then he walked to the camper and sat down on the top step and spoke to Lias through the darkness of the open doorway. 'Reckon you were right. We're wasting our time here. Better move on tomorrow.'

Lias said, 'There's some sort of show being held on Sunday in the next village. 'We'll hang on until then.'

'But we don't have a pitch booked.'

'I did that yesterday.'

'You didn't tell me.'

'Thought you weren't interested.'

Jango said, 'She's gone now. Won't be back.'

'That's all right then. Nothing lost.'

They pulled on to the showground very early in the morning. The venue was attractive, set among expanses of mown grass and surrounded by massed beech and chestnut trees. The arena in which the events of the day were to be enacted was marked out by metal barriers. A loudspeaker

24

system was housed in a shabby caravan. They were not among the first wave of traders to arrive; already the urns were steaming in the tea and coffee booths. The stalls of the car-boot vendors were heaped with worn shoes, tattered paperback novels, broken plastic toys, and the occasional bit of valuable glass or china.

Jango found their allotted space beneath a beech tree. It was one of those warm, still days that sometimes occur early in October. He parked in shade, and Lias and he began to unload the trailer and to erect the trestles and boards which formed their stall. Then they draped the stall and its fitments of shelves with lengths of blue and crimson velvet. From boxes they unwrapped and arranged the china and terracotta oil-burners, the bottles of scented and essential oils, the sacks of brightly coloured potpourri, the fancy baskets, the bunches of silk flowers, the joss sticks and perfumed candles. They worked together without need of consultation.

Other traders were setting up around them. The ice-cream van was only feet away; the double-glazing salesman had already erected his small marquee and was unloading his demonstration doors and windows. Even at this early hour, customers were streaming through the showground. Young parents came pushing buggies and carrying infants in backpacks. Small groups of teenage boys hung around the stalls at which the accurate throwing of a dart or rolling of a ball could win a large stuffed toy gorilla or a bottle of cheap wine.

When the stall was arranged to Lias's satisfaction, Jango withdrew into the camper and began to cook breakfast. Their kind of trade would be slow until mid-morning. Lias set out two folding chairs and a small table in a patch of sunshine. They ate as do men who might not taste hot food again before nightfall. Lias savoured the moment. For him this was the best hour of the day, with the bustle and colour of a market or showground setting up around him; the promise of a good day's trading still to come.

It was at times like this that he remembered his childhood, his beginnings; taking the first meal of the day seated on the ground beside the early morning fire, eating bread fried in bacon fat, and drinking strong sweet tea. They had travelled in Leicestershire in springtime. He recalled a stretch of common wayside, land which lay between Burton-on-the-Wolds and Melton Mowbray. Just thinking about it brought back the almond scent of May blossom, the call of the rooks from their nests in the high elms and himself at the age of ten or so, proud to be trusted to hold the horse's head when the women went hawking around the villages and farms. He remembered wash days, the collecting of wood to build up a great fire, the fetching of water from a nearby stream; the use of separate pails and bowls for the washing of male and female clothing. His grandmother observed strictly the old taboos and laws of the deep Romany. She lived alone in a small, green, bow-top wagon, set a little apart from the main group. Lias was her favourite grandchild. But powerful as she was, his grandmother could not always protect him from his father's moods.

Despair Heron was a hard man. In a people where men regularly beat their wives, and where the women expected to be beaten, he was feared by all for the power of his fists and the violence of his temper. When Lias thought about his mother he remembered a dark and slender girl who rarely spoke; a sweet rounded face. She vanished one summer night when they were travelling in Nottinghamshire. It was whispered among his enemies that Despair Heron had murdered his young wife and buried her body along the roadside.

After his mother's disappearance, Lias was moved out from his father's wagon to live with an aunt and uncle. He attended village schools in the wintertime and frequently in three separate counties. He learned to read and write, to count, and to defend himself against those who called him didicoy. and dirty Gypo. When he was ten years old his father married a Gorgio girl who died exactly four months later giving birth to Jango.

Through the open door of the Winnebago, Lias watched Jango as he washed the breakfast dishes and put them away in their special cupboard. He felt a tenderness towards his brother, a softness he would never be capable of showing. The feeling he had for Jango was expressed in a rough and grudging indulgence for the younger man's wild enthusiasms, his sudden passionate attachments. Lias's love for Jango was an emotion buried deep in him. As deep as the bodies of their dead mothers, left by Despair Heron in unmarked graves in the Nottinghamshire lanes.

The real business of the show began at mid-morning. The marching bands came into the fenced arena, the loudspeaker system roared and crackled with martial music. There was no charge for entry to the showground; the warmth of the sun, the rousing tunes put people in a mood to spend. Long queues had formed at the tea and coffee booths; a crowd was gathered at the stall where slices of hot roast pork and sage and onion stuffing were on offer, folded in a long bread roll.

Lias and Jango dealt with customers three deep around their stall. Jango flirted with the teenaged girls, the young mothers. Lias explained the use of essential oils, the benefits of aromatherapy to middle-aged couples, elderly ladies. They both sold bags of potpourri to pensioners who wished for a small treat, and to schoolgirls attracted by the scents and pretty colours, and eager to spend their pocket money.

The canvas money belts tied about their waists grew heavy with coins, and still the people came. In a lull on that long warm afternoon Lias watched a display of Shire horses in the arena. From his place at the metal barriers, he could hear Jango's laughter. He turned back towards the stall, and there she was. The woman called Maya. Lias felt the short hairs in the nape of his neck begin to rise for fear of her, and instinctively his thumb closed across the two middle fingers of his right hand, leaving the index and little finger extended in the horned sign that is the Gypsy's protection against the evil eye.

Maya

*T*he first time she saw his face he was standing at the arena rail
watching the procession of Shire horses. Even as she talked to the one
called Jango, all her attention was fixed upon the mahogany profile of
his brother, the long lean body of him, the black waving hair scraped
back into a ponytail which reached down past his waistline. He began
to move away from the rail and towards the stall. He walked with the
loose and easy stride of a man relaxed in mind and body. As he came
closer, her heart began to knock alarmingly against her ribs, she began
to experience a mixture of elation and fear. To her certain knowledge
she had never met the man. The glimpse she had had of him at the
inquest and as he stood by her parents' grave had been swift and
blurred by sadness. But now, face to face, she *knew* him. Had always
known the dark and piercing gaze, the broad, high cheekbones, the
thin-lipped mouth.

Jango introduced them. Lias nodded briefly in her direction and at
once turned away to sell lavender oil to an elderly lady. Maya also
retreated. She had an urgent need to be at a distance from him. She
had sensed his rejection of her, for what reason she could not guess.
She walked to the far side of the arena, moving casually from stall to
stall, feigning a composure she did not feel. She picked up and put down
a jar of homemade gooseberry jam, a pot of honey and a heavy fruitcake
on the WVS stall, and then relented and purchased all three. She queued
at the refreshment tent for a styrofoam cup of orange-coloured liquid
and a ham roll. She sat at a white plastic table at the edge of the arena.
The marching bands had returned; between their ranks of gold and blue
and scarlet she could see the brothers – who were, she reminded herself,
really half-brothers – as they moved around their stall. Somewhere in
the showground Alice also wandered. Maya had not yet told her aunt
of the evening meeting with Jango in the Quiet Woman pub. She sipped
her tea and nibbled at the ham roll; the phone call made to Polly the

previous evening had been difficult and inconclusive. 'When are you coming back?' Polly had asked.

'I'm not sure. There's so much to do here.'

'I thought you'd put the house on the market.'

'And so I have.' She paused. 'Well, not any more. I cancelled the advertisement. It's too soon.'

'What do you mean? Why is it too soon? I thought you couldn't wait to be rid of the place?'

'Every room is full of their personal belongings, books and papers, old letters and mementos. I can't just turn all that over to strangers, can I?'

'You could burn it. Have a bonfire in the garden. From things you've said, I gather you have no sentimental feelings about your parents or their belongings.'

'No,' she had said. 'You're right, of course. I'll start on it tomorrow. I'll ring you when it's sorted out.'

'You do that.' Polly had sounded impatient and unusually unsympathetic. 'I need you here, Maya. Jonah is being difficult again. You know what I mean.'

She had known what Polly meant but did not want to think about it, and instead of sorting through the trunks and boxes of her parents' belongings, she had set out with Alice early this Sunday morning to drive around the lanes of Somerset and Dorset.

'A fete of some kind,' Alice had said. 'Somewhere on the other side of Halston.' Once inside the showground they had separated. At intervals Maya had glimpsed Alice laden down with garden produce and assorted items of bric-a-brac. Her last sighting of her aunt had been close to the fortune-teller's tent where she stood in conversation with two ladies of her own age and style.

The bands marched out of the arena, to be replaced by dogs and their owners for a show of obedience tests and tricks. The Gypsy called Lias was drawn back to the rails by the running, leaping dogs. Even with the width of grass between them, she could see him clearly, could not break her gaze away from his features which were, she thought, similar to those of a Red Indian brave. He returned to the stall, and this time it was Jango who took time off to walk away. He came straight to where Maya sat by the refreshment tent. He sat, the chair pulled round to face her. 'Business is slowing down now,' he said. 'But we've had a good day.'

She said, 'It seems an uncertain way to make a living, market trading.'

'Nothing in this life is certain, lady. And if it was, where would the fun be?'

'Lias,' she said. 'Did you and he have different fathers?'

'Same father,' he said, 'different mothers. Lias looks exactly like our father. I favour my mother, and she was Gorgio.'

'It's unusual to see a young man who has grey hair.'

Jango touched the thick silver curls that hung around his collar. The gesture drew her attention to his fair skin and blue eyes. She said, 'You don't look much like a Gypsy.'

'Oh, but that's what I am,' he said softly. 'I'm as deep Romany as Lias. Don't let appearances fool you.' He lit a cigarette. 'Thought you'd be on your way back to the city.'

'I should be. I will be, just as soon as I've sorted out my parents' things.'

He said. 'Have you worked out yet just how we are related to you?'

'No, I haven't. Even if it's true, it doesn't really matter, does it?'

'It might,' he said. 'There's a strong taboo against incest among our people.'

She was never sure exactly when the decision not to leave the house was made. Every time she returned, even after a brief absence of hours, it was to feel more strongly the pull of the neglected gardens, the mystery of rooms as yet unexplored. To form strong attachments to places or people was not in her nature, and yet she found herself explaining, excusing herself, lying a little to Polly in a letter.

> *I think I may be having some kind of slight breakdown. Nothing to get alarmed about. I just need a spell of quiet, on my own, to get my head together. I've made a few discoveries since I've been here. There are things I need to follow up. The coroner brought in a verdict of misadventure on my parents' deaths, but there are still aspects of it all that are puzzling. Don't worry about me, I've seen the local doctor, and Alice comes in every day. I am so sorry to let you down like this, but in my present state I should be useless in the workroom.*

It was not altogether true; she had not visited a doctor, Alice did not visit, and to describe what ailed her now as a breakdown was to question her lifelong sanity. But Polly did not know about the sightings; she would believe that the sudden death of both parents had unhinged her.

And perhaps it had. She would sit in the kitchen in the evenings, in the cushioned wicker chair which had been her father's. The kitchen was the one room in the house where she felt moderately easy. When the autumn evenings closed in early she would light a fire in the iron range, make toast and drink the strong hot tea to which she had become addicted since her visits to Alice. Her days were spent in a slow exploration of the outbuildings and grounds. She neither wanted nor needed the company of others.

One room at a time seemed to be her wisest method. She was in that frail, undermined condition in which too much, too soon might have destroyed her. The beginning of her sickness could be counted from that instant in Chicago when she had seen the car accident in England. She had realised then that the sighting of the crashed and burning Triumph Stag was not part of a national disaster but a personal tragedy and that her vision of it was a new and frightening departure from an aberration which she had come to consider as being almost normal. The inquest verdict of misadventure had further confused and alarmed her; it was a word without meaning, indecisive and threatening. She could have better tolerated accidental death. To return to the house directly from the Yeovil courtroom had, inevitably, linked the fatal accident to her present possession of the place in a way that broke through the carapace of calm that she had, until now, managed to maintain.

She could not bring herself to view or use the bedrooms, although there was a choice of eight. Alice had lent her a folding bed, a pillow and a duvet, which stood in a corner of the kitchen. Her clothes were on hangers in the downstairs cloakroom; she did not linger longer than was absolutely necessary in the antiquated first-floor bathroom.

Bruenette and Geoffrey Pomeroy appeared to have bought the house complete with furnishings and hangings, equipment and knick-knacks. Using a wisdom and a taste she would not have credited them with having, they had changed nothing. Or was it mere inertia that had caused them to leave in place the collected treasures of several generations? It was not until she had slept a whole night through on the makeshift bed in the kitchen corner that Maya found sufficient courage to open up the first door.

It may have been chance that caused her to turn that particular china knob. One step inside and she knew straightaway that this was her mother's special place, that Bruenette had spent many hours here. She walked to the east-facing window and pulled back the heavy green velvet to let in pale November light. It had always been a woman's room. No man ever used that delicate rosewood desk, the fretted cabinets and bookcases, the faded brocade wing chair. The true owner of the room looked down from a portrait which hung above the fireplace. Maya gazed up into the pale, tired face of a Victorian lady, and again she experienced that instant pang of recognition which had struck her on first seeing Lias.

Coming into the little room from the warmth of the kitchen, it struck chill and damp. She lifted the lid of a brass-bound oak coal box and found it ready filled. A match touched to the paper and sticks in the fire grate soon brought warmth and life into the boudoir; for that, she felt sure, was the true function of the room. She returned to the kitchen and washed the coal dust from her fingers. As she dried her hands, a broken fingernail caught and snagged on the towel, and she examined the rough state of her skin, the chipped crimson nail polish, the split cuticles. In a fit of irritation she grabbed a pair of kitchen scissors and cut her long, almond-shaped nails as close to the fingertips as she was able. This act, which two weeks ago she would have regarded as wilful vandalism, seemed now to be a symbolic cutting of more than fingernails. Since coming to the house, working in the garden, the shape of her hands had changed; they looked shorter, more square, workmanlike, similar to those of Polly. For in their partnership, it was Maya who was the designer and Polly who actually worked with the gemstones and precious metals.

Maya went back into the boudoir and sat in the wing chair. The chair was old, the carved mahogany frame early Victorian. In the portrait, the lady of the house was sitting in this chair; the faded beige of the brocade had been a deep gold then. The brass-bound coal box edged into the picture. A cedar tree was visible through tall French doors. From beneath the skirts of a blue silk gown peeped satin covered slippers. The lady sat in a relaxed position, her hands folded in her lap, her gaze fixed upon the cedar tree. Maya smoothed the knees of her blue jeans; she folded her hands in her lap and looked out through the French doors. The cedar tree had reached a great height. She sat for a long time in a meditative state, absorbing the room until it seemed to become a part of her own memory, although she had never set foot in it until today.

Possession of the house deeds gave her no sense of belonging, and yet with every day that passed she slipped more deeply into the heart of the place. Exploration of the kitchen cupboards revealed a box of cleaning materials. Bruenette had not been a domesticated woman. Maya washed and polished the glass in the French doors of the boudoir; she removed the dust of many months from desk and shelves and carpet. A few late-flowering chrysanthemums made a warm arrangement in a crystal vase. Her days were spent in deliberate isolation. In the evenings she now sat in the boudoir, the curtains closed, the fire lit. For company she had the portrait and the tick of the little gilt clock on the mantelpiece.

The quiet time ended. From one day to another the cedar tree was shaken by the great gales of November. The last of the leaves came whirling down, loose tiles from the stable roof crashed into the yard. She huddled closer to the fire and heard the wind roar in the chimney. She thought about Lias who had turned his face away, who had not spoken to her.

Her calm was shattered. She stood up and began to move listlessly about the room. A glass-fronted cabinet held a collection of porcelain figurines; an arrangement of silver snuffboxes stood in a glass-shelved alcove. The porcelain was dusty, the sheen of the silver tarnished. She moved to the desk and began to open drawers. Her mother's notepaper, pale grey and deckle-edged was embossed with the name of the house and its telephone number. It lay neatly stacked alongside an address book, and several sheets of stamps and airmail stickers. Another drawer held household bills stapled neatly together. She leafed through them, appreciating for the first time the high costs of the repair work that had been done to the house. She glanced briefly at the contents of the other drawers, tax details, insurance policies, old correspondence with the solicitor in Yeovil. Nothing of a personal nature. But what had she expected?

She returned to her chair, took a log from the basket and laid it carefully on the glowing coals. The dry wood caught at once, the flames causing shadows to leap across the lamplit room.

Beside her chair stood a box made of satinwood, deep and square and standing on slender incurved legs. At first she had taken it to be a coffee table. Now she lifted the lid, idly, not expecting to find treasure, and saw that it was fitted out with reels of coloured silk and cotton, tiny silver scissors and thimbles, papers of pins and sewing needles, all of which lay in a slotted tray. She removed the tray, still incurious, expecting to find beneath it yet more aids to sewing. But the lower section of the box was crammed with old and musty smelling books. She lifted them, feeling the dried-out leather of their bindings crumble to dust beneath her touch.

The first layer of volumes were farm and house account books, many of which dated back to the mid-eighteen hundreds. Beneath them lay other, more recent records. At the very bottom of the box, two cardboard folders of the kind used by students were wedged tightly together, difficult to dislodge. She pulled hard on the yellow folder so that as it came free, papers from it spilled across the carpet. She picked them up and shuffled them together, noting as she did so the back-sloping and distinctive handwriting that had been her mother's. The swift lurch of her stomach made her drop the folder and its contents, unread, back into the box.

It had taken her a long time to come to the realisation that some people gave her grief, would always give her grief no matter how much she denied it. It needed no more than a glimpse of a face across a room, a street, a sight of that person's handwriting, to feel the pang in her body, the squeezed restriction in her mind. Several minutes passed before she found the courage to pull out the pale blue folder. A quick glance at its contents showed her that these papers had nothing at all to do with her mother, except perhaps for the new and shiny paperclips which held together the strange assortment of torn and grubby scripts.

She closed the lid of the box and laid the blue folder on its surface. At once, she felt the shutter in her mind fly up, leaving her wide open to anything that came. In an effort to escape the threatened sighting, she walked swiftly to the kitchen, poured milk into a saucepan and set it on the Rayburn. She sawed two thick slices from a wholemeal loaf and spread them thickly with the gooseberry jam bought from the WVS stall. With the bread and jam arranged on a white plate, and coffee made in a red mug, she placed her supper on a tray and returned with it to the room she called the boudoir.

As she ate and drank and gazed into the fire, she became preternaturally aware of the folder. To her heightened senses it seemed to pulse with independent life, willing her, against her better judgement, to lift it up, open it, and read.

The papers were dated and filed carefully in order. A quick glance confirmed that all the available writing space had been covered with a painstaking copperplate hand, the ink of which had faded with time to a shade of reddish brown. She sat for a long time, the sense of foreboding growing stronger. The shutter in her mind was all the way up now, she was totally, achingly receptive, and more frightened than she had ever been. Unwillingly, her gaze was drawn to the uppermost paper. With a sense of disbelief she read the name and date which stood above the first lines of writing.

Maya Heron. April 5th 1888.
I learns to write. Not one or two words like before but many. On this day something walks about inside my head and I see the letters behind my eyes. They jump down on to my shoulder. They run down my arm into my fingers. The fingers make the marks upon the paper. I see writ down what I am thinking. It is a very big magic. But it makes my head ache, for I must look in the big dictionary for to find out the proper spelling of some words.

Maya Heron. April 12th 1888.
I wants to show my writing to Evangeline but if I shows it to her she will know my mind and that I cannot bear. When Milady and Guy are not close by she calls me dirty Gypo and hedge-crawler. She don't want me living in this house. Well, I don't want to live here neither. But my

back and legs is still not mended and so here I must bide. I tell her that my Dadus won't leave me here a minute longer than what he got to. But she laughs and says that tribe of mumpers have forgot all about you. I hates Evangeline. I hopes with all my heart that something bad will happen to her.

Maya Heron. April 20th 1888.

I likes to write. I would like to do some every day but I has to pinch the paper from Milord's desk. He would likely give it to me if I asked him but pinching it is better. He won't wallop me even if he catches me thieving. For I am still an invalid and anyhow the gentry don't do their own walloping of *chavvies*. They leaves it to bitches like Evangeline what calls herself governess all because her can read and write and add up.

Maya Heron. April 28th 1888.

This day I find out what it is I do when I write down my thinking. I am KEEPING A DIARY.

Milady KEEPS A DIARY. She writes every day on a silk-covered book what has a golden hasp and a dinky little key. Today I ask her why she writes in the book and she tells me it is an account of what happens in the house and family and how she feels about it. I am sorely wanting to tell her that I too KEEPS A DIARY but I remembers me just in time that my writing is a SECRET.

Evangeline is surprised at how good I am getting at the spelling. You have made great strides just lately, says she. Even your grammar is improved. You are now ahead of Guy and he is three years older than you are. Guy gets very red in the face and is like to cry. I tells him later on that I am not improved but have copied from Lavinia's book. What is not the truth but he feels better. Evangeline truly does not want to praise me but to make Guy look silly. Because she knows that Guy is my TRUE FRIEND and that he stands with me against Lavinia what is his sister but a WICKED BITCH.

Maya Heron. May 1st 1888.

It is two years today, says Guy, since I am come here to this place. For the first year I am bedfast and like to die. For a long time I do not know that I am caught underneath a house roof. I am hurt in all my body and my head is empty. It is better now. The pain is not so bad and my head is full of thinking. I hear Milady say to Doctor Garrett, Maya is a bright child. She learns very fast. Faster than my own two. When she came to us she could not read or write a word. She has become very dear to us. She is like one of the family.

Milady does not know the truth of it. Evangeline and Lavinia act sweet
and kind to me in front of Milady. But Milord and Milady do not come up
very often to the nursery and the schoolroom. Only Guy is always nice to
me. But he is a boy and the oldest of Milady's children.

It pleases me to outstrip Lavinia. She had a long start on me with the
hangers and pothooks and the adding up. Milady says I have learned
more in two years than Lavinia in six.

Oh, but I long to be out on the *drom* again with my Dadus and
Esmeralda. To feel the wind on my face and in my hair. It is two years
since I am come to this place and still I cannot walk further than the
rooms of the house.

They are gone to the May Day high jinks in the village. All are gone
save me and Cook and Annie. They say there is dancing on the village
green round the Maypole. Milord sends lemonade and cider and cakes for
to make a party of it for the village people. Milady says that Jenkins can
carry me down to the carriage so that I can go with them and watch the
fun. I say that I would sooner bide to home. That my back is hurting.

Cook sends Annie up with a glass of cider and some ginger cake.
Annie sees me at my writing but it makes no matter. She only thinks
that I am at my lessons. The Gorgios don't let their kitchen maids learn
reading and writing, says Lavinia, lest they should get ideas above their
station. She looks hard at me while she says this. Ah Maya, says she
all sweet like, you will soon be the only educated Gypsy in the whole
of England. Whatever will your family think of that when they come to
fetch you? If they ever do. Evangeline and she smiles at one another. Guy
sees that I am like to cry. He pats my hand when they are not looking.
Don't take any notice of them, says he.

Two years today it is since I first came here. It was a day like this
one. Blue sky and little white puffball clouds and the sun warm on the
green grass. Our waggons was pulled in to Sheepdip Lane like always
at this time of year. I had gone with my uncle to feed the horses before
breakfast. When Dadus says he would go that day to tend Sir Henry's
stallion I begged to go with him. At first he said no but Esmeralda said
take her with you, Taiso. The Ladyship might have some spare clothes
for to give you. She has a girl about our Maya's size. If she sees our
maid in that old washed-out frock she might find her heart touched.

So I went with Dadus walking through the village where all the people
stopped and stared, for my Dadus is a fine figure of a man and is knowed
all the world over to be the cleverest Romanichal when it comes to the
curing of sick horses.

I remember myself skipping along down that long driveway. I was
thinking about the pretty frock that might soon be mine. Sometimes the

gentry and farmers set their dogs on us. But this is a good place, says Dadus. Sir Henry is a real gent. We can already hear the horse screaming and kicking at his stall. The ostler is real glad to see us. Likewise Milord. Oh, says he, I am so relieved to see you, Mister Heron. We have been up all night with this stallion of mine. I only hope you can tell us what ails him.

My Dadus puts his hands on the horse's neck and talks to him all quiet like in our language. The great black creature falls silent tho' the sweat stands out on him like a white foam. Dadus feels all over the creature's stomach and looks into its mouth. He is about to tell his Lordship what the matter is when a little white yappy dog runs into the stable. It comes jumping and barking round the horse's feet and all at once the great black stallion rears up on his back legs. Dadus is throwed to the floor and I dart out and runs over to him. I hears Sir Henry shouting and then I feels a great pain in my back and head. Then nothing more.

They tells me later that Dadus got many bruises and a smashed arm. His Lordship dragged us both clear of the wild hooves. The horse was shot that day what seems a pity. They had better of shot that little yappy dog. After many months when I was back in my right mind Milady told me how the doctors had said that if they moved me any distance on that day I would surely die.

Evangeline says that to first Milady nursed me with her own two hands which was a wonder, says she, since you are nothing but a thieving Gypsy child. Later on when I am mending a bit, a young girl from the village comes in to tend me. She is a big strong girl. Her name is Susan. We talk to each other. She tells me that the room I lie in is called the nursery what is a special place at the top of the house with bars on the windows like a prison where the gentry keep their *chavvies* so that they don't have to see them very often. Lavinia and Guy are took downstairs once in every day to eat with Milord and Milady. Before they can go downstairs they must be brushed and combed and told their manners like horses what are being put up for auction at a fair. I say to Susan, but Milady is a good woman. It is a hard thing when a mother puts her children from her and leaves them to the likes of that Evangeline for to be looked after. Susan says the gentry got some funny ways. They is not like us poor people.

I ask Susan how much longer will I be trapped underneath this house roof. When you don't need me any more, says she, then you will be ready to go back to your own people.

May 2nd 1888.
You should have come with us to the Mayday dancing, says Lavinia. Your father's tribe is come back to Sheepdip Lane. You could have stayed there

with them. Your back and legs will mend just as well in a waggon as in a fine house. When we are on our own I say to Guy, is this true? They have not yet come to see me. They will, says he. They were just pulling in when we saw them. Give them time. I beg Susan to leave me in the chair by the window so that I may see who comes walking down the long drive.

May 5th 1888.

They are come this morning. Susan has bathed me and washed my hair. I am dressed in a frock of blue all smocked and frilled what was once Lavinia's. Milady comes into the schoolroom. Excuse me, she says to Evangeline, but Maya's Aunt and Papa has come to see her. They are waiting for her in the nursery. Evangeline is all smiles. She even helps me with my crutches. Milady takes me in to Dadus. I will leave you alone together, says she.

Annie has brought a tray up from the kitchen. There is a pint of porter and tea in a pot and a plate with cake on it. Dadus and Esmeralda sit at the table where we children eat our meals. He jumps up when he sees me. His face is all smiles. He holds his arms out. But I am slow on the crutches and the tears are rolling down my face. Ah dordi, says he. Ah maid, what have they done to you? Ah, how we have missed you.

I am angry with him. He puts his arms round me but I am stiff and turn my head away. What is it? says he.

You left me with house dwellers, I cry. Two whole years you left me.

There was no help for it, says Dadus. You were nearly dead. Only his Lordship could pay the gold to the doctor who saved you, and we has hit on hard times and could not get back sooner.

I am not saved, I cry. Look at me. I hang on crutches. I am shut up in this place. I never feel the wind and sun. Better that I had died than have to bide underneath this roof.

Esmeralda says, are they good to you, maid?

They are good, says I, in the way of Gorgios but their ways is not our ways. The food is mostly pudding made of milk and fish what tastes of nothing. I am washed and scrubbed until my skin is fit to drop off. I hold out my arms. Look, says I. See how white I have become. I do not tell them about the lessons. Something holds my tongue when it comes to the reading and writing. I do not speak about Lavinia and Evangeline. I will settle with that pair in my own way.

Doctor Garratt comes. He talks to Dadus and Esmeralda. He shows them the marks on my back and legs. She is mending, says he, but very slowly. Then Dadus says the words that I long to hear.

Can we take her with us, Doctor?

Doctor Garratt says, I do not advise it. The jolting of your waggon, the damp and cold, the hardness of your way of life could kill her in her present weak condition. Then I would sooner die, I shout, than bide here one day longer. Milady comes in just as I am speaking. Ah Maya, says she, looking all upset. We cannot let you go in your present poor state. We feel responsible, you see. Stay with us a little longer until you are truly well and strong. She comes to me and smooths my hair and wipes my wet cheeks. Dadus comes and puts his arm round my shoulders. I am pulled both ways together.

Doctor Garratt says, I advise more exercise for her. Get her out into the sunshine. Let us see how she is by the end of the summer. Perhaps by then she will no longer need the crutches.

I wave from the window to Dadus and Esmeralda as they walk away up the long drive. They will not come back at the summer's end, I know it. In July and August they will be in the North Country for the big horse fair at Appleby. The travelling back to the south will take them many weeks. They will stop on the road to earn food and money at the harvesting and potato picking. It could be nigh on Christmas before they are back here and oh, how shall I bear the long sad days and nights in the house of the Gorgios?

The fire had burned low in the grate. The room was chilly. Maya moved stiffly in the wing chair like a very old person who has sat too long in the same position. She stood, holding on to the cold marble of the mantelpiece. The face of the woman in the portrait seemed to look down on her with sympathy and some surprise. Maya opened the sewing box, lifted out the tray and replaced the folder in the lower compartment.

She walked to the kitchen. From the window she could see the dark bulk of the stable block outlined against the night sky. She recalled the white-barred nursery windows underneath the eaves, the diarist's description of the long rutted drive. But such features were surely to be found in many large old houses.

She went up to the bathroom. Until now, the fixtures and fittings, the Victorian decor had been of little interest to her. As she washed and dried her face and hands, slapped on night cream and braided her long hair, her gaze roved across the mahogany panelling, the blue-flowered porcelain of the lavatory, washbasin and huge clawfooted bath. Was it here that the Gypsy child had been scrubbed and soaked until her skin turned white?

Nine doors opened off the angled corridors of this first floor, and every door was closed. Maya reached out a hand towards the nearest flower-painted doorknob. As she touched the cold china, a shiver trembled through her body. She turned, almost running back towards the stairs and the familiar kitchen. The makeshift bed beside the Rayburn had become her place of safety but sleep did not come easily that night.

The kitchen garden lay beyond the stable block. It was bounded by walls of ancient rose-coloured brick, across which espaliered apricots and peaches spread their branches. A glass-enclosed vinery filled space on the south-facing wall, a potting shed stood in a corner; the greenhouse and cold frames were in a poor state of repair.

The soil of the garden had clearly been cultivated in springtime. Uneven rows of cabbages reached across the width of one bed, what she guessed might be potatoes filled another. Ungathered lettuce, carrots, radishes and beetroot had rotted in their staggered lines. She experienced a vague unwilling tenderness towards the two who had last spring laboured so inexpertly in this quiet plot.

From the potting shed she collected a spade and fork and a wicker basket; the tools when last used had been thrown haphazardly into a corner, clumps of dried soil clung to the tines and blade. She went to the potato patch and drove the fork into ground close to the withered green of the first haulm. The potatoes rose clean and white from the rich soil, and she began to fill the basket.

It was only when she was outside the house and working that she dared to allow herself to think about the writings of the child called Maya Heron. Already there were many questions to be answered. Maya was a name seldom heard in England. Heron was the surname of the Gypsy market-trader brothers, men who claimed a blood relationship to Bruenette but had no proof. The writings had been carefully hoarded, preserved by some unknown persons for more than a hundred years. Someone, quite recently, had fastened them in bundles with new and shiny paperclips, had placed them safely at the bottom of the sewing box, packed into a pale blue folder. Someone had set a certain value on the scribblings of a child long dead. Had Bruenette brought the writings with her from some other place, or had she found them in an attic trunk in this house which was at once a strange and yet familiar refuge?

Maya laboured through the shortening hours of daylight. So much to be done in this garden and she without skill or the most rudimentary knowledge of horticulture. She dragged the basket full of potatoes into the potting shed. Using a scraper and a handful of rags, she cleaned the fork and spade and the other tools until their metal shone and hung them from nails on the shed wall. She tidied the shelves and swept the benches and the plank floor. Walking back into the house, she planned a bonfire for tomorrow.

She lay for a long time in hot water in the stained and ancient bathtub, soaking the ache from muscles not accustomed to heavy labour. She began to think about Polly who no longer phoned; about Alice who lately asked the kind of questions to which Polly would be needing answers. She imagined the collusion between them, their discussions of her. A visit to Alice might be a wise move, so that normality might be established and privacy assured for a few more days or weeks.

Alice was also working in her garden. Her smile, as Maya walked towards her, was edged with relief. 'My dear! How very nice to see you. I was planning to come over, but you know how it is. You'll stay for a bite of lunch, won't you? It's only soup and cheese, I'm afraid.'

Maya followed her aunt into the kitchen. She draped her thin jacket across a chair and sat, while Alice heated soup and sliced cheese and bread. They ate in silence. Alice wore green corduroy trousers, a cream-coloured Guernsey and a green quilted waistcoat. Maya said, 'I need some winter clothes, the things I have are unsuitable for wearing in the country. Especially unsuitable for gardening.'

'So you've started to garden?'

'Well, tidying up really. Pulling out rubbish, having a bonfire, clearing up the fallen leaves.'

'You're getting fond of the place, aren't you?'

'Not exactly fond. I just don't seem able to leave it – yet. I shall sell it eventually, of course. When I've straightened out a few things. I belong in London really.'

As Maya was leaving, Alice said, 'We could shop for winter clothes in Taunton. I could do my Christmas shopping.'

'That would be nice. Ring me when you want to go. My time is at your disposal.' She spoke lightly but Alice did not smile. She stood at the open window of the car looking down at Maya.

'Be careful,' she said. 'Don't get too attached to that place. It has an evil reputation.' She obviously wanted to say more, would have said more, but the car began to move slowly out into the road, and then was gone.

On the twenty-minute drive back to the house, Maya thought about Alice, about the disappointment she must feel at her niece's deliberate withdrawal to a place which she herself feared to visit. Maya turned with relief into the long rutted driveway of the Monks House. London was not where she belonged.

Jango

They returned to Derbyshire in mid-November, he and Lias motoring north on the old Fosse Way, driving through Stow-on-the-Wold and Moreton-in-Marsh, a familiar area for them of the great horse fairs, taking the route they had travelled as children, when the last of the wooden waggons had still found space enough to roll down the English roads and lanes.

Rain beat against the windows of the Winnebago with a force that slowed the action of the windscreen wipers. They drove past sodden fields and brimming ditches, swollen rivers and trees bent double in the thrashing wind. Lias held the heavy vehicle steady on the wet and winding road while Jango, half dozing in the cab's warmth, allowed his thoughts to rove back over recent months.

September had been golden. He remembered how the fields and orchards of Somerset and Dorset had been scented by mushrooms and cider apples. They had pitched overnight in lanes already yellow underfoot with fallen leaves. They had slept under clear skies thick with stars, and woken to misty mornings and the sounds of chiffchaffs seeking woodlice and beetles among the undergrowth of hedge bottoms.

The warm days had continued on into October. They stood markets in little seaside towns and inland cities and retired to whatever overnight pitch it had been possible to find, weary from the long day's trading, their money belts well filled.

They never spoke about the woman called Maya. But Lias knew his brother's habit of falling in love deeply and often with unsuitable females and he guessed the nature of his current preoccupation. What Lias did not comprehend, and Jango was incapable of explaining, was that this time it would all be very different. He had reached a point in his life where his mind turned to marriage, a more settled existence.

He had never thought much about his childhood. He remembered it now as a time of wanderings, of impermanence, uncertainty. Something deep within him regretted those unnamed villages and towns through which his family had passed, the hundreds of fields and lanes in which his first years had been spent. His memories were not so much of places but of people. He remembered his grandparents, the old dark-skinned couple whom he had not in any way resembled; the aunts and uncles and many cousins who noted his Gorgio looks but did not reproach him for them. There was, in fact, an unspoken relief among his family that this second son of Despair Heron favoured in so many ways his town-bred mother.

Lias was Despair's true son, in his looks, the proud way he walked and held his head and shoulders, in the deep Romany of his convictions. But not in his nature or his ways. Oh, he was a hard man, tough in the sense a *chal* of his kind must be in order to survive. But there was a tenderness in Lias which few save Jango ever witnessed.

As they came into Derbyshire, the rain eased. They paused briefly at a village cafe to eat oatcakes with eggs and bacon, and to drink strong sweet tea. Already the air was colder; as they moved northwards there was a smell of snow among the peaty summits. Jango felt the heart-stir that he always experienced on his return to this place. For this was the Dark Peak country, a land of heather moors and grey crags, and sheer rock edges. He had never admitted to anyone, especially not to Lias, how he felt about the wild homestead towards which they now travelled and where they would remain until the springtime.

The land had been bought by Despair Heron in the last years of his life – fifty acres of unproductive High Peak hillside and the derelict stone farmhouse and outbuildings which stood upon it.

They had been travelling south from the great horse fair at Appleby in Yorkshire. They came into Derbyshire on a warm August evening, Lias driving the Land Rover which pulled a custom-built, flashed-out trailer, a luxurious mobile home which had etched glass windows and cream-coloured blinds trimmed with silken bobbles. They were travelling with three other families, all of them close relatives. Despair, seated between Lias and Jango, had signalled that they should halt beside a road sign.

'What's the name of this place?'

Lias, who was good at the reading and writing, had said, 'This whole area is called the Hope Valley.'

Despair had gazed upwards at the bleak hillside and the tumbledown buildings which stood upon it. He noted the stream which still trickled water in this time of summer drought. He pointed to the faded paint on a wooden board which leaned at an angle beside the farmhouse.

'What says the notice?'

'For Sale,' Lias said briefly.

Despair said, 'Switch off your motor. I want to look at this place.' He had bowed his head in a gesture which, with hindsight, now seemed to Jango like one of submission. 'Matter of fact,' said Despair, 'us could bide the night here. Not a living soul to be seen for miles around.'

The Land Rover pulled them easily up the steep slope of the hillside. They pitched in the shadow of a stone-built barn. The children of the company fetched water from the stream. Supper was eaten round a small fire which was contained for safety in a perforated bucket. They sat in the afterglow of a crimson and indigo sunset. The men smoked cigarettes, Aunt Lina puffed on her briar pipe.

Despair Heron said, thoughtfully and slowly, 'A good pitch.' Some minutes later he said, 'I won't be going to Appleby no more.'

'Why not?' Lias asked.

'Too much trouble with the farmers and *gavvers*. I'se getting too old for all that.'

Jango remembered the time, in a village pub, when his father had taken on four farmers, single-handed, and thrashed them.

He said, 'You could still sort 'em out, Dadus, if you wanted.'

'No, boy. Better face it. I'm nearly finished.'

The rest of the company moved out early the next morning. Despair and his sons remained on the good pitch. Lias and Jango fetched water from the stream.

'The old bastard's up to something,' Lias said. 'I've never known him part company with Aunt Lina in all the years we've travelled.'

Jango nodded. 'He was up at daybreak, poking about in that old house and sheds.'

After breakfast was eaten, the dishes washed, the bedding squared away in cupboards, Despair said, 'I've got words to say to you two.' They sat on the short brown turf and lit cigarettes. The sun came up crimson, as it had gone down.

'Rain coming,' said Despair. 'Be a downpour before evening.' For a long time he said nothing and they waited for their father's words. When he spoke the shock was such that they were dumbstruck. 'Times is changing,' he said. 'I've been giving it deep thought. What we needs is our own pitch. Bought and paid for. Somewhere safe to come back to. A place where the bloody *gavvers* and the council people can't touch us.' He pointed with his cigarette, waved it as if it was a magic wand. 'This place,' he said, 'this place'll do me. Miles from anywhere.' His thin lips stretched in a rare tight grin. 'A valley called Hope. Well, I reckon that's a good enough spot for a man called Despair to die in.'

It was Lias who argued with their father. 'So what about freedom?'

he asked. 'All our lives you've told us that the only way to live is to keep on the move. That it's death to a Rom man to be tied down in the one place.'

'We need our own pitch, boy,' Despair repeated. 'Them as got the money, that's what they're doing. Buying a few acres. A place to die peaceful in. Somewhere safe for their children and grandchildren to come back to. A bit of land what they can't turn us from.'

'And have you got enough money?' Lias asked.

The old man nodded and patted the capacious pockets of his poacher's jacket. 'I got more'n enough,' he said.

Lias would not put his name to the legal documents and so the business of buying the holding was all down to Jango. It was he who drove the Land Rover to the solicitor's office. He who, dressed in a good suit, white shirt and blue tie, shot his cuffs in the solicitor's view to reveal a paper-thin Rolex and signed his name with his own gold pen. There was no trace to be seen of his Romany forebears in his collar-length silver curls, blue eyes and fair skin. The fact that he handed over the asking price in Kruger rands caused no obvious surprise. As Despair had said, gold talks in any language.

It took time to transform the derelict two-storey house into a weather-proof habitation. They worked in the winter months, repairing the sagging roof beams, replacing other timbers, digging out a new cesspit. Despair Heron lived to see the farmhouse renovated, the roofs and walls of the outbuildings made good. He never slept beneath those timbers but died as he wanted, on the open hillside. Just moments before his father died, Jango asked the question he had never in his life dared to put.

'Tell me,' he said, 'about my mother.'

The black eyes clouded over, the heavy lids came down and then were raised. 'Your mother? She was a lady. Come from rich folks, she did. Followed me. Followed me all over.' For a long time he did not speak. Then he said, 'I never wanted her. In the end, because my sister Lina said I should, your mother and me jumped the broomstick. She died when you was but days old.'

'Where did she come from? What was her name?'

The breathing was laboured now; it slowed, appeared to cease and then began again. Jango hoped for information, but Despair's only response was, 'Her name was Madeline. She followed me all over.'

Lias

*I*t needed skill and a well-tuned engine to persuade the Winnebago up the steep hillside and in through the double white gates set in a low drystone boundary wall. On the tops of the gatepost perched two carved stone owls.

The farmhouse was built of limestone with the darker shaded gritstone used for lintels and the mullions of windows. The surrounding turf had been replaced by Jango with a wide driveway of smooth black tarmacadam. They had called in a Gorgio builder to supply the refinements of new doors and window frames for the house, a kitchen and a bathroom. The name on the deeds was Jango Heron. His was the enthusiasm, the forward planning of the house; the love. Lias, who owned half of the property with his half-brother, showed no interest in its improvement. He tolerated for Jango's sake the time spent underneath its roof. When spring returned, it was always Lias who said. 'Let's get rolling out of this gaol.'

As Lias stepped down from the Winnebago, the first flakes of snow settled on his lips and eyelids. He stood in the shadow of the van and watched Jango run towards the house door, fumble a key into the lock and enter. Within moments the soft light of oil lamps bloomed in many windows as his brother made the ritual tour. Lias opened the rear door of the van and the dogs jumped down to stand beside him.

The carved stone owls atop the gateposts had been his only contribution to their winter quarters. It seemed fitting to him that the owl, bird of ill omen, should be the guardian of their inheritance from Despair Heron. As he closed the double gates he touched a finger to the caps of snow that had already settled on the owls' heads. If he followed his inclination he would sleep for this first night in the Winnebago. But to do so would upset Jango.

Lias walked with the dogs towards the house, dipped his head beneath the gritstone lintel and closed the door upon the snowy night.

He had done what he could to recreate his bedroom in the style and layout of a *vardo* or the interior of the Winnebago. His bed stood directly underneath the window; the room was unheated, as was the whole house, save for the cast-iron wood-burning range in the kitchen and a vast open fireplace in what Jango chose to call the parlour. The house was solid, draught proof, even on this windy hillside in the bitter winters that were usual in the Dark Peak country. And yet for Lias it was that snugness, the shut-in comfort that he found claustrophobic.

He lay sleepless as he always did on this first night within doors. He suspected that Jango also found difficulty in sleeping but would not admit it. The change had come over Jango as they crossed the boundary into Derbyshire. He began to talk about the house, to worry about it, to exhibit anxieties that were foreign to Lias.

Through the glass of the uncurtained window a crescent moon cast lavender shadows across the snowscape. Lias listened to the sounds made by the house, the creak of timbers which shrank against the falling temperature, the hum of the generator which produced electricity for the freezer cabinets which Jango had insisted must be installed. In all other respects they lived here without the complications of modern gadgets. But in winters when they were cut off by snow and storm, stocks of frozen meat and vegetables were a necessity, said Jango, and not the indulgence which Lias considered them to be.

He lay back on his pillows, lit a cigarette and blew smoke into the semi-darkness. Thoughts came crowding into his mind, memories of summer and autumn, the fields and lanes, the beaches and markets of Dorset and Somerset. For the first time in their life together he understood how it felt to be pulled irresistibly towards a certain place; a certain woman. How it felt to be Jango.

Ten years had passed since that evening when they had come upon the Hope Valley and Despair had gazed up at the house and hillside and seen both as a place of safety for himself and his descendants. What small respect Lias had ever felt for his father died that night. Jango had been a boy of eighteen years, he himself a man of twenty-eight, already set firm in his mould, resistant to the changes certain to be brought about by winters spent in these permanent quarters.

He had thought when Despair died that Jango would agree to sell up, realise on their investment, take the cash and travel. But for reasons known only to himself, Jango had been uncharacteristically determined. He had clung to the chunk of bare hillside, the ugly stone house, as if his life hung in the balance. It had caused the only rift ever to occur between them, but Lias, in the end, had been philosophical about it. And truth to tell it had not turned out too badly. There were profitable bits of business to be done from an isolated site in lonely hills. If he felt like an animal trapped inside a strange skin, then he would endure it. Normality returned with every springtime.

Maya. He drew hard on the hand-rolled cigarette, tamped it out and rolled a fresh one. He could not think about her when he was with Jango. He was grateful that Jango never spoke about her. He lit the cigarette. Only now, in this solitary room, would he let the image of her come back into his mind. He closed his eyes against the moonlight, luxuriating in his memories, reliving his brief sightings of her. He had been close to her just the one time, when Jango had introduced them. He had looked at her and then turned sharply away. But that look had been sufficient. So strong had it been that he could almost persuade himself now that he had buried his face in the fall of white-blonde hair, put his lips to the pale skin of her throat.

He had been married once. A mistake. He was no good to women. He was sufficiently self-aware to know that the violence of his father lived on within himself. He had read about it in a glossy magazine in a dentist's waiting room. How the child who witnesses violence between his parents will himself repeat the pattern in his own life. It was no excuse; he had done those things, he must be accountable for them. It was Jango who had been the lucky one. His young years with their grandparents had been gentle, quiet. He would never hit a woman. Despair had never found a third wife who would risk her life to his murderous fists and temper. Since his own wife's departure, there had been only passing fancies, brief encounters. What he needed, but had so far never found, was a woman of his own sort. One who would match him, blow for blow.

He awoke to the peculiar brilliance of sunlight upon snow. When sleep had finally come, it had been deep and dreamless. Now he struggled, as he always did on this first morning in the house, to place himself among the mahogany chests and wardrobes, the pattern of faded cabbage roses on walls that were higher and wider than those of the Winnebago. He smiled. The brass rails of the bed were tarnished. Before the day was over, Jango, with his polishing cloths and tin of metal polish, would have restored their proper lustre.

In their absence during the spring and summer months the holding was a regular stopping place for family members. Jango had made house rules. The place was to be left exactly as found. Hospitality, he said, was one thing. Taking advantage was another. But no matter how carefully the visiting *raklis* swept and dusted, it never was to Jango's standard. Lias went down to the kitchen to find the flagstones wet from scrubbing, the cooking range newly blackleaded, and breakfast cooking. He pulled out a chair and sat at the table. 'You'll make somebody a wonderful wife,' he said sourly.

Jango tipped eggs and sausages onto a warmed plate and set it before his brother. 'You do your job,' he said mildly, 'and leave me to do mine.' He brought his own breakfast to the table. 'Heavy snow last night. The driveway needs clearing. Lija Heron used all the logs up while he was here. I'll be having words with him when I see him. You'd better get chopping straightaway.'

Lias nodded agreement, deferring to his brother in a way he would not have done while they were on the road. While they lived as Gorgios, it was the Gorgio half of Jango that ordered and decided. In an attempt to assert his authority as elder brother, Lias said, 'We need to talk about business. We shall have to find some new lines to sell.'

'Tonight,' said Jango. 'There are things I have to do today.'

Maya

*T*here were frost ferns on the kitchen window. She had refuelled the Rayburn and maintained a night-long fire in the kitchen fireplace, but while she slept, the intense cold had invaded the house. Her body felt stiff beneath the duvet, her bones ached; she pushed her feet into sandals and pulled the silk wrap tight about her. A spasm of fear writhed in her stomach. She could die in this house, in the month of December, and her body not be found until March or April. She thought that three weeks must have passed, even four, since she had spoken to a relative or friend.

She made coffee, rekindled the remains of the fire with short dry logs, pulled the wicker chair close to the blaze and wrapped her fingers round the brimming coffee mug. The warmth eased her panic. The ache in her bones dulled then disappeared.

The severe cold had come suddenly, and she still lacked proper winter clothing. Her last contact with Alice had been abrupt, unkind, the sort of near-quarrel it is possible to get into on the telephone when the absence of eye contact releases callers from their normal, polite inhibitions.

Maya went to the phone and dialled.

Alice picked up the receiver on the first ring. 'Maya, how nice. I was going to call you. I knew you were all right, of course. I asked the postman and the log man, and they had seen smoke coming from your chimneys.'

'I'm sorry I was so unpleasant to you,' Maya said. 'I get these bad days – you know, when everything looks black. I know that you're right, that I'm too much on my own. But sometimes I can't seem to bear the company of other people. As for staying in this house, well, I have to. I can't leave it now. That's all there is to say.'

'It's all right, Maya. Really it is. I was fussing as usual. I'm happy to see you anytime, but only when you feel like company.'

'I'm feeling like it now. Why don't we make that trip to Taunton? I
need to buy some clothes, and you can do your Christmas shopping.'

'That would be very nice.'

'Can you go this morning?'

'Love to!'

'I'll pick you up around ten.'

The vigilance of the log man and postman at first annoyed and then
reassured her. This was country living, where everyone knew everybody
else's business. How much, she wondered, was known in the village about
Bruenette and Geoffrey, about the history of the house? There were times
when Alice had the look of a woman full of secrets. The time might come
when Alice would say, 'Oh, I could tell you quite a lot.'

They shopped for sweaters, trousers, socks and leather boots. Alice
introduced her to long-sleeved camisoles, winceyette pyjamas, a weighty
dressing gown. She bought a smart quilted jacket in the regulation shade
of country green which matched her new green wellies and the woollen
cap which would hide her long pale hair.

Elated by the spending of so much money in so short a time, they
treated themselves to lunch at the County Hotel. In the afternoon they
would shop for Christmas presents. Maya's list was short. A square of
hand-painted silk for Polly, cigars for Jonah, chocolates for Alice.

The lunch tables of the County Hotel were covered with pink cloths.
A silver centrepiece of freesias gave off an evocative perfume. Maya ate
because the food was set before her; she conversed because Alice asked
her questions she felt obliged to answer. But even as she smiled and
nodded, a part of her mind became separated from what she thought of
as its moorings and floated off to hover just above the freesias. From
this centrepoint she could observe herself, her devious behaviour, the
misleading display of normality in which it seemed she had now become
skilled. She left wide open the shutter in her mind that had been her
only protection against horror. Since she no longer saw the disasters
that happened to other people, all her perceptions had turned inwards.

Alice cut toast into squares and spread them with pâté. Maya
ate melon.

Alice said, 'So what do you do with yourself all day, alone in that
big house?'

'Oh, I keep busy. I've managed to get the garden into some sort of
order. And then there's the decorating. I've emulsioned the kitchen walls
and painted the woodwork. I have this plan to go through the rooms of
the house, one by one, and clean out the cupboards, wash the curtains
– all that sort of thing.'

'My word! That's quite an undertaking. I do admire your energy, but if you'll forgive my asking, to what purpose, Maya? If you don't intend to keep the house?'

Maya said, 'Perhaps I do. I've grown attached to certain aspects of it.'

'And what about Polly and the business?'

'I haven't worked that out yet.'

They drove home through the early twilight of December. Alice stood at her garden gate, her arms full of boxes and packages. 'You'll come to me for Christmas lunch, won't you?' The freezing air had given her face a blue, pinched look. She looked anxious, old.

Maya smiled. 'Of course I will. I'd love to.'

She drove slowly through the village. There were lit-up Christmas trees in gardens and cottage windows, carol singers were about, the school advertised a Nativity play. She thought about the day, about Alice and the questions she had asked, which were always the same questions. Her answers hardly varied by more than a word or two. It was a game they played.

The ache that had pressed all day behind her eyes began to ease as she drove out of the village. As she approached the uphill slope that led to Hunger Hill, the headache lifted. Just to be alone gave her a peculiar pleasure.

The first snowflakes began to fall as she unloaded the car.

The log man had brought applewood on his last visit; the logs burned with a blue flame and a sweet fragrance. Maya stretched her newly slippered feet towards the blaze. Dressed in the winceyette pyjamas, the weighty dressing gown, her supper eaten, the dishes washed and stacked, she had a sense of wellbeing which encouraged risk. For the first time since her initial reading of the diary, she reached into the sewing box and withdrew the pale blue folder.

Maya Heron. June 21st 1888.

I tells them when I first come here that I disremembers when my birthday is but that I think I am aged about eleven years. Today it is Lavinia's birthday. The daughter of the house is fourteen. Milady says that we will also celebrate my birthday on this day. Susan says that it will save them the trouble and expense of having two parties. So today I am thirteen years old. So they say. The day is fine and warm so we has the party in the garden. Tom hangs lanterns in the trees and helps Cook and Annie carry tables and chairs out to the lawn. Tom grumbles that this is not gardener's work, but he winks his eye at me what makes me laugh. There are two birthday cakes. Lavinia and me both have new frocks. Hers is pink to match the icing on her cake. Pink, says I, don't look too good with red hair. My frock is a deep blue like the sky. Guy says it sets my yellow hair off beautifully. His face goes all red after he says that. You better watch out for him, says Susan. You could have some trouble with him in a couple of years.

In a couple of years, say I, my feet will be back on the *drom* with Dadus and Esmeralda and I will be gone far from this place.

Well, you mind my words, says Susan. The gentry is not to be trusted around the lower classes. There's many a poor girl been ruined by a lord's son.

Cook had a hard job to make blue icing for my cake. It turned out looking grey like. But tasted good. Evangeline says to Lavinia but looking at me, I don't know why Milady goes to so much trouble for that ungrateful hedge-hopper. She could have had one of your old frocks for the party. Lavinia says looking side on at me, Mama is a saint. I don't know how she puts up with that child's wicked ways. It seems like we are to be burdened with her for ever. When we are on our own I say to Lavinia, well, fancy now. You is properly on the shelf and no mistake.

I don't know what you mean, says she.

Well, says I, fourteen years old and not yet engaged. If you lived in our *tan* you would have long been promised to some lively fellow. Your fifteenth birthday would have been your wedding day.

Why, that's disgusting, says she. Respectable people don't get married when they are only fifteen.

I puts my head on one side and looks her up and down in that way what drives her mad. Oh, says I, you got no need to worry. There's not a *chal* in our whole company what would take you on even on a dark night. Not with that ginger hair and freckles and your nasty ways.

The new parson comes to the birthday party. He is a young man. His wife is pretty. They come straight to me and shake my hand. I curtsy like Evangeline has showed me.

It is easy to see, says he, that you are your mother's daughter. He smiles to Milady who is also light-haired. Milady tells him no, Maya is our guest. He is shamefaced at the mistake. He has heard about the Gypsy who is foisted on these gentlefolk. But, says he, she has such fair hair. All the Gypsies I have seen are black as midnight.

I curtsies again all sweet and dimples. Oh sir, says I, you have been lucky to have seen the black-haired ones what are good and kind. The light-haired Gypsies like me are the Devil's children. They grows up to be witches.

The parson's face goes all red. Evangeline pulls at my arm. Lavinia says, shame on you, Maya. You have spoiled my party. I throw my right-hand crutch at her. It catches her on the shinbone what is a painful spot. I says to the parson, do you know why I am here? It is because Milord's black stallion tried to kick my brains out. I have not walked properly in two years. I grab up my sticks and go as fast as I can back to the schoolroom. I have not looked at Milady's face.

I lock the door tho' no one comes to find me.

I will not cry tears.

I will make a poppet this night and stick pins in it so that something bad will happen to Lavinia.

July 1st 1888.

Lavinia looks sick. The freckles stand out on her face like brown pebbles on the Chesil seashore. It is nothing of my doing. I am still pinching candle ends when I can find them so that I can make the poppet.

Lavinia lies in bed. She keeps a cotton bag full of hot salt close against her belly. She moans and makes much of what it is that ails her. I say to Evangeline that Lavinia should have felt the stallion's hooves on her back and legs. That is cause enough for crying. Evangeline looks across her shoulder to see if Guy is listening. She whispers to me that Lavinia has that day become a woman. But, says she, I don't imagine that you know what I am talking about.

Of course I know. I have known since I was very young, says I. It means that Lavinia will bleed when the moon is in her quarter. That Lavinia is now ready to be a wife and mother. Her clothes must be washed separately from Guy's. We must never eat any food that she has touched. Among *tatchi* Romanies the true sort, she would be put in a separate tent until she is again clean. We must take care that Guy does not touch her or anything that she has handled. Evangeline is very angry. What nonsense, says she. How could Lavinia's condition possibly hurt Guy? This is some more of your heathen ways. On no account are you to repeat this in the nursery or anywhere else.

Well, don't blame me, I say, if Guy grows weak and fit to die. A man's manhood is soon ruined if he has contact to a *mokardi* woman. It is a lucky chance for me, I tell her, that I am not a boy made to dwell in this house full of women what goes heedless among men when the moon is in their quarter.

Lavinia makes the most of what Evangeline calls her indisposition. She lies abed all day and Annie brings her special treats on a tray with a pretty cloth on it. But this could be a good thing. It means she is well away from Guy and no danger to his manhood.

Guy is coming along very nicely lately. He will be sixteen in August. He has grown tall and his shoulders widen. His voice gets quite deep and there is a soft down on his chin and top lip. He is a very handsome *rai*. He has the red colour of his sister but where she is sandy and frizzy and freckled, Guy has dark red curls and a fresh high colour in his face.

Susan says he is already sweet on me.

Maya Heron. October 1st 1888.

The tutor is back. Mr Purchase was in Italy for the summer long. He has lost his pale sick looks. He is now nearly handsome. Lavinia is to start lessons with him. But I am not. Evangeline says I am too young and anyway it would be a waste of Milord's money for me what can't properly speak the Queen's English to learn French and Latin.

So I am on my own with Evangeline every afternoon. To first I was very worried about this but it have turned out nice. Milady said that we should go out into the fresh air and so improve my walking. Evangeline is not much for the walking, being rather fat. But I is still very slow on my pins so we matches well together.

Maya Heron. October 7th 1888.

They have not come back to get me. I knew they would not be able to but still I hoped. Life is very hard for Dadus and Esmeralda. I only see this lately since I have lived with Milord. I never knowed before how soft and easy is the Gorgio way of living.

Evangeline says even if they came for you, you would only be a burden to them through the winter. I could kill her where she stands in her black boots but I know she speaks the truth of it. I am down in my spirits and sit hours by the window. Some days I can't eat for thinking about Dadus and my own people. I am made to wear Lavinia's old shoes when I go walking with Evangeline who says she will not be seen abroad with a barefoot beggar maid.

Maya Heron. October 10th 1888.

The days are getting colder. This afternoon it rained. Evangeline will not go walking when it rains. I watch from the window. Milady comes up to the nursery. How cosy you look, says she, sitting here in the firelight. She lays her hand upon my head. She knows what ails me. She goes to the big white cupboard where Lavinia's clothes are hung. I have something here to cheer you up, says she. She brings out a winter's cape of dark green velvet with a hood and muff trimmed with white fur. There are high leather boots to match. I tries it all on and everything fits like it was made for me. There are winter dresses made of fine merino wool in colours of cream and dark blue and a lovely bright red. Lavinia has grown so much this summer, says Milady, she will need several new outfits for the winter. Yes, say I, and now she has become a woman Lavinia will stand your watching of her when the *rais* come around. She is already making sheep's eyes at the tutor.

Milady looks startled and then her mouth puckers up like she wants to laugh. You are a wise child, she says to me. Perhaps I should have a word with Lavinia about certain matters.

I am still dressed in the green cape and high boots when Guy comes to his tea. He never speaks or looks at me lately when the others are about. Lavinia and Evangeline are talking in the schoolroom and so we two is on our own.

His face goes first white and then red when he sees me. You look beautiful, says he. I never saw a girl with that shade of hair before. He reaches out his hand and then pulls back. You can touch if you wants to, say I. I won't tell on you. But he puts his hands in his trouser pockets and looks deep into the fire.

So you finds me pretty then, I asks him. But 'tis only your sister's cast-offs what does the trick.

No, says he, it is more than that. He turns round and walks fast towards me but Annie comes in with the tea tray and so now I will never know what Guy intended.

Maya Heron. November 22nd 1888.

Evangeline talks to me when we go walking in the lanes. She says that her days are numbered in the schoolroom. Guy should have been sent away to Sherborne School long since but he was sick of the rheumatic fever when he was little and weak for a long time after. Lavinia is not yet suited to go away from home since she is very sensitive in her feelings. But this state of affairs will not last much longer. I say that Lavinia is a spoilt bitch. If she lived in our *tan* the other maidens would have pulled her hair out by the roots and cured her of her spiteful ways.

Ho ho, says Evangeline, I have heard some spiteful words come from you, miss.

Of course, say I. But I am one against many in this fine house. My Dadus said I must always remember who and what I am.

Oh, you make double sure that we do not forget that, says Evangeline. But she smiles when she speaks.

Away from Lavinia, Evangeline is quite a nice old cow. I shan't make a poppet for her after all.

Maya Heron. December 22nd 1888.

There has been some trouble. Milord finds out that I have pinched his writing paper. He come upon me in his study with my fingers in his desk drawer. I could not deny it. The sheets were in my hand.

Why? said he. Why could you not ask me for it? Paper is expensive but if you need it so badly that you will steal it I will gladly find some for you.

He takes a minute or two to think. I know, says he. I have some old bills and notices that are only printed on the one side. He shakes his head and looks sad. Says he, tell me why you want the paper? I cannot tell him true. How can I say it is to write down for a record all what happens to me in this place so that I do not forget it? So I say I must practise my pothooks and hangers in secret. For if I use the slate, everyone will see how slow I am. I have a wish, I say, to be as clever as Lavinia and Guy.

He smiles. Well, that is a very worthy ambition, says he. I will find you some papers right away.

I say, thank you, Milord. I point my eyes to the ceiling. I say, you won't tell them up there what I am doing. They will make sport with me. A Gypo. Writing.

He says, they are hard on you sometimes.

Says I, Guy is sweet and kind. So is Milady.

And how is your walking coming along? says he. I see you often in the garden. It seems to me that you are improving. He hands me a great sheaf of papers what is empty of writing on the one side. I can hide them under my mattress for tonight but a proper hiding place must be found for them tomorrow.

There were many things she did not believe in; dwelling on the past was one of them, ghosts was another. She believed that she was not a superstitious woman, and yet that night she studied the careful pothooks and hangers of the child called Maya with the feeling of deep dread that always seized her just before a sighting. Now she leaned back quite deliberately into the comfort of the wing chair. Slowly she relaxed her cramped muscles and eased the rigidity of her jaw.

She began to recall that afternoon in Chicago, the sun hot in the blue sky, the Hasidic Jews, dark-garbed and gesticulating in groups upon the pavement. She remembered the voices of Sinatra and Springsteen, lulling her senses so that her mind gave no resistance when the crashing of a car in Dorset was transmitted instantaneously across thousands of miles. That day, that music, had marked the end of normality for her. After other, earlier sightings, and there had been many, she had groped her way back into the world that is inhabited by rational people. But not this time.

She allowed herself, for the first time, to think about her parents. Really think about them, their own deliberate isolation in this house which, for people of their age, was unmanageably large. Everywhere she found the small signs of their neglect: the loose doorknobs, the stiff water taps, the windows which refused to open. She considered her own time in the house, the daily chores of fuelling the Rayburn, cleaning fire grates, bringing in logs and chopping kindling; the long days spent working in the garden. She was considerably younger and fitter, but in the four months of her occupation she had hardly touched the fringe of all that needed to be done. She was careful not to question her sense of obligation to the house, which was more than obligation, something deeper and more urgent. Somewhere behind one of those closed oak doors on the first-floor landing was her parents' bedroom, the wardrobes and drawers still crammed with the clothes they would never wear, the possessions they would never use. The day would come when she would have to enter that room, deal with its contents. But not yet.

Time, she now realised, had ceased to have any significance for her. The world as she had always known it was receding. Soon it would slip away and altogether vanish, and she would be left alone on an island of her own creation. The only area of the day when she might possibly admit to loneliness was this time of early evening when she and Polly, and sometimes Jonah, would gather in her flat or Polly's for an after-work drink and a discussion of the business of the day.

On her thought of Jonah, the telephone shrilled, cutting across the silence of the room. She gripped the chair arms. The handset, made of white bone china embossed with wreaths of painted flowers – her mother's choice no doubt – continued to ring. When she lifted the receiver, it was no surprise to hear his voice.

'Maya?'

'Yes.'

His hesitation at her curt reply was momentary. 'We need you to be here, Maya. Polly says we shouldn't push you on this, but what the hell! You're letting everybody down. You do know that, don't you?'

She said, in a monotone intended to deflect his anger, 'None of your damned business, Jonah.' She paused. 'What I do or don't do is a matter between Polly and me. You are in no way affected by it.'

At once the charm was strong in his voice. His tone dropped down to intimate with a hint of pain, manfully suppressed. 'I miss you, Maya. You can't begin to imagine how much. When you come back, it'll all be very different between us. That's a promise.'

'I'm not planning to return.'

She heard the sharp intake of his breath. She imagined him lying on Polly's tan leather sofa, a glass of something on the floor beside him, a cigarette clamped between his fingers. Because of the nature of the call his face would be more than usually animated, his faun-like features sharpened and pointed into the receiver, the thick brown curls tumbled on his forehead. He said, in tones that were genuinely shocked, 'I can't believe you're doing this to us.'

'Doing what?'

'You know very well what I'm talking about. Polly and I, we're only the workhorses in this operation. You're the designer. Without your artistic flair, our skills are worth next to nothing.'

'That's very flattering,' she said, 'but you have all the designs I did for the American orders.'

'Oh yes. So we do. But what about the spring collection?'

She said, hating the tremor in her voice. 'Did Polly put you up to making this call?'

'Polly and I are concerned about you, Maya. If you're having a breakdown then you should be seeking treatment for it.'

'Polly and you.' Her tone was thoughtful. 'You speak as if the two of you were now equal partners.'

'Well, somebody had to step in, didn't they? Mind you,' he began to speak very slowly and quietly as if her ability to reason had become impaired, 'all that stuff you told me, you know, about Paco, your husband, about the way he died. I remember thinking, even then, there's something odd about Maya. Something that doesn't quite add up.' He paused. 'Don't you ever wonder about it? The way your seat belt wasn't fastened and his was? Pretty crucial point, wasn't it, when the car caught fire?'

Her hands began to shake. She replaced the receiver very carefully on the flowery rest, cutting the connection. For several minutes she sat forward in the chair, staring at the telephone, waiting for the bell to ring. When it did not, she leaned back once more against the cushions. Relief loosened all her joints and muscles; she felt like a rag doll, carelessly abandoned by a destructive child.

From her bed in the corner of the kitchen she could see through the unshuttered window the thick fall of snowflakes. She watched as the sky above the stable block grew steadily lighter, the snowfall thinned and finally ceased. She had slept uneasily and now her limbs felt heavy, her head ached.

She rose, made a large pot of tea and swallowed two aspirin. Paco. As soon as the tale was told she had regretted confiding it to Jonah.

Even then his eyes had grown bright and predatory as he stored away the information for use against a rainy day. Well, that day had come. In spite of the thick woollen dressing gown, the warmth of the kitchen, she began to shiver. The shivering accelerated until her whole body was shaking with an ague so violent that she clung for support to the edge of the kitchen table. When the spasm eased, she moved towards the window. Snow lay deep across the stable yard and kitchen garden; the distant fields and hills were white. Her head felt light and empty, a ready host to painful thoughts, to memories of Paco.

She began to dress, pulling on corduroy trousers and thick socks, and the warm cream Guernsey sweater. She had planned a day of digging in the potato patch but the plot lay two feet under snow. What she needed was physical activity, the kind of muscle-wrenching hard slog that would exhaust her body and dull her mind.

She opened the kitchen door and closed it carefully behind her to conserve the warmth. The air of the hall struck chill against her face. The flower-painted china doorknobs matched exactly the fancy telephone and gleamed whitely in the hall's gloom; she seized the nearest one while her resolution lasted. The knob was predictably loose, the wood of the door and its frame swollen from damp and difficult to open. When it finally gave way she almost fell into the room.

Her first impression was of long neglect. The room smelled musty; reflected brilliant light from the lying snow showed up the thick dust and the bloom of damp on mirrors and furniture. A pale square of Chinese carpet covered most of the parquet; around it stood small companionable groups of unmatched armchairs and low sofas. On a walnut coffee table an ivory and ebony chess set stood in the advancing positions of a game half-played. A harpsichord stood against a wall. A cabinet displayed a collection of old blue Bristol glass.

The room was long, low-ceilinged, its colours faded to a blur of pinks and greys and soft shades of blue and eau-de-Nil. She paused on the threshold, taking in the shabby grandeur of it. She stepped across the fringed edge of the carpet and towards the white marble fireplace above which hung the portrait of a young girl, a tall girl who had not yet quite made the transition into womanhood from childhood. The swing on which she sat hung suspended from the branch of a cedar tree. The same tree, the same branch which featured in Milady's portrait. The girl wore a long green dress of some clinging material which revealed the developing curves of her young body. Her silver-blonde hair fell straight and shining from a centre parting to curve outwards when it touched her shoulders. Her eyes were tawny yellow, tilted cat-like at their outer corners; glowing eyes that held a look of violence and passion.

The shock of recognition was at first so strong that it wiped out thought and feeling. Helpless and mindless, she stood rooted before the painting of a girl who by her colouring and looks might well have been herself at the age of fourteen, fifteen.

Her first returning thought was that someone was playing a monstrous joke upon her, and then dread trickled slowly into her mind, forcing her back from those strange eyes, out of the room and into the safety of the kitchen.

In the warmth and familiarity of her normal surroundings she remembered Alice. Alice, who had more than once seemed on the point of imparting some vital information and then thought better of it; who had warned her that the house was evil, cursed by some long-dead Gypsy.

Maya went into the hall and opened the front door. As the heavy oak swung back, a great mound of drifted snow fell inwards, across her legs and feet. She had already tested the telephone and discovered that the lines were down. There was no way of reaching Alice today, or for many days to come.

A broad band of snow, said the weather forecaster, was still lying across south-west England, the Midlands, and South Yorkshire. Falls would be heavy. Motorists were advised not to travel. Many areas were without telephone or power, and services would not be restored in the foreseeable future.

Her first action on waking was to switch on the kitchen light. The fact that it still worked was reassuring. She cleaned and filled two oil lamps she had found on a back shelf of the pantry. She assembled candles in holders, and placed boxes of matches at strategic points around the rooms that were in use. She had stacked the wood left by the log man in the circular fashion she had once seen in Germany and Austria. One broad round stack stood conveniently close to the kitchen door; a can of paraffin and a funnel stood in a corner of the kitchen. In the cellars, according to Alice, were several hundredweight of coal.

The sense of crisis encouraged by radio and television broadcasts was invigorating. The isolation she had longed for was now complete. Just so long as she did not develop appendicitis or a raging toothache, she would make the most of this time stolen from the world.

She pulled on the green wellies and the shabby Burberry that belonged to Alice, and covered her hair with the woollen cap bought in Taunton. Having lacked the foresight to bring a garden shovel into the kitchen, she took a coal shovel from the fireplace and began to clear a pathway to the barn door. She removed several packs of vegetables and meat from the chest freezer, and examined its remaining contents. If the power should fail, she thought, the outside temperatures should still be low enough to preserve the food.

After many hours of blazing fire in the marble fireplace, the damp in the drawing room had almost disappeared. Maya polished and shampooed, taking pleasure in restoring the shine to wood and silver, bringing back the colours to soiled brocades and carpet. She was now in the grip of the house, enslaved as another woman might be to an exciting lover, a clandestine affair. She was jealous too. She found a deep satisfaction in the thought that her mother had never occupied this room, might have avoided it even. It was as if the precious furnishings, the glass and silver, the portrait of the young girl had come straight from Milady's hands and into her own.

The painting obsessed her. Long after the room had been restored to something close to its former elegance, Maya found herself inventing tasks which would take her within glancing sight of the portrait. In the week before Christmas, when snow still blocked the roads and lanes, and the power lines had finally failed, she moved a small, blue velvet armchair from the boudoir to the drawing room. Close beside the fireplace, and directly underneath the likeness of Maya Heron, Gypsy, she placed the armchair, and the sewing box which held the diaries.

When the Rayburn was fuelled, the coal scuttle filled, the oil lamps lit, she took her supper tray into the drawing room and read.

Maya Heron. December 23rd 1888.

Guy finds me a hiding place for my papers. He shows me a hollow beam in the great barn where he hides his own treasures. He finds me a metal box to keep my writing safe from mice and damp. The box fits in beside his penknife what he is not allowed to have and some bullets what is no use because he does not have a pistol.

Do not read my writing, I tell him. He gets angry. A gentleman of honour, says he, would never touch another person's papers.

I am like to smile at this. For all his talk of honour, Guy is not slow when it comes to the touching and kissing of another person's daughter. I have spied him lately with the gardener's girl.

I have not yet wrote about Christmas because I do not want to think about it. I cannot help but wonder where Dadus and Esmeralda are pitched in this bitter weather. They will have been picking the holly and the mistletoe and selling it down to Taunton. But surely Taunton is many miles away from this place and many steep hills in between.

Maya Heron. December 24th 1888.

We bring in the Christmas tree and set it in a wooden tub in a corner of the drawing room. Milady tells us the story of the Queen's husband called Prince Albert what brought the Christmas tree first to England from a country called Germany.

I am glad he brought it with him. I shall not say so to anybody in this house but I really does love the Christmas tree and the decorating of it. We helps Milady tie on the glass trinkets and fix the candles in their pretty holders. The best minute is when all is finished and the fairy is set atop the tree. Oh my, says Evangeline in her silly voice, I do declare the fairy looks exactly like Miss Lavinia.

Guy has grown very daring of late in more ways than one. Well, says he, in my opinion the fairy looks exactly like Maya. He stands nodding his head with his back to the fire when he says this and with his legs far apart like Milord does when he is talking important business.

What nonsense, cries Lavinia. There is nothing of the fairy about Maya. More of the witch in my opinion.

We puts the presents underneath the tree. We children have been making pen-wipers and handkerchiefs and hair-tidies these many months for to give to others in the house. I goes into the garden before the light fades. I knows a spot where there is two early snowdrops and some pink heather. I makes a little basket out of rushes and lines it all with moss. In it I puts the heather sprigs and snowdrops. It is my own gift for Milady what I shall give to her on Christmas morning.

The fire had died down to a warm glow. She moved, reluctantly, out through the cold hall and into the kitchen, washed her mug and plate and stood them on the drainer. She switched on the radio, careful to conserve the batteries, allowing herself the few minutes of listening time taken up by the reading of the weather forecast. A rapid thaw, said the man, would be setting in, which would continue on into tomorrow, which was Christmas Day. Maya reached out a hand and pressed the small red button, and the sudden silence hung like a shroud between her and the life she had once known. She tried to think about Polly, about Jonah, on this Christmas Eve. She had not known until now that it was actually Christmas, could not visualise the faces of Polly and Jonah or recall their voices.

It took only seconds to snatch up the oil lamp, to step back across the hall and into the drawing room. She opened the folder and with great care removed the brittle faded sheet of the last diary entry she had read. Again she studied the description of that Christmas Eve, the trimming of the tree, the special gift made by the child for the only person in this house who had truly cared about her.

She looked up at the portrait, and the physical likeness still disturbed her. What concerned her more was the way her imagination was now fired at each new reading of the diaries. She was no longer using them as after-supper entertainment, a substitute for television dramas. In a way that was frightening and yet inevitable, she was beginning to experience the emotions, the fears and the hatreds of Maya Heron as if they were her own.

Jango

*W*hen in Derbyshire, Jango wore a tweed slouch hat with a feather in the headband, and high green Barbour boots. His trousers were coarse corduroy, his sweaters knitted by a travelling aunt who was known for her skill at cable pattern. In the worst of the weather he wore a full-length green waxed coat and carried a stout stick.

Looking the part, Lias called it; playing the role of a farmer who owned a patch of barren hillside, and no stock.

Unknown to Lias, Jango often attended local cattle markets. He took a secret, almost guilty pleasure in rubbing shoulders with the old farmers of the district, sitting near to but not with them in the village pubs. Over the years he had come to understand the dialect they spoke, to find some humour in their dry jokes. There were times when he felt himself to be on the edge of some tremendous secret, the truth of which would be vouchsafed to him only in this hard landscape of the Dark Peak. But whenever he found himself teetering on the brink of a discovery, he drew back. Safety for him had always been with Lias. He knew that Lias indulged him, had always indulged him in his small vanities. But when Lias poked fun, it was always gently and without malice. Until now, he could not have imagined a life without his brother. The change had begun with that visit last winter of the stranger, the ex-*gavver*, the man who had posed one question and let loose the possibility of a dozen others.

The car had come down the valley in mid-morning, a black BMW. moving slowly in the pallid sunshine of early March. It had stopped just short of the tarmac drive, the window had wound down and the driver looked up to where Jango stood at the kitchen window.

The car door opened and was swiftly closed when the dogs started barking. The car swung on to and up the driveway and halted beside the open door of the barn where Lias sawed logs.

Visitors were rare and almost always people of their own kind. Lias muttered '*Gavver*' to Jango as the man climbed stiffly from his seat. He was tall, heavy-set, a taciturn type who smiled only with his lips. A typical policeman, possibly detective sergeant, or some Inland Revenue or VAT official. The dogs stood silent beside Lias.

'Mr Heron?'

Lias said, 'Who's asking?'

The man, one hand upon the car's open door, said, 'My name is Thurgood. James Thurgood. I'm a private inquiry agent.' He looked at the dogs. 'Do you think we could go inside and talk? I've been driving since crack of dawn.' He shivered. 'It's bloody cold up in these hills.'

'No need for you to linger then,' said Lias. 'Get in your car and go back to where you came from. You have no business here with us.'

'That's where you're wrong, Mr Heron. I have important business with you. I've driven some three hundred miles to find you, and a relative of yours has paid me good money to ascertain your whereabouts. I think you should at least hear what I have to say.'

Lias stared at him. 'I have you marked down for a copper.'

The man grinned and squared his shoulders. 'Ex-Dorset police. Detective inspector.'

Lias shrugged. 'I'd have thought you to be no more than a sergeant. But even I can be wrong sometimes.' He moved closer to the car, the dogs beside him. 'Listen, Mister bloody Thurgood. I've told you to get off our land and you're still here. That makes it trespass, wouldn't you say, *ex-Detective Inspector*?'

The man climbed back into the car. He slammed the door and switched on the ignition. Through the open window he shouted to Jango, 'Is your name Heron?'

Jango nodded, and a long white envelope skimmed across the grass to land beside his feet.

'Read it, you stupid bloody Gypos,' shouted the ex-policeman. 'That's if you *can* read!'

They watched the black car out of sight round the hillside. Jango fingered and sniffed at the envelope. 'Expensive,' he said. 'Sort of scented too, like a woman wrote it.'

Lias went into that mood of bitter anger that came upon him sometimes. The lines in his face deepened, his fists clenched. 'Burn it,' he said. 'Burn it right now!' He went back into the barn and almost at once there was the ringing sound of axe slicing wood.

Jango took the envelope and laid it on the kitchen table. He walked round it several times like a suspicious dog. Lias had no right to order him to burn it. It was meant for both of them to read, and anyway it was him who took charge when they were in the Dark Peaks.

He made a mug of coffee, lit a cigarette, and sat down at the table. He slit the envelope open with his penknife and withdrew two sheets of closely written paper.

He read slowly, as do those who read only from extreme need and never for pleasure. He looked first at the signature. The writer was a woman. She signed herself Bruenette Pomeroy, born Heron. The script was that of a person accustomed to letter writing. The words used were those of an educated person. He read each line twice over, and then the whole, and then again. She seemed to be saying that she and Lias and Jango Heron were closely related. That it had taken her some years to get the evidence together. Having proved to herself beyond doubt that they shared the same Romany forebears, she proposed that they should meet. She apologised for the private investigator, but referred to him as a last resort. In the final paragraph she addressed them as 'cousins' and begged them to phone her and arrange a meeting.

For several days the letter stayed hidden in his jacket pocket. At intervals he would unfold the sheets of thick white paper and reread the strong back-sloping writing. Discovery came on an evening when Lias, coming silently into the kitchen, looked over his brother's shoulder and snatched the letter from his hand.

'So you had to look at it. Even though I said to burn it.' The dark, high-boned face grew pale with anger and just for a moment Jango feared him.

He said, 'You've no right to give me orders.'

'I wasn't ordering you, *pralo*. I've got a bad feeling about that letter. It would have been better if you'd burned it.'

'It's interesting though.' Jango smiled placatingly. 'You have to say, it's interesting.'

'How so?'

'Well, there's this woman.' He pointed to the embossed address at the top of the sheet. 'Lives in a big house, wouldn't you say, yet reckons her name was Heron, and her mother and grandmother before her. She mentions family, knows all about Despair. She talks about a Django spelled with a D, and a Lias who lived in the old bad times. Dammit, *pralo*, this woman knows more than we do about the past. There's something else. She's wild to meet us. Pays a private eye to find us. So she's wealthy as well as being crazy. Think about it, Lias. She could be worth knowing.'

They had come south in the springtime. In August they moved inland through the county of Dorset, always coming closer to the house of the woman who had said she was their cousin. A meeting had been arranged.

They were driving though the lanes that led to Hunger Hill, following the directions she had given. 'Come to dinner,' she had said on the telephone. 'Eight o'clock sharp.' On a long straight stretch of road, in a fair light, they saw a scarlet Triumph Stag coming towards them at a great speed. They could see a woman's face, her hands on the steering wheel pulling the car hard over so that collision was inevitable. And then the man who sat beside her was pushing her away, grabbing the wheel, swinging the car to the left at the last possible moment. They heard the impact with the tree, the explosion. They left the Winnebago and ran towards the burning Triumph Stag. Together with a tipsy farmer, they dragged the bodies from the fire.

It was the farmer who had looked down into the undamaged faces of the couple as they lay by the hedgeside. Sobered now by shock, he said quietly, 'Oh my God. It's poor Geoff Pomeroy and Bruenette. This will be a terrible shock for Alice.'

Lias
---

*H*e had always known how to handle Jango. The trick had been to instil in the growing child, the adolescent, dreamy boy, a strong respect and love for the deep Romanies of their people, some knowledge of their secret language. By word and example Lias had guided this younger brother in the paths he would have him walk. What he could not pass on was his own hard-edged determination, his single-minded purpose to outwit the Gorgio. Because of this failure, Lias needed always to be mindful of Jango, conscious of his shortcomings, prepared for his occasional stupidity. What he had not allowed for was the private investigator, the letter, the crazy woman who had claimed to be their kin, who had lured them into Dorset and then tried to kill them. The experience had unsettled Jango. Even now, returned to this place where he was usually content, he brooded and was curiously silent. The wild card in Jango was, and always would be, his Gorgio mother.

He had asked about her lately. 'You were ten years old when I was born,' he said. 'You must be able to remember her.'

'You're better off not knowing,' Lias told him. 'It's all in the past; can't make any difference to you now. We've got a good life together, haven't we?' He slapped Jango on the shoulder. 'What say we go over to Sheffield or Manchester? Find us a club, a floorshow, a lady each to spend the night with?'

Jango gave him a long look. 'That's not what I want,' he said. 'Not any more. Things are different with me now.'

Lias knew what he meant. The image of the woman Maya stood between them, her presence so strong that Lias often thought he smelled her perfume, heard her low-pitched voice.

Jango's handsome, gentle face took on a strange expression which Lias could not fathom. 'You'll have to tell me soon about my mother. You're the only one who can, you know that.' And then, with an insight into Lias's mind which he had never previously shown, Jango said, 'It won't make me any the less a Romanichal, any the less your brother, if you tell me about the Gorgio side of my family.'

But Lias had never considered the girl called Madeline to be any part of Jango's family, and it was not the kind of impromptu tale that could be told around the fireside on a stormy evening. He would need to work it out, select and reject, decide how much would be damaging to Jango and how little would be sufficient to soothe his fretting and the painful dissatisfaction that was creeping into their previously carefree lives.

The snow ceased to fall around mid-morning. Lias had cleared the paths to the barn and the outside pump that provided spring water, and filled the log baskets which fuelled the parlour fire and kitchen stove. Jango worked in a corner of the barn, rubbing down the surface of an old pine cupboard he had bought in a village garage sale. The rabbit Lias had caught and skinned just before the snowstorm was simmering with vegetables and herbs in a stove-top casserole. He looked for a valid reason to absent himself from the holding, and reflected that a year ago he would just have walked away without feeling the need for any explanation.

He clicked his fingers to the dogs and they came to his side. He fastened them into coats of thick woollen fleece, for they were valuable assets. He pulled on his heavy leather boots and a jacket of red plaid. To Jango he said, 'The dogs are restless. I'll take them for a bit of a run. Be a shame if they got out of condition, so close to racing.'

Jango nodded but did not look up.

The snow had drifted in the high winds of the night, making depth and consistency deceptive. On the lower reaches of the hills Lias floundered thigh-deep into loose snow, the dogs on their thin legs picking out a route delicately behind him. As they climbed higher, a light powdering was all that they encountered. The dogs ran ahead, returning to him at intervals, but never out of sight or hearing. He began to move with a steady rhythm, following the path that led from Lose Hill up to Back Tor. He thought about other winters. The nineteen sixties. The Beatles, flower power. The death of John F. Kennedy. At the age of eight or nine these happenings had meant nothing to him, and yet, through the talk of the older children in the *tan* and from pictures seen on Aunt Lena's large television set, the memory of them had stayed with him to merge with the other more frightening images of those days. There had been the girl called Madeline who called herself a flower child and talked about her guru. He remembered her thin, childlike body and reddish hair, the way she had never seemed to be properly awake; the way she had sneezed and yawned at certain times, and had at others been quiet and dreamy.

Rumour had it that she had run away from an expensive school and caring family. For many weeks she had followed Despair from one horse fair to another. He was forty years old and she was eighteen. He had married her four months before the birth of Jango. Even now, twenty-eight years on, he could not bring himself to a total recall of the horrors of those four months.

Snow clouds were gathering again above the valley. He had not intended to walk so far; he turned and began the long descent which would bring him back to Jango and the holding. No plan had been formulated, no decision arrived at.

Her name, he remembered, had been Madeline Hathersage. She had told him once that her father was a farmer and wealthy landowner, and that she was her parents' only daughter, but he had not believed her.

It began to snow as he walked the final stretch of path which brought him to the holding. He halted before the last descent and looked down on the squat stone house which Jango loved. He thought about his father, about Despair's choice of a settled home for his two sons. It had seemed at the time to be a spur of the moment decision to settle here in this valley called Hope. But Despair had never been a man who acted without motive.

Polly

She tried to telephone, first Alice and then Maya, but the lines were still down. The plan had been to arrive at the Monks' House without warning on Christmas Eve, bearing gifts and a Harrods hamper. But Jonah had advised against driving in a blizzard.

The thaw had been rapid, total. By the morning of Boxing Day a watery sun shone on the shrinking heaps of dirty snow in London gutters. Out in the country, trees and hedges dripped into ditches which were already flooding across roads and fields. Patches of snow still lay on the blue and distant hills, promising a further fall.

She drove as fast as the road conditions would allow, slowing in villages, getting trapped behind a tractor in narrow winding lanes where passing was impossible. She had never noticed darkness falling in the city, but out here in Sleepy Hollow country the night came down in the middle of the afternoon. It was not until Yeovil was first signposted that Polly pulled into a lay-by and opened the flask of hot coffee and the packet of turkey sandwiches she had slapped together early that morning. She ate and drank as she did most things, nervously but neatly.

Before driving on, she glanced at her reflection in the driving mirror. In the fading light she could just make out her small pale features, and the cap of black hair cut low across her forehead and shaped above her ears. She pulled a lipstick from her jacket pocket and coloured her mouth a rosy pink. The mobile phone lay on the seat beside her. Not really expecting to make the connection, she tried once again to call Alice. The phone was answered on the second ring.

'Alice? Hi! It's Polly, Maya's friend. Look, I'm coming into Yeovil from a place called Sherborne. I seem to remember that I turn off somewhere on this road in order to get to your place.'

'Oh, Polly! You can't think how relieved I am to hear your voice. Yes, yes, you turn left at the sign which says Bradford Abbas, drive straight through that village and then —'

'Yes. I remember now. I'll find you. I'll be with you in about twenty minutes.'

For dinner that evening there was chicken in a casserole and home-baked bread, apple pie and clotted cream, and as much coffee as she could drink. Polly sat among the chintz and watercolour flower paintings. The room was very warm, it smelled of potpourri and beeswax. Her head drooped, until her chin rested on the pink angora of her sweater.

Alice said, 'Why don't you stay here tonight? The lanes up to the Monks' House are bound to be flooded. The power is on again down here in the village, but those lanes are unlit. It could be dangerous, driving in the dark to Maya's place.'

There was a catch in Alice's voice which brought Polly fully awake. 'Has anything happened since you last phoned me?' she asked.

'Nothing specific. It's just that she's becoming more and more remote. I invited her to spend Christmas with me but I could tell that she really didn't want to come. I can imagine her being quite relieved when the blizzard started.'

'You think it's that bad?'

'You haven't seen her for quite some time, have you? I hear things from the log man and the postman. They were used to chatting with Geoffrey and Bruenette, having a cup of tea with them in the kitchen. Maya never opens the door, she leaves letters to be posted on the porch bench. She pays for the logs by leaving cash in an envelope pinned to the barn door.'

Polly said, 'As I told you, she wrote to me soon after she came here. She said that she was having a mild sort of breakdown. That she was seeing a doctor. That she needed some time to herself. Well, I could appreciate that. Her parents had just died, and there had been some bother with Jonah. I've heard nothing from her for several weeks. I planned to come down on Christmas Eve, you know, take her by surprise.'

Alice smiled. 'I'm so glad you're here.'

'But now I feel so guilty. I've been very angry with her. We had these orders, an important deal that could lead to more work, but only if we could deliver goods on time. I asked her to come back to London and so did Jonah. We've worked night and day – but I didn't realise that she was quite so disturbed.' Polly paused. 'She was like this once before, when Paco died. Wanting to hide away, acting sort of disconnected. But I stayed with her that time, kept a watchful eye. I feel now that I've failed her.'

'You and Maya have been friends for a long time?'

'Since boarding school, and then art college. Twenty years or so.'

'Tell me, Polly, who was Paco?'

'Her husband. Has she never told you about him?'

'No. She never has. I didn't know that she had married.'

'He was Spanish. His father owned a restaurant in London. One of those family things, you know. Paco worked for his father. They were on their honeymoon, in Spain. The car crashed on a mountain road. Maya was thrown clear. Paco died.'

'How terrible.'

'Yes, it was. For a long time afterwards Maya acted strangely. She became quiet and withdrawn. I had the feeling that she was very frightened of something or somebody. I tried to make her talk about it but she wouldn't. She was just beginning to recover when this second tragedy happened.'

Alice said, 'I wish I had known all this. Perhaps I could have helped her.'

'She's a difficult person to help. I probably know her better than anybody does, but even with me there is a point beyond which she closes down completely.' Polly pulled herself upright in her chair. The dark arches of her eyebrows came together. She leaned forward, her body tense. She said, 'Maya had this bloody awful childhood. I'm sorry, Alice. I know that Geoffrey Pomeroy was your brother, but how could he have dumped his only child the way he did? Maya hardly remember's living with her parents. If she ever spoke fondly of anyone, it was of neighbours, an au pair called Inge, and her paternal grandparents of course. There was no stability in her life. Her grandparents died when she was twelve years old. School holidays were usually spent at school, even Christmas. The story was that her parents were in South America, that her father worked in Brazil. That he wanted her to have an English education.' Polly sighed. 'Do you know the saddest part of it? She always half believed that they would come back and fetch her. Take her with them to Brazil. For a while she talked to me about it, then she never spoke of them at all. Cards and presents came at birthdays and Christmas, there was a monthly letter from her father. In the end, she threw away everything that came from them unopened. She began to spend holidays at my home when we were both about fourteen. My family sort of adopted her. Then my father died and my mother went to live in New Zealand with my married sister. So there we were, Maya and me, at the age of eighteen, on our own. Her father had set up some sort of trust fund for her. There was always plenty of money but little contact, no love.'

Alice said, 'I always suspected that was how it was. You may find this hard to believe, but my brother had his reasons for leaving Maya here in England. When the arrangements for her care were first set up, it all looked as good as it could be in the circumstances. What Geoffrey had not reckoned with was the death of our parents.'

'I still don't know what possible reason could excuse the leaving of a small girl in the care of elderly relatives and strangers,' Polly protested.

Alice looked down. Her fingers were tightly knotted in her lap. Then she raised her eyes to meet Polly's fierce gaze. She said, slowly and with obvious reluctance, 'Maya was in danger from her mother. Bruenette was unsuited to have the care of children. There was nothing else Geoffrey could have done.'

'Did Maya – does Maya know about all this?'

'I have no idea what Maya knows. I met her for the first time, remember, when you brought her here in August. I find it difficult to talk to her about personal matters.'

Polly said, 'I am going to ask you some questions you may not wish to answer. But I care about Maya. I've looked after her, one way or another, since we were children. Before I go to see her I need to find out, as far as possible, what her real trouble might be.'

'You want to know about Bruenette?'

'That will do to begin with.'

'Did you ever meet Maya's mother?'

'No, I didn't.'

Alice looked at a picture on the far wall, but her gaze was unfocused and strained and Polly wondered what it was she really saw. 'My sister-in-law was a beautiful woman. Exotic. Thick black waving hair, olive skin, great dark eyes. She was tall, voluptuous. Heaven only knows how she came to marry Geoffrey. She was a dancer when he met her, some kind of exhibition dancing, I believe – flamenco, Latin American. Well, she looked like a Gypsy and in many ways behaved like one.'

'So Maya looks nothing like her mother.'

'No,' Alice sounded thoughtful, 'and that was the first of Bruenette's peculiarities as far as Maya was concerned. The child's looks and colouring seemed to revolt and terrify Bruenette. According to my mother, who eventually took care of the baby, Bruenette could hardly bring herself to touch her.' Alice paused. 'She was a very superstitious woman. Oh, it wasn't the usual, "don't walk under ladders" kind of thing. She told the tarot cards and regularly used a Ouija board. She was hung about with amulets and planned her life by means of horoscopes and predictions. If her stars were unfavourable, she refused to leave her bed.'

'She sounds thoroughly unbalanced.'

'It was more than that. My father was a country clergyman, his beliefs

were simple but very strong. He believed Bruenette to be possessed by
the Devil. When Geoffrey's job took him to Brazil, my parents volunteered
to take care of Maya. It seems to have been a solution that suited all of
them – except the child.'

'What you're really saying is that your father thought Bruenette
was crazy.'

Alice nodded but said nothing.

Polly said, 'I have to ask you something else.'

'I can guess what you want to know. Where was I when all this was
going on?'

'Exactly.'

'I'll tell you where I was.' Red colour crept up under the fine, lined
skin. 'I don't know how much you've heard about my life.'

'Maya said you were a violinist.'

'I played with the greatest orchestras in Europe. For many years I
travelled the world. When Maya was six months old I also bore a child.
A boy. He lived two months, just long enough for me to grow to love him.
Then he died. I was touring in America when I became pregnant. The
man was married. He gave me a cheque to cover my hospital expenses
and then he left the orchestra. It was many years before I came back to
England. By that time Maya was grown up. I had kept in touch with my
parents of course, and later on with Geoffrey. It was not until Bruenette
and Geoffrey came to live in Dorset that I began to piece together what
had happened to their daughter.'

Polly said, 'I'm sorry. Me and my big mouth. I had no right —'

'You had every right. There are few enough people who have cared
about Maya, and to be truthful it's helped me to talk to you about it.'
Alice smiled. 'I look at Maya and think that my David would have been
about her age if he had lived. It's one of the reasons I worry so much
about her. About what might be happening to her now.'

Polly looked at Alice, and then away. 'You don't think that Maya might
have inherited her mother's temperament – her strangeness?'

'I don't know what to think.'

'You see, I'm beginning to remember the rare times when the
parents came back to England. They would instruct the school to
put Maya on the London train. She would spend a week with them
in some West End hotel. When she came back to school she would
talk a lot about her father but never, ever, mentioned her mother.
It was after one of those holidays that she began to sleepwalk.
Even then, she would have quiet spells. But I was little more than
a child myself at that time. It's only now that I see how odd it
all was.'

Alice said, 'Would you like me to accompany you to the Monks' House tomorrow morning?'

Polly thanked her but said that she thought it would be better if she arrived alone. 'Two surprise visitors might be more than Maya can cope with at the moment. But I'm planning to stay for at least a fortnight. Perhaps you could come over and have dinner with us.'

'I'd much rather that you came to me. Sunday lunch perhaps?'

'I'll phone you,' said Polly.

The route to the Monks' House, as explained by Alice, lay uphill through narrow twisting lanes. Where snow had lately lain there was mud and water, but the sky was a deep unbroken blue and the air was mild. Weak sunshine filtered through the bare branches of the trees, and even Polly, who was nervous in the country, who feared cows and horses and uninhabited spaces, felt the tension relax in her neck and shoulders. It had all been manageable so far.

Impacted snow still lay in the shaded ruts of the driveway. She drove very slowly, watching first the tall chimneys of the house come into view, and then the roof and upper windows, and finally the full beauty of the building was revealed.

While she was still some distance from the terrace, Polly switched off the engine, lit a cigarette and laid her arms across the steering wheel. Neither Alice nor Maya had prepared her for the charm, the desirability of the Monks' House. Alice, she suspected, was for some reason deeply prejudiced against it. Maya, when she had spoken of her inheritance, had seemed bemused. Polly gazed and envied and thought that she almost understood what it was that held Maya fast in Dorset. But why alone? Why in such unnecessary isolation?

As she watched, the front door opened and Maya stepped into the porch. But not the Maya she remembered. Gone was the elegance, the sophistication. This woman wore corduroy trousers tucked into high boots, and a heavy sweater and quilted waistcoat. Her hair was pulled up and insecurely fastened on top of her head; wisps hung around her face and neck.

Polly stubbed out her cigarette in the ashtray, climbed from the car and stood beside its open door. She longed to run towards Maya, throw her arms round her, but something about the advancing figure held her fast and silent. They stood face to face and neither of them spoke. And then Maya said, 'Why have you come here?' The words were spoken as if Polly was a stranger, an intrusive stranger; her impulse to hug, to comfort, disappeared before the coldness of the greeting.

'Because,' she said, 'I'm concerned about you. I planned to arrive on

Christmas Eve but the blizzard stopped me. I thought it would be nice if we spent the holiday together.'

'I wish you'd warned me of your coming.'

'Warned you? Since when did you and I need to warn one another of our actions? We're supposed to be best friends, business partners.' And now the strange unfocused look on Maya's face angered her. 'For God's sake! Whatever is the matter with you? Don't you hear what I'm saying? We're all very worried about you.'

'We?'

'Alice, Jonah. Me! You said you needed time to yourself. Well, you've had time, a lot of time. There are matters we have to discuss, and if you won't come to London then I have to come here.' Polly gestured at the car. 'And if you think I'm going to drive away now then you're very much mistaken. I'm coming into that house and I'm staying in it until everything is sorted out between us.'

Maya turned and walked away towards the porch. Polly pulled her suitcase from the boot and followed. Alice had warned her that Maya lived and slept in the kitchen of the house, so she was not surprised that it was to this room Maya led her.

'Have you had breakfast?' The small politeness seemed to cause Maya effort.

Polly nodded. She thought it wiser not to say that she had spent the night at Jasmine Cottage and breakfasted with Alice. She said, 'I would love a coffee, and then you can show me your beautiful house.'

'There's not much for you to see.'

Polly laughed. 'Come on, Maya. There must be ten or twelve rooms.'

'I've opened only four doors so far, and two of them were kitchen and bathroom.'

'You mean you've never even peeped inside? For heaven's sake, why not? It's a house not an Advent calendar. You don't have to wait until Christmas before you open all the doors.'

'You wouldn't understand.'

'I understand this much. All that talk of sorting and disposing of your parents' things, you haven't done it, have you? And the tale that you were painting and decorating each room in the house, you haven't done that either.'

Maya gazed vaguely round the kitchen. She said. 'I painted these walls.'

'Well, so I should think! You should also have had a proper kitchen fitted. That sink and drainer look positively archaic, and as for that open fireplace and the water pump,' she smiled disparagingly. 'I'm staying for two weeks. In that time we can plan a really super kitchen.'

In a flat unarguable voice, Maya stated, 'Nothing is to be changed in this house. Ever.'

'But why not?'

'The house does not wish it.'

Polly felt a coldness settle in her chest. She said, falsely bright, 'Well, you had better show me to my room so that I can unpack.'

'There is no room for you, at least not one that's suitable for use. The house is very damp. I'm drying it out slowly.'

'So we'll dry out a bedroom for me.'

Maya looked uncertain. Polly picked up her suitcase and walked into the hall and towards the stairs.

The staircase was graceful, the treads carpeted in deep blue. At the top of the stairs she was faced with a long wide landing from which opened many doors. At the far end of the landing another smaller, less impressive staircase led up to the top floor of the house. Polly's hand went out to the knob of the first door she encountered.

Maya, at her elbow, said, 'That's the bathroom.'

Polly moved on. Maya was no longer at her elbow but standing well back, looking fearful, as if she expected some awful revelation. Polly opened the next door on to a scene of wild disorder; mindless damage had been done here, mirrors smashed, curtains ripped from windows, the surfaces of the dressing table and tallboys, the bedside tables had all been swept clear. Broken lamps and trinkets littered the floor, perfume from smashed bottles had soaked into the carpet, leaving a stale, faintly sickly smell upon the air. Clothes had been pulled from the wardrobes and lay in scattered heaps of silks and tweeds. The room had been beautiful once, furnished with antique mahogany, the hangings and covers in rich jewel colours of crimson, gold and brilliant greens.

Polly turned on Maya who stood silent in the doorway. 'Did you do this?'

The question achieved more than Polly had expected. The vague, disoriented gaze snapped back to full awareness, Maya at once stood taller, more alert, and very angry.

'No, I damn well didn't! How dare you suggest that I might have. Can't you see this is my parents' room. Bruenette had a terrifying temper. This has to be her handiwork.'

'But why?'

Maya shrugged. 'Who knows?' She paused. 'Perhaps you should ask Alice. Alice, I am quite sure, knows all about the goings-on in this place during my parents' occupation and before.'

'You're quite sure that you didn't know the room was in this state?'

Maya shrugged. 'If you don't believe me, there is nothing I can do about it.'

Polly forced a briskness into her voice that she did not feel. The act of destruction had left behind an uneasiness that was still transmitting itself, even to her unimaginative mind. She said, 'I intend to clean this mess up, and then I shall sleep here.'

'No. No, you must not do that. There's no need, there are lots of other bedrooms.'

'But we shall have to deal with all this sooner or later. Your parents' clothes and things have to be disposed of. We might as well have one grand clean-up.' She gazed directly at Maya. 'Might as well get it over with.' She began to pick slivers of glass from the carpet. 'Do you have any bin bags, you know, those big black ones?'

'Yes.'

'Well, go and fetch them. And a bucket of hot water and some cloths. And the vacuum cleaner and some polish.'

Maya left the room. Alone for the first time since entering the house, Polly shivered. The air was very cold, but she knew that the chill she experienced was not altogether due to weather conditions, or the lack of proper heating.

Just to be in her parents' room was clearly almost more than Maya could endure. There were times, as they filled the bin liners with clothing for Oxfam and rubbish for the dustbin, when Polly braced herself for Maya's refusal to continue to help her. But slowly, as the room was restored to a state of order, their tension eased. They began to talk as if this was some ordinary day, some regular task with which they were both familiar.

Maya said, 'You don't really mean to sleep in here, do you?'

'Not if you don't wish it. In fact, no. It was a stupid, tasteless suggestion. I'm sorry I said it.'

The apology seemed to reassure Maya. 'I didn't mean to be unwelcoming. It was a shock to see you. I need to be on my own, I thought you understood that.'

Polly paused in her stripping of the wide bed; she clutched the red and gold quilted bedspread as if it was a tether. She said, quietly but firmly, 'I don't intend to leave, Maya. You had better believe that. There's something funny going on here, and it's really getting to you this time. I saw you in this state after Paco died, but not nearly so ... so ...'

'Crazy?'

Polly did not smile; neither did she offer a denial. 'Your word, Maya. Not mine.' She began to spread the quilt, to smooth it carefully across the bed. 'It's this house, isn't it? Not just the accident, your parents' dying as they did?'

Maya's tone took on the dreamy quality that Polly feared. 'They died as Paco died. Have you taken that in, Polly? I was angry with him just before the car crashed. I was always antagonistic towards my mother and father, but especially so on that Saturday in Chicago.'

Polly held her breath, fearing to interrupt the flow of words.

'It was my birthday. They had ignored that day for many years. Somehow, they discovered I was in America. They sent me flowers. A bouquet, delivered early in the morning. Yellow and white roses. *Their* favourite blooms. I sat in a hotel room and read the card. 'To our beloved daughter on her thirtieth birthday.' I tore those flowers to bits. I shook from head to foot with rage. I wished them both dead, and within a few hours they were.'

Polly said, 'I gave them the name of your hotel. I thought I was helping. Bringing you all together. Your father was so anxious to contact you, he sounded close to tears.'

Maya continued as if Polly had not spoken. 'I killed them,' she said, 'exactly as I killed Paco.'

'That's rubbish! You know it is. What's happened to you, Maya? You were never like this until you came to live here.'

'How do you know what I'm like? When did you ever take the time to notice? You've always seen me as one of your sad deserving cases – and perhaps I was when we were at school and college. I was happy then to have you run my life; you were the only one who took an interest in what happened to me. But I grew up, Polly. I married Paco, and then destroyed him. Things . . . happened to me. Strange and terrifying things.' She began to polish the dressing table, rubbing the wood with hard strokes. 'You came here this morning and straightaway told me how to change the house. But this is *my* house, it's not a joint venture with you like the business, the flat. Like Jonah.'

'Do you want me to leave?'

Maya shrugged. 'You must do as you please. You always do, don't you? There's a linen chest on the landing with sheets and blankets in it. If you mean to stay, choose yourself a bedroom, and air some bedclothes.' She grabbed two overfull bin liners and dragged them from the room.

Polly watched from the window as Maya crossed the muddy yard and threw the bags into the barn. As Polly moved closer to the wall, her knee struck metal. She looked down and there was a radiator. A stone-cold radiator. She followed the pipework back to the kitchen, finding other radiators on the way. When Maya returned from the barn, Polly was switching on heat, refuelling the Rayburn.

She said, 'No wonder this house is so bloody cold. You hadn't switched on the central heating system. Whatever would you do without me, Maya?'

The bedroom Polly chose had once belonged to a young girl. The white curtains and bedspread had the tinge of yellow which comes with great age. When the mattress was aired and the bed made up, she called to Maya. 'Come and see what I found.'

Maya came, reluctantly, not entering the room but observing from the doorway.

'It's a genuine period piece. Do look, it's a Victorian virgin's bower.' She pointed out the shelf which held porcelain-faced dolls, the lace doilies on the dressing table, the trinkets and the embroidered hair-tidy which bore the initial 'L'. 'I wonder who L was?'

'Lavinia,' said Maya.

'So you do know the history of the house? The names of those who lived here long ago?'

'Not really.' Maya began to move away.

Polly experienced a surge of interest, of excitement. 'But you just said —'

'I must have picked it up from Alice,' Maya said quickly. 'She knows all sorts of odd details about local people, past and present.' From the top of the stairs she called back across her shoulder, 'I'm doing sandwiches and soup. If you like, when we've eaten, we could take a walk.'

That first day in the Monk's House set the pattern for the week that followed. The worst of the chill was removed by the central heating. Polly slept long and deeply in the room she thought of as Lavinia's. After breakfast each morning and without permission, she opened up a closed door and forced Maya to confront yet another interior. All the bedrooms were furnished in the dark and heavy Victorian style of the one once occupied by Bruenette and Geoffrey. Together, she and Maya vacuumed and polished. In the spring, promised Polly, she would return with wallpaper and paint. It would be their joint project. Something to plan for. To share. It would be fun, wouldn't it?

The doors that opened off the entrance hall revealed a lobby crammed with fishing gear, raincoats so old that they split when handled, boots that were a uniform shade of mildewed blue. Adjoining was a room which had once been used solely for the arranging of flowers. A deep white sink stood in a corner. Shelves ranged round the walls held vases and bowls of pottery and glass, in many sizes and colours. There was a morning room which Polly found was bright with winter sunshine. One door only, on the ground floor, was locked against her. She asked Maya for the key, but Maya said the key was lost.

On Saturday evening Alice phoned and invited them to Sunday lunch. The call had been arranged by Polly, on the car phone. 'Ring her,' she advised Alice. 'I think she will agree to come. Her behaviour was very odd when I arrived, but she becomes more normal by the day.'

The weather had grown colder. They travelled down to Alice in Polly's car, bumping across frozen ruts. Hoarfrost glistened on the fields and hedges. Maya seemed to be relaxed and happy. All she had needed, thought Polly, was a little cheerful company, some contact with the real world.

After lunch, as they sat round the fire, drinking coffee and chatting, Alice asked, 'Well, what have you two been doing with yourselves?'

Polly answered. 'House-cleaning in the mornings. Walking in the afternoons. In the evenings we're so weary we loll around and doze or watch television.'

'So where have you walked?'

'Hunger Hill,' said Maya. 'It's a fascinating place. I'd driven across it but had never explored there until Polly came.'

Alice said, 'There's a legend concerning Hunger Hill. It's supposed to be haunted. The story is that a Gypsy was murdered on his way to the Pack Monday Fair in Sherborne.'

'When did this happen?' Polly asked.

'Oh, in the late eighteen hundreds, I believe. The murder is said to have been committed in a place known as the Hollow. At certain times of the year the Gypsy's blood is said to stain the rock where his body lay when found.'

Polly leant forward in her chair. 'Was the murderer caught?'

'It would appear not. There are many versions of the tale. A local man was convicted but when they tried to hang him the trap door would not go down and he was eventually released from prison. Another story is that a young woman killed the Gypsy. But I don't imagine that the Dorset constabulary of that time concerned themselves too much about the murder of a vagrant.'

Maya, who had seemed relaxed, almost sleepy, now stood abruptly and moved towards the hall. 'We'd better be going. It gets dark early. Thank you for a lovely lunch, Alice. I'll be in touch.'

In the car, Polly said. 'That was a sudden departure, wasn't it?'

For several seconds Maya did not speak. As they approached Hunger Hill she said, 'If you're game, I'd like to look at the place where the Gypsy was murdered. Perhaps we could go tomorrow morning.'

*   *   *

Overnight the frost had lifted, giving way to a cold and steady rain which soaked the fields and blurred the outlines of the hills. Polly refused to leave the warmth of the house. 'I can just about stand the country when the sun shines. In weather like this I want to hide beneath the duvet.' She regarded Maya curiously. 'I don't know how you can bear it.'

Maya said, 'I've hardly noticed the weather here. Except when it became very cold and I needed to buy warm clothes.' She examined her hands, touching the chapped and roughened skin. She said, unexpectedly, 'I've stopped running, Polly. I'm coming face to face at last with all my old ghosts.'

'That must be hard for you.'

'Certain episodes, for no special reason, get snagged in my mind. I go over and over the same set of memories, without solving anything. Your coming here makes it more difficult to concentrate. You're getting in my way, Polly. I think it's time for you to leave.'

'I can quite see how you might find my presence a distraction,' Polly said calmly. 'But you could be making use of me. Treat me as a sounding board, the way you always do when you're working on an intricate design.' She smiled. 'I don't intend to leave until I'm good and ready.'

They were sitting in the boudoir, one on either side of the log fire. Maya's face in the firelight was pale and unfocused, and the strain about her eyes remained. She said, 'I go over and over the events of that day when Paco died.'

'So why don't you tell me about it?'

'You'll think I'm crazy.'

Polly spoke softly, careful not to break the closeness of the moment. 'I'm willing to suspend my disbelief.'

Maya leaned back in her chair. 'Sometimes I long to talk about those days, recall the feel and colour of them, remember the food we ate, the wine we drank, the quarrels. The hard words we spoke which could never be recalled. Paco. Paco and the Family. They were indivisible, Polly. If you took the one you were lumbered with the whole tribe. For two terrible days before the wedding it seemed that his parents might actually come on the honeymoon with us. But then there was a crisis in the restaurant and the plan was dropped. Even so, we were given a list of relatives to visit while we were in Spain. Paco said it was expected. Two sets of grandparents, several aunts and uncles, cousins by the score.' She paused. 'At first I thought I could be a part of it, that they would be the family I never had. But my Spanish was basic. They spoke very fast in a local dialect. In the end I sat in a corner while Paco had long conversations I couldn't begin to follow. This was our honeymoon, remember, but every day he had a family visit scheduled.'

'Maddening,' said Polly.

'I suppose I was jealous. There were so many of them, and they had one another. I had only Paco. He was the first person in my life who really belonged to me. I know I was over-possessive, but I couldn't seem to help it.'

'So you quarrelled.'

'Bitterly. All the time.' Maya stood up and walked to the window. She looked out at the dripping cedar tree, the soaked lawn. 'The weather was beautiful in Spain.' She returned to her chair. 'It was one of those crisp autumn mornings, cool but sunny. We had stayed overnight in a little hotel in the mountains. It should have been romantic, but by this time I wasn't even speaking to him. I felt so angry and betrayed, as if he had been unfaithful to me.'

'Go on.'

'It's a terrible story, Polly. When you've heard it you may not want to know me any more.'

'Don't be silly.'

Maya leaned her head against the chair back, closed her eyes ... It had rained in the night. There were leaves on the road. Wet leaves. I'd like to say that I skidded on them, but I know I didn't. We were on this road that twisted down round the mountain in a series of hairpin bends. I had insisted on driving because I knew it made him nervous. But I had studied the warnings issued to foreign tourists who were travelling for the first time in Spain. I approached that bend with exaggerated caution, braking and changing down as I went into the corner, carefully hugging the rock face on my right, acutely aware of the ravine which fell away towards the left. As I came out of the bend I remember laughing. There was really nothing to it.

'The cat appeared out of nowhere. I glanced into the driving mirror for just a second, and when I looked back towards the road, there it was, directly in our path. It was large and yellow coloured. Its back was arched, its fur bristled in a halo all round its head and neck. My last thought was surprise at the ill will which came from the creature, the malevolence glowing in its red eyes. My foot went down hard on the brake. I tried to speak but couldn't. I tried to change gear but the gears would not mesh. I tried to believe at first that our slide towards the unfenced drop was accelerated by the wet leaves. Then as we went over the edge I remembered that Paco was fastened safely in his seat belt, and that I was not. I could feel the car falling, and then there was a sort of bump and my head hit the windscreen.

'When I opened my eyes I was lying at the bottom of the ravine. I was aware of pain in my head and hands. I drifted off. I must have lain there for a long time. When I opened my eyes again, sunlight was coming through the overhanging branches. If I glanced sideways I could just make out the stone face of the ravine and the undergrowth which filled the hollow. I remember thinking that it was such a *green* place.

'I looked at my hands. There was a lot of blood, and the fingers of the left hand seemed almost to be detached. The pain of movement was so bad, I fainted.

'When I woke again my head was clearer. Blue lights were revolving high above me, I could hear men's voices and the throb of engines. They were bringing lights to focus on a tree which grew outwards from a fissure in the rock, and then I saw the car, its body wedged between the tree's roots. Some men crawled towards it and others came towards me. But before those men could reach the tree I heard a sound of splitting wood, and then the tree shuddered and I saw the car falling. As it hit the ground there was a noise like an explosion and then it burst into flame, and I knew that Paco was inside. I had wished him dead, and so he was.' Maya gazed into the fire. She was silent for some minutes. When she spoke again her voice was just a whisper.

'I was taken to a hospital. They stitched my head and fingers and gave me a blood transfusion. The policeman who came was middle-aged and plump. He spoke some English. He told me that Paco was already dead when the car exploded. I told him about the wet leaves, the yellow cat. I said, 'If I had fastened my seat belt —'

'Then you also would be dead, señora. It must have been your lucky day.'"

Polly stood up, she moved to the cabinet which held bottles and glasses. She found a bottle of Glenlivet and one of soda water. She said, 'You know that you're talking utter rubbish, don't you? You can't *wish* a person dead. If that were the case, then half of our customers would be six feet under. You know how rabid I can get about the awkward ones.' The drink she handed Maya was almost straight Scotch. She waited until Maya had taken the first sip before sitting down. 'Why didn't you tell me all this when the accident happened? You had arranged to be away for six weeks so when I heard nothing from you I didn't worry. After all, you were on your honeymoon. When you came back and told me that you had been injured in the car crash that killed Paco, well, I just assumed that it was he who had been driving. You said you didn't want to talk about it, and because you were so sad and depressed I thought it better not to press you. Later on – well, the business was really beginning to take off. She paused, hesitated. 'And then there was Jonah.' Polly leaned forward in her chair. 'There's more, isn't there? I can see it in your face.

Look, I know I talk too much, that I often irritate you. But I only want to help. Why don't you let me?'

Maya said, 'There's nothing you can do. Just leave me alone. I'll work things out in my own way.'

Polly drank her Scotch. She said, 'It's this bloody house that's sent you into a depression. You were fine until you came to live here. Come back to London with me, Maya.'

'No. No, I can't do that.'

'But there's nothing here for you. What do you do all day? If you were staying on to put the house in order – well, we've done that. We've polished and scrubbed every corner of it. Except the attics, of course, but as you said, nobody lives in attics.'

'I've become interested lately in family history. Genealogy.' Maya's voice was flat. 'I'm planning a visit to the Records Office in Dorchester. So you see, I have to stay here.'

'All right. All right. I get the message.' Polly forced a smile. 'I'll be leaving in the morning, so you'll be able to take over Lavinia's room instead of sleeping on that awful camp bed in the kitchen. Just promise me one thing. If you need me, call me, and I'll be straight down.' She lifted her glass and drank the remaining Scotch. 'And remember, you can't *wish* a person dead.' She laughed. 'You'd have to be a witch or something to achieve that!'

Maya

She stood in the porch and watched as the small red car drove fast away, splashing the water lying on the rutted drive, while Polly's hand, white and disembodied, waved a final goodbye from the driver's window. There was a last spurt of muddy water, a revving of the engine and then the drive was empty.

Maya lingered in the porch. The silence settled around her like a comfortable garment. The echoes of Polly's voice, instructing and cajoling, would sound in her head for a day or two, and then be stilled.

She went back into the house, closing the thick oak door with a sense of deep relief. They had parted on a warm note, as if much had been achieved in the past days. Maya had promised to work on designs for the spring collection. 'You can draw as well down here as in the office, probably better,' Polly had said, 'and then, if you're busy working, all these foolish guilt feelings about Paco will disappear. Come summer you'll be your old self again. I'll be down in August, we'll decorate those spare rooms. Perhaps we could have a holiday together. Italy is lovely in September.'

Maya went up to the bedroom which had once been Lavinia's. Polly had stripped the bed of sheets and pillowcases and put the used linen in a laundry sack. Maya closed the window, picked up the sack and shut the door with a firm hand. Whatever Polly said, she would not be sleeping in this room.

Back in the kitchen, she began to peel and slice vegetables for soup, to cut bread for toast. This afternoon she would split logs for the evening fire and chop a great boxful of kindling which would last the week through. While the soup began to simmer, she fumbled beneath the tablecloths in a kitchen drawer and withdrew the small brass key which would open the drawing room door.

Her reading of Maya Heron's diaries had already, before Polly's visit,

88

become a ritual event that could not be changed. It needed to be evening before the diary could be broached, with the curtains closed against the night, a log fire burning in the grate, a glass of wine to hand, and the portrait of the writer gazing down upon her with that passionate and threatening expression in her yellow eyes. All day, she anticipated the moment when she would settle down in the blue chair, reach a hand into the sewing box and pull out the thick folder of tattered papers.

Her sense of connection to Maya Heron was growing stronger. The coming of Polly, her distracting presence, had done nothing to weaken the feeling of closeness. Enforced abstinence had in fact sharpened her need. As she lifted the papers from the box, it was as if she brought the living, speaking girl into the room. For now, as she read, she began to think she could hear the Gypsy's husky, low-pitched voice.

Maya Heron. May 14th 1889.

No writing of my diary for a long time. I have been low in spirits. I had thought they might have got some word to me at Christmas. Guy said as how Milord and he saw two wagons crossing Hunger Hill on Christmas Eve. But there was no sign, no message for me from Dadus and Esmeralda.

Lavinia says they have forgotten me altogether. That they will likely be glad to be so easily rid of me. Milady says perhaps they are ill. There is much sickness in the countryside in this hard winter.

I puts on my hard face. I say they will come for me when the flower is on the blackthorn. I am my father's only daughter. He says I am his princess. But in my heart and stomach I feel the twist of pain that tells me they will not be coming in the springtime. And they did not.

I am better in my health. The limp has all but gone. I can even run and romp now with Lavinia and Guy and the gardener's girl what is called Pansy, though Lavinia will not romp much these days. She is coming soon fifteen and fancies herself quite the lady. There is talk of her going to a school in France when she is older, for to be finished off. Finished off? This made me laugh so that I all but choked. You have not even got started yet, say I. I stares at her bony legs and flat skinny chest. Her face goes all red.

Myself I am coming soon fourteen though I heard Milady say to Evangeline that I might actually be one year older than she first thought. I am so well developed. If I pulls back my shoulders and breathe in deep then my bosoms stand out very nicely. The butcher boy eyes me when he brings the meat. So does Guy when he thinks nobody sees him.

June 22nd 1889.

I had such a pain deep in my stomach and my head was all swimmy, and so when I laid poorly on my bed Susan came to find what ailed me. I bet, said she, that your Aunty Mary is coming to see you. Do not be so silly, I say. I have no Aunty Mary. She laughs and pokes me in the ribs with her sharp elbow. Yes you do, says she. All we women have our Aunty Mary what visits once in four weeks. Unless of course we have been naughty with the boys. Oh that, says I. I do not think it so. But it was.

June 24th 1889.

They have made me lie abed. They are feeding me with slops and bringing bags of hot salt for my stomach. Outside the sun is shining and the birds are singing. I sneaked out very early in the morning and ran with my bare feet in the dewy grass. Evangeline spied me from the window. Oh my, cried she, whatever are you thinking of? You will take a chill to your insides and likely die. When we are back in the nursery I sit her down in her chair and tell her how life is for the women in our *tan*. No *rakli*, says I, pays too much heed when Aunty Mary visits. There is much work to be done. Water to be carried, fires to make food to cook and *chavvies* to be looked to. Then there is the calling to be done. There will be no money for bread and tea and bacon if the women do not knock on Gorgio doors and sell their ribbons and lace and clothes pegs. For the men spend all they make in the *kitchima* and comes home drunk when their pockets are empty. So you can see, says I, that there is no time for a Gypsy woman to lie abed with a salt bag on her belly.

Evangeline has a look on her face what tells me that she knows little of how things are for the very poor people of the world. Let me tell you, I goes on, how it is with a girl of our people when she has her baby.

Evangeline claps her hand across her ears. No more, cries she. I will not listen to such indelicate talk. It would be better for you, Maya, if you stayed here with this family. I am sure Milady would employ you in some capacity. How can you even think of returning to those wild heathens and that rough life now that you have lived among the gentry.

My hand itches to slap her thick head. But I do not. I stare at her hard and long and she begins to wriggle. Do not look at me so, she cries, I shall think that you wish me ill. I say to her you are a very silly woman. I wave my hand at the room, at the whole house. You people are prisoners, I cry, and this is your *stiraben*. You dare not leave this place in case somebody robs you of your treasures. Master and maid, you are all trapped. How often have you watched the sunrise? Have you danced in a midsummer meadow when the moon is full? Do you know how good it is to sit around the fire on a winter's night and roast the potatoes you have that day pinched from some farmer's field? Oh yes, you are right, Evangeline, it is a rough life. But we are a free people. Where will you go when you have to leave this safe place? Who will employ you when you get old? We Rom take care of our own. It must be a very bad thing that we have done before we are cast out from the *tan*. So do not talk to me about staying here in this house. Do you think I would ever wash dishes and scrub floors for the Gorgio, no matter how kind and nice they be?

Evangeline says, you would not need to wash dishes. Do you not realise your own worth? You are a very clever girl, Maya. I have taught many high-born children but never one girl as sharp as you. Do you not see that you are educated now? You no longer eat with your fingers or wipe your nose on your coat sleeve. You bath every day and wear the same fine clothes as Miss Lavinia. You are become a lady, Maya, and how will that sit with your own people when you go back to their life?

I am sick to my boots when I hear her words. I am not clever, I cry. I worked hard at the lessons just to spite Lavinia. I hate the reading and the writing and all the fuss with knifes and forks and bathing. But in my heart I know that I am telling lies. I love the reading and the writing, it is such a magic for me. But I will not confess to this. Instead I wipe my nose upon my dress hem. Just to show her.

July 1st 1889.

Guy is to go away in September. He will go to Sherborne School. We are walking by ourselves on Hunger Hill when he tells me this. We have left Evangeline sitting on a bench in the village since she is now too fat to walk uphill.

Says Guy, I shall miss you, Maya.

I shall miss you too, I tell him.

He slips his arm round my waist. He touches my bosom but I moves his hand away. I remembers me of Susan's warning about the sons of gentry.

Will you be my secret sweetheart? asks Guy.

The words make me have a good feeling. I am very lonely. Yes, say I, we shall be secret sweethearts.

But it must be a secret, Guy says. It would not do for anyone to know.

The early days of the new year were dry and windless. A hard frost lay across the land, crisping and whitening every separate blade of grass, silvering the trees and bushes. On Hunger Hill she saw birds to which she could not put a name, varieties of trees she did not recognise. Sometimes she would glimpse some small rodent-like creature as it scuttled under hedges, but she could not have said with certainty if it was rat or weasel, stoat or squirrel.

Maya Heron would have known.

She thought that on this January morning the Gypsy girl walked with her, a derisive smiling doppelgänger, for didn't they recognise one another? Both had been left in childhood among strangers, both had experienced the deadening of feeling which comes with the loss of all hope. More than a hundred years ago Maya Heron had written, 'I am very lonely.' The reading of the diary was now becoming unbearably poignant. There was also the dread she had felt on first handling the papers; a dread that was deepening now into a nameless fear. She was grateful to whoever had clipped the pages into small batches, making a natural pause in the reading, making it easier for her to restrict herself to a single section on any evening.

She stood on a high point of the hill and looked at the road which led down into Yeovil. Strange, she thought, how since her parents' death, Gypsies and talk of Gypsies had come into her life. There were the market traders, Lias and Jango, who had claimed kinship with her and then vanished. There was the tale told by Alice of a Gypsy horse trader, murdered on this hill, on his way to the Pack Monday Fair in Sherborne. It was also Alice who had told her that a long dead Gypsy had put a curse upon the Monks' House and all who lived in it. Alice knew more than she was telling. Much more.

Maya walked without purpose; the object of this particular excursion had been the finding of the Hollow, but alone in the cold bright stillness her courage ebbed. It would have been wiser to come here with Polly who feared nothing and nobody. She imagined the Gypsy, leading his string of horses to the fair across these winding paths, not knowing that his killer waited for him beneath the trees. A little breeze got up, ruffling her hair, chilling the skin of her face, and she shivered.

There was wickedness here on this hill, old wickedness. She turned and walked back to the car; and Maya Heron walked with her.

Traces of Polly faded slowly from the house. It was easy to pack away the forgotten lipstick and night cream left in the bathroom; a few open windows took care of her lingering perfume. Harder to expel were the thoughts and memories that had been stirred up by her presence.

Maya built up the drawing-room fire, poured the wine, held the folder unopened but ready on her knee. She avoided a direct look at the portrait, but knew that Maya Heron watched her. She remembered her mother who had never spoken or acted like other people's mothers. When Bruenette was in the room, other women were extinguished by her.

First childhood memories were of her father's parents. A conservatory filled with green plants, its floor slippery with moss. A kitchen shelf fitted with brass hooks, from which hung the set of porcelain rose-encrusted jugs now owned by Alice. Maya remembered her grandfather's white hair and moustache, her grandmother's soft voice and warm hands.

There was a single early memory of Bruenette. A hot afternoon, a sloping lawn, drinking lemonade with several other people who sat in deckchairs; and she being shown off by her mother to the visiting friends. Bruenette, when in the company of others, had had a soft voice for her child. On that day she had used a rare endearment, and since she never held or kissed Maya, the word had been significant, it had warmed her small heart. In the hours that followed she had waited for the fond term to be repeated. For days she had waited, willing her mother to look lovingly at her, to once more call her darling. It never happened. After a time she began to understand that it never would.

There came a day when she knew she was no longer dependent on anyone for anything; when she knew that she stood alone in the world, that no one would help her, no one could help her. She was not like other people but she did not know quite how she was different. It was to sear her, that knowledge, set her apart.

She lifted her wine glass in a silent toast to Maya Heron, opened the folder and began to read.

Maya Heron. July 3rd 1889.

Guy is gone away to Sherborne School. Susan whispers in my ear that it is all my fault that Guy must go so soon. He should have started to the school in the coming September but Milord thinks it best he is out of the house just so long as I am still here. Susan says there is talk about me in the kitchen. Cook told Annie that I am a wicked temptress. Guy says they are all jealous because I am grown so beautiful. I know it, say I. But how can I help it if my looks draw men's eyes towards me? Guy says he is not yet quite a man. No, say I, but you have the body of a man and a grown man's feelings. I do not understand, I tell him, how this has come to pass but being close to we three women when our Aunty Mary visits has not hindered the growing of your manhood one little bit. Perhaps it is different with Gorgio men.

Before Guy goes away we walk in the garden. He takes me behind the potting shed and says he will prove to me that he is a real man. I do not need such proof, I tell him. I can feel you rising against me when you stand close to me. Go to Pansy the gardener's girl, I cry, if that is what you want. I am a lady now. Evangeline says so. I wear white drawers. Pansy does not wear any. But I am sure you know that.

So he went to Pansy. He took her to the Hollow under Hunger Hill. Pansy told Susan what happened there and Susan told me. I should have known better than to trust the Gorgio. But I had thought that Guy was different.

Lias

Spring arrived late that year in the country of the Dark Peaks. In mid-April, out of clear blue skies, came gusting winds and thick cloud. Within minutes snow was sweeping over Mam Tor, turning green back to white as if winter had never gone away.

Jango took the snowstorm to be an additional sign that they were not yet meant to travel. Lias would, at any other time, have been impatient to be gone, but Tara the greyhound bitch acquired at Christmas in settlement of a large, long-standing debt had whelped in March. The debtor had been a cousin to whom the loan of money had once been made. Lias had profited from the arrangement. The bitch, and the dog which served her, had impeccable pedigrees. Six of the seven puppies would sell for five hundred pounds apiece. The runt of the litter had been claimed by Jango. Together with their winnings on the horse and dog tracks of the northern cities, they had passed a very profitable winter.

The bitch was valuable, the puppies already advertised for sale. It was, said Jango, the sort of business better managed when they were stationary. And so they stayed on through the late, unseasonable snow, the kitchen floor tiles lined with newspaper, and puppies roaming underfoot.

The letter arrived in early May. Such mail as they received was held for them to be collected at the post office in the village. It was Lias, buying cigarettes and groceries in the crowded, multi-purpose little shop, who was handed the long white envelope which was addressed simply to Mr Heron. He pushed the letter unopened into his jacket pocket. He was not curious about the contents. Their correspondence was invariably from officials of one sort or another. He and Jango never wrote personal letters and did not receive them.

He walked back through the soft spring afternoon; on the top of Mam Tor he could see the white patches of snow still lying from the recent storm. It was not until later that night, when Jango had gone to his bed and Lias was giving the puppies their last milky drink of the day, that he remembered the envelope and pulled it from his pocket.

He opened it carelessly, expecting a bill or some typed communication. He unfolded the single sheet of paper. The neat handwritten script surprised him; he studied it briefly without at first taking in a word.

The writer began: 'Dear Mr Heron, you may remember that we met last year in Dorset in the Quiet Woman pub. My mother had written to you—' Quickly Lias pushed the sheet back into the envelope. The letter had clearly been intended for Jango. Well, it was a mistake anyone could make, she had not even used an initial, must have forgotten Jango's first name.

The beating of his heart was pounding in his ears. Just holding the paper which she had held had the power to bring her to him. He could hear those husky cultivated tones with the hint of contempt she had not bothered to conceal. He had caught only a brief snatch of her conversation with his brother, but it had been enough. Slowly he withdrew the letter from the envelope. It was, he thought, no more than his duty to Jango to read whatever this dangerous woman had to say.

The whelping kennel and bed stood in a corner of the barn. He and Jango had built it together, taking pleasure in the joint effort, the shared interest. Jango, who was skilled with the electrics, had rigged up a heat lamp above the kennel. Squares of thick carpet, changed every day and well scrubbed, lined the wide bed, providing insulation. The puppies were fed lately in the kitchen; it was good for them now to be handled, to be away from their mother for short intervals each day. Lias carried them back to the barn. He noted Tara's anxious looks, the way she checked each pup over on its return, sniffing and licking a fussy greeting. Lias fondled the bitch's silky head; with a few exceptions, he preferred dogs to people.

He pulled a straw bale close to the kennel. The heat lamp glowed red above the wide bed. He watched as the sated pups crept close to their mother. He found their milky whiskers and small blunt faces oddly touching. At this point of their development nothing distinguished them as being greyhounds. Only later would the chubby muzzles grow long and pointed; the beautiful clean lines, the deep chests and graceful legs become established.

Sometimes he talked to Tara in the lonely night hours. He spoke to her now, his voice pitched low as she lay half asleep and flanked by puppies. 'You're a pampered lady, do you know that?'

The bitch raised her head, her great liquid eyes sought his face in the semi-darkness.

'When I was a boy there was no whelping kennel then for the

likes of you, no heat lamp, no clean bed. You would have taken
your chances in those days, girl. You'd have dropped your pups
by the roadside or underneath the wagon. The weakest would have
died. The strongest survived. Rule of the road, girl. For women and
for dogs.'

He said to Jango over breakfast, 'Letter came yesterday, addressed to
Mr Heron. I opened it. Turns out it was meant for you.'

'You read it?'

'I read it.'

'So what does it say, this letter?'

'It's from that woman. Maya. The one we met in Dorset.'

Jango corrected him. 'The one that *I* met. You didn't care to.
Remember?'

'She wants to see us. Says she didn't take us seriously at first. But
now that she's done some family research, she thinks that we might,
after all, be related to her. Her only living relative is an aunt on her
father's side. She says that she's anxious now to learn more about her
mother's family.'

Jango smiled. 'Well, well. That's very interesting, eh, *pralo*?'

Lias said, 'So what do you suggest?'

'You're asking me?'

'She's your friend, little brother.' Lias stood. 'Think it over, eh?' His
voice became serious. 'She's a dangerous package. But you know that,
don't you?'

Jango nodded. 'I know it, but does she? She's part Gorgio, remember.
Never lived in the *tan*, had no contact with our people.'

Lias folded his thumb across his middle fingers to make the horned
sign against evil. 'We could go down there, I suppose. No harm in looking,
is there? But we need to be careful. Whether or not she's aware of her
power, she's still a risky one to get close to.'

They worked together on the Winnebago. Lias overhauled the engine,
Jango cleaned and stocked the living quarters. The puppies were
delivered to their new owners, their dew claws clipped, their ears
marked according to the rules of the British Greyhound Racing Board;
their inoculation certificates all in order.

Payment for the puppies was taken in fifty pound notes which were
then stashed in money belts and worn close to the body. Later on, the
cash would be exchanged for gold in various forms. They had learned
a lot from Despair Heron.

The frozen food had all been eaten, the freezers and generator
switched off. Their cousin Lija and his family would soon be pitched
on the hillside to wait for the start of the Appleby fair in July,

secure in the knowledge that from these few acres no official in the land had the power to move them on. The presence of Lija and his dogs and *chavvies* would discourage inquisitive tourists and vandals from the cities. Only Jango would regret the leaving of the Hope Valley.

Jango

*T*he hours of driving were divided equally between them. Lias took the first stint. Jango fastened his seat belt, wound the window down, and watched the house and hillside until a bend in the track took both from his view. He settled back into his seat and glanced swiftly sideways at the impassive profile of his brother; his face might as well have been chipped out of the local gritstone for all the emotion it ever registered. They travelled in silence until they reached the B road that would take them towards Derby and the south-west.

The dog-puppy lay across Jango's knees; from time to time he made small whining noises. He was still missing his mother who had been sold with the rest of the litter. Jango stroked him and fed him scraps of biscuit. Until now he had been nameless, but in view of the small white mark between the eyes he thought the puppy might be called Star. Despair's dogs had never been named. They were called only 'dog' or 'bitch' according to their gender, a practice that had never seemed quite right to Jango.

As they came into Matlock, Lias said, 'Breakfast.' They pulled into a parking space beside a cafe. Jango zipped the puppy inside his jacket, pushing down the small black head and taking a shadowy corner seat which faced away from the counter. He fed the pup surreptitiously with bits of bacon and fried bread.

'You shouldn't do that,' Lias said. 'He'll come to expect it. You'll never get him trained if you spoil him.'

'He's small. He needs feeding up.'

'He's a runt. Feed him every ten minutes and it won't make any difference. He was born small. He'll stay small.'

They got back into the camper. The puppy slept. Jango thought about the words that had just passed between himself and his brother. It was always the same when they were back on the *drom*. Lias setting Jango right, putting him straight. Putting him down.

The puppy had no need of the strict training meant by Lias; he would never be entered for a race.

As the camper moved off, a weariness came over Jango. They came down into leafy Leicestershire where the blossom lay thick on the hawthorn hedges and spring had long become established, all the vivid blues and greens, the soft air and birdsong. It came to him then, the disturbing thought that he had never yet witnessed a springtime in the Dark Peaks. Even this year, when departure had been delayed on account of the puppies, winter had still held fast to the windy edges of Mam Tor and Lose Hill. Only yesterday he had walked on Back Tor. He had looked across to the glory of Kinder Scout. His mind still held the image of deep gorges, littered boulders. He had stood on a windy ridge softened by heather and gazed out at the landscape of sheep tracks and rowan trees, where the grass was still brown and yellow from winter snows. He could still hear the crowing sound of the red grouse; see overhead the sparrowhawk which hovered. He could hear his father's dying words concerning his mother. 'Madeline. She followed me all over.'

He had thought about her often in the hard days of the recent winter. Madeline. A young girl, a Gorgio who had married his middle-aged father; a girl who had died in childbirth, and whose body was buried in some secret place. Lately, when he walked on the high tops, he imagined her, a child, roaming some unknown hillside, her long hair streaming in the wind, her heart light, not knowing that death and Despair Heron were waiting for her. He had studied the old men in the village pubs, the elderly farmers in the cattle markets of Castleton and Hope. Somewhere in the world, in some town or countryside, there might, unknown to him, be a whole family who were close relatives. Gorgios.

All his life he had tried to be like Lias. No, it was more than that; he had tried to *be* Lias. It was Lias aged twelve, thirteen years, and already saturated in the deep Romany beliefs and teachings of Grandmother Heron, who had set his imprint on the motherless Jango. And not just motherless; Jango had known in the way that such children know long before they can walk or talk that his father had no kind thought or word for him; no love. The vanity which had caused Despair to reject the son who resembled his Gorgio mother had been repeated in Lias. He, too, had wanted a son. Jango remembered the dismayed look, the disappointment, when Rowsheen had been presented for the first time to her father. It was Jango who had held the baby, who had said, 'Oh, Lias, she's so beautiful! She's got her mother's blue eyes and red hair.'

Lias had turned away, his hands in his trouser pockets; he had made no move to hold his child and Jango had known then what was in his mind. When Rowsheen was three years old, Sinaminta had taken her daughter and returned to the wagons of her own people. It was fifteen years since Lias had seen his wife and child. He never spoke about them, or allowed any mention of their names by Jango.

They were coming into Bourton-on-the-Water. Lias said, 'We'd better get a sandwich here and let the dogs out for ten minutes.' He nodded towards Star. 'You can leave the runt in the cabin this time.'

Jango pulled up the zip on his blouson jacket and pushed the pup down inside it. This time Star knew what it was that he must do. The small head disappeared from view and Jango smiled. A smart dog learned discretion early. Lias noticed his actions but said nothing, although he closed the door on his side of the camper with unnecessary force. Jango smiled again. Through his shirt front he could feel the warmth of the puppy's body. Oh well, he could live with a little show of temper from his brother. He thought about the woman Maya, and without examining too deeply the nature of his thought he reflected that if it ever came to a contest between himself and Lias, his love for his brother and his equal fear of him might be difficult to deal with.

Lias always drove fast and with total concentration, his knuckles white around the steering wheel as if his will alone maintained the progress of the Winnebago. Jango was totally relaxed when driving. He did not hunch across the wheel but sat well back in his seat, body and hands unclenched, his speed slow. Spring had scarcely touched the high places of the Dark Peaks, but here in the West Country it was almost high summer. Jango drove carefully between hedges thick with dog roses; the scent of cow parsley tickled in his nostrils. He could see the slow turning of the new-cut hay in distant fields. The transition to warmth, which always happened and should have been expected, was shocking to him this year. He felt the prickle of sweat across his chest and forehead. He was aware of Lias shrugging off his fleece-lined jacket. Jango slowed and halted. He removed his own jacket and laid it on the cabin floor. He set Star down upon the jacket and sternly bid him 'Stay'. He saw his brother's grin of approval. 'That's better,' Lias said. 'It's time you showed him who's boss.'

They were into Somerset before Lias picked up the mobile phone and dialled her number. 'Maya? Lias Heron here. We're in your area, just passing through. You mentioned in your letter that you'd like a meeting.' He listened, nodded. 'OK. That's fine. See you in the morning then.'

Maya

*T*he sound of his voice brought his image before her, the deep abrupt tones matched his dark looks. She had not believed that the brothers would call her. There had been no response to her letter to Jango and she knew that they were literate, they had read her mother's letter; and she had seen the mobile phone in the pocket of the Armani jacket. But their lack of interest now had, on reflection, been no real surprise. Her behaviour back in August had been cool to the point of rudeness. Remembering her airs and graces then, the mockery of her words to Jango, she felt ashamed and unexpectedly apprehensive. Far back in her mind had been a hope, after the letter was posted, that they would not respond. There had been a curious sense of power about them, particularly Lias; a dangerous power that seemed directed straight at her as if, for all the smiles and pleasant words, they wished her ill.

Her fingers touched the handset, and then she realised that she could not call them back. They had never given her their number. She could, she supposed, say that she had changed her mind, that there was nothing to be gained by talking further. She studied her reflection in Milady's gilt-framed mirror and saw that her hair needed washing, that her shirt and jeans were stained and shabby from working in the garden. She decided on a long soak in a scented bath, a special rinse to make her hair shine. Not since the time of Paco's courtship of her had she cared so much how she looked to any man.

She went up to the bathroom and stood before the full-length rust-pocked mirror. She stripped off her clothing, pulling and unbuttoning in great haste, like a child ripping Christmas wrapping from a present. She looked at her body, the elongated neck and full breasts, the narrow waist and hips, the long legs. Her skin was creamy and unblemished, she had never borne a child or had an operation. All her scars were on the inside. The mirror image of herself was mesmeric; she tried to turn away, but each time she moved, the shade of Lias came to stand at her shoulder, his naked body a dark and shocking contrast to her pallor. She knew that it was a trick of her mind that brought the Gypsy to stand beside her; it had happened before, this involuntary summoning up of apparitions. She tried not think about the implications of such a power, if power it was.

As well as the lipstick and night cream, Polly had left behind a squat blue bottle of expensive bath essence, as if she was stating her intention to return. Maya lay breathing in the scented steam until the water grew cool. She washed her hair and doused it with the special rinse. She pulled on a plain cream jogging suit and left her damp hair lying loose on her shoulders. Her feet were pushing into moccasins when she heard the clatter of the door knocker. She moved to an upper window which gave a good view of the driveway. The Winnebago camper labelled LIAS 7 was parked only feet away from her front door.

She stood well back behind the curtains. As the men moved out from the porch and back towards the camper, she had a foreshortened view of their heads, one black, one silver. Seeing them together she realised how similar they were in height and build, both tall, broad in the shoulder, narrow-hipped, long-legged. A shock of excitement ran through her body; she forgot that she had regretted the writing of the letter, that she had feared their coming, especially Lias. She watched as they returned to the Winnebago, saw them open up the cabin doors and prepare to climb inside. Her hand went out swiftly to the brass catch, she pushed open the window. 'I am sorry,' she called. 'I didn't hear you knocking.' Without a word to each other or to her, they slammed shut the doors and began to walk slowly back towards the porch. She ran to the staircase, her moccasined feet slipping dangerously on the polished boards. When she invited them to enter the dark hall, they refused.

The formality of Jango's first words made her smile. 'We don't wish to cause you any trouble. We intended to call here in the morning, as arranged. But we've had problems finding a parking place for the camper. It's getting late and we've had a longish drive. We were wondering if —'

'Of course,' she said. 'Why not? There's plenty of space here.' She beckoned them to follow, and led them past the stable block and out into the paddock.

'We shall need water,' said Lias.

She pointed to a tap set in the stable wall. 'But you're welcome to stay in the house if you'd like to.'

'No.' said Lias. 'We don't stay in houses, except when we are forced to, in bad winters. Even then, I prefer the Winnebago.'

'Ah yes,' she said. 'I should have known that. Well, you're welcome to park there for as long as you wish.'

103

'You've no objection to a fire?'

'A fire?'

'We'll contain it in a bucket. We won't leave any rubbish. You won't know that we've been here.'

'A fire will be fine,' she said, not knowing quite what they meant. 'Make yourselves at home,' she said. 'If there's anything you need I'll be in the kitchen.'

She returned to the house, walking slowly and conscious that they watched her. She pushed her hands through her drying hair and shook it back across her shoulders in the provocative gesture she had seen used by very young girls. I am behaving, she thought, like an adolescent, acting as I never did when I *was* a young girl.

From the room that had been Lavinia's she could see the stable block and the adjoining paddock. She made coffee and sipped it while she watched from behind the curtain at the open bedroom window. She had offered them shelter but not food and drink. But she was sure they were men who would be willing to accept only what they had specifically requested.

Two greyhounds roamed the paddock; they were followed by a small black puppy which pushed its way excitedly through the long grass. From the trailer, Jango unloaded a sheet of flat grey metal; on it he placed a bucket-like container with holes punched in its sides. Lias brought paper and a sack of chopped wood. He laid the fire but did not light it. The brothers did not speak to one another, they performed their separate tasks without consultation, and she saw how such mutual confidence could only have grown out of lifelong dependence, lifelong trust. For the first time in her life she became aware of her own total self-absorption. At the root of all her thoughts lay herself, her needs and longings, her own pain. She wondered how this state of narcissism had come about, how long it could continue. The sudden insight caused her an acute discomfort and she turned her attention back to the men in the paddock.

There was light now in the Winnebago. A meal was in preparation, she could see the one called Jango busy with bowls and saucepans. It was Lias who called to the two dogs and the puppy. He set three bowls of food close to the camper steps and watched while the dogs ate; when they were finished he removed the bowls, struck a match and lit the wood and paper in the bucket. He went back into the camper and fetched two low wooden stools which he set down beside the fire. Jango came down the steps, cutlery and a plate of food in either hand. He handed a plate and fork to Lias, they sat down close to the fire and began to eat.

The strangeness of the scene brought her out from behind the curtain.

She leaned her elbows on the windowsill and frankly watched them. The soft blue light of the spring evening was fading fast into deeper shadows, but the air was still mild. They had no need of a fire for warmth, they could have eaten their meal more comfortably inside the camper. The dogs, even the puppy, lay quietly beside the fire. Only now did the brothers speak to one another; she could see the movements of their lips, the animation of their features. In her life she had often felt excluded when in the company of others, she was not gregarious, not a joiner. Across the space which lay between the window and the camper she could sense the powerful bond between the brothers, a link that any woman who lived with either of them would at first resent and then long to sever. Even now, when she hardly knew them, a bitter envy of their closeness possessed her.

It would, she thought, have to be a reckless and foolish woman who ever dared to try to separate them.

She went down to the kitchen and stood beside the camp bed. The best view of the stable block and paddock was from the window of the room that had been Lavinia's. Within minutes she had transferred the duvet and pillows from the kitchen to the lace-trimmed bedroom, and packed away the folding bed into a cupboard.

She found it difficult to sleep in the strange room; she had left the window open and the unfamiliar sounds of the night alarmed her, the high scream of an animal in pain, the repeated call of what might have been an owl. And yet she could not bring herself to close the window. From time to time she rose from her bed and gazed down at the paddock and the camper.

The two men sat for a long time beside their fire. They smoked cigarettes. Lias filled his cup repeatedly from a large brown teapot. Jango drank straight from a green glass bottle. Their voices rose and fell at first in argument and then in appeasement, but they were too far away for her to hear their words. It was some time after midnight when they built up the fire and moved into the camper. She expected them to stay there, but they re-emerged, each man wrapped in a blanket and carrying what looked like groundsheets and extra blankets. They lay down, one on each side of the fire. The two greyhounds lay at Lias's feet, the puppy snuggled up to Jango.

She awoke towards morning. Her dreams had been anxious but unremembered. She lay for a while only half-aware, watching pink light streak the eastern sky, and then she recalled the presence of the men in the paddock. She rose and walked slowly to the window.

Lias, dressed in jeans and T-shirt but barefoot, was filling a kettle at the stable tap. Jango still slept, the puppy close beside his head. Lias, the filled kettle in his hand, came to stand beneath her bedroom window. She looked down on the sharp planes of his upturned face and knew that she was lost.

'We'll be moving out within the hour,' he told her.

She wanted to ask him, what about our meeting? But pride would not let her put the question.

'Will you be coming back?' She could hear the anxiety in her voice and was embarrassed by it.

He nodded. 'All right if we leave a few bits and pieces here?' he asked.

'Fine,' she said, and turned back into the room.

The telephone rang as she was eating breakfast. It was Alice, speaking in the high bright tone which meant that she was seeking information. 'I hear that you have visitors,' she said. The jungle telegraph, which operated over a ten-mile radius of Hunger Hill, was working well; the postman had called early that morning and the Winnebago camper was too large to be denied.

'Yes,' said Maya. A sudden irritation, a wish to shock was pushing her towards an answer she might well regret. 'Two men, two Gypsies. Bruenette wrote to them just before the accident. She believed she was their cousin.' The forced laughter sounded foolish in her own ears. 'It's quite ridiculous, of course. My mother was always unbalanced, she had these strange convictions – well, I don't need to tell you, do I?'

Alice said, 'What are they called, these two Gypsy men?'

'Well, they have these outlandish first names. Jango and Lias. Their surname is Heron.'

Alice did not reply at once. She said at last, 'Your mother's name was Heron before she married Geoffrey.'

'Oh. I didn't know that.' It was not altogether true, but if Alice could be sparing with her confidences, so could Maya, and guessing wasn't knowing, was it?

'Maya, look here, I think you and I should have a talk about this. When can you come over?'

She answered with amazing swiftness, the lie ready on her tongue. 'Not this week for certain. I've advertised for someone to help in the garden. I have a few people coming out to see me. So I'll be stuck here for the next few days.'

'In that case I shall have to come to you. In the meantime, don't get involved with these men. I mean it, Maya. Some things are better left alone. It would be a pity to upset your peace of mind just when you seem to be improving.' Alice paused. 'If you really want help in the garden I can send old Mr Parsons over to you. He used to work at the Monks' House years ago.'

Maya would have liked to question Alice but feared the answers she might get. The garden waited for her. She returned to the task which the coming of the brothers had interrupted. As she dug beneath the apple trees, turning the dark soil, pulling out the chickweed and the couch grass, her anger with Alice began to dissipate. The memory of Lias's upturned face stayed with her. There was nothing she would not do to please him, if he asked her; although she thought he was probably a man who took what he wanted without bothering to ask. She tried not to think about him. When evening came she found herself listening for the return of the Winnebago. Only a reading from Maya Heron's diary would be sufficiently gripping to distract her mind.

Maya Heron. August 12th 1889.

Guy came back from Sherborne School two weeks since. In that time he has scarce spoken to me. He is with Pansy every day. I know it from her sly looks and smiles what she gives me every time we meet. I find out the candle ends and make a poppet. I never did use the poppet on Lavinia which is just as well for I need it now for what Milord would call *a worthy cause*.

Lavinia is gone off to be finished. Evangeline has found a new post. She is to teach the children of a family what is related to Milord. So now it is just me and Milady, what is very nice. I am allowed to help her with letter writing. I do the flowers every day. She is showing me how to do fine sewing. I have quite took over the mending of the household linen what was Evangeline's job when she was here. I sit most days with Milady in the boudoir. Her in her gold chair and me on a footstool at her feet. She tells me all about when she was a young girl and I tell her about life in the *tan*.

I think Milady is keeping me close by her because she does not trust Guy to be near me.

Or mayhap it is me she does not trust.

Maya Heron. September 1st 1889.

The Lovell family is come to Sheepdip Lane. They leaves a sign beside the house gate that they wants to see me. Milady says how clever it is of them to leave such a sign with bits of stick. I look in the long cheval mirror what shows me myself from head to foot. I see how different I am become. What will the Lovells make of me? I hunt in the wardrobes for some torn and faded gown but of course in this house there is none. I even think to ask Pansy if I can borrow one of her dresses what is sure to be washed out and shabby. But I see that I am much fuller in the figure than Pansy and so no use to ask.

In the end I go down to Sheepdip Lane in my very finest rig-out. After all, I did not ask to be left amongst the Gorgio gentlefolk. It is not my fault if they have changed me and made me over into their ways.

It goes very ill with the Lovells. They are down on their luck. Two horses have died and they have had a bad summer. To first they will not have it that I am truly Maya Heron daughter of Taiso. The women finger my lavender silk gown trimmed with the fine lace and ribbons and my hands that show no sign of rough work. The *chavvies* touch my kid leather shoes. The men and boys in the *tan* give me the sort of lewd up and down looks what they would never dare to send if they were not sure and certain that I was a Gorgio. It rocks them all back in their boots when I begin to speak the Romanes to them. I reminds them of things past that only Maya Heron could know about. I scolds and swears at them. I say I cannot help the way I look. Have I not been forced to live for many years in the house of the Gorgio Milord, who would not have me looking down-at-heel in his fine house.

To last they believe me. They give me the message. Dadus and Esmeralda will be coming to fetch me. They are already on the road from the Appleby horse fair. If all goes well they could be here by the end of November.

I go back to the house. I tell Milady what has come to pass. I say I shall not be here with you for much longer.

Guy is with her when I say this. A long look passes betwixt him and me. A warm look what says that he is still my secret sweetheart.

Maya Heron. September 15th 1889.

Guy goes back next week to Sherborne. I help Milady pack his trunk. I sew missing buttons back on to his shirts and jackets. It is such a joy for me to do this for him. Like as if we are already wedded. But I do not say this to Milady.

Today Milady showed me photographs in an album. Most were groups of miserable lords and ladies, with stiff necks and mad eyes, and faces sour like lemons. But these were her relations so I held my tongue. One photograph was sweetly pretty. It was the wedding of Milord and Lady. He was a soldier looking very fine, she made a lovely bride in a white gown. They stood underneath a canopy of crossed swords which seemed a risky thing to do.

I said to Milady, you both are very young in this photograph.

Not so young, she said. Henry was thirty years old and I was twenty-seven.

Why did you wait so long? I asked her. You had plenty of money.

She answered me in that voice people use when they mean you to hear more than they are saying. Maya, she said, it is not good to marry when you are very young. It is better to wait until you have some experience of life. Until you have learned a little wisdom. I know, said she, that it is different with your people. But Guy – and now she fixes me with both her eyes – Guy will not be ready to marry for many years yet. First of all he will have to finish his schooling. After that he is to go into the Army. He will join his father's old Regiment of Guards. His uncle is a brigadier. Guy will see foreign service in many parts of the world before he is ready to settle down.

And what does Guy say to all this? I ask her.

My son knows his duty, says Milady. Both to his family and his Queen.

This makes me wild. The ways of my people are better than your ways, I shout out. Guy has his natural urges. What is he supposed to do about them? It is safer and better to be wed. Especially for such as Guy.

What do you mean? Milady cries. Guy has only just turned seventeen. He is but a mere boy. He is too young for what you term his natural urges.

Although she is a woman grown and with children of her own I see that in some ways she is but a child. He has strong passions, I tell her. I run from the boudoir and into the garden. I stay absent for a long time. I am feared to say more. When I come back to the house I find Susan carrying her clothes and things upstairs and placing them in the nursery bedroom what stands next to mine. She has been told to keep open at all times the door between her room and mine. Orders, says Susan. I don't know what you have been saying and doing but my mistress means to keep a careful watch on you in future and no mistake. She winks her eye. Whatever have you been up to, eh Maya? Master Guy got a wigging too. Now I wonder why?

I only spoke the truth, say I.

There will be trouble yet, says Susan. You mark my words.

Maya Heron. September 22nd 1889.

Guy is gone this day to Sherborne. There was no chance to say goodbye. I watched his going from the nursery window. He gazed up at me and raised his hand and with this I had to be content. When the carriage was gone I said to Milady, you can move Susan back to her own room now. I know that you will not believe this, ma'am, but it is not me that means danger to your son.

She gave me that sad look of hers what is more hurtful than anger.

Oh Maya, said she, you really do not know your own power, do you? His father and I have had much trouble with Guy lately. I do not understand the reason for it but I am quite sure that somehow you are at the centre of it.

Maya Heron. September 23rd 1889.

Last night I had bad dreams, leastways it always feels like a dream but as usual this morning I am told that I have sleepwalked. I dreamed about Guy. I saw his future life and it was so terrible that when I woke up I was weeping. I cannot get out of my head the words spoken to me yesterday by Milady. *His father and I have had much trouble with Guy lately. I am quite sure that somehow you are at the centre of it.*

Maya Heron. October 1st 1889.

I am no longer happy in this house. I had never thought to miss Evangeline and Lavinia but without them there is no spark, no fire, no chance to use what Susan calls my wicked tongue. The absence of Guy is like a great hole deep inside me. I know now that though he is Gorgio and will one day be a Milord like his father, Guy is and always will be the one true love of my life. No matter what Milady says, none of this is my fault. I did not ask the stallion to kick me. I did not ask to be left with this family for so many years. I did not want to be changed in my ways or to love their son. After seeing the Lovell family I know that I am now neither altogether Rom nor Gorgio. But it has all happened and there is nothing I can do to change it.

When Milord and Lady are not at home I walk through the rooms of the house from top to bottom. I will need to remember this place so that I may think about Guy living in it when I am far from here.

I am to have my portrait painted. The artist who painted Milady and her children is to make my likeness. I do not understand why. I would have thought this family would be only too happy to forget me. I am to wear my favourite green dress, and pose on the garden swing before the weather turns colder. I have no heart for any of this. In a few more weeks my father and aunt will be coming to claim me. I shall never more see Guy whom I love more than my own life.

Maya Heron. October 2nd 1889.

Strange things happen. There is some mischief afoot and I do not know what it is. I was sitting on the garden swing while the artist made my likeness from his paint pots when I heard voices on the far side of the high hedge of the laurels. It was Tom the gardener and one other whose voice I did not know. I heard Tom say, if it be true then I shall kill him with my bare hands. The other man said, hold hard, Tom. We do not know for sure and she won't tell us. No sense in you landing up in Shepton Mallett gaol and swinging from the gibbet, is there?

I could not think what trouble ailed poor Tom, that he who is so mild and quiet should have his mind turned towards murder. But today I heard some other news. Cook says that Tom's daughter Pansy has been sent away to stay with her grandmother who lives a great distance – all of twenty miles – from this village. I am dumbfounded that Cook who says she does not gossip is the one to tell me this. Why? I ask. Why would Pansy go away so sudden? Cook smiles and lifts her fat shoulder and lays a finger alongside her nose in that way she has when she is minded to be perverse. *Tell me*, says I. I fix my eyes upon her and she starts to shake. No, Maya, she calls out, don't look at me so wicked. I will tell you but you must not say a word to anybody.

I have heard, says Cook, that silly Pansy is in the family way and the man is one who will not marry her no matter what. They say he is from a well-off family. I reckon, says Cook, it could be one of the Earl's sons. They is known to be a wild lot. Poor Tom is like to lose his mind. Well, it's all her own fault, says Cook. She was after Master Guy all summer and him only just out of short trousers.

I turn from Cook and walk into the garden. I sit in the vinery where it is green and quiet. Oh no, I think it is not a man so high born as an Earl's son what has done for poor Pansy. The trouble lies much closer to home and Tom knows who the man is. Except that the father of Pansy's child is not yet quite a man but still a schoolboy and the length of his trousers won't have mattered to either of them. I am surprised that Cook who seems to notice nothing is so well informed.

I go and seek out Susan who is ironing in the laundry room. I say, if you are ever asked about Master Guy and Pansy you are not to say one word of what happened between them on Hunger Hill in summer.

Susan thumps the iron down hard upon the trivet. Well, you are too late, Maya, she cries. I have told it already. I thought it only right that Tom should know. Specially since that half-daft Pansy won't say who the father is.

I go back into the house. Milord and Lady are not yet home from visiting. I drag my body up the staircase to the nursery. I feel as broken as I did when I first came here when the stallion had trampled on my head and back. My heart is sick. I lie down on my bed and wrap the quilt round me. If I had tears inside me I would weep. But I do not seem to have any.

Later on I watch from the window as the sky grows dark. The stars come out and a great moon rises in the heavens. I see the side lamps of Milord's carriage coming up the drive. I hear the clop of horses and then Milady's laughter as they walk into the house.

So nobody has yet dared to tell them the truth about Guy although by this time all the village knows it.

Maya Heron. October 3rd 1889.

Today is Sunday. We walk down to morning service. I sits as always with the family in their special pew what has got its own little door and a strip of blue carpet on the floor. The servants sit all together just below us. I look down on to Tom's grey hair all slicked down with water and his wife's blue bonnet and their seven children, the youngest still a babe in arms. I feel my stomach churning like a butter maker. I am pulled all ways at once and do not hear one word of the sermon.

As we are leaving the church Tom stands direct before Milord. I hear Milord say, very well, Stagg. If it is so urgent as you say I will see you directly after luncheon. Be up at the house at two thirty sharp.

I cannot eat. I beg to be excused. They think it is my Aunty Mary come to visit. I hide in the flower room from where I can hear what passes between Milord and Tom.

Tom comes at sharp two thirty. To first I cannot make out what they say. Then I hear Milord shout loud as if he is in great pain. Are you certain of this, Stagg?

Tom says, on my life, Milord. When we asked her straight out my Pansy said that it were Master Guy and none other. It seems, Milord, that all the village and the household servants knowed about it. Saving you and me, sir, and Cook what says she don't never listen to gossip so nobody told her.

Milord says, don't worry about this, Stagg. Your daughter and her child will be well provided for. This is no fault of yours. Your job and house are here for as long as you want it. As for my son, you can leave his punishment safely in my hands. He will be dealt with this day, make no mistake about that.

Within minutes the small brougham stands before the front door. I bides in the flower room sitting on the floor, my back against the wall. Through the wall I can hear Milady weeping. I know that I should go to her but cannot bring myself to do it. I think back over all that happened. At last I hear the carriage wheels. The door slams shut and Milord is back. He says to Milady, leave us, my dear. This is business only I can deal with.

The voices are very quiet at first. Then I hear Milord say, answer me, sir. I want the truth.

Guy cries out in an awful voice and all at once he sounds like a man

112

and not a boy. It was not my fault, Father. You should never have brought Maya Heron here. She tempted me and then turned me away. She drove me crazy, Father. So I went to Pansy, who was more than willing, I might say. You would not be making all this fuss if the girl in trouble was Maya. She is only a Gypsy. She could have been sent back to her father's wagons and nobody in the village any the wiser.

Milord roared out, enough. Hold your tongue, sir. How dare you malign these innocent girls to excuse your own guilt. I could have borne the wickedness of your behaviour but your lies and excuses I will not, cannot possibly, condone.

There is a silence and then I hear Guy cry out, oh no. Oh Father. Please no.

I hear a swishing sound and then Guy starts to scream. I run from the flower room and see Milady stumbling fast down the stairs. She and I stand together before the shut study door. Milady says, oh my God. Miles is using the horse whip on him. She looks at me. She says, what has happened to my family since you came here?

Maya Heron. October 6th 1889.

The portrait is finished. I find it strange to look upon. It is my face and body, the colour of my hair and eyes. But the artist has painted in all my bad feelings. It is there on the canvas for everyone to see. It is a greater magic even than this writing I am doing. I look at the picture and recognise my soul. I go to the boudoir and study the picture of Milady and I see that we are very different people. I say to Milady, burn it. I am not as that artist has made me seem. I am as you are, ma'am. I am good and gentle. But even as I speak I know that this is not the truth. Towards one person only in this world have I felt gentleness and goodness and he is in great trouble and I cannot help him. Poor Guy has laid abed for nearly two weeks. The doctor has called most every day. They say in the kitchen that Milord has almost done for Guy and that Milady will never forgive that beating.

Milord has gone away to London. I am forbidden to see or speak to Guy. Tom digs beneath the apple trees as if nothing terrible has happened.

Maya Heron. October 7th 1889.

Susan comes running to me early this morning. Good news for you, she cries. Wagons came into Sheepdip Lane last night. I was stopped by a Gypsy woman as I came up the drive. She said, tell Maya Heron that her aunty and father is waiting for her.

I stand at the nursery window. The day I have waited for is here at last. They have come to take me with them. I am not forgotten. But I am not the Romany *chavvie* who was once carried dying into this house. Neither am I a *tatchi* Gorgio. Or a daughter of a Milord. Or a gentlewoman.

Milady comes up to the nursery. She puts her arm about my waist and I see that I am now a whole head taller than she is. I feel the tears start in my eyes. She has been as a mother to me.

Take with you everything I have given you, she says. She unclasps the gold pendant which hangs about her neck and fastens it round my throat. For a keepsake, she says. Remember me kindly, Maya. You are as God has made you. I have the portrait to remind me of you.

She helps me to pack the clothes and slippers, the good boots and finery. I put in the box the writings I have done and the paper I have not yet used. She brings me a big bottle of black ink and some quills and these are the greatest gifts she could have made me. I ask if I might see Guy for just one minute. No, says Milady. It is better that you go quickly now. Guy is no longer your concern. You will do better to forget him. Promise me, Maya, that you will never more approach him for any reason.

I look down on to the driveway where Dadus and Esmeralda are waiting for me. I say I promise I will never approach Guy for any reason. These are the last words that I shall write in the house of the Gorgio. But I have made no vow to Milady of what might come to pass if Guy were ever in the future to approach me.

Mr Parsons the gardener came on a bicycle. He was a small man, old, rosy-faced and chatty. He had worked at the Monks' House when a boy. Tuberculosis, he explained, had prevented him from serving his country in the last war. But he remembered the airmen who had convalesced in the house at that time. Poor devils, he said, who had hidden their burned limbs and destroyed faces from the village folk.

The Monks' House, Maya thought, had been a refuge for many people. Maya Heron had recovered here and then gone back to the wagons of her people. She herself had lately been in some sort of retreat, like a nun who needed time and seclusion for the contemplation of her soul.

The house, said Mr Parsons, had been in the possession of the same family for as far back as records went. Over the years it had been leased by those who had inherited but did not wish to live there. He looked sideways at Maya. Well, the house, he said, had gained a funny reputation in the time of Sir Henry and Lady Anne. But it was only their direct descendants who ever saw and heard strange things. He paused and appeared to wait for Maya to claim or deny a blood link with the family; a talent for seeing visions. When she said nothing, he continued in a knowing tone, 'It must have been nice for your mother,' he said, 'to be back here again after so many years.'

'What do you mean?' she asked him. 'I don't understand you.'

'Mrs Pomeroy, your mother. She was often here when she was little.'

'In this house?'

'Why, yes.'

'I didn't know that.' She saw that he was embarrassed for her, and began to push his bicycle back towards the drive.

'Three days a week then,' he said, 'just until I get this lot sorted. You'll never manage all the planting and weeding on your own. After that – well, we'll see. One day a week ought to do it.' He touched a finger to his forehead in an old-fashioned gesture. 'I'll see you again come Tuesday, ma'am.'

Mornings and evenings she walked to the paddock. She stood in the long lush grass beside the metal sheet and perforated bucket, and studied the assorted tools and chopped sticks left there by the brothers.

A white mist lay in the hollows and corners of distant meadows. The colours and smells of early summer made her body ache with a deep pain she recognised as being desire. Lias came to her in sleep, in dreams that did not end with waking. She had felt no resentment at his sudden arrival at the Monks' House and his even more abrupt departure. He would be one of those men who never apologised or offered explanations. She had exchanged her preoccupation with herself for an obsession with an unknown man that was so strong it was becoming almost indecent.

Alice came on the fourth morning of the brothers' absence; she moved from the Rover to the paddock fence. Maya went to stand beside her. Together they gazed at the perforated bucket.

'Gypsies, you said.' Alice spoke in a flat voice which was intended to conceal her feelings, but failed.

'Yes,' Maya said. 'But well-heeled ones. They appear to have a taste for the luxuries of life. Designer clothes. Gold jewellery. They travel in an enormous camper-wagon of American manufacture, with two greyhounds and a puppy.'

'Flashy,' said Alice.

'You could say that, I suppose. But flashy with a certain style.'

'They've made quite an impression on you.'

Maya said, 'Would you like some tea?'

'That would be nice. Perhaps we could have it outside. I see that you've put the summer chairs and table on the terrace.'

Maya set a tea tray with an embroidered cloth she had found in a dresser drawer, and flowered china from a high cupboard. She put scones on a plate, and jam and butter into small pots. She poured milk into a jug, and put cubed white sugar in a bowl with silver sugar tongs beside it. Alice smiled her approval.

'Are your Gypsy friends so civilised?' she asked.

Maya thought about the big brown teapot and the green glass bottle. 'I haven't noticed,' she said.

'Why are you letting them stay here, Maya?'

'Because they asked me. They're perfectly harmless.'

'How can you know that?'

'Oh, for heaven's sake, Alice! I didn't think you were so prejudiced.'

'I'm not. Well, perhaps a little. But a woman alone, in a house filled with valuable objects, you could be in all kinds of danger.'

Maya said, 'According to the letter written to them by my mother, the Heron brothers almost certainly have a moral if not a legal claim to some of the contents of the house.'

'Is that why they are here?'

'They haven't said so.'

'Oh, they will!'

'Look,' said Maya. 'I wrote to them. I suggested a meeting. There are certain things I need to know, and I believe that they are the only ones who have the answers.' She paused and looked across the teacups. 'Unless of course you would care to tell me all that *you* know. And you do know quite a lot, don't you, Alice, especially about Bruenette?'

Alice rattled her teacup back into the saucer. She said, 'Go back to London, Maya. You should never have stayed here in the first place. Your mother should not have willed you the Monks' House. She was not a considerate woman and she could never have foreseen the disastrous effects it would have upon you.'

'What disastrous effects, Alice?' Maya spoke softly. 'All that's happened is that I've become more thoughtful, more aware of many things since I first came here.' She stretched her arms above her head, leaned back in her chair and smiled. 'I feel so alive. The past is done with, over. I begin to see a future. Don't spoil it for me. Please don't spoil it.'

Alice said, 'It's the dark one, isn't it? The one who looks like an Ashanti god. I saw them, you know, that day we visited the fete in Halston. I saw you watching him there.'

Maya stood abruptly. 'Thank you for sending Mr Parsons up here. He's to come three times a week until the garden is in proper shape. I'll come down to see you soon. Meanwhile, don't worry about me.'

They came back in the evening of the fifth day of their absence. She watched them from behind the curtain of her bedroom window. Their every movement was economical, controlled. First the release and feeding of the dogs. Then the lighting of the fire and the preparation of a meal. Once again they ate beside the leaping flames. It was not until Jango brought the green glass bottle and the teapot, and the cigarettes were lit, that she approached the paddock gate and waited to be noticed. If Lias realised her presence there, he have no sign. It was Jango who smiled and beckoned her in, who offered the choice of elderflower wine or herbal tea. He also volunteered the wooden stool, but she chose to sit cross-legged on the grass.

The pouring of the wine, her tasting and approval of it helped to overcome the awkwardness between them. For although they were camping on her land, and with her permission, it was made clear in a way she could never have explained that she was their invited guest and that this was a favour extended by them to very few.

The silence lengthened to a point where it seemed that none of them would ever speak. She sipped the wine which tasted innocuous and faintly sweet. Jango offered her a cigarette which she declined. She saw that he was a nervous smoker, dragging smoke down hard and fast into his lungs, and exhaling through his nostrils. He also drank the elderflower wine, glass after glass as if consumed by thirst.

She searched for an acceptable subject of conversation but whatever came into her mind seemed either over-inquisitive or insulting. She was also becoming aware of the insidious power of the wine. In the end it was Lias who said, 'You wanted to see us. To talk.'

'Yes,' she said. She lifted her gaze to meet his and the contact between them was like a flash fire. She glanced swiftly, almost furtively at Jango but his head was bent to the small black puppy which lay across his knees. 'My mother,' she began, 'my mother told me nothing of this Romany – this Gypsy connection. Even now, having seen the letter she wrote you, I still find it difficult to understand.'

Lias said, 'Well, you would, wouldn't you? Hardly your scene, is it?' He looked meaningfully towards the house. 'Like something from a storybook, eh? The lady of the manor accosted by the itinerant Gypos, the dirty didicoys.' He rose and threw a handful of dry wood on the fire. Sparks and flames leaped upwards into the blue dusk. In the orange glow his features had a cruel aspect, and yet she suspected that he spoke without total conviction, that he was taunting her for his own amusement.

'Oh my!' she said. 'How you do love to wallow in self-pity.' She nodded towards the Winnebago camper. 'Seventy-five thousand pounds worth of vehicle there, and then there's your land and the farmhouse in Derbyshire.

If this is the lifestyle of an itinerant Gypsy, then it seems I was born to the wrong side of the family.'

Lias said, 'You're well-informed. Courtesy, I would guess, of Detective Thurgood.'

'It was my mother who employed the detective, I'll remind you. And let's get one thing straight. I am in no way remotely like my mother. I've worked for my living since I was eighteen. Worked damned hard at what I do.'

'And what do you do?'

'I design and manufacture jewellery with a partner in London.'

Lias first looked blankly at her, then amused. 'So you string beads together,' he said softly. 'Well, well, Cousin Maya, that surely makes you one of us.'

'I shall accept that as a compliment, Cousin Lias.'

It was not the answer he expected. His heavy eyebrows came together. He turned towards Jango. He said, a sharp edge to his voice, 'You're very quiet, *pralo*. Why don't you take a turn at conversation with the lady? Ask her why she wanted us to come here.'

Jango smiled, and she looked at him properly for the first time. A strong face, heavy-featured and handsome, but with a sweet curve to the mouth that hinted at humour and gentleness. She realised then that the brothers were totally dissimilar. Their way of life was all they had in common. She turned to Jango as if he was a salve that would soothe a deep burn. Lias rose and walked away towards the camper. He did not say goodnight.

In the days that followed she saw them at irregular intervals. There was no pattern to their comings and going. The uncertainty of it all disturbed her. No matter what task she set her hand to, Lias swirled like an undercurrent just beneath the surface of her consciousness. In the hours that he was absent from the paddock, time had no meaning. When he returned it was as if the freeze-frame button had been pressed to reactivate the video that was her life.

Jango found reasons to come knocking at the kitchen door. The black puppy sometimes escaped, squeezing his rounded body underneath the lowest bar of the paddock gate. She would find him in the hall, or curled asleep in the wicker chair that had once been her father's. She always kept the puppy with her at such times, knowing that Jango would soon follow. To have contact with Jango was to maintain a direct line to Lias. Jango came at first to the outer door, and then into the kitchen. He would lift the pup from the chair and then sit down, the dog laid across his knee. He had a taste for the hot strong coffee which she provided. He was an easy man to be with at such times, good-natured, smiling; one who moved slowly through the world. She liked his deep voice, the lazy way he had of speaking. She asked him many questions.

She said, one morning, 'Your brother is quite welcome to come over for coffee.'

Jango laughed. 'You won't catch Lias underneath a roof, especially in spring and summer.'

'So how does he cope in winter, in your farmhouse?'

'Badly, I suppose. I don't pay much attention to it. If I do, it only encourages him to moan the more. He says that living in a house gives him the feeling that he is already buried but not quite dead.'

'And so, are you affected by this claustrophobia?'

'I'm not. Not really. I couldn't live in towns, mind you. And I'd surely die in a city. But truth to tell, I like my house in the Dark Peaks. I like doing things to it – you know, mending and renovating. I'm learning to repair our drystone walls. There's this old boy in the village who's showing me how it's done. It's a dying skill, you know, drystone walling.'

She refilled his coffee cup, content to keep him with her. Much of their talk was inconsequential, but occasionally she learned something significant.

On the day before the brothers' departure for the fairs and markets of the coastal towns, Jango said, 'We might run across Lias's wife, Sinaminta, and his daughter Rowsheen. We often see Sinaminta, she tells fortunes and sells charms. But the last time we saw Rowsheen she was three years old. We never speak to them, of course.'

They pulled out early in the morning; she heard them go but did not watch. It was late in the day when she found courage to visit the paddock. The metal sheet and the perforated bucket still stood like a promise among the green grass.

Maya Heron. October 8th 1889.

I am so mixed in my feelings I scarce know how to write it. Today I came back to Sheepdip Lane with Dadus and Esmeralda. We were all heavy laden with the gifts from Milady. As we walk I see that I am now taller than my aunt and near as tall as Dadus who I once thought to be a giant. They both eye me as if I am a stranger to them in my fine gown and good boots.

Dadus says, do you remember the last time we walked this road together? You held my hand that day. You skipped and sang alongside me. You were my princess then, Maya, though your frock was patched and faded. Yes, say I. I do remember and all that seems like another life now.

I see that Esmeralda is troubled in her mind. It was not our fault, says she, that you were left so long with the gentry. To first you were very sick. Later on we had our own troubles and could not get to you.

Yes, I say. It was not your fault. But in my heart I am thinking that the truth was they had forgotten about me. If they had truly wanted me back they would have found a way to get me.

As we come into Sheepdip Lane I feel a pull at my heartstrings. The wagons stand in a long row side-on to the hawthorne hedge. It is just as I have seen it in my dreams. There are fires burning. The blue smoke rises straight and true, a sign what foretells hard frost. Some *chavvies* are fighting just beyond the wagons. I see them rolling together in the mud. They swear at each other using the curse words learned from their fathers. It is all the same as it ever was and yet I do not seem to truly recognise it.

We come to Esmeralda's wagon. I see the green and yellow paintwork, the brass cages hanging all around the door and the little brown songbirds hopping on their perches.

I see that the Lovells are of the company. I recognise their plain green *vardos* and the young women who stand beside them. They were all children when I last saw them. Now they are watching me pass by, their babies slung across their hips in pinned-up blankets.

The Lovells have no word of welcome for me. Likewise do not many other people, some who I do not remember and some I do. We walk in silence to my father's wagon. My heart is so full it is like to burst. I see the shining red and green of fresh paint. The great carved golden crown set above the door. The carvings on either side are of horses' heads, swags of leaves and leaping long-dogs all picked out in gold paint. Dadus shares his wagon now with Chesi and Black Ingram. They are brothers linked to us by blood but very distant.

We are to stay in the village until the potatoes and sugar beets are lifted. There is much work for us all, says Esmeralda, and in a few weeks comes the Pack Monday Fair in Sherborne which should help to fill our pockets and bellies for a part of the winter. She looks sideways at my gown and boots when she says this and I am as mortified as she meant I should be.

I am to share the wagon of Esmeralda and her two daughters.

Maya Heron. October 9th 1889.

My cousins are nervous when I take the paper and pen and ink from the box. They will not bide inside the wagon while I am at my writing. The *chavvies* peep in at the door and run away. The men and young women sidle by, looking and yet not looking. The old ones have called a Council of the Elders to talk it all over. The reading and writing has upset them more than my good clothes.

Yesterday I called my girl cousins to the *vardo* and shared my gowns between them. For myself I kept only the green, and the lavender silk, and the cream merino wool. Also the green velvet cape and high boots. Already their silk gowns have a crust of dried mud around the hemlines. I see at breakfast time my cousins wiping the bacon fat from their fingers on to the good silk. But still it is the first time in their lives that they are silk clad and they step out like queens in the village when they go hawking their bits of lace and clothes pegs.

Since my gift of the gowns they smile at me. But still they treat me as a stranger. As a Gorgio.

Maya Heron. October 10th 1889.

A strange thing has happened. In the night when I could not sleep I remembered my kitten. I am not used to sleeping in a bed with two other people. My cousins talk in their sleep and pull the bedclothes from me. As I lay awake the thought of my little cat Minta came back to my head and this was for the very first time since I had been kicked by Milord's horse.

I got up very early. I fetched wood and water. I lit the fire and set the kettle to boil. As I worked I called to Minta, but quietly so as not to rouse the *tan*. No cat came to me. As we walked to the potato field I asked my aunt about the cat. She said I should go to Dadus about it. Such matters were not for her to tell. I worked in the potato field until midday and then I fell over in a dead faint.

Maya Heron. October 11th 1889.

Dadus says I am not to do field work any more. It is plain, says he, that I am not yet properly healed from the kicks of the black stallion. There is much muttering and dark looks around the fire at supper time. But my father is their King and what he says is law. My cousin Starina whispers to me when we are abed that she too could wish for a kick from a black horse if it meant no more sugar beet or potato picking.

I ask Dadus straight out what has happened to my kitten Minta. To first he looks away and will not talk about it. I remind him how I loved the kitten. How I fed it with scraps of my food and slept with it on my pillow. I am sad and lonely here, I tell him. I have been away too long. They do not like me any more. It is as if I am a Gorgio come to live among them.

I will tell you about the cat, says he. But it is a very queer story. You will maybe take a shock when you hear about it. You remember how you were damaged by Milord's horse in mid-morning? It was night when Esmeralda and I came back to the *tan*. We were both in a fine old state, I can tell you, girl. We thought for sure you were a goner. We had just told the company the dreadful news when Wisdom Lovell cried out, oh my dear God. Look at that kitten. Ah Taiso, it's the one that is always with your Maya. Whatever can have happened to it? I picked up the kitten and it was in a sorry state. Its head and back were trampled and broken and a mass of bleeding. Esmeralda whispers to me, ah dordi dordi. The cat has the exact same damage to its body as our Maya.

Well, she takes the kitten to her wagon and tends it and feeds it. The kitten does not mend for a long time. But here is the funny thing. As you got better, Maya, so did your cat. When you walked for the first time, so did Minta. In the end I went to old Grandmother Ingram and asked her what she thought. She said to me, Taiso, 'tis a wonderful thing and a terrible thing what have happened in your family. I have seen such a thing before in my long life but not often. Your Maya is a true *chovihani*. Well, she always had the looks of one with that white hair and the amber-yellow eyes. But this damage to the kitten proves it. Your grandmother looks me straight in the eye. She says that cat is Maya's *familiar*. What happens to Maya happens also to Minta.

But nobody saw the kitten getting hurt, I tell her.

Of course not, says Grandmother Ingram. That's the way it always is with *chovihanis*.

These words of my father strike deep into my soul. I feel cold from my head to my feet. Where is Minta now? I ask.

In my wagon, says Dadus. I thought it better that you should not see her too soon.

Take me, I say. Show her to me.

My cat knows me straightaway. She comes at once into my arms and her whole body shakes with pleasure. She has grown large in spite of the smashed head and back but when she walks I see that she drags herself along and it is painful for her. I take her to Esmeralda's wagon. I touch the cat's hurt head and spine and as I stroke her my hands grow very hot and I feel a goodness go out from my body and into hers.

She sleeps for a long time and I hold her as I would a sick child. When she wakes she jumps down from the wagon as easily as she did when a kitten. When she walks she no longer drags her body. I do not understand this. I only know that it has happened.

Word gets round the *tan* that I have magic in my fingers. That I have mended the cat that could scarce walk. We are a people full of secrets. Nothing is ever spoken straight or outright. I remember Milord's ways. How he demanded the truth no matter what the cost. I go to my

Grandmother Ingram. There is much talk about me, I tell her. They are saying that I have strange powers. But I do not believe it.

She is silent for a long time. Then she says, it makes no odds what you believe or don't believe. You were ever a headstrong child and living with the Gorgio gentry has turned your mind against your own blood kin. You are much changed, Maya.

No, I cry out. I am still a *tatchi* Romany. I always will be.

She shakes her head. There is a terrible power in her face and I am afeared. She says, we have heard tell about the young red-haired *rai* who lives up at the big house. The Gorgio men who drink in the *kitchima* say that he is sweet on the yellow-haired yellow-eyed Gypsy known as Maya. That he has already had his way with her. There have been fisticuffs over the matter between the village men and our men.

Lies, I cry. Whatever would the likes of Guy want with a Gypsy maid? He is a Lord's son. He can have his pick of all the women of England.

Grandmother Ingram takes my hands in both of hers. She looks deep into my eyes. She says, well, it pleases me to hear you say that. But there is something you must know, she tells me. You have said that you are a *tatchi* Romany and this is the truth. You are also a *chovihani*. It is not something you can choose or not choose to be. It has come down to you through the blood of your mother's family. There have been many *chovihanis* in the Ingram line.

I say, but what does it mean?

She smiles at me then. I cannot tell you, says she. That is for you to find out. But I think that in your heart you know already.

Maya Heron. October 12th 1889.

Esmeralda goes with her daughters to the Pack Monday Fair. They do not ask me to go with them. It is took for granted that I will stay here in the *tan* and tend the fire and mind the youngest *chavvies*. Although nobody says a word, I know why I am left behind. Guy is a student in the great school in Sherborne. Students will be roving through the fair, and it is forbidden that he and I should ever meet.

It is easier to write when the *tan* is empty. Even Dadus who is proud of all I do does not altogether trust the reading and writing.

I think about the school in Sherborne where Guy lives. I know the place. I have seen it many times when we passed through that town on the way to Yeovil. I can see in my head the great stone walls, the heavy doors and many windows. Guy will be lonely there and thinking to be home. He will be wanting me, as I long for him.

As I dream of Guy, the picture changes in my head. The school becomes a gaol, and Guy locked up inside it. I see a gibbet and a noose. I do not want to see these things. I write them down so that they are on the paper and no longer behind my eyes.

It is quiet here in Sheepdip Lane. The *chavvies* are sleeping and Grandmother nods and dreams where she leans on the steps of her wagon. I sit underneath a beech tree. The copper-coloured leaves fall on my head and all around me. I feel a great change coming over me. It is as if the telling by Grandmother Ingram that I am a *chovihani* has opened up some deep place inside me, so that I see everything more clearly.

The sleepwalking, the pictures in my head, the cloudy visions that I have told myself were no more than childish fancies, all these things I see now were only signs of what was still to come. Grandmother says that while I lived underneath the Gorgio roof my true nature could not show itself.

Maya Heron. October 13th 1889.

There was little sleep last night for any of us. The women came back from the fair well pleased with the day and the filled money bags. But the men as always took their profits to the *kitchima* in the village and did not return until they were drunk and their pockets were empty. This made for trouble in the families. The women screamed and chided their sons and husbands. The men beat their wives and Ashela Lovell hit her man across the head with a kettle iron. He promised to murder her. But today she is tending him lovingly with poultices and soft words and he is grateful to her.

I am able to write these things because I know that none of them will ever read this. It hurts me to say so but I begin to see my people now as the Gorgio must see them. At last I understand why in those first years with Milady my own ways and temper seemed so shocking to the household. I remember how often I threw on to the nursery fire the good leather shoes they bought me. How I went barefoot into the drawing room and shamed them when their friends came to visit. How I wiped my nose and fingers on the clean nice gowns. How I spat out the strange tasting foods that I had never before seen. I also see how it was that Evangeline was so strict and hard on me. Today I watch the *chavvies* in the *tan*. I see how they roam about and fight. How they speak back as if they are their parents' equal. How they are seldom checked or disciplined but indulged as if each one were precious even though there are often fifteen others in the family. All these things I had forgotten or perhaps I never really knew them. After all, I was but a child and unobservant when I fell under Milady's spell. When I learned the Gorgio way of living.

They say that I am a *chovihani* but it is more like I who have been bewitched and by the Gorgio gentry. Whatever shall I do about it? I cannot easily put away what I have spent some four or five years in the learning. All the time I need to be watchful of my people. They are resentful towards me over almost everything I do. I must take care not to use long words when I speak. I must not brush my hair or wash my face and body oftener than do my cousins. Starina taunts me. Says she, your skin is white enough already, Maya. Would you scrub it even paler?

It is true what they say. I am become quite unlike my own people. I think long and hard about this. Since Dadus will not have me doing field work, I sit alone in the *tan* in daytime. I mind the little ones. I tend the fire. I make ready the supper. I write these pages. But it is not enough for me. My head needs to be busy. I have read the books Milady gave me until I know each single word. Sometimes my thoughts are wild and crazy. I think to run away to Sherborne, to find Guy in the great school but I know I must not.

In the night when I cannot sleep I creep from the bed and sit on the steps of the wagon. The moonlight is cold and I hear the vixen calling for her mate up on Hunger Hill. My body burns for Guy as if I am took with the fever. I wrap my arms round myself and rock and moan and then I feel that strangers' eyes are watching me. I look up and see that Chesi Ingram stands beneath the beech tree. He is tall and slender. The black curls hang like grapes across his ears and forehead. I see the flash of white around his dark eyes. He is good-looking and he knows it. He does not come close but his whisper reaches to where I sit. He speaks to me in the old language of our people. He says, you are sick now with love for the red-polled Gorgio, but never fear, Maya, I am the one that you will be promised to in marriage.

This time she knew that several weeks must pass before the brothers would return. The knowledge did not make their absence easier to bear. All at once the house became burdensome, she longed to be free like them, to turn an ignition key and escape. Lyme Regis seemed a likely place for them to be.

Driving through the heat haze of the early morning, she wondered what she would do if she found them, selling their wares in some seaside market. Jango would be friendly, welcoming. Lias would look into her face and know what it was that had brought her halfway across Dorset. Men like Lias always knew the exact effect they had upon women.

By the time she reached Lyme Regis, she thought that she no longer wished to see him.

She stood for a long time on the Cob and looked down into the blue-green water. As always, once away from the house she could dare to think about Maya Heron, about the diary entries, the tone of which was changing, taking on a depth and maturity which made the reading more than ever compulsive.

'I see everything more clearly,' Maya had written. 'The sleepwalking, the pictures in my head, the cloudy visions that I have told myself were no more than childish fancies. All these things I see now were only signs of what was still to come.'

Poor troubled girl; her confusion and pain were as fresh and real on the mildewed scraps of paper as if the words had been put down only yesterday. They might well have been written a century later by a second Maya. The thought took her unawares; she was unprepared for the flood of emotion that it released. She wrapped her arms about her body and shivered in spite of the hot day.

She watched the little boats go in and out of Lyme Bay. The sun was fierce now across her shoulders; she loosened and shook out her long hair as a protection against its rays, and then walked slowly back towards the shingle. The light reflected off the water was so brilliant that it dazzled. She went into a cafe that overlooked the harbour and the sudden dimness caused a temporary blindness. She fumbled her way towards a table, sat down and ordered coffee.

Looking out from the gloom of the cafe made the glittering bay more bearable, less overwhelming. She thought about the darkness in her life, the way it seemed to follow her around. It always had. She got caught up in other people's tragedies, their blackness rubbed off on her. In the years when she had experienced the 'sightings', the sudden deaths by violence of people who were strangers to her, she had carried in silence the burden of those horrors. But since the deaths of her parents, all her visions had been personal, her perceptions turned inwards, and now paradoxically she wanted to talk about it all. She wanted to tell Jango Heron about the diary, about the Gypsy Maya Heron and her love for Guy. About her own fears.

It was as she drove out of Lyme that the pale bulk of the Winnebago caught her attention. It was parked beneath trees in a lane that led down to a farmstead. She slowed and then halted, and was not surprised when Lias Heron walked towards her.

As she waited for him she became acutely aware of the small sounds of the night, of the luminous sky above the ocean; of the hair still loose across her shoulders and the burn of her skin from the hot sunlight of the day.

He came slowly through the blue dusk, and she saw that something had changed in him since their last meeting. Lias moved like a man who was dreaming; she had the feeling that since the day he had driven away from the Monks' House, he had been her shadow, following and watching, knowing her every thought and feeling. She stepped out of the car and stood, one hand resting on the bonnet. When he stood before her, she saw that he was fractionally taller than Jango. She needed to look upwards to read his face.

He said, 'You took your time. What kept you?'

She said, 'You're very sure of yourself, aren't you?'

She was used to gentleness in men. Paco had been hesitant in bed. Even Jonah had approached her with a certain caution. Lias Heron gripped her upper arm and led her to the shadows of the high hedge. She stumbled and felt the cutting edge of grass on her bare legs. Without loosening his hold he knelt and pulled her down to face him. As he leaned in towards her she caught the smoky smell of his hair, a hint of expensive aftershave, the sharp musk of his skin, which alerted her own senses.

He thrust his hands into the hair that lay above her ears, pulling at her head so that it was angled backwards. He began to kiss the base of her throat and the inch of skin directly underneath her chin. When he reached her mouth she clenched her teeth against him. At once his fingers twisted in her hair. He shook her and her teeth parted. She bit his lower lip and felt his warm blood in her mouth. His hands moved from her head, he gripped her shoulders until she cried out with the pain. She wanted him inside her as she had never wanted Paco or Jonah. He touched her breasts and she felt her nipples harden in his fingers. She was tearing at the hooks which held the waistband of her skirt when yellow lights bloomed on the far side of the hedge. A car door slammed, men's voices called goodnight.

Lias whispered, 'Jango! Back from the pub. He always takes a taxi.' The fingers that had held her now pushed her violently away. Lias stood, careful to remain in deep shadow. She could just make out the flat planes of his face, the high cheekbones, and the thick swing of the ponytail across his back.

'Get up from there!' His tone was sharp. 'Into your car and go! There's no call for Jango to know you ever came here.'

She rose, obediently, stupidly, and combed her fingers through her wild hair. Her face burned at his whiplash words. She hooked the skirt round her waist and pushed the blouse inside the waistband. She watched Jango's unsteady progress down the lane and into the Winnebago camper, and still her heartbeat pounded in her throat.

The curse came out of nowhere. The words were in her mouth and on her lips without premeditation. She spoke quietly and coldly in a voice she did not recognise as hers. 'God damn you,' she said. 'God damn you to hell, Lias Heron. Touch me again and you're a dead man.'

She turned to go but the sudden terror in his face delayed her.

His right hand was raised, the fingers arranged in a curious pointing gesture.

'*Chovihani!*' he shouted. 'Get away from me.'

Afterwards, when she thought about that night, she wondered at her lack of feeling. There should have been anger, self-loathing, but there was nothing. She had no memory of returning to the car, or of driving inland through the deep lanes and sleeping villages. She must have studied signposts, for the route she took was unfamiliar to her.

Some awareness returned as she approached the first slopes of Hunger Hill. But all that seemed real was her hands on the steering wheel, the rush of night air from the open windows. All that she wanted was to be inside the Monks' House, with the doors barred against the world.

Overnight the weather changed. She woke to a mist of rain sifting in at the bedroom window. As she rose to close the casement, the Winnebago pulled into the paddock. Only Jango sat in the forward cabin; she stood behind the curtain and saw him jump down on to the grass, followed by the greyhounds and the puppy. He walked round to the side door, opened it and pulled down the expanding steps. Something about him, a greater self-assurance, told her that Lias was not with him. She pulled on jeans and a clean but faded shirt, and tied her hair back with a scrap of chiffon. She switched on the coffee percolator, sliced bread for toast and opened wide the kitchen door.

The puppy came in almost straightaway, his small fat body squirming and wriggling with pleasure when she touched his head and spoke his name. From the kitchen window she could see Jango filling a water container at the stable tap. She opened the casement and called out, 'I'm cooking breakfast if you'd like to join me.'

He nodded and smiled. 'Give me ten minutes,' he shouted, 'and I'll be with you.'

She made him the sort of breakfast that she thought he regularly cooked for himself and Lias. He looked across the table at her single slice of toast.

'I'm not hungry,' she said. 'I stayed out in the sun too long yesterday.'

'I thought you looked pale,' he said. 'Better take it easy for a day or two.' He fed the puppy scraps of bacon from his plate. 'You don't mind, do you?' he asked. 'Lias gets mad when I give him tidbits.'

She smiled. 'Lias isn't here,' she said.

They ate in silence, she refilled his cup with hot strong coffee as soon as it was empty. He laid the knife and fork across his plate. 'That was good,' he said. 'I can't remember the last time a lady cooked breakfast for me.'

'Lady?' she said. 'I'm your cousin. Or at least I think I am.'

'Yes. We ought to talk about that. After all, that's why we came here, it's why you asked us to come down.' He paused and glanced across his shoulder as if he might be overheard. 'It's Lias. He's not keen on talking about family matters. When that private detective brought your mother's letter to us, Lias took it very badly. Really didn't want to know.'

She said, 'So why do you think he's come here now?'

He bent down, picked Star up and laid him across his knee. She saw the red colour that had crept under Jango's tanned skin. 'You never know where you are with Lias. He's changeable, see. Take last night, for instance. We'd had a good day's selling. I'd called in at a pub close to the lane where we were pulled in. When I got back he was in a right old temper. He said he'd had word from a pal that his wife and daughter were *dukkerin* a bit further down the coast. Well, Lias had never thought much of Sinaminta's fortune-telling. I suppose when he heard that Rowsheen was at it too, well, he just lost his rag about it. He said that he was going to see them both. I could hardly believe him. He's never been anywhere near them in fifteen years. Oh, he always knows where they are. Keeps one finger on them, you might say. But not to *see* them.' Jango touched the white star on the puppy's head. 'So I dropped him off in Weymouth early this morning. He said he'd make his own way back here, didn't say when though. I asked him what I should do in the meantime. It needs two of us to run the stall. Take a holiday, he said. You've never had one of those in all your life.'

Although Jango's tone was deliberately offhand, she could see that he was troubled. 'Perhaps,' she said, 'perhaps he just wants to have some time alone. Perhaps he needs to sort his thoughts out. He might be thinking of going back to live with his wife and daughter.'

'Never! When those two were together they damn near murdered one another. He said that Sinaminta turned the child against him. He'd not go back to her. As for needing time alone, no traveller could ever stand the strain of that. We need to keep together. No, there's something else that's eating up Lias.' He set the puppy down and watched him walk away towards the door. He said, carefully not looking at her, 'Lias had a visitor last night. I was pretty drunk when I got back to the van, but I'm sure I remember a little black car standing at the roadside.'

'Somebody visiting the farm?' she suggested.

'Could be, I reckon. But drunk as I was. I could tell that there was something else had really got to Lias. You don't live all your life with a person and not get to know them through and through.'

'I wouldn't know,' she said. 'I was never lucky enough to live for very long with anybody.'

He said, as if considering her life for the first time, 'Yes. You've got a sad sort of look about you. You never smile much.' He paused. 'I was going to say you're a typical Gorgio, but you're not that either, are you?'

'No,' she said quietly. 'I don't believe I am. Perhaps we could talk about that. As you said, it's the reason you came down here.' She smiled at him, deliberately provocative, across the table. 'Come over tomorrow evening and I'll cook you dinner.'

He looked doubtful, uneasy. 'I don't know as I should. Not without Lias. He'll want to be in on all this, it being family business.'

When she spoke, her tone was even gentler. 'Sod bloody Lias! I'm sick of hearing you say his name. You make me feel that he's sitting here with us, even when he isn't. It's you I'm inviting, Jango. It's you I want to talk to.'

Jango

The meal was set out on a round white table which stood underneath a beech tree in a cool corner of the garden. The table was covered with a blue cloth; it held a wooden bowl filled with salad, a platter of ham and cold chicken, and potatoes baked in their jackets and drenched in melting butter. Maya had, she told him, made the summer pudding with fruits discovered in the freezer; berries picked from the nearby bushes and frozen last year by her mother. The mother who, he thought, had later tried to run down Lias and himself but had died instead, together with her husband.

There was a pitcher of double cream to go with the pudding; a rare request to the milkman, Maya told him, which together with the reappearance of the Winnebago camper would be bound to cause gossip in the village.

Jango, by arrangement, had brought two bottles of his own potent elderflower wine.

They ate in silence, but it was not the awkward hush of that first evening when it had seemed that none of them might ever speak. Maya and he were at ease with one another. It made for an atmosphere in which either of them could ask questions. They fed the puppy bits of ham and chicken. After two glasses of wine Jango said, 'So what do you want to know?'

He had expected her to ask about the Heron family, the Ingrams. The names that had been spelled out in her mother's letter of inquiry.

She said, echoing his recent thought, 'What exactly happened when my mother tried to kill you and Lias?'

He took a long draught of the wine. He breathed in deeply and was slow about the exhalation. 'What makes you think she tried to kill us?'

Her yellow eyes grew cloudy, he began to see pictures in their depths and forced his gaze away.

'I saw it happen, Jango. Every awful detail. I could tell you the colour of the shirt you were wearing.'

He half rose in his chair. 'No,' he shouted, 'that's not possible; you were in America. I heard you say so at the inquest.' He sat down and poured more wine, unable to control the trembling in his fingers.

'Ah yes,' she said, 'that inquest. Lucky, wasn't it, that you and Lias were not called?'

'Lucky? Not really. That old farmer told them all they wanted to know. He was a local, see. They trusted him, believed him. They could see that we were travellers. They always know.'

'What happened?' she repeated. 'What happened when she tried to kill you?'

He felt cold although the night was warm. Beneath the cover of the table his fingers formed the horned sign against evil that was his only protection against her. He said, 'You really saw what happened? From Chicago, America, you saw it?'

'I saw it.'

'Yes,' he said. 'Your grandmother and great-grandmother had the same gift of "seeing". God help them!' The gaze he turned upon her now was full of pity. 'That's an uncomfortable place you stand in.'

'Yes,' she said. 'It's caused me a few problems over the years.'

'Did your mother never explain it to you?'

'My mother never spoke to me at all if she could help it.'

'You know what you are, don't you?' There was fear in his face.

'No,' she said. 'What am I?'

'You're a *chovihani* – a witch. Oh, it's not your fault. It's like getting red hair or brown eyes. Nothing you can do about it.'

'A *chovihani*,' she said softly. 'Yes, I've seen that word written down. Just recently I heard it spoken.'

'Where did you hear it?'

'I think it was on a television programme, a documentary on Gypsies.'

He admired the swiftness of her responses, her capacity for lying. It would be Lias who had called her *chovihani*; and the small black foreign car seen yesterday evening would be the one beside which he had parked last autumn in the forecourt of the Quiet Woman pub in Halstock. The only advantage he could count on in his dealing with her was his ability to sense when she spoke the truth.

They sat on through the twilight. The puppy slept in the grass beside his feet. Across the table the skin of Maya's face gleamed like a pearl. The white-gold hair was loose across her shoulders, she wore a dress of green and clinging silk, and golden sandals.

She leaned over and touched his hand. 'Tell me about them,' she said. 'Those old Gypsies who were my mother's people.'

'You should be talking to Lias. He knows much more than I do. See, he's ten years older —'

'It's you I'm asking.'

'Oh well. There was a lot of intermarrying. Herons and Ingrams. and here and there a Hawkins or a Penfold. But never very close relations, mind you. There's a powerful taboo against incest among travelling people. Well, there needs to be if you think about it. Especially in the old days when families of sixteen or more lived in a single wagon and a couple of benders.'

'Benders?'

'Six or eight hazel wands,' he said, 'bent double, with each end driven into the ground. Chuck a few blankets over the top, and a good tarpaulin, and you've got as cosy a home as any man could wish for.'

'Did you ever live in a bender?'

'Born in one, so I'm told.' He grinned. 'When I get a bit above myself, like the time I bought the Armani jacket, Lias reminds me – you were born on the straw, boy, in a dinky little bender, it's a *tatchi* Romany you are, and don't you forget it.'

'What about your mother'

'Gorgio. I never knew her. Died soon after I was born. Something funny there, I've always thought. Lias won't talk about her. All I've got is a name. Madeline. I asked my father about her just before he died. But nothing he said could help me to trace her beginnings or her family.'

'So who brought you up?'

He laughed and refilled his wine glass. 'Gypsy kids don't get 'brought up' in your sense of the language. There's hardly any discipline in the *tan*. They watch their elders and then do the same as they do. You learn just as soon as you can walk that life's a bitch, and your fists and boots are going to be your only weapons. You learn to lie and cheat the Gorgio because he's always got a down on you, and he'll lock you up given half a chance. You take whatever comes easy to your hand, but you won't find many travellers living on state benefits, 'ceptin' them as lives in the permanent camps, poor devils. We're a dying breed. There used to be dignity for our old ones, and a decent spell of hop-picking and harvesting in the season for the young men. But that was a long time ago, when the knife-grinder was welcome everywhere he went, likewise the tin smith who patched up poor folks' pans and kettles. Nowadays it's laying tarmac on people's driveways and digging over their gardens; selling a bit of scrap here and there, putting a bet on a fast dog.'

'But not for you and Lias.'

'We had Despair. Oh, all right, he was a bastard. But he was a clever bastard. Money stuck to his fingers. Give him education and there's no knowing what he could have been. Lias is the same. He's got the knack. Can't hardly read nor write properly but he rarely backs a loser, be it horse or dog. Oh, he's got a long head on him, has our Lias.'

'And you?'

'I'm what you could call semi-educated. Went to school – went to twenty or more different schools. I never admitted this to anyone before, but I really liked the learning. Especially the reading.'

'You read a lot?'

'I pick up books around the markets. Old stuff, second-hand.'

He relaxed again into his chair. He had led her away from the question he most feared to answer, the question of her mother. They spoke about books and he could see her surprise at his unexpected knowledge; and while they talked a part of his mind broke free and roved back over all the girls that he had once known. The hundred times and more that he had thought himself in love. He remembered the tales he had heard about the ways and the powers of the *chovihani*. He looked at the face and body of Maya, and it seemed to him that she hovered and began to float towards him in the blue dusk. He felt a sharp sweat break out along his hairline. He wanted her more keenly than he had ever wanted any woman. But still he feared her. When her fingers touched his face he said, 'The other night. In Lyme Regis. It was your car, wasn't it? It was you with Lias.' He smiled. 'How else would you have known that we were pitched beside a farm?'

'Yes,' she murmured, 'but nothing happened. I just chanced to be passing and recognised your camper. It was just a friendly visit.'

He wanted to believe her, but he knew she lied.

When she pulled him gently in towards the house, he went with her.

Maya

She was not sure what she had intended when she took his arm and led him to the house. Perhaps she had meant to seduce Lias's baby brother. Vengeance had been in her mind. He came without protest, but she sensed an unwillingness in him that was close to panic. He said, as they came into the kitchen, 'What about the dirty dishes? I'll bring them in and wash them for you.'

'No,' she said, 'you're my guest. I'll deal with the dishes in the morning.' They faced one another across the kitchen table. He had drunk the greater part of the elderflower wine but it had not relaxed him. She remembered that night in the Quiet Woman pub. She said, 'I've got Bacardi if you'd like some.'   She walked across the dark hall and opened the door of the room she called the drawing room. He followed close behind her. She flicked a switch and lights came on. His eyes contracted at the brilliance of the crystal chandelier. She indicated that he should sit in the blue velvet chair that was her usual place in this room. The Bacardi she gave him was straight. without lemon or Coke. He sat down, still dazed by the bright light. The Bacardi glass was halfway to his lips when he gazed upwards and saw the portrait of Maya Heron. His fingers tightened to whiteness round the stem of the glass. He turned his head to where she sat on the sofa, and Maya thought that he had the look of a man who was temporarily blinded.

'You?' he said.

'No. Not me. That portrait was painted more than a hundred years ago.'

'She's your living likeness.' He took a long swig of the drink, his gaze still fixed on the image of Maya Heron. 'But you know who she is.'

'Not really. How could I? I didn't even know that my parents owned this house until after they were dead. As for the previous owners, well, I'm still finding out about them.'

The Bacardi had relaxed him a little. He said, 'There's so much that

135

we don't know. Lias says it's best to leave the past alone, best to keep old troubles buried deep.'

She said, 'Buried troubles have a habit of getting resurrected.'

Her gaze went to the inlaid workbox which held Maya Heron's diaries, and on which now stood the Bacardi bottle and Jango's empty glass. She looked up into the painted eyes of the Gypsy girl, and allowed herself, for the first time, to remember last night's rejection by Lias Heron. 'You took your time,' he had said. 'What kept you?' She recalled the way his fingers had twisted in her hair. When she had showered that morning, the bruises he had left were blue-black on her breasts and shoulders. He had called up an equal violence in her. She had wanted to lacerate him, do him physical damage; draw blood. Even now, in this quiet room, the memory of the flat planes of his face, the sweet high cheekbones, the thick swing of the ponytail across his shoulders roused in her a deep thrust of desire which sent her towards Jango.

'Get up from there,' Lias had said. 'There's no need for Jango to know you ever came here.'

She knelt beside the blue velvet chair. She sensed Jango's fear of her and sought to reassure him. The fingers of his right hand were locked into the strange fist that she had noticed on previous occasions. When she tried to prise loose the rigid thumb and fingers, he cried out. 'For God's sake, don't do that!'

'Why not?'

'You'll bring down bad luck on the both us.'

'Superstition!' she said. 'My father described it as being the religion of the weak-minded.'

He stood. He looked first at the portrait and then at her. 'But you believe in it,' he said. ''Spite of your college education, and your London business and your fine house, you believe in it because you have to. It's in your blood and bones. It's just taking you a long time to admit it.'

She heard the kitchen door close carefully behind him. His steps ground through the gravel of the yard and then went silent when he reached the paddock grass.

There was more to Jango than she had thought. He was not, after all, his brother's shadow.

It was that time of the year when the skies are never quite dark. She took a tray into the garden and collected the supper dishes. After they were washed and dried and put away in cupboards, she went up to her room and stood for a long time at the window. Down in the paddock Jango followed his nightly ritual before sleeping. It was not until he had wrapped the blanket round him and lay down beside the glowing embers of his fire that she acknowledged she would not sleep that night.

Weeks had passed since she last read the diaries of Maya Heron. The Bacardi bottle and Jango's glass still stood on the inlaid workbox. He would probably say that it was bad luck for them both to drink from the same glass. But on this particular night she hardly cared.

Maya Heron. November 21st 1889.

We should have left this place long since and moved nearer in to Taunton but a sickness struck which meant that we were held fast for these many weeks. Two newborn and their mothers died of the fever and we buried them out along the road to Sherborne what will make for easy visiting of them when we come back this way next year. The mothers and babes when they died were still living in the benders what were set aside for the birthing and the following weeks when the mothers were still *mokardi* from childbirth. So no need for us to fire the wagons, what is a blessing. Only the mothers' clothes have needed to be burnt and their dishes smashed and buried.

The sickness did not touch me or Starina. We helped to tend the others. Starina and I fetched wood and water for the whole *tan*. Render Penfold who is but ten years old but clever with the snares and traps kept us in meat for the pot, and his little brother Churi brought us potatoes and vegetables and we did not ask once where he had found them.

It fell to me to wash and wrap the two newborn ready for burial. It is the saddest task that my hands have ever known.

Maya Heron. December 20th 1889.

We are still held fast here. It is like the life has gone out of us and nobody sings or whistles.

Maya Heron. December 25th 1889.

Christmas Day. Last night Milady came down to the *tan*. Tom brought her in the carriage what was full of blankets and shoes and clothes, and meat and puddings from Cook's kitchen.

I hid myself inside the wagon and would not come out although Milady called my name. How could I let her see me in my sorry state? After she had gone I found a box standing on the steps. She had brought me clothes and books and a whole batch of paper to write on, with ink and quills.

When I saw these gifts I wept.

Early this morning I scoured out the woodlands. I found snowdrops and some flowering cherry. I made a little mossy basket and took it to the big house. I left it on the doorstep. Milady will know that the gift was mine.

I think about Guy but there is only sadness in the thoughts. Grandmother Ingram says that in April I will have my fifteenth birthday. Dadus says that it is high time I was wed. Starina says that Chesi Ingram has been chosen for me, that he is already sweet on me and can hardly wait till April.

I tell Starina all about Guy who is and always will be my true love. I say if I cannot have him, what matters it who I am to wed.

Maya Heron. January 1st 1890.

So today we begin a new year. I have the date right because Parson told us so in his sermon. Since we are caught fast in this village and pitched on Milord's land we are obliged to go to Milord's church. We sit in the backmost pews. I am hopeful for a sight of Guy. I put on the green velvet cloak what I have managed so far to keep decent. The boots are shabby looking but not to be seen when I am sitting in the pew.

Milord and Milady come into church followed by Lavinia and Guy. I keep my head low as they pass by as if I am praying. But I watch them between my fingers. Lavinia is grown taller and skinnier than ever. But Guy has come to his full manhood. He steps out strong and head high. His red curls are the colour of a ripe horse-chestnut. I remember private things about Guy what would shock Parson Hodges.

Chesi Ingram sits beside me. He watches me watching Guy, but there is nothing he can do about it. Looking is not touching. Late in the afternoon I see the brougham pass by the end of the lane. It carries Guy and his boxes back to Sherborne School.

Maya Heron. January 16th 1890.

They say that I have the 'touch' and mayhap it is true. It is for certain I have not lacked practice of my skill this winter. The old ones say I ease the pain in their stiff joints. The young ones bring me their babes and *chavvies* to have their fevers cooled. The maidens ask me for love potions. If I could oblige you, I tell them, I would make such a thing for myself for I surely need it more than any of you.

I know now that I have the gift of 'seeing'. It is an awesome thing. There are times when I could wish to be without it. They say that it has come down to me through Grandmother Ingram and my mother and that I shall pass it on to my own daughters and their children. Perhaps it would be better if I died childless and so end the matter. But such is not to be my fate. I have looked into my years that are still to come. I see that I shall be wed soon with Chesi Ingram. But the single child I shall bear will not be his.

Maya Heron. February 20th 1890.

It rains every day. The wagon wheels sink in mud up to their axles. The sickness has left us, but it has cost us dear. There is nothing left that we can barter. All of my fine clothes have been *chopped* in the village for medicine and food. Except for the cream merino wool dress and the green silk what I hid because I could not bear to part with them.

Grandmother Ingram calls a meeting of the Council. The Elders sit around the fire and decide what will happen in the months to come. My name, so I am told later by Esmeralda, was on everybody's lips. To first, it is decided for certain that I am to wed in midsummer with Chesi Ingram. Meantime, I am to go *dukkerin* around the villages and at the upcoming hiring fairs. This is the quickest and surest way of making money, I am told, and since the last of the coins have been spent on doctors' medicine for Lovells' youngest, how can I refuse?

Maya Heron. February 28th 1890.

Grandmother Ingram instructs me in the *dukkerin*. It is not enough, says she, to have the 'sight'. The Gorgios will expect a good show for their silver coin. There must be different stories told for different women. For the young ones I must spin a tale of romance and of handsome suitors or broken hearts and happy endings. Women in their middle years are more concerned with money and the good marriages of their children.

All that the Gorgio women truly want to hear is that their husbands are faithful to them. They need to be told that they themselves are handsome or misunderstood or about to witness some miracle or other. They live lives of misery, says Grandmother Ingram, shut up like cattle in their smelly houses. The Gypsy who comes to tell them their future – their *exciting* future – will not be turned away.

I say to Grandmother Ingram, but anyone can do that. Any *rakli* who is so minded can spin a tale of romance.

True enough, says she. But because you have the 'sight' you will find that in amongst all the flummery will be a seam of truth. As you tell the women what they long to hear, something else will trip across your tongue. You will hear yourself speaking strange words about matters and people that you cannot know. And yet you *know* these things and it will all be a wonder and a fearful business to you. As time passes, your powers will grow stronger. The bloodline in you is the purest I have ever seen. When you were a *chavvie* Maya, when that white-silk hair grew down to your shoulders and then curled outwards, I knew it for a sign. When your eyes changed from the first blue of all babies to that yellow amber colour, I had started already to wonder about you.

She put the clay pipe to her lips and the tobacco glowed red through the blue smoke that rose around her head.

She says, you know that you are to wed at midsummer with Chesi Ingram?

Yes, say I.

There is no need for me to tell you how you must behave, says she. You will not be alone with him at any time from now until the wedding. He will not touch you nor you he.

I say, I would not wish to be alone with him. I could not stand to touch him, or to have him touch me.

He is a good man, says Grandmother.

Has he no fear of marriage to a *chovihani*? I ask her.

She laughs. He sees it as a sign that your money bag will never be empty. He has a strong fancy too for your pale looks what are not to the taste of every Romanichal.

Oh, say I, well perhaps I should be grateful to him. But he had better be careful of me. I have no good feelings for him and I think he knows this.

Grandmother raises her first finger at me and I am as a child again. You will marry Chesi and you will be his true wife. You are in great danger, Maya, from the red-headed Lord's son. Your only safety is with your own people.

I bow my head before her but I am full of bitterness and pain. I did not ask to be left so long in Milord's house. I did not ask that my mind should be split down the middle so that I no longer know who or what I am. Whatever I do in the future it will not be my fault.

If I could only see Guy. But I am watched now night and day by Chesi and his brother. They do not trust me and I do not trust myself.

I look at my Grandmother and I see my own fine hair, but on her it is a blue-white colour now in its thick braids. We have the same yellow-amber eyes and the same cast of features. She is a tall woman and though she is old her back is still straight and her head held high. I feel a great love for her.

I say, I know you are only thinking of my own good and I will marry Chesi and try to be a good wife to him. But even as I speak my thumb and little finger fold across my hand to make the sign that wards off Evil.

Maya Heron. 25th March 1890.

In with the paper and the ink left me by Milady was a calendar so that I might tell the days. I show it to Starina who laughs and says, what need have we for such things? We know the days by the skies, the weather, the flowers and the little birds coming and going.

I point to the numbers on the paper. See, I say, how this tells you exactly how much time has passed.

Exactly? she asks. What is this word, exactly? When was any Romanichal ever exactly about anything? You have grown very strange, Maya. While you spend time at the reading and writing and the counting of the days, you miss the lark's song and the first violets in the woods, and the sweet winds on your face.

I think about her words. What she says is true. So I walk in the woods, but alone, for I no longer care for the company of others. I find the first violets, I hear birdsong. I feel the sweet winds on my face. But it is my head that tells me it is nearly springtime, because next week will be April. These things I have learned in the house of the Gorgios, and because of Guy I cannot put that learning from me. Grandmother says I am in great danger from him. This is true, I know it for myself.

Maya Heron. April 15th 1890.

The courtship has started. We sit facing one another each evening in Grandmother's *vardo*. He looks at me. I look out of the window. We hardly speak. What shall I say to him or he to me? Grandmother sits on the steps in the open doorway, so there is no way out of there for us until she so chooses. After a whole week of silence, Chesi starts to talk, but softly, and because of her deafness Grandmother does not hear his words.

I had not known he was so quiet spoken. Most Romanichals have big loud voices and plenty of swagger. He says, Starina tells me that you do not want this wedding.

I look quick to where Grandmother hooks a fine lace collar, but she has not heard him. I say, Starina is sweet on you, Chesi. She wants you for herself. This is a lie, but he is not to know this.

That is no answer, Maya.

Then hear this, I tell him, but speaking sweet and smiling. You must know what they say about me. That I am a *chovihani*, that I have the 'sight'. That I have it in my power to cure or kill. I lean forward so that my face is close to his. Do you not fear me, Chesi? Do you never look at me and think that Maya the witch could be your death?

I had meant only to warn him, to frighten him, to change his warm feelings towards me. But it was *I* who felt the fear. Even as I spoke I saw the blood run red upon him. I saw the deep wounds in his throat, his face as white as marble gravestones. I began to shake with an ague I could not stop.

Chesi called to Grandmother, Maya is sick. It is the fever that has got her. They take me back to Esmeralda's wagon and I am put to bed with many blankets and one of Esmeralda's potions. In the morning I am back to my own self again. But it is not the fever I am sick of.

Maya Heron. April 20th 1890.

Guy is home because of Easter. And now I feel the winds soft on my face and now I hear the lark sing.

There are times in the day when I can slip away. I have found out just lately that to be a *chovihani* is not altogether a bad thing. The others take one or two steps back from me when I speak. Just so long as I am not together with my future husband I may go and do very much what I please, except for the watchful eyes of Chesi and his brother. I go to Hunger Hill. It is a wild sweet morning. Great puffball white clouds blow across the blue sky. The grass is green and cropped as velvet by farmers' sheep. The dew is cool to my bare feet. I loosen my hair from its tidy braids and let it go free down to my waist. I am wearing the last of my good summer dresses, the green silk I wore when my likeness was painted.

I go down into the Hollow. I look all about me lest Chesi should have followed. I step carefully onto the stony incline, for my bare feet soles after long years in shoes are still tender. I come into the green gloom where the leafy branches bend over to meet one another. I sit on the side of the gorge in the stony cleft what is shaped like an armchair. I remember the first time I came here holding on to Guy's hand. We were but *chavvies* then but already I loved him. I think about Chesi. He is still fixed on marriage. Well, I have given him fair warning.

Starina tells me she has heard the Elders talking. In a few days we are to leave this village and go over the border into Somerset. It is a bad thing to stay too long in the same *atchin-tan*. The constable is all against us. Some of the farmers blame us when their crops and cattle die. Only because of Milord have we been able to stay this long.

The birdsong grows silent. I hear a stone roll on the path. A twig cracks. Only a Gorgio can make so much din in a quiet place. I see first a head of red curls, then a pair of broad shoulders. It is Guy.

As he comes up the path I go to meet him. When we stand together I see that I am almost his height. We are shy to first with one another.

He says, it has taken you long enough to come here. I have looked for you every day.

It is not easy, I tell him. I am to be married so they watch me all the time. Today our men are in the woods hauling timber for your father. Even so I do not trust Chesi Ingram not to follow me. He is the one I am promised to. We are to wed at midsummer. I look into Guy's face to see how he will take the news. His skin is red and then a sick white.

No, he shouts, I will not allow it. You promised me.

No, say I, it is you what promised me. Secret sweethearts, you said, and then you went and lay with that silly Pansy. She earned you a walloping from your father. They say the child she bore is yours.

He says, it was all your fault. You pushed me away. You roused me then you told me to go to Pansy. He takes me by the shoulders and shakes me so that my head rocks. Tell the truth now, he shouts, if you know what the truth is. But that is not your way, is it? You Gypsies, you lie all the time.

At once we are children again, taunting one another. I call him carrot-head and mother's darling. I push him in the middle of his chest and he is unbalanced and falls backwards. He swears a very bad word. His hands are cut and bleed a little. Oh-ho, say I, so that is the language you learn in your fine school. He gets up and comes towards me. And then we are tumbling and shoving one another like we did all those years ago when Evangeline said that it was horseplay and not ladylike to behave so.

I put out my foot and trip him. Again he falls heavy, and this time he grabs at my shoulder taking me down with him.

We lie still, the breath knocked from our chests. And then it comes to both of us at the same time that I am lying underneath him. My frock has rucked up in the struggle and is now round my middle. I am no longer living in Milady's nursery. Under the dress I wear no drawers, not a stitch on all my body save for the green dress.

The sun has gone in. It is as dim as evening under the trees between the great rocks. I feel him move against me and I ache inside. We do not look at one another.

All of a sudden I am taken with a madness. I rip at his clothes until Guy is as bare-skinned as I am. And all the time I am thinking that I knew how this must happen one day, and in this certain fashion.

There was pain to first. And then a singing joy and such a pleasure that I cried out loud. Yet there was still a sadness in me. I wanted him and yet I did not want him. Even as we lay together I could not forget that he was a Lord's son and I was a Gypsy. That he had always taken what he wanted. But I remembered who and what *I* was. I am the *chovihani*. I have the 'touch', the 'sight', the POWER.

I knew that later on I would say that none of this was my fault, and he would say that it was mine. The day will come when one of us is lying. I will say that Guy seduced me.

But did he?

Maya Heron. May 1st 1890.

A week ago we moved out of Dorset. Somerset is kinder to our people.
There is field work for us all on this farmer's land and as much buttermilk
and potatoes from the farm wife as we can make use of.

I dress every day in the green silk and a new white apron. Starina's
little sister Lura puts flowers in my braids. In my basket I carry lace,
and lucky hares' and rabbits' feet. Word has gone out around the villages
and farms that I have the 'gift'. That I can tell the future. Chesi should
be pleased at the money in my waistbag.

Chesi and I still sit each evening in Grandmother's wagon. The lace
collar she hooks is coming close to finished. It is for me to wear on my
wedding day.

On the night before we left Dorset, while the company was busy with
the packing, I slipped away to the Hollow and Guy was waiting for me.
We lay together for the last time, and I knew on that evening that I will
always love him.

I look at Chesi and Guy is in my heart. Sometimes I cannot hold the
tears back. Chesi says in that soft voice of his, you are thinking of him,
aren't you? When you think about him I could kill you both. So I tell
him lies. No, I say, it is just that I am weary. My leg is hurting where
the stallion kicked me. It is only you I think of, Chesi.

He is at once all sweetness. When you are my wife, he says, it will be
a heaven. I will treat you like a princess. I will never once come drunk
from the *kitchima*. I will never beat you.

I look at his black curls, his dark eyes and copper-coloured face and I
see what lies behind the bones and skin. I see clear into the jealous, bitter
pain that burns him up. Ah yes, I think. You will come home drunk, and
you will beat me. But not for long, my fine Romanichal. It will be for a
little time and then it will be over.

I don't know why I think these things. The words come to my head
and it is all as Grandmother said it would be with a true *chovihani*.

To see the future is a wonder and a fearful thing.

Maya Heron. May 5th 1890.

Starina is to marry Black Ingram. So we shall be sisters-in-law as well
as cousins. It seems that for them, all was decided long ago, as it was for
me and Chesi. But for these two there will be no long courtship evenings
in Grandmother's wagon. For them it will be a time of loving underneath
the stars. They are to run away together to a secret place. They will live in
a bender far from the *tan* for six weeks or more. If after that time they are
still sweet on each other and suited, they will return to their families and a
wedding will be held. The parents will act very angry towards them, but

it is all for show. The elopement is what the parents have wanted and expected. But they can never say so. All of this is told me by Starina while we sit by the hedge making baskets of green rushes and filling them with flowers to sell in the town.

So why, I ask, have I not been told all this before? If I could only run away with Chesi I could mayhap lose him on some quiet road. Oh, I should have known all this, I tell Starina. See how much time I have wasted sitting in that wagon.

No, she says. It is different with you, Maya. Five years you were away from us. What can you know of our ways? She bends her face low across the basket she is weaving and does not want to look at me. Two more things, says she. First off, you are a *chovihani* and Uncle Taiso is our King. So your wedding must be something extra.

And the second thing?

Ah well, she says, there is this business of the young Lord up to the big house. That is the real trouble for the Elders to get over.   My heart stops beating in my chest. What business? I ask offhand, as if it is nothing to me.

Starina says, there has been talk in the village, the servants in the house have said that this Guy is hot-blooded and that you are too knowing for your young years. They say in the *tan* that it was the Milord who asked your father to come and take you back to your own people. For your own safe good, for he did not trust his son and you together.

I shout at her, my father fetched me because he wanted me back. I am so mad with Starina I could do murder to her.

Of course, says she. But now you must stay close inside the company. It would not do for you to run away with Chesi. You must stop in the *tan* where your father and grandmother can watch you. If you went off with Chesi you might run to the young Lord instead and never come back. That would be the finish of you, Maya.

While my fingers weave the rushes, my head is racing like a long-dog. Now I see it all. All of them are lying to me, even my father. Ah dordi, how I am deceived. But then I think of the times I was with Guy in the Hollow. I remember the green silk rucked up round my middle, and the sweet pain he gave me, and afterwards the singing joy, and I know that from that day onwards it was already too late for the Elders to say what I should or should not do.

Before they run away together, I ask Starina if she truly loves Black. Of course, says she, I would not otherwise go with him.

She had fallen asleep in the blue chair, the folder which held the diary spread out before her on the workbox. She came awake suddenly, and this time her disorientation was severe. With her eyes wide open to the dawn light she remained deep inside that old time of wild and dangerous people who made their own laws, observed their own taboos. A company of outlaws who judged and punished according to their own beliefs, while caught up in, and constricted by, the bonds of superstition.

She had read each diary entry slowly, and twice over. The sense of approaching tragedy grew stronger with each reading. She viewed the folder now with an even greater dread and a kind of fascinated horror. Somewhere among the mildew spots, the laborious pothooks and hangers, would be the secret of Bruenette and her crazy actions; and perhaps an explanation of the link between the Heron brothers and herself.

She showered and put on fresh clothes. The puppy, hearing her movements in the kitchen, came scratching at the door but she did not let him in.

Ten minutes after Jango and the Winnebago had left the paddock, she was in her car and headed towards Weymouth.

The flyers which advertised the circus appeared with increasing frequency as she approached the coast. She followed the arrows for no better reason than that they pointed forwards. A circus was not a likely place of trade for Lias Heron and his kin.

A small fair stood in the field that was next to the broad space which held the big top and its vans and animal cages. She drove in past showmen's trailers and the generators which powered the roundabouts and rides and the lighting system.

The fairground was stirring into gradual movement. A miniature ride of painted horses was attracting small children and their parents. A single booth had just opened for the sale of Coca-Cola and ice cream, coffee and doughnuts. She bought coffee and a doughnut, carried her breakfast to a gap in the hedge from which she could observe the dormant circus, and sat down on the sun-scorched grass.

But now there was movement and shouting on the far side of the big top. People she had thought to be still sleeping were cleaning out cages, carrying hay and straw bales, using water hoses. The faint sounds of music and laughter reached her as she drank her coffee. A young girl rode bareback on a white horse. As the rider came closer, Maya felt a coldness in her chest that almost stopped her breathing. The girl was Bruenette. Bruenette as Maya remembered her from her own childhood. As she approached, Maya had a full uninterrupted view of the voluptuous figure, the waist-length black and curling hair, the fine dark eyes set slantwise over the high cheekbones, her copper-coloured skin.

146

At the shock of recognition which showed on Maya's face, the girl smiled. 'Sorry I startled you,' she said, and then, 'I don't know you, do I?' Her voice was low-pitched, sweet and husky.

'No, you don't know me. But you remind me of someone.'

'Perhaps you saw my picture on the posters. I'm billed as Juanita but my proper name is Rowsheen.'

'Does your mother tell fortunes?'

'That's right. She's with the fair, I'm with the circus.'

Maya said, 'I think I know your father.'

The full lips ceased to smile. The girl spat sideways on to the grass. 'Poor you,' she said. 'Poor you.'

Her plans had been vague; she had thought to spend a day in Weymouth, to watch the ocean and think about her life. But the meeting with Lias Heron's daughter, who looked like Bruenette but who also closely resembled Lias, had unnerved her so much that all she could do was to turn the car round and drive back to the Monks' House.

As she negotiated the last bend in the drive, she saw the scarlet colour of Polly's car, and Polly herself sitting in the porch.

Polly had promised to visit in the spring but had telephoned in April with excuses that Maya had been only too happy to accept. Now, in late September, here she was, unheralded and unexpected. Maya drove on round the side of the house to park in the barn's shade. The walk back to the porch gave her time to arrange her thoughts, her face. She greeted Polly with pleasure if not enthusiasm. They embraced, briefly, and then surveyed one another. Maya thought how much thinner and strained Polly looked, but did not say so.

Polly said, admiringly, 'Well! Look at you! All tanned and glowing. Country living obviously suits you. Or are you in love? Don't answer that. I'm almost dead on my feet. Show me to Lavinia's room, there's a darling. I'll sleep for an hour or two and then we'll have a session. Catch up on all the news.'

Maya said, 'I'm sleeping in Lavinia's room these days.'

She carried Polly's bag into the house, and together they collected sheets and pillowcases, towels and duvet, and took them to a room that overlooked the driveway.

'Wake me at teatime.' Polly said. 'I can only stay the one night and there is quite a lot I need to say to you.'

While Polly slept, Maya washed salad and baked a batch of scones. She set the garden table with the flowered china, feeling an unusual need to convince and impress, in case Polly should doubt the quality of her present lifestyle.

Polly came yawning and stretching into the garden. She said, 'The smell of baking woke me.' She halted beside the table. 'Oh my! Things have certainly looked up since I was last here.' She sat. 'You've changed, Maya. I don't quite know how, but whatever it is, it's a great improvement. It also makes what I have to say a little easier.'

Maya pushed cream and jam, and a dish of still-warm scones across the table. She said, 'I can guess what it is you have to tell me. You want me out of the business, and I don't blame you.'

'I was hoping you'd say that, but I wasn't sure.' She paused. 'There's something else. I'm going to marry Jonah.' She bit into a scone, chewed and swallowed. 'Oh, I know he's a bastard. But I've grown sort of used to him. Anyway, from what I hear, you've found a bastard of your own.'

'I don't know what you mean.'

'Come off it, Maya. Your Gypsies are back. There's a fire bucket and a Winnebago, and two bloody great greyhounds in the paddock.' She smiled. 'No wonder you took Lavinia's room. For the view, I assume. Oh, I don't blame you. He looks a real hunk. Those silver curls look stunning with his tanned face, and those shoulders!'

'You've talked to Alice.'

'Well, yes. We do converse from time to time on the telephone.'

Maya said, 'Which is more than she and I do. Since Jango and Lias arrived, my dear aunt has chosen to act all offended and disapproving. I was going to tell you about my lodgers. I didn't know that Jango was back. I was listening to the radio while I prepared tea. I didn't hear the arrival of the Winnebago.'

Polly said, 'Jango? Singular?'

'His brother Lias is away at the moment, visiting his wife and daughter.' Maya's tone was defiant, challenging.

Polly raised her eyebrows. 'So which one is it?'

'Neither.'

'I don't believe you.'

'Suit yourself.'

The silence between them was uncomfortable. Polly said, 'I really came to talk about the business. You agree that things can't go on as they are?'

'It's my fault,' said Maya. 'I should have sorted it all out long ago. Tell me what you want me to do, and I'll do it.'

'I – that is we – would like to buy you out.'

'Fine. Draw up the necessary papers and I'll sign them.'

'Just like that?'

'Just like that.'

'Maya, look, there was a time, not so long ago, when the business was your whole life. I don't want you to feel —'

'I don't. Stop worrying. Something happened when my parents died. I can't explain it to you, because I don't yet understand it. I'm carrying out an investigation. It takes up all my energy and time. I'll be relieved to hand over my share of the business. I really can't be bothered with it.'

'I don't believe you said that. But you did, so I must accept it. At least you're no longer in that awful state of depression. In fact you're more alive than I have ever seen you!'

The impulse to confide was brief and easily controlled. There had been a time when she and Polly had told each other everything. But that had been in childhood and adolescence.

Polly said, 'You don't mind about Jonah, do you?'

'No,' she said. 'Jonah was never important in my life. I hope you'll be happy with him.' She could have said that Jonah was dangerous, evil, a blackmailer. But there are certain things about a man that a woman must be left to discover for herself.

They talked late into the evening about old times and people they had known. The distance that had grown between them was barely noticeable, but it was there. After breakfast the next morning, with the kitchen door kept closed against the puppy, Maya signed away her share of the jewellery business. The financial settlement was generous. Lias Heron, she thought, would be pleased, if he knew, that she carried so much money in her waist bag.

She said goodbye to Polly with promises to visit her in London. As she turned back towards the house, the Winnebago camper pulled out of the paddock. Jango smiled and waved as he drove by, but did not speak.

Maya Heron. June 21st 1890.
Starina and Black are returned from the elopement. I had not thought to miss her so. She is the only one I can talk to in the *tan*, although I do not tell her too much. I hear my father and Esmeralda scolding the pair but there is a smile behind their hard words. So how went it with you and Black? I ask her. She smiles like a cat what has supped on cream, but she will not tell me. You will know soon enough how it is with a man, says she. We are to have a double wedding on Sunday. Me and you with Black and Chesi.

I smile on the inside of my face. Starina thinks she has the better of me, so does my father and Esmeralda. They have kept my wedding day a secret. But for Starina I would still have been in the dark about it.

June 25th 1890.

There is money enough found for the weddings. My father sells a horse, and the Ingrams have painted up a flat-cart and *chopped* it for a broken-down *vardo* for a start for Starina and Black. With Starina and me gone, my aunt Esmeralda will be left alone with Lura. My father is to move in with Grandmother Ingram so that Chesi and I may have the big King's wagon. I am told it is a mark of my worth to the family that my father is gone to live with his mother-in-law so that I might have his *vardo*. Grandmother has made me a wedding dress of blue silk with puff sleeves and long skirts. Starina has the same, only pink. I have no heart or stomach for any of it. I only want it to be over.

Maya Heron. June 30th 1890.

It is late, but there is still light enough for me to write by. Well, it is done and I was wed yesterday to Chesi Ingram. The day was hot and did not start well. Evangeline would have said that my nerves were all wrought up. I felt sick in my stomach and likely to faint off. The blue dress had been stitched some weeks since. When I came to put it on I found it had been cut too small and was tight across the chest and stomach. So I *chopped* with Starina and I wore the pink frock what was bigger, even though I feared that the exchange would bring ill luck down on us.

A great company of our people is pitched in the farmer's lane and fields. Even the village folk came out to see a double Gypsy wedding. Let us give them a good show, said my father, and there was much eating and drinking, and the Buckleys brought their fiddles and made music for the dancing. For an hour or two I forgot about Chesi and the shadow that lay on him. I too danced and laughed until the real business of the day began.

My father did the talking. He wished the four of us long life together, and many children. We stood before him and he took his silver knife and cut my wrist and Chesi's. Then he put our wrists together so that the blood could run as one. He did the same for Black and Starina. Then we ran, hand in hand and two by two, through the clearing and jumped across the fire, and it was all over.

Chesi has gone to the *kitchima*. I was glad to see him go. Black and Starina are like lovebirds in their broken-down waggon. I cannot write when Chesi is nearby. He is saying now that the reading and writing is not for such as us. It is, says he, the Devil's work. You could be right, I tell him. For it takes one Devil to know another Devil. Already we are at each other's throats.

I come now to the part I do not want to think about. But it must go out of my head and on to the paper lest I get no peace. Chesi knew at once that he was not the first man I had laid with. He rolled away from me last night and the light from the fire outside came in at the window, enough for me to see his face, and I thought then that he would try to kill me. He stood beside the bed and held the pointed knife close to my face. So you are the whore they say you are, says he in his soft voice. There were tears on his face and I saw then he would not have the heart to kill me. I had no answer for him and so I covered myself and waited for the beating that I knew must come. But Chesi is a smart man and a proud one. He would not wish the family to know his shame. Chesi knows where to punch and kick so that blue marks do not show. When I had trouble walking through the *tan* this morning, when my legs were weak and my back bent over, the men smiled into their teacups and told each other how strong in love must be the ways of Chesi Ingram, and how lucky the woman who had won the hot passions of such a Romanichal.

But Chesi was right to beat me. He does not know yet just how right he was.

Maya Ingram. August 29th 1890.

I have not wrote these many weeks. Just to see the pen and ink and paper makes my husband like a madman. But for the next five days or more he is away with Black to a horse fair on the far side of the world. All of twenty miles, says Starina, who is sad to be alone.

The trouble grows worse between me and Chesi.

You have lied to me, says he. You have shamed me before my family. I had thought you clean and decent. He points to my swollen belly. That is no child of mine, that is Gorgio spawn you carry. And to think how I loved you. The tears come as ready to his eyes as his fists to my stomach.

I have never lied, I tell him. If you had asked I would have told you. You have never loved me, Chesi. You thought by marrying me you did a clever thing. You believed that a *chovihani* will always have silver in her waist bag. You thought I would put food in your mouth, clothes on your back, money in your pocket for drinking and betting. Well, you are not so clever as you think. My father wanted a husband for me, and you were more than willing. You and I had been promised to each other, so they say, a long time ago. You knew all about Guy and me, so what were you expecting?

He rocks himself back and forward. Ah dordi, he cries, whatever shall I do?

I say, you will do what you have to do, and so will I. I do not love you, I do not like you, but you are my wedded husband, and my child will bear your name. There is nothing you can say to change that.

They will all know, says he, that I am not the father. How shall I ever hold my head up?

Only if you are fool enough to tell, I say. I shall keep my mouth shut, so must you. Have no fears, my manniken, I tell him, I will work for you and keep you in the style you had expected. As for the child, it will be all mine and no charge upon you. I put my face up close to his. I say, if you strike me again and I lose my child, I will change you to a toad and stamp you underneath my heel.

He is like to die of fear. He kicks out at my little cat Minta.

Have a care, I say. The cat is my *familiar*. She has powers of her own.

Witch, he shouts, using the Gorgio word which has no music in its sound.

I do not know if I could do to him the thing I promised. But he has not touched me since. Nor Minta.

Maya Ingram. September 30th 1890.

Two days ago we moved back into Sheepdip Lane. My father sees no danger from Guy now that I am wed. The calendar says that Chesi and Black have been away from us for five weeks. Starina moons about like a sick cow. She is sure that some bad thing has befallen both of them. Don't fret yourself, I tell her. Bad pennies always turn up.

She wails at me, how can you speak so of Chesi when you are carrying his child? You are a hard woman, Maya. But, ah dordi, how I envy you that baby. How I wish I was myself in your happy state.

I am thinking to myself that I know why Chesi stays away. It would be better for me if he never returns.

A child will happen to you soon enough, I tell Starina. Unless of course Black means to go away regularly from you for weeks at a time. Starina has not yet worked out that I am too far gone for the baby to be Chesi's. The older women in the *tan* watch my stomach but do not speak their thoughts. My little cat Minta is soon to have kittens for the first time. This is seen by the company as yet another sign that Minta is my *familiar*, and that I am the true *chovihani*. They all fear me more with every day that passes.

Maya Ingram. October 2nd 1890.

I must not think of Guy, but every time the child moves inside me I can seem to hear Guy's voice and see his red curls and blue eyes. I go out *dukkerin* every day. Churi Lovell drives me in the flat-cart. I am now known far and wide as one who can read palms and cast spells. It is not unpleasant for a Romanichi such as I to stand so high among the Gorgio.

Maya Ingram. October 7th 1890.

They are back. They came last night, very late, leading what Chesi describes as a 'fine string of horses'. To my eye the poor beasts are spavined, broken-winded, lame and some so old that they can scarce walk. But the brothers are skilled in the doctoring of such creatures. Black and Chesi are full of tricks. I have seen them file down the long teeth that show great age in a horse, so that the buyer thinks he gets a younger bargain, or poke a slow pony slyly with a knife point so that it rears up and seems to be mettlesome to a Gorgio buyer.

Chesi does not share my bed. He sleeps on the waggon floor but only he and I know this. Starina's waggon stands next to mine. She waits upon Black since his return as if he is pure gold. She takes off his boots what are in tatters after the long trek. She bathes his feet and binds them in clean rags. She all but spoons the food into his mouth. It is as though if she takes her eye off him for only a second, he will vanish. Chesi takes off his own boots. I say, there is stew in the pot if you are hungry, but I do not go to the fire and bring the food to him. He would like to beat me, but I see in his face that he remembers my promise to change him to a toad and kill him if he ever again lifted his hand or foot against me. He takes a bowl and fetches stew. He says, my brother is the lucky one.

No, say I, not lucky. Your brother has a true heart. All Starina brought to him was a worn-out *vardo*. Black wed with my cousin for love of her. Not for the silver in her waist bag.

Chesi says, I have no need of your silver. I will have plenty of my own when I sell the horses at the Pack Fair in Sherborne next Monday.

Maya Ingram. October 8th 1890.

Guy is home for the weekend. It is Starina who sees him and brings me a note which of course means nothing to her. What does he say? she pesters.

Oh, he just writes that he is thinking of me.

It would not do to tell her that Guy says he will wait for me in the Hollow, after church on Sunday evening. Oh, I always knew in my heart that Guy would not forsake me in my awful trouble. He is still my secret sweetheart.

Maya Ingram. Tuesday.

A bad thing has happened. It is so terrible that I cannot write it. But I know that I must set it down, lest I forget exactly what was done and not done. I will start with the easy bit and mayhap find courage for the writing of the rest of it.

I went up to Hunger Hill on Sunday evening. I saw Black and Chesi's horses tethered on the hillside grazing, but my heart was full of Guy and so thought nothing of the horses.

Guy waited for me in the Hollow. I cannot tell how sweet it was to see him, to hear his voice. I wore my cloak of green velvet, but he saw straight away how things are with me. He took both my hands in his. He said, it is my child, Maya.

Yes, I told him. Yes, it is your child.

He put his arms round me then, and I wept on his shoulder.

Tell me what you would have me do, says Guy, and I will do it. Come back to the house with me, says he. We will tell my mother what has happened. My mother loves you like a daughter. She would never turn you away. She will care for you. After all, it is her grandchild.

Too late, say I, I am already wed with Chesi Ingram. But I remember too how Pansy's baby was also Milady's grandchild and Milady did not take it.

Even as I speak his name, Chesi stands above us. He looks down from the high slope of the Hollow, the string of ponies roped behind him. And now I know what it is I should have remembered. No horse dealer who is going to a fair will wait until morning to make the journey with his horses. Chesi, also on his way to Hunger Hill to fetch his stock, has watched me come into the Hollow.

I see the red colour leave Guy's face. My own blood sinks towards my feet. Chesi loops the leading ropes round a birch tree. He comes down towards us. It is falling dusk beneath the overhang but I can see the pointed knife blade in his hand. He does not speak. He pushes me hard so that I fall against a rock, and then he crouches low and springs at Guy.

Guy calls out to me, run, Maya, run.

I get to my feet and the child inside me rolls and tumbles. A sharp pain in my side makes me fearful, and I scramble from that dark place and back on to the hilltop. I bide very still and listen. Sounds come clear on the night air. I hear grunting but no words, and then a crashing of footsteps, and a breaking of bushes and I know that it is Guy who runs for home and safety. I wait for a short time but Chesi does not come. He will be waiting for me in the Hollow, the knife ready in his hand. And this time his anger will be such that he will use it on me. I begin to walk back to the *tan*, moving very slowly for I am much afeared, and the child inside me turns and twists as if it would break free from my body.

I am coming into Sheepdip Lane when I meet Black Ingram. Where is my brother? says he. He was off to bring the ponies long since, something must have happened to him.

Nothing happened, say I. You must have missed him. I saw him only minutes ago setting out with his string of old donkeys along the road to Sherborne.

I cannot now explain what made me lie to Black. I watched him out of sight along the Sherborne Road and then went into my waggon. I sit all night by the open door, and when the first light breaks I go slowly back up to the Hollow.

It is that time of the year when the sun hangs low in the heaven. The red berries of hip and haw are thick on the hedges. Down in the Hollow the fallen leaves have made a bed for Chesi. He lies on his side, knees drawn up, body curled together like a sleeping child. I kneel down beside him. I look at his black curls, the long lashes of his closed eyes, the skin of his face what is no longer copper-coloured but a dirty white. He is dressed up for the fair. He wears his long dark green jacket with the poachers' pockets and silver coins for buttons. The trousers are to match, with seven rows of fine stitching at the cuffs and pockets. His boots are soft brown leather. The *diklo* knotted at his throat had been a striped green and yellow, but I see that it is now dark red and stiff with Chesi's blood. There is also blood on the rock behind him.

To first I could not bring myself to touch him. But in the end I eased the *diklo* from his neck and saw the single stab hole. He opened his eyes as I leaned across him and I saw that his death was very near. His blood had soaked the ground about him and turned the fallen leaves to red. He said, your lover did this to me. Bring Black so that I can tell him what has happened here. Your fine Gorgio shall hang high for murder in Shepton Mallett gaol.

I knew then that I could not let him live long enough to name Guy. Without thought or doubt I pulled my paring knife from my boot top. It was then that Chesi cursed me and all my descendants. A terrible, evil curse what I can never put to paper.

I drove the knife many times into his throat until he breathed no more, and then I closed his eyelids. I let the horses loose so that they might graze and drink. I was on my way back to Sheepdip Lane when the weariness caught me. I pulled the cloak around me, lay down underneath a furze bush, and slept.

It was Black who found his brother. A farmer had complained that the horses were loose across the hill. One little coloured pony had strayed into the Hollow and Black had gone to get him. I heard Black moaning and weeping as he came into the *tan*. He had carried Chesi on his shoulders all that long way from Hunger Hill. I went out to meet Black. It would have looked strange if I had stayed inside my waggon. Black stood in the middle of the clearing, holding Chesi in his arms. I walked to him on shaking legs.

This is your doing, he said. My poor brother foretold that you would be the death of him.

What has happened? I cried. Who has done this to my husband? I felt the blood leave my head and I fell upon the ground. The women lifted me with gentle hands and took me to my waggon. Among our people a time of solitude is allowed to the bereaved one. I closed my curtains and lay down on the bed which Chesi had not shared with me for even one night. All my thoughts were for Guy. I went over every word and movement until I was sure in my head that nobody had seen us meet, save Chesi. There was no way that blame could fall on Guy, and if it should, then I would tell the constable that it was I who finished off my husband.

Black Ingram was the first to come knocking on the door of the poor grieving widow. He came alone, bearing food and strong tea sent by Starina.

You think yourself clever, says he, but I know you, Maya Heron. My poor brother told me everything, and I shall tell the constable. I will see to it that you and your lover hang high from the gibbet in the gaol at Shepton.

No, I say, you will keep a still tongue if you are a wise man. I fix him with my two eyes, and he cannot look away. I say, I believe that you and Starina would like to have a family. A big one.

He does not give me answer.

If that is your wish, say I, then you will keep your mouth shut. I have the power to give life and the power to take it. You know this to be true, I tell him. Remember Lovell's youngest? The one who was sick of the croup, who stopped breathing and was dead? Do you recall, Black, how they fetched me to the child and I breathed into its mouth, and that dead child took a long sigh and came back to life? That same child plays now with its brothers and sisters. If you would see your own live children playing in the *tan* then you will keep your own counsel over me and Chesi.

He says nothing, and then he says, we have set up a bender at the lane's end. Chesi lies inside it. The men and me will take turns at keeping vigil until the funeral. Will I send Starina to you? He backs away from me. He says, for Starina's sake I shall say nothing. But my brother's curse is on you.

Starina comes. She brings bread and strong sweet tea and sits with me while I eat and drink. For the child's sake, she tells me. You must think of the child. It is all that you have now.

What is happening? I ask her. I heard strangers in the *tan*. Their voices woke me.

It was the constable from Sherborne and a gentleman what wore a frockcoat. They wanted to see Black, to find out what had happened in the Hollow. The constable wanted to see you too, Maya. But Black told him how you were in the family way and crazed with grief, and no sense to be had from you this day, no matter what the questions.

Starina went away, and again I slept. I am so bone weary I could shut my eyes and never open them again. I think about Chesi, lying in the bender at the lane's end. I remember the time of the great sickness when I washed the newborn dead and made them ready for burial. But this is different.

I lose all track of time. I think it was the next day when my father came into my waggon. I say, you can have your *vardo* back now, Dadus. I have no more need of it. A bender will do for me, in my condition.

My father's face is grey coloured. He looks like an old man. He says, I did wrong, girl. I should never have put you together with Chesi.

I say, the wrong was done five years ago when you left me with the Milord. I will tell you the truth, Father. This child is not Chesi's.

My father nods as if he knows already. He says, there is great trouble for that family in the Monks' House. It was their red-haired son what killed your poor husband.

My blood runs cold. I say, no, Dadus. Whoever told you such a lie?

It is no lie, says he. The gardener up to the big house was coming up through the Hollow on his way from work. He saw all what happened. He heard the young Lord telling you to run away and when you was gone he saw how that young man put a knife in Chesi's throat and killed him. The gardener said it happened all so fast there was nothing he could do. The constable have took the Lord's son to the prison at Shepton. The talk in the *kitchima* is that this Guy will hang. He was seen by others, with blood about his person. And that blood was Chesi Ingram's. The young Lord is not liked among the village people. He could well hang even though the dead man is a Gypsy.

I say, make the bender ready for me. I cannot bear to stay inside this *vardo*. Do it quickly, Dadus, for I am like to lose my mind.

He makes to go. He says, will I send your Aunt Esmeralda to you?

No, I say, I will have Starina and no other at this sorry time.

Maya Heron. October 12th 1890.

I learn for the first time in my life about funerals. I find out from Starina what is happening to Chesi in his private bender. Starina thinks to give me comfort in the telling. She builds up the fire in the stove and boils a great pot of strong tea, for I am cold to my very core. I lie on the bed under many blankets and my cousin sits beside me. The curtains are closed and I see her sweet face in the fireglow. If she only knew what I had done. But she does not know and Black will never dare to say.

Starina tells me it was known in the camp that death would be coming soon to one of us. Grandmother Ingram had heard the death-bird singing for a week or more. There were others who had heard it too. From the minute Chesi's body was carried home by Black, that bird had not been seen or heard. Starina says that I can rest easy that all that should be done for Chesi is being done. He lies in a coffin made big enough to hold his Spanish leather saddle, what he won by a wager from Comfort Smith. Also packed with him for his trip to the other world is two gold coins and his wedding shirt of blue silk. A candle burns at Chesi's head, and vigil is kept up by a rota of three women, and by Black who is the closest to him.

Starina says that because Chesi's death was not like a usual dying, to first there was great fear in the *tan* and only Black would touch the corpse, and was not *atrashed*. The Elders had a meeting. It was decided that Chesi's spirit would be still very angry from the way he had been torn from life, and that it would be dangerous for any one of us to touch him. So an old Gorgio woman was brought out from the village. She was told to wash the blood from Chesi's face and neck and close his mouth. He was already dressed in his best clothes and boots, so nothing else need be interfered with. A brand new *diklo* has been laid across his throat to cover the stab holes, says Starina, and his hair combed. When you go to see him, says she, you will hardly know that he is dead.

Black has kept the three days' watch beside his brother's body, and Starina has scarce stirred from my side. She is more dear to me than any sister. I would never have lied to her, save to keep Guy from the hangman. Even now, I must count every word I speak lest I say too much and the constable hears about it. I am a very good liar, and Starina is not.

The company come to my *vardo* early in the morning. They stand silent in the clearing, every one of them, from the oldest to the babes in arms. Grandmother Ingram calls out to me and I rise from my bed and open the half-door. She says, it is time for you to say goodbye to Chesi. We shall bury him beside the crossroads over by Bradford Abbas.

I begin to shake.

Grandmother says, come, child. He was your husband. His spirit will find no rest if you do not see him for the last time.

No, I say, I cannot see him. I am sick. I must keep to my bed.

I see the faces change. The women mutter between themselves. The men spit upon the ground. My grandmother turns away, and they all follow.

Starina touches my hand, she leads me back to the bed and covers me with blankets. She says, I must go with them, Maya.

Yes, say I, it is for the best. Black will need you on this day.

She says, when I come back I will help you to your new home. They have already built a bender for you.

The funeral procession must needs pass by my waggon on its way to the crossroads. They make a pause before my door, and I stay behind the curtains. But Chesi's vengeful spirit finds me, as Black had meant it should do. I feel it come in through the barred door and take possession of my soul and body, and then I know the bitter truth. Chesi Ingram and I are now as one in Death as we never were in Life.

I have lost track of time, but the great gales blow and so it must be November. The company have moved from Sheepdip Lane because of danger from Chesi's ghost. They have made their winter quarters in a worked-out quarry on the far side of the hill. My bender is set much further from the new *tan* than I had thought to find it. Esmeralda says, you know it is the custom for a woman to live alone just before she gives birth and for six weeks after?

I say, yes, I know it. But my child will not be born for many weeks yet.

She will not meet my eyes. It is for the best, says she, that you are here and separate.

My father has built well. The bender stands in a sheltered spot and on high ground. Eight good wands of hazel hold up a covering of blankets, and a top layer of tarred cloth what will keep the rain out. There is a deep layer of clean straw for me to sleep on, and a box to keep my clothes and dishes, and my papers. Starina comes night and morning. She brings food and water. My father has stacked wood so that my fire might burn by day and night. When the sticks are all used up I am to tell Starina. There is no call, says he, for me to come to the *tan*. So they do not yet mean for me to die. I am to have the life kept in me until the child is born and they can see the colour of it.

The constable comes. He brings with him a gentleman who wears a dark cape. They stand beside my fire. They say how they have asked for Black and Starina to be present at this meeting. I say there is nothing I can tell them, but I can see they think I lie.

Black comes, and Starina looking white and fearful. The constable says to me, when was the last time you saw your husband?

I touch my swollen belly and my head. I have been sick from shock, I tell him. It is not easy to remember, but I must have seen him on that last evening when he went to fetch the horses from the hill.

The gentleman says, now tell me, Mrs Ingram, how well are you acquainted with the young Lord Guy of the Monks' House?

I look downwards at my folded hands. I say all meek and quiet, as you must know, sir, I was cared for by that dear kind family for nigh on five years. I growed up alongside his young Lordship. But o'course I never did forget my place, or that I was a Gypsy. I never got to know him well. Well, I wouldn't, would I?

He smiles down on me. I have said the very words he wants to hear. He gives the constable a long look. He says, I think I have heard all I need to here. There is nothing to be gained by further questions.

But the policeman does not give way so easy. He turns to Black. He says, was your brother still alive when you found him?

Tears come in Black's eyes. Like I told you before, sir, there was no life left in Chesi when I got there. Before God, sir, I cannot bear to think on it.

The gentleman speaks next. Tell me, young man, just how would you say your brother died?

Why, from the knife wounds, your honour. His neck was like a colander. You must have seen it for yourself.

Oh yes. I saw it. But did it not strike you as odd that your brother had so many wounds? He had also taken a severe blow to the head when he fell back on the rock. In my opinion that blow alone would have been enough to kill him. But someone was very determined to have him dead, and I cannot help but wonder why?

Black looks at the ground and not at me. He says, we have talked about that very thing, sir, among ourselves. We think some villain was out that night to steal my brother's valuable horses.

The gentleman smiles. In that case, says he, there must have been two murderers. For one wound was made with a stiletto, and all the others with the broad blade of a paring knife.

The gentleman is very near the truth. That paring knife is the one I use when making clothes pins.

I take a deep breath. I say to the gentleman, it is very good of you, your honour, to take so much trouble over my poor dead husband. It is not the usual way of things, hereabouts, when it is a Gypsy what is killed or robbed.

He looks long into my face. He says, perhaps you have not heard, Mrs Ingram. Lord Guy has been apprehended and charged with your husband's murder. It is not your husband who concerns me. I am a lawyer. I represent Lord Guy and his family.

I say, I am sure Lord Guy did not kill my husband, and since I speak only the bitter truth it shows on my face and in my voice, so that even the constable believes me in that moment.

He rubs his hand across his face. He says to the lawyer, it's a bad case, Mr Jennings, and no mistake. The gardener won't be shaken on his sworn statement. It's a poor lookout for his young Lordship.

Black says, it will turn out yet to be some wicked horse thief. Who else would want my brother dead?

They all go away. I build up the fire and warm the stew Starina brought me. I am so weary lately that I sleep the day through. It is growing *dimpsey* when I wake. I can just make out two people coming up the hillside. As they draw near I see it is the groom from the Monks' House, and with him, wrapped in cloak and hood, is Milady.

Oh ma'am, I cry, you should not have come here.

She says, I am perfectly safe with Watkins. I had to see you, Maya.

I say, tell your man to leave us.

She instructs him to wait for her in the carriage. He goes unwillingly. I fetch a straw bale to the fireside and she sits down. I hang my head before her.

She says in her gentle way, what do you do here all day, and by yourself?

I say, I keep up my reading and writing, but I mostly dream, ma'am. I go back to my young days in the *tan* when my life was easy. Then I think about my time in your house and all your goodness to me. Further than that I cannot go.

She says, bad things have happened since you left us.

I feel the tears come and I cannot halt them. She comes to me and puts her arms round me. She says, cry, child. It will do you good. You have much to weep for.

It is my own fault, I tell her. I have done a wicked thing and all to help Guy. I killed my husband so that Guy should not be blamed. But it all went wrong and the police have taken Guy, and oh, I love him so. Whatever shall I do?

She strokes my head as she did all those years ago in the nursery. She says, you are not to blame yourself. This whole sorry business is my son's fault. He is headstrong and wilful and will not be advised.

But he is your child, I say. How can you say that?

You are also my child, says she, and I will tell you a strange thing, Maya. I never cared for my children with my own two hands. They were given up at birth to nursemaids. But you – I nursed you night and day when you were injured. I saved your life, the doctor said, and so that made you mine. She turns me round to face her. You must let me help you now. When is the child due?

161

Somewhere around Christmas, I think. Or maybe after that.

And how will you manage?

I smile. As any other Gypsy woman. It will be born here, on the straw, as is our custom. Starina will help me when my time comes.

Milady says, this is my son's child. My grandchild. She twists her hands together. Come back with me now to the Monks' House. We will do up the nursery together.

I say, Pansy also had your son's child.

No, says Milady. Did you not hear? Pansy admitted in the end that she had lied. But not until after we had paid her a good sum of money.

I look at Milady and I think that someone clever in her family has misled her. After all, it is Pansy's father who has named Guy to the constable. And why else should he do that, without a strong grudge?

I say, I cannot come with you, ma'am. The child is Guy's but it is mine too. It must be born according to the customs of my people.

She says, you have been through so much in these last weeks. Supposing the child is weak and sickly? She waves a hand at the bender, the straw bed, the fire. A baby could die in such circumstances.

I take her hand. Thank you, I say, for your kind offer. But if my child is strong it will survive. If it is sickly then it is better dead. There is no room for weaklings among my people. I have one favour to ask of you, ma'am. As you know, since the days I learned to write, in your house, I have kept a record of what has happened to me. The time is coming when I shall have no means for such a habit, but I would ask you to hold my papers safe in the next months. If you are willing, I will send Starina to you with the tin box.

Milady says, when Starina comes I will have ready clothes for the child and for you. You are sadly ill-clad, Maya, considering your condition and this bitter weather. Where is your warm, green velvet cloak?

I think of the green cloak, soaked with Chesi's blood where I had leaned across him. I say, it got roasted, ma'am, when I stood too close up against a fierce fire.

There are times when even I can tell the near truth. I remember how that cloak burned slowly and with a dark smoke. Black Ingram watched the destroying of it with me. He stood at my shoulder and whispered in my ear, go away from us, Maya. There is no place for you in this family.

I said, there is no place for such as I in all the world.

As I write I see the yellow sky, and the snow clouds piling up above the hilltop. I think of Chesi in his grave, and of poor Guy in his prison cell. I think that the child and I will not live through this winter.

If we die together, she and I, it will all be for the best.

*   *   *

Her hand reached out for the folder and found it empty, as she knew it must be. She re-read the final page of Maya Heron's diary and would not believe that it had ended so inconclusively. And yet, how could such a record have continued? The physical deprivation, the powerful emotions of that situation had made the very act of putting pen to paper an awesome and rare achievement.

She willed herself to calmness. Her wristwatch said two in the morning, and there was no point in going to bed for she would not sleep. Exhaustion had brought her to a pitch where awareness was heightened. The portrait on the wall took on an extra dimension. Reason told her that Maya Heron's child must have survived that bitter winter, must have grown to womanhood and borne children of her own. How else could she account for her own existence, and that of Lias and Jango Heron? Her final acceptance of Maya Heron, as great-grandmother, Gypsy and witch, was total now, as Bruenette had clearly planned it should be.

But what had happened next?

She opened the workbox and began methodically to remove and examine each green ledger and notebook, and the yellow folder which appeared to hold nothing of interest save a thick file of letters, written in her mother's hand. She moved through the house, searching drawers and cupboards, not sure exactly what it was she sought. Was there still a tin box hidden somewhere? Or another folder of fragile papers clipped neatly together in some unlikely corner?

A pink dawn came up behind the stable block and she pulled back the curtains and switched off the table lamp. Up in her bedroom she closed the casement of the window against the chilly morning. The weak rays of the climbing sun lit up two blanket-clad figures down in the paddock lying beside the burnt-out fire.

So Lias was back! His dark head was identifiable against the red plaid blanket. She leaned her elbows on the windowsill and watched him; she imagined herself lying with him in the blanket, his hands on her body.

She turned abruptly and went down to the kitchen. Remember Maya Heron, she told herself. Murder once done can be repeated. Some families accumulated evil. It was passed along from one generation to another. A terrible inheritance that could not be avoided. She had suspected lately that the brothers, who usually shared everything in life, might be capable of jealousy and worse when it came to possession of a woman.

Mr Parsons the gardener had lit a bonfire. Maya had not slept but she did not feel tired. Sweeping up the fallen leaves that covered the lawn, wheeling garden rubbish, she breathed in the evocative smell of wood smoke and went over in her mind the possible hiding places of further diary entries. When she paid Mr Parsons for his morning's work, she said, 'Have you lived in this area for a long time?'

'All my life, ma'am, and I'll be eighty-one next week.'

'Did you ever hear the story of the Gypsy who was murdered on his way to the Pack Monday Fair in Sherborne?'

He smiled. 'Oh, I've heard it. Happened in my father's time, that did. A funny old place, the Hollow. When I was a boy the tale was that it was haunted. A ghost-like coach and horses was supposed to go galloping through there. And then, o'course, there was the Gypsy.'

She said, 'I've heard there was a curse concerning this house and its owners.'

The look he gave her was a mixture of sympathy and suspicion. 'Who told you that, ma'am?'

'My Aunt Alice.'

'Hmm,' he said. 'Well, you don't want to go bothering yourself about all that. I'm not saying that some bad things didn't happen hereabouts. But that's all in the past now. None of that need concern you, ma'am.'

She said, 'Did you work here in my parents' time?'

His fingers tightened round the handlebars of his bicycle. He took a few steps away from her. 'Just for a few months. Just to get the place in order. After that, they managed on their own.'

'My mother,' she said. 'Would you say that she was happy here?'

'Happy?' He made a pretence of considering her question. 'Well, I wouldn't exactly say happy. She was always busy about the place – a bit too busy, if you get my drift. She said to me once, 'You know, Parsons, this house means more to me than anything else in the whole world.' Now that's not right, ma'am, if you don't mind my saying. After all, 'tis only wood and stone when all's said and done.'

She said, 'You told me once that my mother lived here when she was a child.'

His reluctance to speak further was obvious.

'Please,' she said. 'I really want to know.'

'Well, all right. See, she didn't altogether live here. More like visited from time to time. Come to see her great-grandmother, she did. I was a young apprentice gardener in them days. I'd see them bring her to the door and leave her, and then, a couple of months later, they'd be back to fetch her.'

'Who? Who brought her here?'

He looked uncomfortable. He said, 'Why, them Gypsies, ma'am. The ones she mostly lived with.' He sought to reassure her. 'But make no mistake, your mother was the proper little lady, even in them days. Fancied herself a sort of princess, she did. Well, she was schooled by Lady Anne, see. Learned her manners here in this place.'

'Lady Anne? She must have been very old by that time, to be a great-grandmother, I mean.'

'Oh yes, ma'am. Ninety-six years old when she died, spite of all the trouble she'd seen.' He smiled as if to comfort her for the unsavoury information she had forced him to impart. 'Your mother was a wonderful consolation to her. Such a beautiful child, always laughing and dancing round the house and gardens.'

'So what happened after Lady Anne died?'

He began to walk away. 'I don't know, ma'am. I got married and went to work up at the Earl's place.' He paused. 'If you want to know more, then I reckon you had better ask your Aunty Alice. I've got the feeling that I might have said too much already. Just remember, ma'am, you made me tell you.'

She went back into the house. Without washing her hands or removing her boots, she made straight for the boudoir and stood beneath the portrait of Lady Anne. And now the pale and gentle features took on a new significance. She had never envisaged that Milady might still have been living, and in the Monks' House, in the time of Bruenette's childhood. But there was still a missing generation. What had been the name of Bruenette's mother, the child who had been conceived in the Hollow and who had inadvertently been the cause of the death of the Gypsy, Chesi Ingram? The questions crowded in upon her. She went back to the kitchen and sat down in the wicker chair that had been her father's. She had a sense of being on the edge of some monstrous revelation that might well destroy her. But she had come too far now to turn back. The dry sobs took her by surprise; her body shuddered but there were no tears. The arm that went round her shoulders made her catch her breath. He had come in silently, the puppy at his heels.

Jango's voice, infinitely tender, said, 'What is it, Maya?'

She could not answer, but stood abruptly and made to walk away. He blocked her exit from the kitchen. 'No,' he said. 'It always ends up like this when I want to talk to you. This time you're going to sit down and listen to me.' He pushed her back into the chair. He said, 'Hot, strong tea. Better even than Bacardi when you've had a shock.'

She watched as he plugged in the kettle, fetched milk from the fridge, and mugs and teabags from a cupboard.

She said, 'I haven't had a shock.'

'Look, lady. I know shock when I see it. Your face has got the same look as our Lias when he's put five hundred sovs on a horse to win and the bloody nag comes in second.'

165

Her sudden laughter was involuntary; it released her deep tensions and set tears flowing. She turned her face away, uncomfortable that he should see her weep.

He switched off the kettle and came to kneel beside her. He held her cold hands and chafed them between his own. He said, 'Why don't you tell me about it? You'll have to talk to somebody, sometime. It might as well be me. After all, I am sort of family.'

His concern, his unembarrassed tenderness, was more than she could bear. Suddenly weak, she slumped against him, and he held her. Her face was bent to his face, she felt his lips brush her ear, her eyelid, and then settle on her mouth. He kissed her long and slowly, and she did not resist him. He was the first to move away.

He said, 'There you are, see. It always helps to kiss it better.'

She felt comforted, reassured. 'Make that tea,' she told him, 'and then I think we have to talk. But not here.'

The Quiet Woman pub was almost empty on that rainy evening. They sat beneath the same pink-shaded lamp. Jango ordered sandwiches and a pot of coffee. The tension she had witnessed in him at the time of their first meeting was absent now. He had worn the Armani jacket then, almost as if it was a badge which gave him special powers. He had drunk the Bacardi defiantly, wishing to impress her with his capacity for it. He sat opposite her now, wearing old jeans and a sweater, and she thought, but he's a nice man, a truly good man, and he tries to hide the truth of it behind a tough façade. She recalled her own style on that other evening, the coral shirt and tailored trousers, the jewellery that she had also intended should make a statement. Now she, too, wore her oldest jeans, and a shirt that had faded in the sunshine of a Dorset summer.

She poured coffee into thick white cups. She said, 'I wasn't very nice to you the last time we sat here.'

He smiled. 'No, but you were pretty miserable then. Your parents had just died.'

'That, and other things.'

'I think you'd better start telling me about those things. We've reached this point before and you've always copped out.'

She drank coffee and bit into a sandwich in order to gain time. She had asked about Lias on the drive to Halstock. 'He hitched a lift back to Weymouth early this morning,' Jango told her. 'A cousin of ours picked him up at the end of your driveway. But he'll be back in time for the Pack Fair on Monday.'

She set down her coffee cup. He was watching her, his head tipped a little to one side. She said abruptly, 'I'm in deep trouble. I may be losing my mind even. I think it's possible that I might be some sort of witch or suffering from an inherited mental condition.'

She waited for his laughter, for mockery, incredulity. But his face was solemn, his eyes wary, and she knew then that she could trust him.

'Yes,' he said. 'Well, given your ancestry, it's very likely.' He paused. 'How long have you suspected that you might be a *chovihani?*'

'I've known since I was a child that there was something odd about me. I sort of saw things that other people couldn't see. It cut me off from normal relationships. I was afraid to get close to other people in case they found out that I was peculiar.'

'Not peculiar,' he said. 'Gifted.'

'It's a gift I would rather not have had.' She spooned sugar into her cooling coffee and stirred it. 'I think I might need psychiatric treatment. You know, electric shocks, all that stuff.'

He did not answer straightaway. When he spoke his voice was different, authoritative, as if he had known other witches and had reassured them. 'First off,' he said, 'you have to accept yourself for what you are. It's no big deal. We all have special powers. Look at Lias. A real disaster with women, but with dogs and horses, why, the man is magic! As for me, well, I'm that rare breed, a literate Gypsy. I'm good with my hands too. I can mend 'most anything that's broken.' He reached across the table and touched her fingers. 'What you really need,' he said, 'is not a shrink, but a man in your bed at night. I see your downstairs light burning until all hours.' He blushed as he spoke, and his shyness endeared him to her.

'I was married once.'

'Divorced now?'

'No. I killed him. We quarrelled and I wished him dead, and two hours later he was.'

He accepted her statement without question. 'Ah, yes,' he said. 'You have to be careful what you wish for. Sometimes you get more than you intended.'

'That's why I live alone now. Isolation is safer.' She heard herself confessing many of her best-kept secrets, and having once begun she feared that it would be impossible to stop.

He said, 'You didn't sleep at all last night.'

'I was reading.'

'Must be something pretty riveting.'

'Oh, it is.' She saw how tensely he waited for her to continue, but she could not. The diary had become a part of her very root and core. She could not bring herself to share the magic of it. Not even with him.

His tone was gentle but insistent. He said, 'You still don't trust me, do you?' There was pain in his eyes and face. He was a man who was unpractised in deception. He could not dissemble. He was vulnerable, and she could have as easily hurt the puppy, Star, as she could cause Jango pain.

She said, 'You're not the first literate Gypsy in the Heron family.' She picked up a sandwich and began to shred the beef and bread. 'When I first moved into this house I found some old record-books and papers. There was a diary that covered several years. The writer of it was called Maya Heron.'

He said, 'The Gypsy in the portrait?'

'Yes.'

'That must have been a shock for you. She's your living image.'

'The contents of the diary are even more alarming. She was not only a witch, but a self-confessed murderess.'

He smiled. 'Why should you have been alarmed? In the past half-hour you have told me that you are guilty of both those crimes.'

'Yes,' she said. 'I know I have. But can't you see how frightening it is to have my – well, to have my evilness confirmed? It's as if I was programmed somewhere down the genetic line to be like her. To *be* her. To *do* what she did. It means that I am not a free agent. So much of what happened in her life has been repeated in mine. A disrupted childhood, a sense of abandonment, a disastrous marriage. It's all in there. Jango!' She paused and pushed the breadcrumbs around the plate. 'The worst of it is the diary ends at the point when she has murdered her husband, her lover is imprisoned for that killing, and she is about to give birth to that lover's child.'

He said, 'No wonder you were up all night!'

'There has to be more information somewhere in the house. This diary is a collection of scruffy bits of paper placed in a folder. But fastened together with brand-new shiny paperclips.'

'Your mother?'

'Yes, of course. My mother willed the house and its contents to me. She bargained on me finding the folder, reading its contents.'

'And why do you think she took so much trouble to make sure all that happened?'

Something in his voice made her glance up sharply. 'You know more than I do,' she accused him. She watched the indecision, the reluctance, chase across his features. 'I've been honest with you,' she said. 'I think you owe me the same consideration.'

'That accident,' he said. 'The car crash last August. Your mother drove at us head on. My God, you should have seen her face! It was your father who saved us, but in doing so he killed the both of them.'

'But why?' she whispered. 'She was always a bit – odd – but not really wicked.' She thought that he still held something back. Something so dreadful that he could not bring himself to tell her.

He said. 'I've thought a lot about it. Especially since I got to know you. There has to be a pattern in there somewhere. First of all she buys the Monks' House. Then, you tell me, she hid this diary where you would be sure to find it. So it seems that she wanted you to know exactly who you are and where you came from. Then she comes looking for Lias and me. Hires a private *gavver*, even. When she has us marked out, she invites us to dinner at a certain time and place. Then she aims her sports car at us and tries to kill us.'

'It doesn't make sense, Jango.'

'Perhaps we've only got half the picture.'

She said, 'It's the other half that really scares me. I have this awful feeling that the worst is still to come.'

'We could look for it together,' he said. 'After all, it concerns Lias and me just as much as it concerns you. She was our relative too, remember.'

'We need to find out first what happened next to Maya Heron.'

He said, 'I could help you search the house.'

'I already did that.'

'Then do it again, with me.'

They had travelled in her car to the Quiet Woman pub. The return drive through the mild October night was slow and pleasant. Lias waited for them at the paddock gate. He nodded briefly to Maya and spoke sharply to Jango.

'Early start in the morning. We're going to the wholesalers in Taunton. It's Pack Monday Fair in a couple of days, in case you've forgotten.'

Maya stood between them, caught in the anger of Lias, the resentment of Jango. It seemed wise to walk away. She called goodnight to them across her shoulder. If they answered she did not hear it.

It was two days later, when she had ceased to search the house and barn, when she had given up all hope of ever finding further information on Maya Heron, that her mind went back to the yellow folder of letters, written in Bruenette's hand. This time she looked without flinching at her mother's powerful back-sloping script. The package of letters was held together by faded pink chocolate-box ribbon. The topmost one began 'Dear Geoffrey . . .' She lifted the thin sheaf of letters and saw that immediately beneath them lay other papers, thick yellowed pages, the left-hand edges of which were jagged and uneven, as if they had been hacked by scissors from a book. As with Maya Heron's diary, these sheets were also clipped together in separate sections by the same new and shiny paperclips, but in this case the writing was angular and practised. She reached further into the workbox. Not all of the small leatherbound volumes, she now discovered, were as she had thought, household and farm account books. A quick examination revealed that twelve of them were personal records. She had found Milady's journal! But as with Maya Heron's diary, the hand of Bruenette had been at work, and here were the expected gaps in every volume, rough-cut edges where kitchen scissors had removed the pages Bruenette had presumably considered to be relevant to her own family.

This script was easier to read than that of the first Maya. The paper, although old, had not been exposed to the hazards of weather and life in a Gypsy settlement, the ink was less faded. Her mind grappled hazily with the implications of the find. She began to realise that if the child carried by Maya Heron had in fact been fathered by Guy, then this journal had been written by her own and Jango and Lias's great-great-grandmother.

The topmost sheet was dated November 29th 1890.

Today I found Maya!
Watkins took me in the brougham. We drove for a long time around the lanes that skirt the quarry, for I had been told it was to this new location that the Herons and the Ingrams had moved in the past weeks. I had thought to find Maya living close by to the main camp, but I had forgotten that because of her coming confinement she would now be obliged to remain at some distance from the menfolk.

Even so, I was shocked to observe the wide distance that has been set between my poor dear girl and her family. Watkins and I had searched for at least an hour when at last we spied smoke rising from a fire, and a small brown tent that was barely visible in a deep cleft of the hillside. The best I can say about her state is that it is only marginally better than that of our own livestock on the home farm. She has a fire, and straw to sleep on. Food and water are taken to her daily. The tent is weatherproof – or so she says.

But she is alone. Alone and in a strange and dangerous frame of mind. I fear for her sanity, and the safe delivery of her baby in such conditions.

I prevailed upon Watkins to take me on further, up to the worked-out quarry, although he was very reluctant so to do and remained at my side throughout the visit. We came into the camp as dusk was falling. I had visited these same families when they were resident in Sheepdip Lane. On those occasions I had found them welcoming and pleasant, but now everything was changed. In fact, I believe that had not Maya's father been present, Watkins and I would have been driven out by their fierce dogs, of which they have many! As it was, we walked towards them with not a small amount of trepidation, and I saw them for the first time as a dangerous and threatening band of people. There were some thirty or more souls present in the old quarry workings. Tents had been set up beneath overhangs of stone, and several fires burned. Small children, wreathed in smoke, tended to these fires with handfuls of sticks, while their mothers occupied themselves with frying pans and great kettles and pots which were suspended just above the flames by means of an iron tripod. In the background I could make out the dark bulk of their wagons and the tethered horses.

We paused some yards short of the nearmost tent. The low growling of the dogs made us fearful of proceeding further. But despite my anxiety I could not help but appreciate the uniqueness of the scene. Even as we watched, the menfolk came to squat around the fires, their dark and arrogant faces lifted to the glow, making a picture that would stay with me for ever. Still though we stood, we were at last spotted by a child who pointed us out to his father, and so brought the gaze of the whole company to fall upon us. I thought it prudent to reassure them of our good intent. I called out, 'It is Lady Anne here, from the Monks' House. I wish to speak with Mr Taiso Heron.'

Maya's father came forward. He expressed concern that I was so far from home on such a damp, cold evening. He was polite but unfriendly.

'Your worry would be better spent on your poor daughter,' I soon informed him.

His handsome face changed expression in an instant. 'My daughter is my own business, madam,' he told me.

'She is also mine,' I said. 'For five years I tended her more dearly than if she were my own.'

'I don't deny that,' he said, 'but as you and I both know, some wicked things have come to pass of late in these parts. It would be better, begging your Ladyship's pardon, if there was to be no more contact between our two families.' His words were simple, but there was menace in his voice.

I said, 'I will speak plainly to you, Mr Heron. I want you to persuade your daughter to come back and live with us at the Monks' House. I wish to take care of her – and the coming child.'

Again his face grew dark and threatening. 'Never,' he said. 'My girl has suffered mischief enough already at your hands. When she lived with you, why, her mind was turned against her own kind. Leave her be, my Lady. We take care of our own, in our own way.' He smiled, almost as if by so doing he could reassure me. 'As for the *chavvie*, do you think I would hand over my first grandchild to be raised as a Gorgio?'

'It is my grandchild too,' I reminded him.

'Ah,' he said. 'but we don't know that yet, do we? Not for certain.' He began to speak softly although none of his people was in earshot. 'If the child be fair or dark, why then it will be one of us, and welcome. But if my daughter should birth a red-polled brat, in that case it will be one of yours, my Lady, and you will be welcome to it!'

'Then you will not help me, Mr Heron?'

'You are beyond help,' he told me. 'You and your family. Did you not hear about the curse that was laid upon you by my poor son-in-law as he lay dying?'

'No,' I said, 'and how, may I ask, did you come to know about it?'

'From your own servant, madam. The gardening mush who stood by and did nothing while your son stuck the knife in Chesi's neck.'

I said to Taiso Heron, 'I am a Christian woman. I do not believe in curses.'

'Oh, you will, my Lady. If the coming child has red hair then you will surely believe upon it.'

She began to remove the paperclip from the first batch of pages, intending to read further, but she could not continue. The final paragraph still held her attention. So Maya and Guy had been twice cursed by Chesi Ingram. There was a time when she would have dismissed as pitiful such superstitious claptrap. Now she was unsure. Sometimes lately she surprised herself. She wondered how much of her present doubt was self-delusion and how much genuine conviction. The woman who had come a year ago to attend her parents' funeral had been confident, ambitious, level-headed. But since living in the Monks' House she had lost her certainties. The layers of her former life were stripped away, so that now she was able to admit that anything was possible.

She had also learned how to be alone, to be thoughtful; how it felt to desire a man, although she suspected that man to be violent and dangerous.

But there was still confusion.

She went into the kitchen. A note had been slipped underneath the door. 'Pack Monday Fair tomorrow,' Jango had written. 'Why don't you come over?

The Winnebago had left for Sherborne on the previous evening. The sight of the empty paddock on that October morning had its usual unsettling effect. Dressed in jeans, and a thick sweater and the quilted waistcoat, Maya pointed the car towards Sherborne and the fair.

The morning was cool, the skies grey and overcast. She had risen at six; by seven o'clock she was driving out past Hunger Hill and Sheepdip Lane. She thought about Chesi Ingram who, one hundred years ago, had gone out to fetch his horses from this hill and had met death instead. Her sense of living in two worlds at once was growing stronger. Perhaps the day would come when she could no longer distinguish between them. Lady Anne, and Guy and Maya, were as real to her as Alice and Jango and Lias.

She parked her car on the outskirts of Sherborne and walked slowly down to where heavy vans and trailers edged cautiously through the narrowness of medieval Cheap Street. By nine o'clock most of the stalls were set up and trading with early shoppers. The golden stone of the ancient buildings made a curious backdrop for the more garish of the stalls which displayed cheap plastic toys, fluorescent jackets, candyfloss and hot dogs. The fair was vast, it extended through the main streets of the town and would continue trading until late that evening. She took notice of the traders, most of them young and enthusiastic. Jango and Lias were not pitched in Cheap Street; she would find them later in the day.

She discovered a cafe, from the upper windows of which it was possible to view the street. The coffee was hot and strong; she pushed open the casement and tried to imagine the scene as it must have been a hundred years ago. There would have been the Gypsies trading their horses; their women telling fortunes and hawking their lace and ribbons. Naphtha flares would have illuminated the stalls. There would have been the cheap-jacks and thimble-riggers, the knife-throwers and the boxing booths. The goods on offer would have been made of wool and cotton; the toys carved from wood. Mr Parsons had told her that in his grandfather's time a sheep sale had been held on this day in Hound Street. But the Pack Monday Fair, he said, dated back to the twelfth century.

Down in the street the smaller stalls were still being set up. She began to watch, idly at first and then with growing interest, the lady with the handbags. She was blonde, slim, attractive, and probably mature underneath the heavy make-up. Dressed in a severe black jacket and trousers, heavy gold chains hung about her neck; she was not wearing the usual traders' money belt but a gold lamé bag on a chain across her shoulder. A lady of considerable style!

Her stall was tiny; the usual bare boards were laid across trestles and compressed into a corner. From a bin liner she took several lengths of heavy black silk and strips of gold and silver lamé. From another bag came a number of expandable boxes. The boxes were set up heightways on the stall in diminishing sizes; over them was draped the lenghts of lamé and black silk. From other bin liners came the handbags, large and small; black leather embossed with gold and silver motifs, tiny purses suspended on long cords and embroidered with diamanté. There was a special display of gold and silver evening bags.

Even before the stall was properly arranged for business, customers began to gather. The goods were of a quality and sophistication rarely seen in a country market. Maya went down into the street. Seen close to, the black, gold and silver stall was even more attractive. It now also held a small display of fashion watches. To a group of young girls the stallholder was saying, 'Cartier, my darlings! On my life, genuine Cartier!' Her husky voice was the product of a lifetime's habit of cigarettes and whisky. The village girls, intrigued by the woman's unusual appearance, and never having heard of Cartier watches, departed giggling.

The stallholder turned to Maya. 'Would you believe these people, darling! I just sold a Gucci bag to a woman, bronze quilted silk it was, exquisite, and do you know what she did? She opened it up and dumped onions and carrots in it! Seventeen quid she paid me for it. I ask you, sweetheart! Like I said to her, you could have bought a bloody plastic carrier for two pee.'

Maya said, 'You've come quite a distance, I imagine.'

'Pimlico. Left home at four this morning. Rotten journey. Then when I get here I find they've given me this God-awful pitch.'

'Your display looks wonderful.'

'Oh, I'm ashamed of it, darling. You should just see it when I'm firing on all cylinders. But the heart's gone out of me this morning. Nothing but bloody hassles. I've parked the car in the front bit of that old abbey.' She smiled. 'Probably pinched the parking spot of some bishop or other.' She pulled coins from her pocket. 'I'm that thirsty I'm spitting feathers. You wouldn't fetch me a Coke, would you, sweetheart?'

Maya bought a can of Coke from a shop in an adjoining street. She returned to the stall to find the woman exchanging her plain black jacket for an amazing blouson of diamanté-studded gold silk. She twirled and chuckled. 'Showtime! This'll bring in the punters, sweetheart, you'll see.'

Maya handed her the can of Coke. As she began to walk away, she saw the woman grab the sleeve of a very young policeman. 'I've left my car by the bishop's front door,' she said. 'What would you reckon my chances are of copping a ticket?'

The Gypsy women were recognisable by their dark, braided hair and the indefinable style with which they wore their clothes, so that the most ordinary garments took on a raffish, exotic look. Two were carrying baskets which held foil-wrapped bunches of white heather. Maya followed them at a distance. In the street that led down to the abbey the women disappeared, each into a small blue trailer. Ranged alongside each caravan were noticeboards which informed the customer that here was 'A TRUE ENGLISH ROMANY GYPSY. I AM ABLE TO ASSIST YOU IN YOUR TROUBLES. I HAVE THE TRUE GIFT OF SEEING PASSED DOWN THROUGH SEVERAL GENERATIONS. COME IN AND SPEAK TO SINAMINTA IF YOU WANT TO KNOW YOUR FUTURE'.

Maya walked away, fascinated but fearful. She returned five minutes later and tapped on the trailer door. The door was opened by a tall and slender woman. Her black hair fell in ringlets to her shoulders, her skin was a warm-tinted shade of olive and her eyes were a keen slate-grey.

She welcomed Maya in. 'Have you had your fortune told before, lady?'

'No,' said Maya, 'never.'

The woman was dignified. She applied financial pressure as if conferring a favour. 'Five pounds for one hand. Ten pounds for two hands. Twenty for the crystal ball.'

Maya opted for two hands, a ten pound note was handed over, and she was invited to sit down. The furnishings of the trailer were luxurious. The seating was upholstered in a blue brocade which was protected by covers of thick clear plastic. The window blinds were a deeper shade of blue ruched silk, and the carpeting was dark blue.

There was no hint of magic in the set-up, and yet the woman was impressive. She spoke with the soft accent of the County Kerry Irish.

'So you've come then? I knew you would, sooner or later.'

'You know me?'

'O'course I know you! Because I don't live with my dear lawful husband that don't mean that I'm in the dark about what the bastard gets up to. I knew that you'd be bound to come to me: they all do in the end. You're a woman, see. Instinct have brought you knocking on my door. Nothing ever gets past Sinaminta. lady. Specially where Lias is concerned.' She smiled and took Maya's right hand, palm upwards. 'Yous'll want to know all about him. Well, o'course you do. Any woman fancies a fellah, she wants to find out his whole life story. And who better to tell her than the poor bitch what is married to him.'

Maya said, 'And what makes you think I fancy him?'

The grey eyes seemed to look into her soul. 'Oh, you hates him too.' Sinaminta leaned forward, and said abruptly, 'Well, come on, tell the God's truth now, lady. Tell me how you hates that dear, dear man.' She laughed, a soft chuckling sound deep in her throat. 'I'll tell you all of it for your ten pounds. A swine is my Lias. Cruel and vicious, like Despair, his father. Stay with him long enough, lady, and he'll leave his brand mark on yez.' She pushed back the sleeves of her yellow sweater and Maya saw the long red puckered scars that ran from wrist to elbow and beyond. Sinaminta nodded at Maya's shocked expression. 'He's a liar, too. What's he told you? Some fanciful tale that you and him are cousins?' She looked briefly into Maya's palm. 'He's not your cousin, lady. Oh dear me, no! What he really is to you is not for me to tell. But believe me, he is *not your cousin*. You want my advice, you keep away from Lias Heron. He's done murder in his time. lady. It's in his blood, see. Nice girl like you, it's a wicked shame, ah, to be sure it is.'

Maya stood, she took a step towards the door but Sinaminta gripped her elbow. 'Something else about you, lady. I can feel it, see. You've got the gift. I'm right, eh?'

Maya looked at her and a kind of recognition passed between them. 'Thank you,' she said drily, 'for warning me off Lias. It was worth all of the ten pounds.'

Sinaminta said, 'Ah, but I make it my business to keep track of Lias's women.'

'I'm not his woman.'

'But you do keep chasing after the dear man. You're here today looking for him, aren't you?'

As Maya stepped down from the trailer she was still conscious of the slate-grey gaze. She marvelled at Sinaminta's unique ability to stir up fear and doubt and charge highly for the service. She tried to analyse the woman's quality. It was not perception. Perception required a certain sophistication, and Sinaminta was uncomplicated. Or was she? There was a knowingness about her, as if she had access to channels of information not open to less gifted mortals.

Maya walked out of the fair and back to her parked car. The scent of sandalwood was strong on the mild, still air. The potpourri stall must be close by but she no longer had the impulse or the energy to find it.

She drove with care, her mind deliberately blank. As she turned into the drive, the grey cloud lifted to reveal a crimson sunset which lit up the windows of the Monks' House as if a fire raged within its walls. She brought sticks and paper and a basket full of logs, and built a blaze in the drawing-room fireplace. There was no question of her sleeping that night.

The mistake had been to visit Sinaminta. The confrontation had been intended as a statement to herself that Lias was no longer of significance in her life. Now she must pay the price; for in spite of her scepticism towards fortune-tellers, the woman and her words had slipped sideways into her head and would not be dislodged. Sinaminta had joined the parade of ghosts that came nightly to haunt her. At first she had not felt frightened by them. They were no more than the whisper of a presence on the air, shadows on the edge of vision. Fear had come later, when she could no longer control the images that filled her mind; when the ghost of Chesi Ingram and his string of horses stumbled slowly through her dreams.

She went out of the house wearing only a towelling robe and sandals. The night was cold, the first frost of winter lay white across the paddock grass, but she hardly noticed. From the gate she could see the lit windows of the Winnebago. She watched for a long time, but only a single shadow fell across the drawn blinds. By the outline she was sure that it was Jango in the camper. When the shadow ceased to move she walked to his door and tapped upon it.

He opened up and she stepped in. He did not ask the reason for her visit, but drew her inside as if she was expected. The camper felt overheated; a lamp gave a diffused light. There was a tangle of coloured blankets on the bunk bed; he had knotted a towel, for decency's sake, round his middle. A part of her mind took in the masculine, squared-away tidiness of the limited space even while her hands were at his waist, loosening the towel. He released the belt of her robe and slid the garment from her shoulders. They approached each other slowly. They lay down together in the tumbled blankets and touched one another like people who could hardly believe what was happening to them. She whispered. 'Do you believe that the dead can influence the living?'

'Yes,' he said, 'but it makes no matter. You and I are alive *now*.'

She had not recognised the latent passion in him, had believed him to be shy all the way through. Well, sometimes a woman was mistaken in a man. Jango was skilled in all the ways of love, inventive, amazing her with a practised tenderness, and the curious love-words that he murmured in the old language of his people.

They slept towards dawn and woke only minutes later to see Lias staring down upon them. A jerk of his thumb and the one word 'Out!' had her reaching for her robe and through the door.

Jango

*H*e had thought at first that Lias meant to kill him. Murder had looked out of his brother's eyes, a swift gleam, instantly hooded, but it had been there. Even now, with Lias gone and the camper quiet, Jango felt uneasy. He felt as he had when a small child, told that he had done something wrong but not understanding what his fault was.

All through that long night he and Maya had loved one another. For him it was as if she was his first and only. She cancelled out all others. He forgot that she was a *chovihani*, that she was dangerous to love. He knew her now in ways he would never know, or want to know, any other woman. She had him sealed and packaged, made exclusive only unto her. He remembered with shame how he had wakened to find Lias standing over him and Maya already running out of the door. Humiliation had seen him speechless; he sat on the edge of the bunk bed, head in hands, while Lias poured words of hate into his ears. To his mind at that moment, dazed with loving and exhaustion, the words had made no sense. Now he began to think about them.

He rose and belted on a dressing gown. He shook the kettle, and finding water in it he lit the burner and spooned coffee into a mug. He took the coffee and a blanket and sat on the camper steps. The paddock grass was spiked with hoarfrost, a red sun coming up behind the Monks' House. He remembered their first days in the paddock. He had passed hours just looking at the house, had been like a child curious and greedy, staring in at a toyshop window. He had made guesses. How many rooms in the house? What kind of furnishings? What colours? What did she do all day in that vast place? When she had asked him into the kitchen he had been disappointed. He was not sure what level of luxury he had expected. What he saw was the same old-fashioned open-fired stove and stripped pine furniture as in his Derbyshire farmhouse.

Lias had said, 'You've been sniffing around her from the first minute that you saw her. I told you then that she was not for you. You didn't listen, did you? World is full of bloody women and you had to go for the one who is bound to destroy you.'

'Destroy me? Why destroy me?'

'She's a blood relative. You know that. You know no good can come of it.'

'A cousin. Nothing wrong in marrying a cousin. Happens all the time. You know it does.'

'Not *this* cousin. Our father and her mother were brother and sister. There's bad blood in that line of the family.' Lias had paused then, had said with unusual honesty, 'Look at me if you don't believe it. I'm a wicked sod. I try not to be, but it always seems to come out wrong.'

He had felt sorry for Lias in that moment. What he said was true. His temperament had ruined his life. His fists had taken him to prison. Jango said, 'I'm not like you. If there's bad blood then I seem to have escaped it.'

Lias looked away then, did not answer. He sat, almost collapsed, on to the facing bunk and Jango saw the sudden greyness of his brother's skin, his sick eyes. For a moment it seemed as if Lias was about to tell him something. But the moment passed.

Jango said, 'You know what your trouble is, don't you? You want her for yourself. You tried it on with her, didn't you, and she sent you packing?'

'Did she say so?'

'She didn't have to. If you can read me, *pralo*, then I can also read you. I've seen you before when there's a woman in your sights. I know how you are at such times. You're crazy for her – and she chose me.'

It was then that Lias really lost it. He slipped back into the old language, used words that Jango only half understood. He pounded the bunk with his clenched fists, then he grabbed a binliner and stuffed it full of boots and garments. He pulled a fistful of banknotes from his money belt and flung them down on the bunk. 'You're on your own in future,' he said. 'God help you!'

Jango heard him telephoning their cousin Riley who was still in Weymouth, heard him asking for a lift to Sherborne. 'You planning to go back to Sinaminta?'

Lias stared at him then as if they were strangers. 'None of your business,' he said. 'You and I are finished.'

Jango's thoughts went back to Maya and the house. In his mind the two were indivisible. It had been on a still night when there was no moon that she had invited him into the drawing room and he had seen the portrait of the Gypsy girl. He had sat on an antique chair and saw by lamplight the muted textures and colours of the lovely room. He had seen this kind of set-up only in books and on television. Now he was actually inside the toyshop. But not allowed to touch. The touching had come later, delighting and amazing him. Just when he had decided it was Lias that she wanted.

It was Star who saved their embarrassment. Maya came to the camper carrying the puppy; they joked uneasily about his wandering habits, the way he scrounged two breakfasts. She sat down on the grey quilted leather from which the coloured blankets of the previous night had been folded away. She studied the layout of the Winnebago, loving the leather upholstery, intrigued by the many cupboards, the galley with its stove and sink unit, the bathroom which held shower and toilet. She admired the luxury of the fittings. Custom-made, he told her, according to Lias's specifications. The mention of his brother's name sent them skidding into silence.

She said, 'Was it very bad?'

'The worst ever.'

'I'm so sorry. I should never have come here.'

'It's as much my place as his.'

She said, 'But that's not the problem, is it?'

'No,' he said. 'He objects to the fact that we are first cousins. He says that your mother and my father were brother and sister. That there's bad blood in both of us.'

'How does he know that? He never met my parents.'

Jango said, 'Good point. I'm beginning to think there's a lot Lias knows but never tells.' He suspected from the way she would not meet his gaze that Maya also kept her secrets.

She said, 'Do you think he'll come back?'

'I don't know. This is the first time we've quarrelled, really quarrelled. I think he may have gone back to Sinaminta. He's visited her lately.'

'I met her at the fair. She told my fortune – or that's what she pretended. Her main intention was to warn me about Lias.'

'Warn you off him, you mean. The woman still wants him, always did, always will. Jealousy is her problem and, to be fair, he always gave her plenty of provocation.'

'She showed me her scarred arms. How could he do that to a woman?'

'He didn't. She worked one time in a circus. Got too confident with the big cats. What you saw were claw marks. She tells everybody that Lias caused them. Lias is rough with women, but he's no sadist.'

'What are we going to do?' She spoke so softly that he strained to hear her. He saw love in her face and he wanted to go to her, to hold her.

But he stayed in his place. He needed to know for certain that her trust in him was total.

He said, 'That diary you told me about. I would really like to read it.'

'Why yes,' she said. 'Of course. Why not?' Her ready acquiescence did not altogether mask her faint reluctance. She seemed to guess his thoughts, for she added swiftly, 'By the way, I found Lady Anne's journal.'

'I hoped we might have searched for it together.'

'I came across it accidentally.'

He thought it might be almost true. Concealment, lies and half-truths had become so habitual to her that she hardly noticed.

The diary of Maya Heron, which she had studied in fear and over many months, was read by him in a single evening. It was late when she came to the Winnebago. Her gaze went at once to the pale-blue folder lying open on the bunk. She said, 'So what do you think?'

'Hard to find the words. Terrifying? Wonderful? If Maya Heron really was our great-grandmother, and if the child was Guy's, then ...' He waved a hand towards the Monks' House.

'Exactly,' she said. 'It's as much your inheritance and Lias's as it is mine. I'd already worked that out for myself.'

He said, 'That's not what I meant. What would Lias and I do with that great pile of stone?'

'It's worth a great deal of money.'

'We don't need that sort of money.'

'What do you need, Jango?'

He held her hands as if the touching could aid communication. He looked towards the folder. 'I need to know more. I need to find out about Despair. There's violence in that writing, and a lot of hatred. What an inheritance. No wonder Lias is the way he is. No wonder my father killed my mother.'

'And my mother tried to kill you and Lias.' Her face was very pale, her fingers cold.

'And Despair and Bruenette were brother and sister.'

'We still have to read Lady Anne's journal.'

He turned to a locker and began to pull out the coloured blankets. 'Tomorrow,' he said.

Maya

She woke early to the sounds of birds. Even in this dark November, in gales and drenching rain, there was still a pre-dawn stirring among the trees and hedges, small twittering sounds that reached her in the camper, which would have been inaudible within the house. She lay, propped on the bright square patchwork cushions which served Jango as pillows, and watched him as he slept. He had told her once that he could not live alone, that a lifetime's habit of communal living had left him ill-equipped for solitude. She had seen how he and Lias, although no longer attached to the main group of their family, kept up a constant habit of visiting and contact with cousins, aunts and uncles. In the past two weeks she had learned many things about him. How he liked to wake slowly, coming gradually back into himself, his life.

It was she who was expected to make the early morning tea, and she loved the novelty of it, the few steps that took her to the bright and shining galley, and back again to the shared bed, cosy with the lamp lit and the heaters purring.

The close confinement of the trailer, which she would once have found claustrophobic, was now a comfort and a reassurance. From the windows of the Winnebago she watched the Monks' House emerge through a misty dawn. She viewed the house as she had never seen it as it must appear to Jango, a cold and inhospitable pile of masonry and timber, a container for valuable furniture and unhappy people. She began to see how a limited space could become a whole world, holding all she could desire or need.

How simple would it be to walk away from all that held her in this place? To travel light would be to follow Jango; to live his life; to be like Maya Heron and her people.

She thought about love. Some people, the lucky ones, were programmed for it from conception. Longed for and cherished while as yet unborn.

She wondered what Bruenette, who had never given her love, had wanted from her daughter when she sent the birthday roses? What vision of revenge, what dream of retribution had been in her mother's mind when she seeded the Monks' House with the written records of her family's crimes and passions. Maya tried to push Bruenette from her thoughts, but the painful memories of childhood were tangled up in the recent images of Lias and Rowsheen. The physical likeness between the three of them was striking. The threat was in their linked inheritance of arrogance, their piercing looks of sinister directness; their tendencies to violence, to murder. She put a hand out to touch Jango and saw that he was awake and watching her, saw again how unlike he was to his brother, to those other long dead Herons.

She said, 'You once told me that you resemble your mother.'

He shrugged. 'So they say, but how would I know?' There was something needy in his face, a naked longing that made them equal.

She said, 'You're missing Lias, aren't you?'

'I would rather not have quarrelled with him.'

'My fault,' she said.

'No. Not your fault. It was bound to happen some time. Things were awkward between us all last winter.' She thought he might have explained further, but he did not. She made a pot of coffee and a plate of buttered toast, and took the tray back to the bed.

'Lias,' she said. 'I think you're better off without him.'

'No. That's not true, never could be.' His fingers curled round the coffee mug. 'Listen,' he said, 'I'll tell you about Lias and me. Everything good in my young life came from him. He was mother and father to me. I would have died without him.'

She waited, wanting to know more but unable to ask. She rarely shared her thoughts, her deepest anxieties, with anybody.

He said, 'Lias told me once how it was when I was born. Seems they were a long way from a town and my mother was in a bad state. Should have been in hospital. Nobody in the *tan* appears to have bothered much about her. Not even the women. She was only a kid, seventeen or so. I was born Romany fashion, on the straw, in a bender. Lias said she bled to death, slowly. Took four days for her to die. Towards the end they got a doctor to her. But it was too late. Our Aunt Lena had just given birth to Lija, so she took me and fed me. But apart from that I was Lias's problem. Lias told me once exactly how it was. After my mother died, Despair turned his face away, couldn't bear to look at me. He wrapped me in my mother's woollen cardigan and handed me to Lias. Told him to take me to a Gorgio house and leave me on the doorstep.' Jango's voice was bitter. 'As if I was nothing to do with him. As if I was not his own son.

'Lias was barely ten years old and lonely. He could just about remember his own mother dying. He made up his mind that he would try to keep me, like you would a stray puppy or a kitten. It was summertime, warm and dry. He hid me, sometimes in the empty food box under the wagon or, when he could persuade them, with the other women in the *tan* for a few hours. He tried to talk our grandmother into taking me, but she wouldn't. They were all mortally afraid of Despair. It still surprises me that Aunt Lena dared to continue to feed me. I reckon I must have been weaned pretty early as it was.' He smiled. 'Of course, once I began to move around, the game was really up. One extra tiny baby crying in the *tan* was never noticed, but a fair-haired, fair-skinned, blue-eyed toddler? Poor Lias. He had to own up to Despair, and that meant trouble. But by this time the other women, as well as Aunt Lena and Grandmother, had taken quite a fancy to me. Despair could see how he would lose face among them if he tried again to kick me out. So I stayed. Just as long as I was Lias's responsibility and not my father's. It was not till I was in my teens that Despair began to take notice of me. I was good with the horses, see, could ride anything, break any wild *gry* that I sat on. He liked that. Towards the end of his life he did some strange things. He bought the Derbyshire plot and put it in my name. Lias agrees that half of it is his, just to make me feel easier about it. But he would never live there permanently, no matter what. It was as if my father was trying to make up to me for something lost.' He paused. 'Like your mother leaving you the Monks House.'

She said, 'I've been thinking about that. Only hatred of me could have made her will me the house and then put those diaries where I was bound to find them.'

He said, 'All right, so she planned to upset you. Why not turn her malice back upon her? People can only really hurt you if you let them. She might even have thought she was doing you a favour, showing you your roots.'

'The best place for roots is safely buried six feet under.'

He laughed and put his arms round her. The rain poured down the windows, a gust of wind rocked the Winnebago. He said, 'Let's stay in bed today. Let's read the journal. See what Lady Anne has to say about the Heron family.'

They sat, cross-legged among the blankets, the yellowed pages spread around them. Maya passed the entry for December 1st 1890 across to Jango. He noticed her sudden pallor, her reluctance to begin the reading. He said, 'What is it?'

Her shoulders moved as if she carried something too heavy to be borne. 'I've already glanced at that first entry. You'll find Lady

Anne's account of what took place quite different to that of Maya Heron.'

'Well, that's not surprising, is it? She was an educated woman, and much older.'

She picked up the entry for December 28th 1890 and removed the paperclip. She said, 'If I had to do this on my own, if I wasn't here with you, I don't believe I could go on reading any of this. In fact, I still have the feeling that it would be better if we burned it – now.'

He shuffled the papers together and set his hand upon them. 'Do as you please,' he told her. 'Burn them if you want to. But not until after you and I have read them.'

December 1st 1890

My husband went this day to visit Guy in Shepton Mallett gaol. He reports that our son is greatly demoralised and cast down, he has already confessed to the stabbing of Chesi Heron and is resigned to the inevitable consequences. It is only now that I tell my husband that Maya Heron has also confessed to me that she is guilty of the same murder. That she took it upon herself to extinguish what life was left in her husband when she found him dying, so that the poor man should not survive long enough to implicate Guy in any way. My husband thinks long and hard about this. He says that such a moot point as to which of them is truly guilty will be a lawyer's delight. Such a trial could drag on indefinitely and result in the both of them being hanged. Or neither.

My reaction is instinctive. I can see that Henry is inclined to turn Maya in to the constable. I tell him I will not permit her to be taken. She is about to give birth to our grandchild. Do you wish to be responsible for the death of *three* human souls? I ask him. Henry is a good man, but Solomon he is not! He says that he will talk to the lawyer; that when I have seen the abominable conditions in which our boy now languishes, I may feel less inclined to spare the Gypsy girl who has caused us so much grief. I think about Maya, alone on her bed of straw, in a frail tent on that bleak hillside, all her brave and shining spirit dimmed to nothing, and I remember the accident that brought her into our lives and hearts.

Memory, I now find, is strange and selective. I was present in the stables when the accident happened. The dog which caused the stallion to rear up was Patch, my own pet. I see again the ragged child dart forward and throw herself across her father's body to protect him from the hooves. I recall how, many days later, when the injuries to her head were somewhat settled, I took warm water in a bowl and gently washed her blood-caked hair. I spread the long damp tresses across the pillow, and as the hair dried I saw, for the first time, the beauty of it. Thick and silky; it was the colour of buttermilk, with a hint of silver. Together with her small, triangular face, the full red lips and wide-spaced yellow eyes, the child was not pretty; oh, but she had that fey and haunting quality that later on would turn to beauty, such a lovliness that draws the eye and charms the soul!

Her injuries were severe but her courage was remarkable. She was like a small, fierce wildcat, rejecting every comfort and solace that we offered. I watched her, but secretly, as she regained sufficient movement in her legs to leave the nursery and explore the house. I saw her fascination with the quality and quantity of our possessions. She would touch a finger to delicate glass and decorated china, and then count up on her fingers the number of our plates and cups and saucers. I heard her say in tones of disbelief to Cook, 'They've got *seven* teapots!' For a year at least she refused to so much as hold a knife and fork, and ate defiantly with her fingers. She burned each pair of shoes we gave her, she spat upon the floor; and the more disruptive she became, the more I loved her. When she saw that I was not to be shocked, why then she loved me too.

It was the power of her intelligence which first brought her to my husband's notice. She stole paper from his study, and then lied as convincingly as any adult to excuse her little crime. But he was not deceived. Poor man! It was hard for him to accept that this wild and naughty Gypsy child was superior in intellect to his own children.

He is as yet unaware of my intention to bring Maya back to the Monks' House. But, once she is installed with her baby in the old nursery, I trust that he will come round. After all, what have we two left in life but the hope of this promised grandchild? Our own children have proved to be a bitter disappointment. Our only daughter Lavinia has expressed her intention of remaining in Paris when her time at finishing school is expired.

As for our son, I cannot bear to think about his future prospects. His case is to be heard at the next sitting of the Assize Court. It comforts me greatly that he has begged his father to make sure of Maya's safety. I had not expected so much decency from him.

December 28th 1890

It has been a sad and bitter Christmas. Lavinia had promised to spend a few weeks with us but she did not come. Henry is closeted for hours with the lawyer and other gentlemen who are strangers to me, and to whom I am not, it seems, ever to be introduced.

The subject of their talk is Guy. There are clearly some plans afoot, but I am not to be privy to them. So I will turn my thoughts and energies to Maya, since it seems that no one else will.

When I distributed our usual Christmas parcels among former and present employees, I took the opportunity to make veiled inquiries about the Heron family, but learned little of consequence. There were the usual exaggerated tales of ghosts seen in the Hollow. The blood of Chesi Heron is said still to mark a certain rock formation there, in spite of heavy rain. As to Maya, she is said by the villagers to have borne variously a dead child, a child hideously deformed, and a child with skin so black it must in origin be Negroid or born of the Devil. She is said to be dead; living, but in the poor house; incarcerated with her child in the Shepton Mallett House of Correction.

The blizzard has raged for many days, pinning me close to the house. The resultant snowdrifts have made a search for my poor girl impossible. But Watkins says a thaw is imminent.

February 2nd 1891

Henry has finally seen fit to apprise me of our son's position. It would seem that after much deliberation, Henry and his visitors have concluded that Guy will not receive a fair hearing in this County of Dorset, his father being wealthy and of high position, and Guy himself ill-thought of hereabouts. I am not impressed by these arguments, but I am a mere woman. The upshot of it all is that Guy is to be transferred to the prison in Exeter, where it is assumed he will be given a fairer hearing. Henry does not look me in the eye when imparting this curious decision. When I dare to demur, he says with some heat that I blamed him years ago when he was strict with Guy and thrashed him. Now he is doing his best for the boy but still I argue with him!

Henry leaves the house in high dudgeon, and without farewell. I summon Watkins and inquire as to the state of the lanes around Hunger Hill and the old quarry.

'Barely passable, ma'am,' he says. But seeing my distress, and knowing the reason for it, he adds, 'But we can try, if your Ladyship is so minded.'

We drove out shortly after noon, taking the small brougham and our steadiest horse. The thaw had come suddenly, but all the lying water is on lower ground. Snow still lies on the hills and around the quarry, but we took a path much used by cattle and horse-drawn carts and so proceeded.

We achieved the old quarry workings without too much difficulty but found only a few children present who could not or would not answer my questions.

I said to Watkins that we must go higher into the hills, to the place where we had last seen Maya. I had dressed on this occasion for that precise purpose, wearing many petticoats and some high riding boots once worn by Lavinia. But still the cold and damp seemed to penetrate my bones. It was only the thought of Maya and a newborn infant living outdoors in such conditions that spurred me on to further searching.

When we reached the cleft in the hillside we found the bender tent gone. All that remained was the ring of stones that had contained the fire, and a heap of grey ash.

I found it difficult to hold back tears.

February 10th 1891

My son is to be moved to Exeter within the week. Henry prevails upon me to visit Guy in Shepton Mallett. The great grey prison stands close against the church, although this proximity to Heavenly Things does not seem to have engendered mercy in the hearts of the gaolers. Rather the reverse being the case. In all my life I shall never forget the coldness of that awful place, the stench, and the unnatural absence of the sound of human voices. Prisoners are not even allowed the small dispensation of normal discourse, in addition to all their other most horrible privations.

I found my son much changed. He is thin to the point of emaciation, his head shaved close to the bone, while a great red beard has grown out to obliterate his features and mark the pallor of his skin. He wears the rough grey uniform issued to convicts, and truth to tell I would not have known him.

Our meeting was painful. There was nothing we could say to one another that would diminish our sorrow. He inquired after Maya. Since Henry stood close by, I was obliged to confess in my husband's presence that I had sought my girl and failed to find her. She is also on my mind night and day, but think it wiser not to say so.

Guy's case is to be heard down at the Exeter Assizes within three weeks. Henry tells him that he has personally arranged that Guy's living conditions will be somewhat less harsh in the larger prison. I can only hope that my husband knows what he is about when meddling in these matters. I have a deep suspicion that Henry is up to something!

It is when we are leaving that we meet a line of women, each of whom, we are told by the turnkey, have that very day been apprehended in the commission of a crime. These poor souls are fainting and unsteady from hunger and exhaustion. We stand aside to let them pass, and so great is my anger at their plight that I can scarce contain it. At the end of the line comes a tall, thin figure, with a blanket pinned about her hips which almost certainly contains a baby. At first sight I do not recognise her. Her hair is dark and matted to her head with filth. Her face and limbs are blue with bruises, and yet still she moves with that loose-limbed ease of a woman used to walking great distances over rough terrain. As her gaze swivels sideways to meet mine I recognise those high cheekbones, the slantwise set of those yellow eyes, their fire and passion which no prison can extinguish.

'Maya!' I cry out, and move towards her. But the turnkey leaps between us, and she is gone.

I insist upon speech with the Governor and will not be denied. I demand from him the reason for the incarceration of Maya Heron. The answer is vagrancy, found wandering with her newborn child and no means of subsistence or of paying the court's fine of a guinea.

'She is bruised. You have beaten her,' I say.

'No,' says he, 'it is the other women. They say she is a witch.'

I look to Henry and he at once slaps down two sovereigns. We are permitted to take her straightaway with us.

We wrap her in a travelling rug and settle her in the carriage, and in all this time I have not so much as glimpsed the child, but considering the condition of Maya I deem it wiser to be patient. She flinches at my slightest touch and will not look me in the eyes. She cowers in a corner of the brougham. The drive home in the darkness seems unending. Maya will not speak a single word. Cook and Susan run out to meet us.

'It is Maya and her baby,' I tell them. 'We need hot water and nourishment, and the nursery made ready.'

They rush to do my bidding, and together we divest my poor girl of her stinking rags and bring her to the hip bath before the kitchen fire. I myself unpin the blanket and lift out the baby. I am back at once these twenty years! It is Guy, but female, delicate and pretty in spite of the filth and lice upon her tiny body. While Cook and Susan minister to Maya, I lower the infant into the first warm soapy water her small form has ever known. As the grime comes away from her hair and skin, I see how truly beautiful she is. Rose-petal complexion, great blue eyes, and a riot of red curls upon her head.

'Oh thank you, Mr Heron,' I whisper to her. 'Oh thank you, Taiso! We most certainly have here a red-polled brat and she is not one of yours but is *very* welcome to us!'

Susan runs to the attics and returns with a box full of baby clothes that were my own children's! She sets them to air across the brass rail of the fireguard. When the baby is dressed all in white and placed in a basket, she looks a perfect picture!

My heart is so full I cannot speak.

Meanwhile, poor Maya is not so easily improved. It takes three changes of water before Cook and I are satisfied that her hair and body are clean and free of vermin. I bring her one of my own warm nightgowns, slippers and a thick robe. Cook sits her at the table and sets before her a thick and nourishing soup. It seems at first that Maya will not eat, but Cook says, 'Come on now, maid! If you don't eat up proper, you'll never manage to feed that baby.'

So Maya ate, and all but fell to sleep across the kitchen table. As we laid her in her old nursery bed, the child at her breast, I said, 'The baby's name, Maya. What is it?'

She opened her eyes and said the one word, 'KERELINDA.' It was the first and only word that was to come from Maya over several days.

March 5th 1891

We have a child in the house again, and oh, the wonder of it! There is that special baby fragrance on the air that is like no other. I believe she is more than two months old, but would pass for two weeks, so malnourished is she. But with her mother's improved health the infant starts slowly to grow. She rarely cries but watches us from wide-open eyes. It is as if her terrible introduction to the world has silenced her in some way. I wait for, would welcome even, a normal lusty scream! But she stays silent.

The silence of Maya is even more distressing. She who prattled endlessly in childhood has been utterly mute these past three weeks. The questions crowd upon my lips but I dare not utter. I recall again that time when she first lay in this nursery. On that occasion it was her body which was damaged; now it is her very soul and mind that seem all but destroyed. Her animation is solely for the child. She eats, but only to secure a sufficient quantity and quality of breast milk. She bathes because Susan leads her by the hand to the warmed water in the hip bath. She sits for hours in the old white rocker beside the nursery window, the child in her arms: and who knows what awful memories, what painful thoughts go through her head. There is nothing in this world that I would not do to help her. But the doctor says that she is in a state of fugue, and will only emerge from it in her own good time.

Meanwhile, I have my darling, my exquisite little Kerelinda, here at last beneath my roof; and I will never let her go.

March 20th 1891

We come to Exeter. Our hotel is close beside the Assize Court. A great crowd had gathered to see Guy's arrival in what is called a Black Maria. He is brought instead in an ordinary carriage to avoid a disturbance in the streets. Henry points out that if this is the state of affairs in Exeter, where Guy is hardly known, how much worse would it all have been in Shepton Mallett.

'It is our name,' says Henry, 'and our position in the world that is causing so much scandal in the daily papers.'

Our solicitor agrees. 'After all,' he says, 'the dead man was nothing but a vagrant and a rascal. A Gypsy horse thief.'

I say, but quietly. 'He was still a fellow human. He had the same right to his life as you and I, and you did not know him for a thief.'

The trial lasts but a day. Against the lawyers' advice, Guy offers no defence.

The jury is absent for twenty minutes. The judge puts on his black cap. I hear those awful words. 'And you will be taken from this place – to a place of execution – you will be hanged by the neck – until you are dead.'

I see Guy's face. There is relief upon his features at the sentence, and then I know what has been his purpose from the outset. All his actions and words have been measured towards one end only. The protection of Maya and their daughter. He has ensured that no blame shall fall upon her for her husband's murder. Maya goes free, and so does Kerelinda. I had misjudged Guy.

April 12th 1891

We are again in Exeter.

There are two condemned cells in the prison, both furnished more comfortably than the usual convicts' bare cell. Guy points out to us the bed instead of a plank, the table and chairs. He is allowed to eat almost anything he fancies in this three weeks before the execution. Two warders are always present when we visit. Guy asks about Maya, and I am able to tell him at least that she is safe with us inside the Monks' House, and that his baby daughter is named Kerelinda, that she is beautiful and perfect and his living image. I try to control my tears for his sake, but it is not always possible so to do.

I do not understand my husband. He is not at all cast down at Guy's awful plight, but rushes daily about this city in a most cheerful manner. He explains that he is meeting several influential men. That I am not to worry. All will be well in the end, that I should have faith in him. Guy bears up well, considering his circumstances. How sad it is that

I could not feel pride in him until he sat in the condemned cell of Exeter gaol.

April 19th 1891

I walk about this city in an effort to distract my mind from what must happen tomorrow. I look at the great Ham-stone abbey, I explore as far as St David's Hill and the railway station. When I return to our hotel I remember little of what I saw in these peregrinations.

I am strung so tight in my nerves I fear that I shall snap in two halves. There is no point in going to my bed. I cannot bear to think of Guy's state of mind. I shall not sleep this night, but will keep this last vigil with him. I remember the day of his birth. His happy childhood. Tomorrow. Ah, dear God. I cannot bear to think about tomorrow.

April 20th 1891

I must write about this day exactly as it happened. It is a tale that will be told many times by other people, with exaggeration in the newspapers, but mine will be the only true account.

Executions are performed early in the morning. Henry was strangely insistent that he and I should be present in the prison buildings by the appointed time of eight o'clock. I had hoped that such permission would not be granted, but so great was the sympathy felt towards us that we were allowed to watch from a window which overlooked the garden. A cruel dispensation!

The prison bell began to toll as Guy emerged into the garden. He was dressed in the yellow garb of a convicted murderer, his arms pinioned to his sides by a thick belt of straps buckled at his waist. His hands were similarly strapped. With him, before and behind, walked the Governor, the Executioner, several warders and the Chaplain. They marched him towards a shed, the doors of which stood open. I could see the beam from which the rope was hanging, I could imagine the trapdoor placed directly beneath it.

I was told later that even as Guy walked, the burial service was read aloud by the Chaplain. A grim accompaniment to a man's last moments! It was at this point that I fainted.

I came to myself to find that I was lying on a sofa. My husband still stood at the window, but now he was in a state of great excitement and elation. He turned to me and shouted. 'They have tried to hang him – but they could not! The mechanism would not work. Three times they tried, but still the trapdoor would not fall!'

'What does this mean?' I whispered.

'It means that three times on the scaffold are the lawful limits. Guy will not hang on this day, nor any other!'

I could not at first believe that Henry had the right of it. But it was true. Word of the abortive hanging spread rapidly throughout the prison. There was, we were told, great disturbance and excitement among the convicts, and some time elapsed before order was restored.

We were advised to return to our hotel, and to come back to the prison in the morning, when the Governor would speak to us.

April 21st 1891

A beautiful spring morning, and we go light-hearted to the gaol. Our son still lives and cannot now ever suffer execution. We have audience with the Governor. Henry asks what will happen to Guy. We are told that twenty years of penal servitude is a possible outcome. It seems there is a precedent for such a mischance – on a previous occasion the murderous mechanism of the trapdoor did not function and the poor fellow thus tormented was released to spend the rest of his years in solitary confinement in the prison of Parkhurst.

But today even this gloomy prospect cannot cast us down. We plead to be allowed to see Guy and our request is granted. We find him still in the condemned cell. He embraced us both, and tears flowed. He seemed bemused and somewhat incoherent. It took some time for Henry and me to elicit from him clearly what had happened in that awful shed. It would seem that his most vivid memory is of standing on the trapdoor and the rope being placed about his neck, and a close-fitting bag pulled over head and face. He recalls the rope being tightened, the tolling of the bell and a sound beneath his feet of metal rasping against metal. He felt a slight movement beneath his body and then nothing more. The rope remained round his neck, the bag across his face, and all around him shouting and stamping of feet as warders leaped on the trapdoor in a vain effort to move it. He stood for several awful minutes on that trapdoor and was finally led out to wait a few feet off, while further efforts were made to release the hanging mechanism. Guy reports to us on the nervous and upset state of the Governor and Chaplain, and the warders who surrounded him at this terrible time.

For the second time he was led back, still blindfolded and strapped, to the place of execution. Another ten minutes of thumping and struggle by the warders, but still the trapdoor would not give.

Again he was led outside. This time a carpenter was brought from the prison workshop and Guy heard the sounds of hammering and chopping.

Yet a third time he was taken back and placed upon the trapdoor. Yet

193

a third time attempts were made to draw the bolt, and he did begin to fall, but only a few inches. The rope was removed from his neck, the strapping unbuckled, the bag taken from his head and face. He saw the parlous state of the officials, some of whom were weeping. He also wept, only wanting the dreadful business to be over. Then the prison bell ceased to toll, and he was informed that he would not be hanged that day, nor at any future time.

Henry leaves considerable sums of money with the warders in order to ensure Guy's comfort. His state is to remain one of solitary confinement, so we promise to bring him a chess set, and several books.

As the money changes hands I remember my husband's odd behaviour in preceding weeks and I begin to wonder. But of course such suspicions on my part are pointless now, and can achieve nothing. So I put them from my mind and rejoice in Guy's deliverance, for the truth of what happened between my son and Chesi Ingram was never told to that jury of twelve good men and true. It was Chesi who attacked first, forcing Guy to defend himself, and though it pains me to write this, it was Maya, in defence of Guy, who inflicted the final, mortal stab wounds.

My son has one request of me before we part. He asks for a sketch of Maya and Kerelinda, so that he might always have their likeness with him; for he does not expect to ever see either of them in this life, and perhaps it will be better so.

August 2nd 1891

They are bringing in the harvest on the home farm. I carry Kerelinda to the end of the drive, and we watch the loaded wagons as they go swaying down the lane. The child has grown like a flower in the summer weather, she is now a sweet and heavy burden to my arms. There are other wagons, Gypsy wagons, lately come to Sheepdip Lane. It would appear that Taiso Heron is still certain of his welcome here, in our midst, in spite of all that has passed between us. Or mayhap his conscience pricks him regarding his daughter. He might even own to a degree of curiosity about Kerelinda.

I have alerted all my household to be especially vigilant while the Herons and Ingrams are among us. Since the care of the baby rests mainly in my own hands, it is up to me to ensure that she remains safe within the Monks' House and gardens. But there have been times of late when Maya grows restless and unpredictable; when she takes Kerelinda into the deep woods and stays away till nightfall. It is at such times that Taiso Heron, should the fancy take him, might snatch the child and keep her for his own. The man is unpredictable, and blood is blood, after all.

Guy's future is settled, if 'future' be the correct word for such a plight. His sentence of twenty years is to be served in Dartmoor. He is at present obliged to do 'hard labour', but Henry is hopeful that in due time, and because of Guy's youth and education, some more suitable task will be found for him to do. When we are low in spirits at the thought of our poor son, we remember that lonely waiting grave lined with quicklime which we glimpsed briefly at Exeter prison. At least Guy still lives and breathes in this world.

September 12th 1891

Maya still improves, but slowly. I have thought it wiser to leave her strictly to herself, to do or not do as she so pleases. Nowadays she comes of her own accord into the kitchen to pick up some task which will assist Cook. The job of silver cleaning she has taken over altogether, also the cutting and arranging of the flowers. What she will *not* do is put pen to paper, or read books or magazines. The whole nursery suite on the top floor is private to her and Kerelinda, and I must confess it is becoming my own very favourite place in the whole house! I have told her about Guy and the failure of the hanging mechanism, but she made no sign that she had heard a word of it.

The artist came yesterday to make sketches of Maya and Kerelinda. Several charming studies were completed, and Henry is to take them to Guy within the next days.

Maya will not speak of Guy or her own people. When she talks at all it is mostly to the child and in the Romany tongue. Sometimes I worry as to what we should or should not tell to Kerelinda when she is old enough to ask questions about her birth, and her mother and father. Henry says we should not lie to her. I say that neither should we feel compelled to tell her the whole truth.

October 8th 1891

The Herons and Ingrams had gone away from Sheepdip Lane, but now they are back for the Pack Monday Fair. John, the gardener's boy, observed them last evening at the crossroads where Chesi Ingram lies buried. John says they were sitting by the wayside, drinking tea and singing sad hymns. When he asked them what they were about, they said they were 'visiting' their poor murdered brother and praying for his soul. I can only hope that Maya does not see or hear any part of this strange rigmarole.

Today Kerelinda stands alone for the very first time on her sturdy little legs in the middle of the lawn! I hold my breath and do not dare approach her. I wait to see if she will take a step forward, but she decides against this. She sits down again in the long grass and laughs at a hopping blackbird. A more happy and contented child I never saw!

October 10th 1891

Eve of Pack Monday Fair, and Maya is missing! I rush to the nursery, but Kerelinda sleeps sweetly in her cradle. John and Watkins search first of all our land and buildings. I instruct them to go to Hunger Hill and the Hollow, but I can see they are unwilling to venture where, on the eve of this first anniversary of Chesi Ingram's death, they might meet the Herons and the Ingrams. I say that they must search for Maya, but I am not sure that they will.

October 12th 1891

Maya stayed away from us for two days and two nights. We decided to behave as if nothing untoward had happened when she returned late this afternoon, walking through the kitchen and up the back staircase, without a word to anyone. Her clothing was torn and stained as if she had forced a path through brambles; her hands and face bore scratches, and her hair was wild. Her bare feet were thick with the white dust of the quarry. A large yellow cat trotted at her heels and would not be turned away. But she bathed of her own accord and put on fresh clothes and when I carried a supper tray to her, her hair was still damp from washing. She had taken the child into her own bed and they lay curled together. When Maya saw me she sat up and smiled; for the first time in a year she smiled in the old way that lit her face up. 'Don't worry about me,' she said, 'don't be so anxious.' I heard the first warmth in her voice since her return.

'But I do worry about you. You are so silent and withdrawn. I wonder often what your thoughts are. You never speak of Kerelinda's birth, or what brought you to the prison.'

She says, with that simplicity which is her hallmark, 'You had but to ask, ma'am.'

I am not so sure that this is the case but I take advantage of the moment. I say, 'You have been away two days and nights.'

'I knew my baby would be safe.'

'That is not the issue, Maya. It was your safety that concerned us.'

She gestured towards the rocking chair. 'They would not let Minta go with me when I left the *tan*. I have great need of her. I went to find her.'

I look to the chair standing in the shadows, and see the huge yellow cat curled up on the cushions.

'Why?' I ask, 'Why do you need a cat? Surely you have all you could possibly want here with us?'

'I am a *chovihani* – a witch. Minta is my *familiar*. She gives me strength.'

At these words my blood runs cold. She speaks with such simple conviction I could almost believe her. But I have other, more pressing questions. 'Kerelinda's birth. What happened?'

She leaned back into the pillows, and I saw her features sharpen with the memory. 'As you know, ma'am; it was meant that Starina should be with me in the bender when my time was come. But there were days when I grew restless and like to lose my mind at the thought of Guy locked up in Shepton. I had a need that morning to walk free under the skies lest I go mad. I saw the snow clouds gathering but I paid no heed. I was somewhere along the way to Bradford Abbas when the first pains caught me – and the first snow. I waited a while and by easy stages I got myself back closer to the quarry and the *tan*. Then the waters broke and I could go no further. I found a hedge, much overgrown and with a dry ditch. I crept into its shelter, for by this time it blew a blizzard and was very cold. I lay there the day long. Oh, ma'am, I was so frightened. The pains came and went, and I thought for sure the child was dead. It was late afternoon and the light fading when I spied Starina on her way up to the bender with my supper in a basket. I dragged myself from the hedge bottom and called to her. When she saw my state she wanted to bring out the older women from the *tan*. But I begged her not to leave me, and anyway they would not have come.

'Starina said, "Oh dordi, I have never birthed a baby with the mother lying underneath a hedge."

'"Well, neither have I," I told her, "so we shall both learn something new this day."

'It was as if the child knew help had come at last, for the pains grew strong again. She was born by the light of the moon striking off the snow. We put her inside of my clothing, next to my skin, and the cloak wrapped around us. Starina brought us back to the bender, and she made a great fire and some hot food. It was by firelight that I first saw my baby's face and her red curls, and I knew then that whatever happened, I still had a part of Guy with me.'

Tears filled my eyes but I would not weep in Maya's presence. To make her the object of my sympathy and pity would be to diminish her in her own eyes, and she did not deserve that. I took her hand and held it. I said, 'You did very well. You and Starina. Guy would be proud of you, *will* be proud of you when I write and tell him of your bravery.'

She smiled, and I saw how much my words had pleased her. She stroked the baby's head and face. She said, 'I have told you the best

197

part. Now comes the bad time.' She took a deep breath and closed her eyelids, as if she could not bear to watch my face.

'Starina stayed with me while the food and firewood lasted. She went down to the *tan* on the second morning. When she came back my father was with her. He would not touch the baby but said that I should show her to him. I moved out of the bender and into the cold light of the snows. I knew what he wanted, what he had come for. I pulled back the covering from Kerelinda's head, and the red curls burned in the sunlight as if they were afire. I looked up at my father and saw a terrible sight. He was growing old before my very eyes. All the bones of his face seemed to fall inwards. His colour was an awful grey. He turned from me with not a word. He spoke only to Starina. "Back to your husband this very minute. You have been too long away from Black!"

'Starina stood, not moving or speaking.

'"Come with me now," my father told her, "or nevermore."

'"Go," I said to her.

'"But what will become of you?"

'I looked to my father. "I will go to Lady Anne. I will go where I am loved and wanted."

'Starina kissed me and went off weeping. My father turned away and did not look back. I was frightened to be on my own, but they had brought plenty of firewood and food and I thought that in a day or two I could come down to the Monks' House. But it snowed again, and this time it was over the hedgetops and the small trees. All the tracks were covered. My supplies ran out. I stayed in the bender a day and a night without food or fire, and then I knew that I must move on or we both should perish.

'I walked for a long time. I was all but dead when this band of mumpers found me. They were hedge-hoppers, didicoys, not *tatchi* Romanies. They first robbed me of the gold pendant that you gave me, but they let me sit awhiles beside their fire and gave me tea and bread. They were a very poor and wild bunch. I knew they meant me ill and so I left them. I came to a village and a church. I crept in at the church door. The parson was a young man. He promised food and shelter if I would let him christen Kerelinda. I was glad enough to hand the baby to him, for by this time I was weak and all spent out. He was pouring water on her head when the constable came into the church. There was an argument between them. The constable said I was one of the tribe of mumpers he had just caught with stolen goods outside the village. He took from his pocket my golden locket and showed it to the parson.

'"That's mine," I told him. "Lady Anne gave it to me."

'He laughed then, and looked me up and down. "Name and address?"

'I said, "My name is Maya Heron. I am on my way to the Monks' House to stay with Lady Anne.'

'He turned to the parson. "A liar and a thief, as well as a vagrant."

'I looked to the parson but saw he would not help me.

'"I am arresting you on a charge of vagrancy," the policeman said, "and that's only the beginning!"'

Maya paused and opened her eyes. 'And that's how I came to the House of Correction in Shepton Mallett, where you found us, ma'am.'

I put my arms round her and held her close. When I was able to speak I said. 'You are safe now, you and Kerelinda. You will stay here always, both of you. You are my very dearest daughter. You must never again call me ma'am, or Milady. I would be pleased if you will call me Mother.'

Jango passed a hand across his face; he shuffled together the papers they had read and fastened them with the clip. He said. 'I think our ancestor is going to be all right, don't you? It's all getting better for her. That Lady Anne – she's really something.'

Maya said, 'I'm not so sure.'

'But why not? Master Guy is locked up all nice and tidy on Dartmoor. Lavinia is miles away in Paris. Lady Anne is absolutely potty about that baby. Seems to me that our great-grandmother is on a winner. She's right in there, among the rich folks. How can she lose?'

'She's already lost everything that matters to her. Her family have thrown her out; Guy is put away for twenty years, and in a place so awful that few long-term prisoners ever lived to complete their sentence. And then there's Chesi Ingram's curse.'

'Yes,' Jango said. 'I'd forgotten about that. What do you suppose it was, specifically?'

'It concerned the descendants of Guy and Maya, according to the diary.' Maya shrugged. 'It must have been bad, for there's something seriously amiss with all of us. Think about Bruenette and Despair. Consider Lias and me.' She looked searchingly at Jango. 'Only you seem to have turned out to be normal and decent. Why do you suppose that is?'

'Don't sell yourself short. I've been thinking it over. I reckon most of that stuff you told me – about your husband and the visions – well, it could have been an over-active imagination and you being lonely and not having any closeness to your parents.'

'No,' she said. 'Even when I was very small my mother told me that I was a bad girl. As I grew older I could feel the badness growing too.'

He touched her arm and his hand was gentle. He said, 'I wish there was some way I could help you, make it up to you, what you've missed.'

She turned towards him, put her hand over his hand. 'You are helping.'

The rain still fell, the skies grew darker. Star and the greyhounds lay curled together on their strip of carpet. Jango switched on extra lamps; he made sandwiches, and tea in the big brown teapot. The Winnebago felt like a home. It was as if Lias had never lived there.

January 1st 1895

We continue to keep Kerelinda's birthday on this first day of the year. I should really go to the village church once described to me by Maya and check the date of my little one's christening. But still it would not give us her exact date of birth, and in any case, it is not so important.

Today she is four years old, never quiet, never still, oh but a truly blithe spirit! Happy the day long and such a joy to all of us!

I am sad to record that Maya continues strange in her mind. Sometimes she is with us, and yet not with us. Only with Kerelinda is she altogether normal. I am truly thankful that when Maya goes wandering, both in her head and across the countryside, she does not take the child with her. I still fear the power and influence of the Ingrams and Herons over Maya. In spite of all his hard words on the subject of Kerelinda, it is my constant dread that Taiso Heron will one day seek to lure Kerelinda away from me and into his own wagons.

January 1st 1900

The first day of the new century and I am still not recovered from the shock of the deaths of both Henry and Guy in the past year. A letter came from Lavinia at Christmas, but she does not visit. It is in my mind to sign the whole of my property and fortune over to Maya and Kerelinda. They are the only ones in the world who care about me.

The troubles with Kerelinda grow ever worse. She is nine years old today. I have bought her a pony, which is her heart's desire. But she was insistent that I purchase same from Taiso Heron, the man she calls Grandfather. When I remonstrated with her over her choice of pony, she informed me sweetly that the Heron horses were what she termed 'coloured' and much sought after. Taiso Heron had promised to give her a Spanish saddle as a birthday gift. I can only hope that now she has her own pony resident in our paddock, her temptation to disobey my rule will be at an end, and she will desist from sneaking off to the Ingram and Heron wagons when they are in our vicinity. Meanwhile, her schooling is seen to by her mother and my own self. She is like Guy in that she lacks application and ambition. We bring her each morning to her books amid tears and lamentations. It is only the promise of freedom to 'run wild' in the afternoons that persuades her at all to take up the pencil.

Maya herself is no real example to her daughter. But for the schooling of Kerelinda, she neither writes nor reads any more. I have grown used to her wandering ways, to her unexplained absences and silences; but of her utter devotion to the child there is no doubt. I have considered the matter of a boarding school for Kerelinda, but dare not broach the subject. The Romany way of rearing children is to grant them absolute freedom and licence to be naughty. This is so much at odds with my own beliefs that I find it hard to stomach.

But, I ask myself, were our ways with Lavinia and Guy any more successful?

January 1st 1904

It is her birthday and Kerelinda has been missing from the house since Christmas Eve! Were it not for the fact that I know her whereabouts, half the police force of the West Country would be searching for her. But I am only too well aware of my granddaughter's hiding place. She is to be found, as on so many previous occasions, in the wagons of the Herons and the Ingrams. Today she is thirteen. Watkins takes me to the camp in the old quarry. I had prevailed upon Maya to accompany me, but she would not. Kerelinda has told me that when her mother wanders, Maya sits but a few yards from the Herons' stopping place but is never acknowledged by them. I am sure that Taiso Heron does not care for Kerelinda, but encourages her visits just to spite his daughter and myself.

Well, he has succeeded! I am never so distraught, so unhappy, as at these times when the child is with what she calls 'her jolly, happy family'.

I find her seated on the ground beside a fire. She cuts and peels lengths of stick for clothes pegs. She describes her task to me in the Romany language. 'I'm *chinnen the cosht*,' she calls out, laughing and unruffled, as if I had given my permission for her to be there. I can see that to exchange words with Kerelinda will be useless. I make straight for Taiso Heron who watches from the steps of his wagon.

'Give back my granddaughter,' I say. 'You have charmed her away from her mother and me.'

'As you did yourself, my Lady, when you took my daughter from me and spoiled her life.' He speaks softly but in deadly earnest.

'It is not the same,' I tell him.

'Ah, but it is, my Lady. You have the two of them. and I have none.'

'You never wanted Kerelinda. You said so.'

He smiles. 'But Kerelinda wants us. Now ain't that a funny outcome, madam?'

I can see that further speech with him is pointless. As I walk away I call out to my grandchild, 'Come home, Kerelinda. Your mother needs you!'

Her rosy face is lit with laughter. The red curls tumble on her shoulders. 'Tomorrow,' she shouts, 'or maybe the next day. Don't fuss so, Grandmother!'

April 12th 1907

Fifteen years old – and she is married! I do not know how I am to bear her loss. I tell myself it is my own fault, I should have been more strict. But is it possible to lock up sunshine, to imprison quicksilver? There was no holding on to her once her mind was made up that she would go.

The boy she has married is a Heron. Eighteen years old and handsome, and his name is GOLDEN. She is, of course, with child, but that was no surprise. It was a Gypsy wedding and we were not invited. What shocks me most is Maya's attitude to all this. It is almost as if she takes gratification from her daughter's wilfulness, her wildness. Her sole comment has been, 'It is the right thing. It is as it should be. Kerelinda belongs in the *tan*. They are her people.'

I say, 'But what of me? I am also her family.'

She says, 'My girl was becoming a burden to you. She is growing into her powers. Had you not noticed?'

'What powers?'

'Why, of a *chovihani*!'

'That silly rubbish! Listen,' I tell her. 'That talk of witches and magic is no more than wicked superstition. Can you not see why your father and his relatives filled your young mind with such nonsense? It gave them power over you. It allowed them to direct you in a certain way, to bend you to their will. The greatest advantage to them was your ability to make money, which I am sure always ended up in their pockets. They deceived you, Maya.'

It was as if she had not heard a single word. 'Kerelinda will be safe with Golden,' she continued. 'There is Chesi Ingram's curse still to be considered. That danger has not yet altogether been worked out. I can never forget that.'

She picked up her shawl from the chair and flung it round her shoulders. I watched her graceful, long-limbed stride as she moved through the paddock and into the meadows. I did not need to wonder in which direction she was headed.

The tea had cooled, the sandwiches curled at their edges. The dogs became restless and Maya opened the door and let them loose into the paddock. She stood for a moment and breathed in the cold air. The rain had given way to blue and wintry skies. She looked across to the Monks' House and saw it as a prison to which she would never return.

Jango laid down the final journal entry of that batch. He said. 'Maya Heron couldn't stay away from the *tan*, and yet she no longer fitted into either life.'

'Yes,' she said, 'and Guy was dead, so no hope for her there. But she approved of Kerelinda's marriage to a Heron. Said that it was right and proper.'

He smiled and tapped the folder. 'Oh; she was still a *tatchi* Romany; and she may have envied Kerelinda. After all, the girl had escaped, back into a more easy-going way of life. A life that she herself was born to.'

'You could be right. But there's a sense in those recent journal entries of Maya's growing madness. She seems to cause havoc in every life that touches hers, and yet none of it is deliberate. She carries bad luck with her.'

'As you imagine you do, in your own life.'

'It's not imagination, Jango.' She stuffed the papers back into the folder. 'I want it all to come right for her in the end. But I know it isn't going to. I don't see how it can.'

He shivered. 'Let's get away from it for a few hours. We could find a place that does those Dorset cream teas they're always banging on about in these parts.'

She said, 'I'd like to go to the Records Office. They hold most of the old baptismal ledgers. Lady Anne reports that Kerelinda was christened. If I could find some written verification of that, then I might feel some sense of reality about it all. Might be able to break out of the nightmare I'm trapped in.'

They drove to the Records Office in her car. She requested the baptismal registers for several villages in the vicinity of Hunger Hill. They sat at a mahogany table and spoke only in the regulation whispers permitted to researchers. The air in the room was hot and heavy. Jango turned the pages in a mesmeric silence. They studied the scrawled and blotted entries of long-dead village clergymen, with little hope of finding Maya Heron and her baby.

So that when the name they sought appeared, they passed it over. Jango had already moved on two pages when they stared at one another and he leafed rapidly backwards.

It had merited a half page to itself, as if the netting of a Gypsy soul deserved special mention.

Born to Maya Heron – A Strolling Manner of Woman
A Female child – name of Kerelinda
[Father not known]
Aforesaid child being born underneath a Hedge in the neighbourhood
of Hunger Hill and Bradford Abbas, in the time of the Great
Blizzard, in this Year of Our Lord 1891.
'A Brand Plucked from the Burning.'

Jango said, 'Ah, but was she? Plucked from the burning?'

'Why do you think Maya had her christened? I think it was for more than a few minutes' shelter in a church porch. She would have hoped to weaken the power of Chesi Ingram's curse with prayers and holy water.'

'You are obsessed with that curse.'

'It's ruined every one of Guy's descendants down the bloodlines. Something bad must also have happened to Kerelinda's children.'

He said, very quietly. 'They were Despair and Bruenette.'

'Exactly.'

'So how shall we find out what happened to them if it's not in the journal?'

'Through my Aunt Alice. I'm becoming convinced that she knows something so unspeakable about my mother that she can't allow herself to have contact with me any more, in case I ask too many questions.'

Jango said, 'I'm willing to stop this reading now, if you are.'

'No.' she said. 'We lost that option when we went to bed together.'

They began to read again that evening.

Jango pulled out the paperclips and handed Maya the first of the four remaining pages. She said, 'Look at the date! We've moved on by ten years.'

September 20th 1917

After ten years of marriage, and many stillborn births, Kerelinda has at last borne a live child.

She brings the baby to us. It is a strong and handsome boy, dark-haired, dark eyes, with the copper-coloured skin which is the mark of a true Heron.

They have called him Despair, which she says is a Heron family name but is to my mind the very *worst of omens* in the circumstances.

Kerelinda has been well cared for during her confinement and the lying-in. She comes to us all aglow with pride and good health. I say, perhaps more sharply than I ought, 'You should have seen your poor dear mother after your own birth. She was in prison and almost dead when your Grandfather Henry and I found her, and brought her home.'

I see bewilderment and pain on Kerelinda's face, but her curiosity is roused. Motherhood has awakened her tardy interest in her own beginnings.

She says to me, 'My father was your only son. It is time you told me all about him. Whenever I ask, you say that I must wait till I am older. Well, I am twenty-six now, almost an old woman. I mean to know, Grandmother!'

Maya grows pale and rushes from the room. I hear the kitchen door slam and her running footsteps on the asphalt.

I say. 'See what you have done. You have upset your mother.'

'I don't care,' she shouts. 'It is always all secrets with the two of you. Anyone would think it was murder you are hiding.'

The baby wakes and cries and my granddaughter also rushes from the room and across the fields towards the Heron wagons.

I sit in my blue chair and strive for calm. I look up at Maya's portrait and remember that she, too, in her way, was as beautiful and wild as Kerelinda.

It would appear that Taiso Heron and his tribe have not yet passed on word to Kerelinda of the awful heritage Guy left her. For this much I am thankful. If it be left in my hands, I will never tell her.

It comes to my mind that the boy called Despair is my great-grandson, and that he is *not* one of *my* kind, but what Maya would call a *tatchi* Romany.

May God help the child!

September 24th 1927

Almost ten years to the day, and Kerelinda brings a second baby to us. We had thought Despair would be her one and only, but now, in her middle-age, she has borne a daughter! The child has the Heron colouring and handsome looks. The hair and skin shades of Guy and Maya are not repeated in any of their descendants, which seems to me a *good thing*. Kerelinda says that Despair is devoted to his baby sister, and cannot bear to be parted from her. Her name is Bruenette, another traditional Heron name. But Golden is a good man and they are a happy little family; and I am grateful for it. The wagons are about to move out from Sheepdip Lane. It will be some time before we see them all again.

Maya is, as usual at these times of parting, quite distraught.

January 5th 1929

I cannot bear to write this, yet I must.

Kerelinda and Golden are dead. By some miracle the children are yet alive. Taiso Heron also perished in the flames.

I had always thought those wooden wagons dangerous. A fire took hold while they slept. A spark from the stove, it is thought, and the whole structure, tinder-dry, went up like matchwood. Taiso Heron lost his life while saving the children. Of his bravery there can be no question, tho' I doubt he rescued Despair and Bruenette for my sake! It has been a terrible time for all of us.

Maya has all but lost her mind. She says it is all the fault of Chesi Ingram. Despair is taken care of by Lena, his father's sister. Bruenette is with another Gypsy family who also have a small girl. I had wanted to take Bruenette and keep her here with us but Maya is adamant on the subject and will only allow the child to visit us at intervals.

I do not always understand poor Maya.

October 10th 1930

They are back for the Pack Monday Fair. Bruenette is to stay with us for a whole month! She is just three years old and has Kerelinda's happy smile and spirit. In all other respects she is pure Heron, pure Romany, with the beautiful looks of the Heron women. She is also as wild and undisciplined as was my dear Maya when she first came here. Both children still grieve for their parents. Perhaps I am grown wiser with the years, or it is the dulling effect of my great age, but I am now able to accept without criticism the unruly ways of this precious Gypsy great-grandchild of mine.

April 2nd 1934

The Herons brought Bruenette to us this morning. She will be here for the celebration of my ninetieth birthday. At the age of almost seven years she is wonderful and intelligent company for me. Maya takes little interest in her. My poor girl wanders greatly in her mind, and lives almost completely in the past.

Despair, aged seventeen, is the most beautiful young man I have ever seen. He visits us but rarely, and when he does I am struck afresh each time by his charm and his endearing manner. Bruenette and Despair see little of each other, and soon not at all. My great-grandson is a brilliant horseman. He is to travel overseas with the Sangers' Circus, and tells me that already his is the STAR TURN of the evening's entertainment. He is sure the Americans will love him!

Jango spoke into the silence. 'So that's it?'

'Yes,' she said. 'There's no more information anywhere. I've looked.'

He grabbed up the swatch of papers and shook them. 'How in the hell did my father come to change from the golden boy described here to the miserable old sod I knew all my life?'

'I can say much the same about my mother, and she was such a liar! She was never in an orphanage, never unloved and unwanted. Even supposing she was ashamed of her Gypsy parentage, she was still the natural great-granddaughter of a titled lady, granddaughter of a lord. Why did she never tell me about them?'

He said, 'Why did your father never tell you? He was born in these parts. He must have known.'

'You're right. He not only condoned her lies, he took great care that I should never learn the truth about her. It explains the boarding schools I was shunted off to, my lack of contact with Alice. But why, Jango? What can they possibly have had to hide that was so terrible?'

He said, 'And there's all that stuff you told me about the way she couldn't bear to touch you . . .' His voice faltered, suspicion twisted his mouth and fear looked out of his eyes.

She said, 'You know something bad. Or you've guessed. I've seen that look on your face before.'

'No! What could I know? I'm in the same state of ignorance as you are. I never knew Despair was in the circus, that he'd been in America. I know even less about my mother than you do about yours.'

'It's not your mother we're concerned with, Jango. It's Despair and Bruenette.' She paused. 'It's got something to do with the fact that they were Kerelinda's children, and with that old curse.'

She put out a hand to touch him. but he flinched and moved out of her reach.

'We're both very tired,' he said. 'We need to sleep. I want to take you visiting in the morning. There's a traveller family you really ought to meet.'

He slept that night on the far bunk that belonged to Lias.

Breakfast was eaten in an awkward silence. They spoke to the dogs but not to one another. Pride would not allow her to ask him what was wrong. She went over to the house, picked up the milk and bread and letters. When she returned to the paddock, he sat in the cabin of the Winnebago. He opened the passenger door and gestured her inside.

She said, 'Why take the camper? It's simpler to use my car.'

'We're visiting relatives,' he said briefly. 'They don't know yet that you and I are together.'

She could not see his point but did not wish to argue with him. They drove for several miles, out of Dorset and into Cotswold country. The Winnebago was manoeuvred down lanes so narrow that its paintwork was brushed on either side by leafless branches. She wondered what would happen if they should meet a vehicle travelling in the opposite direction. They came at last to a stretch of what Jango said was common land. She saw a smouldering fire, an assortment of shabby modern trailers, and one beautiful little bow-top wagon, its green canvas taut and fresh, its paintwork gleaming. All down the connecting lanes stood lines of tethered, coloured ponies. Grubby, tow-haired children played games with two treadless car tyres and a broom handle. Four teenage boys were peeling sticks and making clothes pegs.

Jango halted the Winnebago just short of the bow-top. A very old woman emerged from the half-door; her seamed face was split by a toothless grin, her clothes a colourful selection of jumble sale bargains.

'Jango!' she cried.

'Aunt Kezie,' he shouted. There was a special kind of affection in their greeting of one another. The woman spoke a mixture of Romany and English. Jango answered her only in English. He introduced Maya simply as a descendant of the Ingram and Heron families. The fire was stirred into a blaze; mugs of sweetened, orange-coloured tea were pushed into their hands. They sat on upturned wooden crates and talked about distant relatives and friends. Jango asked about his cousins and their children. He said, 'You've bought two more trailers since I saw you last.'

'Yes,' said his aunt. 'Well, see, our Random's gels and lads was getting bigger. Time to separate 'em. Us needed to sort out the sleeping quarters.' Her voice became a whisper. 'You knows how perticler us is 'bout all o' that sorta thing.'

Jango nodded, rose, and made to leave. He had the look of a man whose mission is accomplished.

'You's never going a-ready?' his aunt said. 'Our Job and Wisdom'll be here soon, and the women.'

Jango said. 'I'll be back.' He touched a forefinger to the side of his nose. 'Got a bit of business to attend to down the country.'

'I understands you, my lovely,' said his aunt. 'You come back soon, you hear me, and bring your beautiful lady with you!'

They drove away, the dogs and children running behind the camper for the length of the lane.

They returned to the paddock by way of the Quiet Woman pub. It was not until the drinks were served, the supper ordered, that they spoke to one another on the subject of the visit.

She said, 'So what was that all about?'

'About nothing.'

'Oh, come on, Jango! You didn't drive all those miles just to show me Gypsies making clothes pegs.'

He rounded on her then, more angry than she thought he had any cause to be. 'That's exactly what I did. I've had this feeling lately that you think all Gypsies are filthy rich. I wanted to show you the other side of the travelling way of life.'

She thought he lied to cover some purpose of his own. She said gently. 'They are very poor, but I knew that all travellers are not like you and Lias.'

Again, he was fiercely defensive. 'They make their own way in the world, that little family! They draw no state benefits, except a quick stay in a hospital, and that's not often. The kids are a bit scruffy, but they're beautiful, and strong and healthy. Like their parents, they'll grow up to call no man master.' He struck the table a soft blow with his clenched fist. 'I also wanted you to know that without my presence there, you would never have come within spitting distance of them – unless they were trying to sell you something. The way they live now, proud and isolated, that was how Lias and I lived in our early years. Somehow, I don't know how, Despair suddenly got rich; gold stitched into his body belt and a custom-built, flashed-out trailer, and a few years later the land bought in the Dark Peaks.'

'While your aunt and cousins stayed – independent?'

He said, 'They're more Lias's relatives than mine. Aunt Kezie is Lias's mother's sister. But yes, they've kept true to the old ways. I feel sort of awkward when I'm around them. Like they are the diamonds and I'm just glass.' He was drinking Bacardi. When he looked at her, his face was expectant, quizzical, and then disappointed, as if she had failed him in some way. He said, 'Is there nothing else you want to ask about Kezie and her family?'

'No,' she said, 'but you'd better go easy on the rum. I don't think I can handle a vehicle the size of the Winnebago.'

'I drive better when I'm drunk.'

'That's what my mother used to say.'

His expression changed again to one of bitter anger. 'Don't dare compare me to your bloody mother,' he shouted. 'She's the cause of all our problems.'

She had never seen him like this. She tried to work out what it was she had done, or not done, to upset him. They were quarrelling without reason. Tears pricked behind her eyelids. She pushed the food around her plate, chewed and swallowed, hardly knowing what it was she ate. Covertly she watched him: the denim-clad legs, skewed sideways because

209

they were too long to fit beneath the table; the narrow hips, deep chest, wide shoulders, the collar-length silver hair, the blue eyes and tanned face. Jango. The first man who had shown her gentleness and taught her passion. Who had offered her safety and contentment. She could no longer imagine a life without him. She said, impulsively across the table, 'I do believe I love you.'

His gaze met her gaze, all pretence abandoned. 'For God's sake,' he whispered, 'don't ever again say that to me.'

Lias was perched on the barred gate of the paddock, his body a dark hunched blur against the night sky, his cigarette a glowing point of light. They had parked the Winnebago, lit the lamps and drawn the curtains before he stepped in through the door.

The dogs went straight to him, tails wagging, bodies wriggling in an ecstasy of welcome, marking by contrast the stunned silences of Maya and Jango.

Lias sat down on his own bunk, staking out his territory.

'Kettle on?' he inquired of Jango, and to Maya he said, 'The box of teabags marked Chrysanthemum is my brand.'

When the mug was in his hand and a fresh cigarette between his fingers he said, 'Well, isn't this cosy?' He nodded towards Maya. 'Living with you, is she? Like, as in, carnal knowledge of?'

Jango muttered, 'Cut it out, Lias. None of your bloody business.'

'Oh no? Let me remind you little brother, *pralo* of mine, that your woman is occupying my half of the Winnebago. Without my permission or approval.'

Jango said, 'I thought you'd gone back to Sinaminta. I thought we could maybe work out some sort of deal, some cash arrangement so that I could keep the camper.'

Until then, the mood had still been light, the voices quiet, the tones bantering. Now, something dark and threatening began to grow between the brothers. All their concentration was fixed on one another, so that Maya felt like an observant ghost. A knot of fear tightened in her stomach, a prickle of sweat formed along her hairline.

Lias said, 'Get rid of her.'

'Why should I?'

'Because I'm telling you she's trouble. We've been through all this before. For Christ's sake, man, you know exactly what she is. She's poison; you know it.'

Jango said, 'That silly rubbish? Your talk of witches is no more than clapped-out superstition. Can't you see what those old ones were up to when they filled their daughters' heads with such nonsense? It gave the power to the parents; it meant that they could send the chosen girl out fortune-telling, which put money in the family purse. With a bit of persuasion, she would begin to believe in her own propaganda; begin to think she saw visions, that she could heal the sick. It's all a con, Lias! It always was. You have to be simple-minded to believe it.'

Lias's astonishment showed in the way he set his mug down carefully on the table, in the sudden hooding of his gaze, his hesitation. He said, 'I thought I had taught you better than that.'

Jango's voice was bitter. 'Oh yes, you taught me. Every bloody thought inside my head began its life in *your* head. Maybe I've been brainwashed too, just like the poor old *chovihanis*.

Lias said, 'I don't know you any more.'

'I don't know myself. I need time to sort out what I think, what I want to do.'

Lias stood. He walked to the door. 'Don't be too long about it, Jango. There's some things won't bear the waiting. Know what I mean?'

Without Lias the camper seemed larger, brighter, the air easier to breathe. She went into the recess of the galley. In the polished bottoms of the hanging copper saucepans she could see her pale reflection repeated half a dozen times. They had spoken about her as if she was not present, and yet surprisingly she felt no anger.

The surprise had been Jango's rebellion against his brother. He had spoken on the subject of witches with such conviction that she wondered if he realised that he quoted Lady Anne almost word for word. No matter how she tried, she could not believe in this theory of coercion and exploitation. It had never in her own life been suggested to her that she might, if she wanted, have the ability to see tragic events even as they happened, and in a different time zone. And yet she had seen them, unprompted; could still see them if she so allowed. But it hardly seemed the moment to point this out to Jango.

She washed the mugs and dried them, and placed them in a cupboard. She was aware of Jango taking blankets and pillows from a locker, and knew without looking that he had already settled down to sleep on Lias's bunk. She switched off the lamps and pulled back the curtains. The moon rode high in a clear sky, turning the golden stone of the Monks' House into silver. She knew that if she allowed the shutter in her mind to open, she would 'see' old Lady Anne and middle-aged Maya, the young Kerelinda and her baby son Despair; all of them walking the gardens and paddock, or running in the fields, towards the Herons' wagons; the child Bruenette playing on the garden swing.

Clouds veiled the moon, closing off the Monks' House from her view.

She guessed that Jango feigned sleep because he could no longer bring himself to touch her. She felt cold and sick. Like Maya Heron, she had only to love a man and he would be destroyed. Out in the dark night she suspected that Lias crouched beneath a hedge, keeping watch, for some reason of his own, on the Winnebago camper.

The moon came out from behind the clouds, and she remembered Alice. Alice, who was her father's sister. Who must have known Bruenette more intimately than she would admit.

Alice, who knew more than she ever told, and who must now be persuaded to share that knowledge.

Sleep did not come and Maya rose towards dawn, moving quietly about the camper, making strong thick coffee and drinking it black, thinking all the time about what it was she had to do. She pulled on corduroys and an Arran sweater, and tied her hair back with a ribbon.

Jango slept with an arm curled about his head as if warding off a blow. She needed him awake and involved, but knew better than to rouse him from a deep sleep. She pulled the blanket up about his shoulders and checked that there was sufficient water in the kettle for his morning tea. As she moved towards the door, the dogs rose from their rug, tails wagging. She allowed them an urgent five minutes in the paddock grass and then recalled them. The morning air was fresh and very cold.

At this early hour Alice was already working in the garden. A wheelbarrow heaped with leaves stood beside a smouldering bonfire, a rake leaned against a birch tree. As Maya stepped from the car, the tall thin figure of her aunt emerged from the greenhouse and came towards her.

'Maya!' Alice paused. 'Oh, my dear. You don't look well. Has something happened? Come into the house. I'll make some tea.' Still talking nervously, she led the way into the kitchen.

Seated among the sitting-room chintz and flower paintings, warming her fingers on the teacup, Maya realised how much she feared what was about to come – the agony of certain knowledge. It was not too late. She could explain her presence to Alice with some trivial query, make a swift departure. Jango could be easily persuaded to burn the diaries; to forget their content. They could drive north together. Get married.

But then she thought of his recent sudden coldness towards her, his change from ardent lover to barely civil stranger. She should never have confided in him. She looked at Alice, at the way she sat taut and upright in her chair, and she knew that this moment had also been long expected and feared by her father's sister.

There was surely some gentle way of broaching the matter, but still the question came out coldly. She said, 'I want to know everything you know about my mother.'

Her aunt's face seemed to crumple inwards, the features imploding like some half-demolished building. She did not speak because she could not. Maya heard herself apologising.

'I'm sorry to put you through this, but no one else has the information that I need.' She continued to explain, giving Alice time in which she could recover. 'I've spent months, more than a year now, wondering and worrying. There's something seriously wrong with me, Alice. I've read the diaries, but you know all about them, don't you? Going all the way back to the first Maya, there's a broad streak of lunacy in the Heron women. Something passed down through the female line. It's all there, on record. Kerelinda didn't live long enough to suffer from it; well, she got lucky and died early. But there's Maya Heron and Bruenette, both seriously unbalanced. And now me. I've looked up the hereditary diseases that end in madness. There's Huntingdon's chorea. That's the very worst one. Incurable, untreatable, and certain to be passed on to fifty per cent of all descendants. I'm the right age for that one. It usually shows up in the late twenties or early thirties. Or there's schizophrenia. You could say I might have been marginally schizoid all my life. I see visions and hear voices.' She paused. 'Or there's premature senile dementia. It's been known to occur even in people in their early thirties. If I have something dodgy in my genes I ought to know about it. I could at least be seeking treatment, making provision for an uncertain future, making sure I never pass it on to another generation.'

As she spoke she remembered the fear in Jango's face, the way he had recoiled from her, as if he had suddenly suspected some taint. She said, 'Somewhere along the line I feel that I'm missing a vital bit of information. I wish —'

'Are those young men still camped in your paddock?' Alice interrupted.

'Hardly,' she lied. 'They sort of come and go. I rarely see them.'

Some colour came back into Alice's face, she breathed in, then said quickly on an expelled breath, 'You are not my niece, Maya. There is no blood relationship between us, and you are not suffering from any inherited disease. Your only problem is that you have been lied to all your life.'

The words had no meaning. Maya repeated them inside her head. She said, feeling stupid. 'I don't think I understand you.'

Alice said, slowly, using simple, spaced out words, 'You – are – not – my – brother's – child. Geoffrey was sterile. You were also conceived at a time when your – when he and Bruenette were not together. It happened while Geoff was working in Alaska. Your mother usually

213

travelled around with him, but the living conditions were primitive and so she stayed that year in England. He came home four weeks before your birth.'

Maya set the teacup down unsteadily onto the saucer. 'So who am I?'

'What difference can it make now?'

'I have to know, Alice. All my life I've suspected there was something wrong. My father – Geoffrey – tolerated me. Bruenette hated me! You know she did. She couldn't bear to touch me. What happened? What did I do wrong? I've always thought it was my own fault that my mother couldn't love me.'

'You did nothing wrong. The sin was theirs, not yours.'

'What sin?'

Alice bit her lower lip. She said, 'Don't make me do this, Maya.'

'Alice!'

Alice leaned forward, her long thin arms wrapped round her body. 'Always remember,' she said, 'that you made me tell you.'

Mr Parsons, the gardener, had used those same words not so long ago when speaking of Bruenette. Maya wondered how many people knew about the secret thing, or guessed it.

Alice said in a flat voice, 'Your natural father was your mother's brother.'

Once again the words lacked meaning. For some purpose of her own, Alice was seeking to mislead her. Maya laughed, uncertainly, trying to diffuse the tension. 'But surely that's a contradictory statement? There's nothing *natural* about *incest*.'

The word, once spoken, seemed to take on its own momentum. It grew large and loud, bounced from the walls, echoed through the house, shook the garden trees. *Incest*. The unthinkable, the unimaginable sin. The crime which was never condoned among Gypsies, as Jango, by visiting his relatives only yesterday, had been trying to demonstrate to her. She remembered his inquiring looks. Had he wanted to discuss the subject with her, to prepare her for this revelation?

She said, 'You are saying that Despair Heron was my father.'

'Yes.'

'Which means that Jango and Lias Heron are my half-brothers.'

'Yes.' Alice sighed. 'Now you can see why I tried to discourage your association with them.'

'You should have told me.'

'I hoped they would go away,' said Alice. 'That you need never know the truth of it.'

It seemed that the human brain could absorb only so much horror at once; she attempted, unsuccessfully, to deal with both the past and present implications of her situation.

She thought about the two men who were her half-brothers, and felt the bile rise hot and bitter in her throat. She ran from the kitchen. That night, in the lane in Lyme Regis, Lias had known, would have compounded the sin of their father if Jango's return from the pub hadn't stopped him. But he had hated her then for being who she was, for tempting him. He would always hate her, wish to punish her. Jango had not known; not then. But it hardly mattered any more. It was all too late.

Maya gagged and clutched the porcelain bowl in Alice's blue and white bathroom, remembering the nights spent in Jango's arms, his bed. She splashed cold water on her face, and stood on trembling legs. She went back to the kitchen.

The coffee pot and brandy bottle stood together on the kitchen table. Alice poured the unusual combination, and they both drank. Maya said, 'You had better tell me all of it, beginning with my mother's childhood.'

'You've read Lady Anne's journals?'

'I've read the sections Bruenette intended I should read.'

Alice nodded. 'Your mother visited the Monks' House at least three times every year, until Lady Anne died. The house and lands had been bequeathed to Maya Heron, but the daughter, Lavinia, had the will revoked on the grounds that Maya was insane, and that Lady Anne, when she made the will, was too old to know what she was doing. There was no problem with the courts. After all, Maya was only a Gypsy. Two days after the court hearing, Maya was found dead in the Hollow. It was thought she had suffered a stroke, but I have never quite believed that. Bruenette always thought that her grandmother took poison, that she no longer wished to live without Lady Anne, and away from the Monks' House.' Alice paused.

'The deaths of these two women, coming close together, and the fact that she could no longer visit the Monks' House, was the second major trauma of Bruenette's young life. She had already lost both parents in a wagon fire. Despair was her only surviving close relative, and he was much older. When he joined the circus, she was left with a succession of aunts who had large families of their own.'

Maya said, 'I can see now why she wanted to buy back the Monks' House; and she wasn't altogether lying when she said she was brought up by strangers.'

Alice nodded. 'And you have to remember that Bruenette was also Guy's granddaughter. While Despair was pure Heron, pure Romany, his little sister had a strong dash of Guy's aristocratic blood, and it began to show as she grew up. Bruenette had come a long way from the Gypsy wagons when Geoffrey met her.' Alice sipped at her brandy-laced coffee. 'She was extraordinarily beautiful. I often wondered why she married him. He met her just after the war in London. She was performing with a troupe of flamenco dancers. He was still in the Army. They were married within weeks of meeting. He became a mining engineer and she always travelled with him. They both wanted children. When it didn't happen they began to visit doctors and hospitals. It was then they discovered that the fault lay with Geoff. When he went on the Alaskan trip, she refused to go with him. She would never admit it, but I have always believed that she made a deliberate decision then to get pregnant in his absence.'

'But surely not with her own brother?'

Alice, shocked, said, 'Oh no! When Despair last saw Bruenette she was five, maybe six years old. She had forgotten all about him and he about her. They met as total strangers. Twenty-seven years is a long time, they were not likely to recognise each other.'

'Where? When did they meet?'

'At Newmarket racecourse. In the bar. Where else? They were instantly attracted. He was a widower, she was footloose and looking for excitement. She told me how they recognised some kind of bond, but the possibility of a blood relationship never occurred to either of them. They spent three nights together. She told him her name was Lola, he said his name was John. She said she was an actress. He said he was a trainer with a racing stable. Both of them were lying, playing games, having an adventure, a fling. It was on their last morning, in the hotel dining room, that a friend recognised Bruenette and spoke her name across the tables.' Alice shook her head. 'All those years later, when she was telling me about it, the shock of what happened next was still there in her eyes.

'The man who said his name was John now stared at her, white-faced. He said, "I once had a little sister called Bruenette." She told me how she looked at him then, feature by feature, and could not believe that she had missed the similarities between them, the dark colouring, the broad high cheekbones, the unusual height.

'Bruenette said, "You are Despair. You are my brother," and he did not deny it.'

Alice poured coffee and drank it. She said, 'In truly horrific situations, full realisation comes only slowly. That's how it was with them. Your mother told me how they continued to butter toast and eat it, drink tea. It was as if the words brother and sister had no meaning for them, and then it seemed to have occurred to them both at the same instant that she might be pregnant. They began to question one another then about the past, and the answers tallied. They confirmed for each other that they were the children, the only living descendants, of Golden and Kerelinda Heron grandchildren of Guy and Maya, great-grandchildren of Lady Anne; both of them born in the old tradition, on the straw, in a bender tent. Mutual revulsion also set in simultaneously. They packed, left the hotel, and went their separate ways without an exchange of addresses or the details of their present lives.'

'And what about my – about Geoffrey?'

'You were born a month after he came back from Alaska. Bruenette told him she had been raped by a stranger. I think by that time she really believed this was the case. Geoff was horrified but sympathetic and supportive.'

'She could have had an abortion.'

'That was not so simple thirty years ago. And she was very superstitious; her life was ruled by a system of peculiar beliefs. She believed abortion to be murder, even in a case of incest.'

'Even so, I should never have been born.'

'No, Maya! You must never think that. You were the most wonderful thing that ever happened to Geoff. When Bruenette refused to hold you, touch you, my brother saw her behaviour as a perfectly understandable mental breakdown. He took six months' leave and cared for you himself. But she didn't improve. The fact that he loved you caused more trouble between them. She wanted to put you up for adoption but he wouldn't allow it. So began the long trail of nursemaids, au pairs, relatives, and minders; and then the boarding school which solved most problems.' Alice hesitated.

Maya said. 'What is it?'

'On one occasion you met your father.'

'I don't remember.'

'You were three, maybe four years old, a lovely child with your ash-blonde hair and huge eyes. Bruenette and Geoff were motoring to Scotland, a rare holiday, and Geoff had insisted that you go with them. They came across this horse fair somewhere in Yorkshire. They stopped for an hour, and there on the street of this little town Appleby they came face to face with Despair Heron. He tipped his hat to Bruenette but did not speak. When they returned to their parked car, he was waiting for them. He claimed you as his daughter, asked your name, was told, and said Bruenette had named you well, that you were the living likeness of an earlier Maya. Geoffrey was distraught and extremely frightened. The man was menacing; Geoff believed him capable of kidnap – anything! So he offered Despair Heron money to leave them alone, believing him to be the rapist and fearing any further contact with him might send your mother right over the edge. Bruenette confirmed the man was your father but did not confess to Geoff that they were brother and sister.

'Geoffrey paid him a lot of cash, all in gold as the man demanded. Well, the man kept his word. They heard no more from him. But all through the negotiations, Despair's young son was present, the boy he called Lias.'

Maya said, 'Who would then have been ten, eleven years old?' She followed Alice's defensive gesture and wrapped her arms close about her body. 'That bastard,' she whispered. 'Lias knew who I was from the beginning. He remembered and recognised me as his sister.'

'How involved are you with them?'

'With Lias not at all. With Jango, as involved as it's possible to be.'

'That is what I feared. I've been so stupid, Maya. I should have told you sooner. But you seemed to be in such a fragile state when you first came here. It appeared to be wiser to wait. I hoped that I need never tell you.'

Maya rose and placed an arm round Alice's shoulders. 'Don't blame yourself. I love him so much it would probably have happened anyway, even if I'd known.'

Alice smiled at the blatant lie. 'Thank you,' she said. The smile became rueful. 'My own baby died in infancy; had he lived he would have been about your age. I had always thought of you as Geoff's daughter because that is the way he saw you. I suppose when my brother died and I finally met you. I hoped you would be a replacement for my lost child. But then I became frightened, of what you might discover, of what you might demand to know. It seemed wiser to put some distance between us.' She sighed. 'Old sins throw long shadows.'

The dogs ran loose in the paddock, a fire burned in the perforated bucket. A coloured horse she had failed to notice on her early morning departure was grazing in the adjoining meadow. She felt relief at the continued presence of the camper, and then fear at the coming confrontation. Lias had lied and concealed, as had Alice, but more dangerously, and for all of Jango's lifetime. The pain and revulsion between herself and Jango lay too deep for argument and recriminations, and yet she knew that she would blame and argue.

She halted at the camper steps. Anything could happen now between the brothers. Her brothers. Their bloodlines carried violence. Murder could be done. She recalled the tale of Chesi Ingram and his dying curses. Was this to be the culmination of that old evil? The breath caught in her throat. She suppressed the need to kneel down in the grass and vomit. She could barricade herself inside the Monks' House but sooner or later they would have to talk to one another.

She pushed open the door and stepped inside. The air was blue with cigarette smoke. Jango sat on his bunk, the coffee pot and Bacardi bottle at his elbow. His face, open and vulnerable, turned towards her as she entered, and she felt a rush of tenderness towards him which swiftly passed. Lias emerged from the shower room. His bare feet made damp tracks on the carpet, a towel was knotted at his middle, and the swinging braid of wet hair shed droplets as he pulled jeans and a sweater from a cupboard. As Lias stepped back into the shower room, Jango made to speak, but she said, 'Wait! Not a single word until he is with us.'

The passenger seat was set on a pivot, so that when required it could be turned from its forward-looking position in the driving cabin to face back and become a part of the camper's living space.

Maya touched the button which swung the seat round. Jango and Lias sat, each on his own bunk. She took her unaccustomed place, facing them as a judge might face the accused in a courtroom.

She said, 'I've talked to Alice. I know the truth now. All of it.'

Her words were directed towards Lias. She saw his stillness, the animal wariness of his eyes; an odour of fear came from his still damp body. She knew then she had him trapped and bound. Her words dropped like single stones into deep water.

'You're an evil man,' she told him. The bitterness burned on her tongue, scorching the words. She turned towards Jango. 'I don't need to tell Lias what I learned today. He knows, has known, since he was twelve years old.'

Her voice sharpened to a keener pitch. 'Remember me, Lias, *pralo mine*? Remember me, *dear brother*, in the car park at Appleby, and Despair, *our father*, bargaining for Kruger rands on his promise not to snatch me from my mother? Surely you had not forgotten Maya, your little sister, the child who made your family wealthy?'

Jango's face reflected his stupefaction. She knew the feeling well, had experienced it several times herself this morning. She saw Jango wait for some denial from Lias. But there was none. She watched him try to work it out, first the implications of what she had said, and then the inevitable conclusions.

Jango rose and moved towards Lias; he stood over him and looked down into the grey of his brother's skin, the sudden ageing thinness of his facial bones. He said quietly, 'What's she saying, Lias?'

Maya spoke into the silence. 'Oh come on, Jango! Don't play the innocent. It's too late for that. You know damn well what I'm saying.

I don't know exactly when you were sure I was your sister, or what made you suspect it, and it doesn't matter any more. But don't start lying to me now.' She could hear the contempt growing in her voice but could not control it. 'Well, as Lias once said, isn't this cosy? One happy little family. Brothers and sister, finally reunited. A story worthy of a TV documentary. Except that two of them have been to bed together; several times. And the other one was saved from committing deliberate incest by the unexpected arrival home of his brother who, though drunk at the time, might just have noticed something untoward.'

She turned again to Jango. As she started to speak, Lias interrupted. 'Leave him be,' he shouted. 'He's done nothing. Knows nothing. I may have dropped him a few hints just lately that you might be a bit more than a cousin. He brooded on it.' To Jango he said, 'Sit down. We can sort this out between us, you and me. This woman is nothing. We can up and leave this place right now. Be as we were. We once had a good life together.'

Overhead a helicopter from the base at Yeovilton droned through grey cloud. She could hear the coughing engine of the woodman's truck as he delivered the logs she would never burn. At the door, the puppy Star whined to be admitted, but no one moved.

The Winnebago had become a capsule, a sealed tomb. They watched and waited, each unwilling to be the one who broke the silence.

Jango said, 'It's over, Lias. Things can never be the same. Never mind what I suspected, I need to know all the truth now.'

Maya said, 'All right, I'll spell it out for you again, Jango. My mother, your father. Brother and sister. Well, we already knew that much. What we did not know was that those two conceived a child together. Oh, they didn't know it was incest, but even so, a child was born. I was that child. Which means that all three of us have Despair Heron for a father; and he was a blackmailer, and worse.'

Lias spoke in a soft voice full of menace. 'You patronising bitch! How dare you make judgements about a man you never knew. What can you know about our life? Have you ever gone barefoot, cold and hungry? That day in Appleby, my father saw a rich man who could well afford to cough up a few gold pieces, a man who was actually offering him money to go away. That Gorgio man was holding the hand of Despair's little daughter. If he wanted to keep her, then let him pay for the happiness she gave him. Nobody got hurt. We ate well for the first time in months. Jango was two years old. Geoff Pomeroy's cash bought the first pair of shoes that baby ever had. It set us up in a decent trailer. Despair took good care of that gold, made it grow. Years later that same money bought the Derbyshire land and farmhouse. If you're dishing out blame,' he sneered, 'then save it for your crazy mother. She threatened us that time in Appleby. She told Despair that he had ruined her life; that one day, no matter how long it took her, she would seek out his male children and kill them. I was twelve years old and she looked straight at me as she said it.'

Maya said, 'Her life *was* ruined. And so was mine.'

'And what about our father's life? He had broken the strongest taboo of his people. If word of it had got out, he would have been cast off from the family to live among didicoys and mumpers. He was no more to blame for what happened than she was.' Lias stood, moved to the window which faced the Monks' House. 'It was Chesi's curse working out. Incest was exactly what he wished upon the Herons. The most terrible curse one Romany can put upon another. Despair was a hard man, but breaking the taboo destroyed him.'

She heard the threat of tears in Lias's voice and pity for him touched her. 'And you?' she asked. 'What about you?'

'Me? Oh, I've been careful. Bloody careful! I've stuck to the dark-haired, dark-skinned variety of woman. I learned from Despair's mistake, see. I remembered your blonde looks, your face; fixed them in my mind. I also remembered the way my father described the first Maya's looks. Hair like spun gold, he said, slanty eyes the colour of old honey. I felt safe from you because I knew that I would recognise you, if and when I saw you. When your mother put that detective on us, when she sent the letter, I guessed then that the curse was starting to work out.' He paused. 'But many years had passed, and I'd got careless. So I let Jango persuade me down to Dorset, and I was curious too. And then I saw you at the funeral and I thought, well, what's the harm in it? I let Jango make the first moves towards you. It was no more than a game, to start with. I intended to startle you one day. Say, hello, little sister! And then I realised that I was attracted to you. My God! Can you imagine how that made me feel? Guilt and shame don't sit well on a man of my sort. I have to believe in myself or I'm finished. That night in the lane, I could easily have killed you just for being there. And then there was your mother's death still heavy on my mind, and the problem of Jango.'

Lias moved from the window and sat on his bunk. His face was closed, his eyes blank.

Jango said, 'So I was a problem, was I? Well, I wondered when we'd get around to me. So far all I've heard is your name and Despair's.' He still spoke in the low voice that showed how tightly he contained his anger. But then control slipped. He shouted, 'Christ Almighty! What about me, you bastard? What about my guilt, my shame? You knew what was likely to happen, and you never did more than chuck out the odd hint, the sodding Gypsies' warning! She's poison, you said. Keep away from her, you said. What you didn't say was keep your flies fastened this time, Jango, this one is different. She's your sister!'

Lias stared down at his clenched fists, at the falling tears that wet his fingers. The words did not come easily, his voice was rough, unsteady.

'There's stuff you don't understand, *pralo*. Stuff I could never seem to tell you. Madeline, your mother, was a druggie when she came to Despair. Flower children they were called, back in the sixties. Most of the time she was out of her skull. When her labour started, the other women wouldn't help her. Despair was away, up the country. Probably took off on purpose when her time was near. I was all she had. I was just a boy. A child. Oh, I'd seen puppies born, foals and kittens.' He rubbed his hands across his face. 'I dragged you out of her, Jango. Feet first, I dragged you out of her body. I saved your life and took hers. And that made you all mine. I knew from the minute I saw your screwed-up ugly little face that I would never give you up. Oh, the women came around just as soon as you were born, and a few days later Madeline was dead. When Despair came back he wanted to dump you. So I hid you away—'

'What do you mean? Dump me?' When Lias did not answer, Jango said, 'Please, Lias!'

'I needed you. I was like Despair, cursed, awkward, a bit of a loner. Later on, as you got older, I thought, if you knew who you were, that you were not my brother but total Gorgio, then you might go away. I liked things the way they were. No matter what happened, it was always going to be the two of us – brothers! Except that we never were. How could we be? Despair was not your father.'

'So tell me. Tell me how I'm total Gorgio.'

Lias laughed. 'I used to watch you up in Derbyshire, dressed in your Barbour and green wellies, slouch hat and knobbly stick; happy, rubbing shoulders with the farmers in the cattle markets. I used to think, it well could be that our Jango is standing alongside his real daddy. Don't seem so funny to me now.' He laughed again, hard and bitter. 'Madeline's family came down to Stow, to look for their daughter. When Despair said that she had died the previous week in childbirth, they wanted to take you back with them. Despair said that I would bring you to their hotel the next morning. Well, I never found them, did I? I never even looked. I hid you in the food box of the wagon. We moved out that same day and had travelled many miles when Aunt Lena heard you crying.'

'Did my mother tell you who my father was?'

'Some farmer's son, about to be married to another girl, and too spineless to own to what he had done. That's why she ran away, took up with Despair; smoked and sniffed whatever it was. I was the only

222

one she had to talk to. I liked her, Jango. She was a sweet girl. I never really knew my mother, and Despair wasn't much of a father. But you know that.'

Lias moved uneasily. 'One thing Despair did that was right and proper. He tried to make up to you for what you had lost. He bought that land and house in the Dark Peaks. Just before he died he said I should tell you the truth about your birth. That your folks still live thereabouts.'

'But you couldn't do it?'

'I'm sorry, Jango.'

It had all been said.

They sat, heads bent, shoulders bowed, careful not to look at one another. The Bacardi bottle and coffee pot were empty. Lias alone had wept, which seemed to refute her hatred of him. Her surreptitious glance crept across his slumped body, his defeated aspect, and her mind and heart whispered, 'Brother. This man is your brother.' It was not yet time to reach out a hand, to try to mend the broken edges. But she knew that time would come; if they both were to survive the past hour, it had to. More important, more alarming, was the chasm between the two men who had been for Jango's lifetime the only family either of them had known.

She raised her head. She said, 'Brother is just a word. It can mean a lot, or it can mean nothing. It doesn't have to be a relationship by blood alone, it can be a shared childhood, loyalty to each other; just simply love.'

The heads remained bowed and she thought she had failed. Then she saw Jango's tentative smile, Lias's hesitant nod of acceptance. It would take time. They were men. Pride would have to be satisfied, past omissions justified and dealt with. But their welding held fast. Nothing now could separate them except the physical space of their future lives.

Lias rose, and Jango followed. They stood face to face. Lias held out his arms and they held one another.

From the open door, across his shoulder, Lias said, 'Be good to each other. I'll be with Sinaminta and Rowsheen if you ever want me.'

It was too soon to be alone together; in the close confinement of the camper, good will at least between the occupants was essential for survival. Jango had resumed his pretence of deep sleep. Before Lias had mounted the coloured horse and galloped from the meadow, the blankets already covered Jango's averted head.

She emptied the ashtrays, threw out the empty rum bottles, washed the coffee pot and mugs. She fed the dogs and filled the kettle. A caretaking visit to the Monks' House was becoming urgent, but she could not bring herself to leave him. The small domestic noises of her continued presence spoke the words she could not bring herself to say. When there was nothing left for her to do, everything polished, scoured and tidied, she showered and put on a robe and lay down beside him.

The exhaustion that comes from shock and deep emotion soon made their pretence at sleep a reality. When they woke it was already evening and they were locked together as if they had already made love while still unconscious. They lay for a long time, not moving, listening to the night sounds, a hooting owl, a baying fox, the soft breathing of the dogs.

She said, 'We can begin again.'

'Yes,' he said.

'It won't be easy.'

'No.'

'If you really want to.'

'I want to.' He stroked her face, her hair. He said, 'You do understand the new situation, don't you? Things have turned round. Seems like you're the *tatchi* blood, Romany after all, and I'm the rotten Gorgio.'

'We'll cope,' she said, and kissed him silent.

Jango

*N*ovember again, but the weather this year was cold and sunny. He observed himself with some amusement, behaving like a tour guide, introducing her to the villages of Stow and Moreton, telling her of the horse fairs of his childhood, taking her into cafes he had visited with Lias. He described the Fosse Way as being the main artery of the communication system of the Roman legions, used when they needed to move men and equipment from fort to fort.

He maintained a low and steady speed because that was how she liked it. She found it, she told him, an awesome experience to have seventy-two feet of heavy vehicle riding behind them on the narrow road. He pointed out that many transport vehicles were heavier, longer than the Winnebago. But this is our home, she said. It's everything we have.

It pleased him to hear her say that, even though it was not altogether true, for either of them. Details and photographs of the Monks' House were already on display in a Yeovil estate agent's window. For Sale or To Let. Considering the state of the housing market, he thought, the place could still be on offer two years hence. Meantime, Mr Parson's granddaughter and her husband had agreed to live in the house and caretake. I just want to forget about it, Maya had said. I shall never go back there.

And still he could not resist the occasional sideways glance towards her, nor yet feel certain about her continued presence at his side.

The sun still shone as far north as Matlock. He took her to the cafe which served hot oatcakes with the eggs and bacon. The wind blew cold off the Heights of Abraham, and they ran shivering and laughing into the steamy warmth. The cafe owner recognised him. She winked and smiled. 'I see you haven't brought the pup in with you this time.'

'No,' he laughed, embarrassed. 'He's grown too big to fit inside my jacket.'

They settled themselves at a window table. Maya said, 'What was that all about?'

'Lias said I shouldn't bring Star in here when we came down last spring. I zipped him inside my jacket and fed him bacon scraps'. He nodded towards the counter. 'I thought she hadn't noticed.'

They drank scalding tea and held hands across the table. The American tourists who filled the town in spring and summer had dwindled to a hardy few. Jango and Maya were the only customers; the service was swift, the plates piled high with the all-day breakfast.

Maya ate with obvious hunger and enjoyment. He reached out a finger and wiped a smudge of butter from her upper lip. But he saw the way she looked at the vase of plastic daffodils, and the red and green plastic tomato which contained vinegary ketchup. He said. 'Not really your sort of place, this?'

'Oh,' she said, 'I've seen worse. I once ate in a truckers' diner on the way to Chicago. It was much like this place except they poured maple syrup over the eggs and sausages. My guide said everyone should eat at least once in a lifetime in such a dive.' Her amused tone became laughter. 'For the experience,' she said.

There was a moment of absolute silence; it was as if the world stopped.

He said, his voice subdued, 'Lias and I always eat in this sort of cafe when we're on the road. And not for the experience but because it suits us. Because we're the sort of people who only feel at ease in these kinds of places.' The paper tablecloth was patterned with yellow cabbage roses. He began to touch them, count them, carefully not looking at her. 'Are you sure you know what you're doing, Maya? You've walked away from your life and bang into mine, and we haven't begun yet to talk about it.'

He rolled the plastic tomato between his fingers. He said, 'You won't find much gracious living in the Dark Peaks. The only business trips I make are to the horse racing and the greyhound tracks. The only visitors we'll have will be my – your aunts and cousins. They usually come by in April. They pitch in the lea of the hill. They cook on an open fire. They mostly can't read or write. They're true travelling people, decent and good-hearted. But they are not your kind of people, and you ought to think about that.' He set the ketchup holder back in the middle of the table. He said, 'As for me, well, I can't change. I'm plain and simple, no fancy tricks. No trimmings.'

'I know,' she murmured, and he heard the shame behind the words. 'You don't have to explain yourself. You're the most uncomplicated person I have ever known. I'm the one who has the problem. I have a thirty-year accumulation of pretence and false values to get rid of.'

She looked into his eyes and he saw her fear.

She said, 'I know I can change, because I have to. But you'll have to be patient with me. I know I was only playing at being a traveller when the camper was parked so conveniently in the paddock, when I could go back to the Monks' House any time I wanted. I know there are going to be times when I come out with the sort of stupid. crass remark that I did just now. Perhaps if you were to laugh at me when I do that, tell me to shut up, remind me that I'm not Lady Anne but Maya, the child of Gypsies.'

The first flakes of snow began to fall as they came into the Hope Valley. It was like a re-run of last year's arrival, except that it was Maya who sat beside him as he inched the Winnebago up the hillside and in through the white gates. Maya who stayed in the cabin and watched him run towards the house, open the door and enter.

He moved from room to room, lighting the oil lamps, putting a match flame to the ready-laid sticks and paper in the parlour fireplace and the kitchen stove. He watched from an upper window as she climbed down from the cabin and stood for a moment, touching the stone owls on the gateposts.

The light from the house picked out the sheen of her pale skin, the gloss of the drawn-back white-blonde hair. As her head bent into the wind and the whirling snowflakes, she seemed hardly real, but a woman conjured from his imagination. And then he saw her turn to perform the action which was automatic to every thinking country dweller.

She closed the double, white-painted gates and secured the padlock.

As she came into the house he was waiting for her. He pulled her hard to him, acutely conscious, even through their padded jackets and thick trousers, of the length of her body tight against his. He kissed her, tasting a trace of the cafe butter still on her lips. He rocked her back and forth. 'Last winter,' he said, 'when Lias and I came back here, I thought about you all the time. I pretended you were here. I imagined me showing you the house, the barn; the two of us walking up to Mam Tor, and on Kinder Scout. I wanted you to see what I see, hear what I hear.' He began to stammer a little. 'But – but maybe I was wrong. Maybe that's not what you would like, want – I don't know. You've been to other countries, places I haven't. Perhaps the Dark Peaks won't look so magical to you. Perhaps it'll all look sort of ordinary.'

She stirred in his arms, then took one step back so that she might see his face. She said, 'The light was fading as we came up the valley, but what I saw was beautiful. I didn't want to look too closely or to comment on it. I want to wait for morning, to have you show it to me. I want to see it first as you see it.' She glanced away, suddenly shy. 'There's something else. You're a very special breed of man. Whatever else Lias did, he reared you well. I not only love you, I like you. I never imagined that happening with a man.' She gripped his jacket sleeves and shook him. 'Now show me this house of yours.'

So he showed her the broad oaken floorboards he had sanded and polished; the tables and cabinets he had stripped and restored, the inglenook fireplace he had dug out from behind lath and plaster, the cell-like bedroom which held only his wide bed and a chair.

He said. 'It's all a bit bare,' noticing for the first time that it was. 'We could go shopping for a few cushions and curtains in Sheffield; a sofa perhaps and some carpet.'

She said, 'I don't want you to change anything for my sake. You don't have to please me. This is your place, your home.'

'But I want to change things. I want to make a life with you.' He could hear the doubt in his voice and saw that she had also heard it. But the doubt was all on her account and not his own.

She put her arms round him. 'Time,' she said. 'We have to give it time.' The snow was falling thickly now, the light almost gone. 'Let's agree to stay together until springtime, and then see how we feel about each other then. Sometimes,' she said, 'there is a temptation to bury painful things deep so as not to think about them. We mustn't do that. What we learned from Alice, Lias – we have to come to terms with all of that. But if we try to do it separately and in silence it will divide us in the end.'

He said, 'I'm not much good at talking about personal matters.'

'You're not ready to talk yet; neither am I. Let's leave it for a while. Meanwhile, let's go to Sheffield when the roads are clear. Buy a sofa or two and some carpet.'

The grass on the high tops was still brown and yellow from the winter snows. They sat in a cleft between tumbled rock, sheltered from the wind, the slanting April sun warm across their shoulders.

He said, 'I think about my mother every time I come up here.' He gestured towards the grey stone villages in the valley. 'She was born down there. She must have played up here as a child, picked the wild flowers. Perhaps she walked here on a first date with my father. I've begun to think about him just lately. It's a damned funny feeling. They were younger than I am now when she found out she was pregnant. I find myself inventing how it went between them. She would have cried when she told him about me; he would have been scared witless, and mad as all hell. There he was, about to be married to another girl and my mother no more than a nuisance, an embarrassment to him. He will have married the other one, of course. I've got sisters and brothers down there who will never know me. I wonder if he ever thinks about us, about Madeline and me.'

'What would you say to him,' she murmured, 'if you met him?'

His fingers curled into fists. 'To begin with, I'd kick the shit out of him. Then I'd tell him what happened to her, to me.'

'That wouldn't solve anything.'

'It would make me feel better.'

'And what about Madeline's parents? People seem to live to great ages in this part of the world. Have you thought about your grandparents, still living down there?'

'Lias said they wanted me. That they travelled to Stow, came to the trailer, talked Despair into handing me over.'

She said, 'It must have been terrible for them when they waited for you in their hotel room and then discovered that Despair and all his family had vanished.'

'Yes,' he said. 'I never thought about how it was for them. A dead daughter and a lost grandson must have taken some getting over.'

'Perhaps they've never recovered from it.'

'You reckon?'

'They may believe that one day you'll walk in at their door. They would be in their seventies now. They could be clinging on to life, just waiting for you.'

'How can we find them?'

'The way we found Maya Heron, through the local Records Office. But it will be easier in their case. They'll be people of some standing in their own community. Their name will be well known. Country people tend to stay in the one place.'

'And my father?'

'Find your grandparents and you'll find him.'

He said, 'Well, we seem to be talking about it, don't we?'

'It's the right time,' she said. 'It was all too raw and close back in November.'

She leaned back against the sun-warmed rock and began to tell him about Wapping, about the oily rainbows on the river's surface, the converted warehouse in which she had once lived and worked; her black and silver flat. She recalled the menace of Jonah, the claustrophobic quality of her friendship with Polly; the magnified importance of what she had believed to be a career that was going somewhere.

She looked out across the windy ridge softened by heather, at the landscape of sheep tracks and rowan trees. Overhead a sparrowhawk hovered, she could hear the crowing sound made by the red grouse. She said, 'This place must be absolutely beautiful in summer.'

'Yes,' he said. 'I expect it is. I've only ever seen it in the winter and the early spring.'

She said, 'We don't have to leave it if you don't want to. We could look for your grandparents. Do some more work on the house. Make a garden.'

'You'd be bored out of your mind.'

'No, I wouldn't.' She spoke hesitantly, not looking at him. 'When I was at the Pack Monday Fair last year, I saw this amazing lady selling gold and silver handbags —'

'I remember her,' he interrupted. 'She put on quite a show.'

'I'd like to do that, Jango. Have a market stall, travel around. Oh, not all the time. But there will be days when we get restless. Just occasionally I'd like to wear a diamanté studded jacket, and pile my hair high on my head, sell fake Cartier watches and Gucci handbags and call everybody sweetheart.'

'You would?' The delight in his voice explained his unspoken fears. 'Well, why not? Lias will know the best wholesalers for that line of —'

'No,' she said. 'Not Lias. It's just you and me now.' She rose, took his hand, and pulled him upright. 'Come on,' she said. 'Let's go home and do some phoning around to handbag manufacturers.'

He walked to the village shop to collect the post. Sometimes, in their isolation, they would muddle the days. He had thought it was Saturday but a sight of the counter crammed with copies of the heavy newspapers told him it was Sunday.

The shop was crowded with young people wearing anoraks and stout boots and carrying backpacks. They came in all seasons, those who tramped and climbed for a day or two and then went back to the city. He picked up the letters and a handful of chocolate-covered marzipan bars, her favourite. He bought cigarettes for himself and fuel for his lighter. Their main shopping was done once monthly over in Sheffield; it was then they stocked the freezers, made contact with the world. He had hoped it would never end, this quiet secret time. But the crowded shop told him that the month was May. The display of tourist postcards had been renewed on the revolving rack. There were sandwiches on sale at the far end of the shop, ice cream and hot chocolate, tea and coffee.

He bought a carton of the strong orange-coloured tea, the sort of deadly brew loved by Lias. He began to think about the man who had always been his brother, and who was not his brother. All winter long he had felt the pain of that separation, as if the living flesh had been sliced through, leaving him bleeding. Something deep inside him was still bruised by the knowledge that he was not, as he had always believed, part of a strong and caring family, but a single entity, a one off, belonging to no one.

Six weeks had passed since Maya had talked to him about his grandparents. He had rejected all her attempts to bring him to the local Records Office. He nursed a mutinous, childish anger against his mother's people. If they had really wanted him, he reasoned, they would have tried to find him. Even Despair, who was not his father, had bought him a hillside, so that he might be near them.

He walked until his legs ached and the dogs' heads drooped from weariness. The evenings were drawing out, the mornings lighter. He sat on a rocky height that faced the house, and watched the lights come on as Maya moved from room to room. It was that time of the year when Lias would be growing restless.

He saw her standing at the bedroom window looking out towards the facing heights. He knew that she could not see him in the darkness, and yet he knew she sensed that he was near.

Women were wiser than men, more adaptable, more willing to forgive and begin again. He wondered at her ability to turn her life around, to say, as she had lately, so my mother and father were brother and sister, it's not the first time such a thing has happened, it won't be the last. But I am here, alive and healthy. It can only ruin the rest of my life if I allow it to. She was full of plans; all her days occupied with making the house into a home. Curtains and cushions, green plants on windowsills, rugs on the polished boards, copper pans and spice jars in the kitchen. She had dug out a garden from the flinty hillside; if it were possible for flowers to grow there, she would make it happen.

Her stock of gold and silver handbags was bought and stored in an upstairs room, ready for when he should say the word and take her to the northern fairs and markets.

He knew now that she loved him; he believed at last that she would stay. They might even marry, have children. It would all be up to her.

There was a farm, an isolated steading even among these lonely hills and valleys. He had lately walked the lanes around that farmhouse, observed the elderly couple setting off for the cattle market, watched the young men, obviously two grandsons, who drove the tractor, milked the cows and shepherded the flocks. He had noted their height and build, their long, curling, prematurely silver hair, the faces that were like his own.

He stood up, and the dogs rose with him. He began to walk towards the lighted windows of the house. He could feel the heart softening inside him, the hardness melting, the raw places healing.

He had not yet told Maya about the farmhouse, about the young but grey-haired men. He patted the marzipan bars in his jacket pocket and smiled in the darkness.

It should be an interesting evening.